Poverty wants some,
luxury many,
and avarice all things.

~Lucius Annaeus Seneca
(5 BC – 65 AD)

Clubman

by

Ronald Stephen Reiniger

720 – Sixth Street, Box # 5
New Westminster, BC
V3C 3C5   CANADA

Title: Clubman
Author: Ronald Stephen Reiniger
Cover Art: "Office Party Dimension 7" © Candice James
Layout and Design: Candice James
Editor: Candice James

www.silverbowpublishing.com
info@silverbowpublishing.com
© Silver Bow Publishing 2020
isbn: 9781774031261 book
isbn: 9781774031278 e book

Library and Archives Canada Cataloguing in Publication

Title: Clubman / by Ronald Stephen Reiniger.
Names: Reiniger, Ronald Stephen, 1960- author.
Identifiers: Canadiana (print) 20200331477 | Canadiana (ebook) 20200331507 | ISBN 9781774031261
  (softcover) | ISBN 9781774031278 (EPUB)
Classification: LCC PS8635.E4775 C58 2020 | DDC C813/.6—dc23

For Carol –
My passion, my rock.

6

PROLOGUE

Sean Tifflen, Chester Moehr and Geoff Favelle had developed their conglomerate, LNa, over the past twenty years. They had their hands in many businesses: Real Estate development and management, a commercial fishing fleet, a large farming operation where they raised hogs and recently, they had expanded it into growing and processing berries. They also owned a large shipping business that included two oil supertankers.

What was shielded from the public was their illegal endeavors. They built their business on murder, and they were the largest illegal drug wholesalers and smugglers in Western Canada.

Chapter One

Present Day

Sean Tifflen was a large Caucasian male: 6'2", late 30's, very fit, dark neatly cut hair, dressed in an expensive suit and tailored white shirt. Chester Moehr, was a few years older and nowhere near as muscular as Sean, but he had a magnetism about him. This, plus the discerning quality of his clothes, easily identified him as the head honcho. Today the two of them were leaving the hustle and big city eyes of Vancouver for the sleepy little town of Penticton, BC where they would take off in a private Eurocopter, quietly and discreetly, from the Penticton airport far from the ever-watchful eyes of big city law.

On the drive to Penticton, Chester and Sean enjoyed some small talk before Chester's face took on a more serious tone. He shifted in his seat, then turned his eyes square onto Sean's,

"I have a question for you."

"Shoot," Sean said guardedly, but didn't show his nervousness.

"This is not an offer, so don't take this as a sure thing," Chester paused and shifted again " One of the things I've been pondering is spending more time on my yacht. I realize it's there I'm at my happiest," he paused again and repositioned himself more comfortably. "However, to do that, I would have to step back from the daily hands-on aspect of the business. I haven't spoken to anyone about this. I wanted to get your opinion first, so, what would you think if I stepped back and you assumed greater control of our operation?" Chester lifted an eyebrow quizzically.

Sean was stunned, "Wow, I haven't really ever thought about that scenario. You've always been the leader, even before we officially formed LNa." Sean sat back and steepled his fingers, "My initial reaction would be to say yes, I would love the opportunity." Sean twisted a bit in his seat, gazed out the window momentarily then back at Chester, "are you serious?"

Chester enjoyed Sean's shock factor response but was even more pleased with the smile spreading across his face. There it was again, that million-dollar smile. "As I said, nothing has been decided. It's just something

I've been mulling over. I would still be involved, but more like a consulting partner, rather than senior managing partner. I am pleased with your quick and positive response but before I make a final decision, we would need approval from the Club, and of course we'd need to get Geoff's thoughts as well. In the meantime, would you please keep it to yourself until I've made a final decision?"

Sean nodded and sat in silence for a moment, digesting what Chester had just said. He forced a look of consternation hoping it would cover up the feeling of bitterness creeping through his bones. So, Chester still wanted to be involved. Sean didn't like that, not even a little bit, but he forced a smile, "My lips are sealed Chester."

They sat in silence as the rocking movement of the car started to play with the residue of their early morning waking and their eyes slowly closed as they appeared to drift off to slumber of sorts. Chester was actually playing the scene over in his mind - the conversation and Sean's reactions. Peeking through one eye, he saw Sean slumped down in light sleep, only to be awakened when the car slowed down and turned off the main highway.

***

Penticton is in the middle of wine country in the southern Okanagan valley, nestled between Lake Okanagan and Skaha Lake. Tourists flocked to this area to relax in the warm summer sunshine or to enjoy the temperate winters, with close access to nearby ski resorts.

While many people loved this area, Chester was not a fan of the arid, barren land; it reminded him of his childhood, growing up on the prairies. He much preferred the rich green forests closer to the coast. This, however, was a perfect location to catch their ride as it was close to the Big White ski resort.

On the way towards Big White, there was a small remote campground at Chute Lake, where they had scheduled their early morning secluded meeting. It would have been much quicker and more convenient to fly from Vancouver airport or even from Chester's estate in Anmore, but the Penticton airport was far enough away from the city to provide the required discretion needed to be able to leave and return unnoticed.

***

Chester and Sean walked from the car to the awaiting helicopter. The pilots were already getting seated, so the men were greeted by a slender, pleasant looking lady.

"Good Morning Mr. Moehr. My name is Marci. We hope to make your brief flight as comfortable as possible, please let me know if there is anything I can do for you."

"Thank you, Marci," Chester smiled warmly.

As they boarded, they took the front seats on this eight-seat helicopter, while three men boarded and took their seats directly behind Chester and Sean. The bodyguards did not say anything, but through their suits you could tell they were carrying guns. The AS450 helicopter was specially fitted with luxury upgrades, large comfortable leather seats and the entire cabin was leather-lined in a colour that coordinated fashionably with the seats.

What you couldn't see was what was behind the leather lining. A sound dampening system of fabrics and honeycombed material that made the cabin almost soundproof. Helicopters are traditionally very noisy, but in this aircraft, they would ride in air-conditioned comfort and easily converse without the use of headphones.

As the helicopter lifted off, Chester was gazing out the window at the scene unfolding below. The mountains framed Lake Okanagan on both sides, as the long thin lake snaked its way north through mountain passes and a light breeze created small wavelets that glistened like diamonds in the sunlight.

The wineries and orchards skirted the lake as people slowly made their way to their early morning meetings. This tranquil setting, with the low thumping noise from the rotor blades, should have been enjoyable. Instead, Chester was preoccupied and although he was looking, he did not see the spectacular views below. He knew, within the next couple of hours, he may encounter the greatest danger he had ever faced in his life.

Chester's great passion in life was Success...with a capital "S". Even as a young lad, his competitive spirit was evident. He always had to be the best, even when racing with his cousin across the field; he had to be first. When playing hockey, he truly suffered anytime his team lost; and his teammates suffered through his wrath as he chastised them for their poor play. Later in life, he achieved financial success. Coming from humble beginnings, he had worked diligently, smartly and ruthlessly. Today his wealth was approaching one billion dollars. Much of it was hidden in offshore accounts and sheltered from various taxation and law enforcement agencies. Most people's appetite for success would be satiated with such abundance, but Chester still lusted for more. Once they landed at their destination, he would have to put his keen senses to use to prevent his possible demise. He had taken precautions, but in the back of his mind he wondered what he may have missed. Now though, he had a chance for some respite before landing. Chester melted back into his chair and closed his eyes. Thirty minutes to relax. He heard a whisper of movement as Marci moved past him to Sean.

"May I get you a drink?"

"Just water," Sean replied, too loudly.

Sean probably wanted whiskey—he hated flying—but knew Chester wouldn't approve. He needed Chester to know he was alert and on duty.

"A drink, Sir?" The sudden closeness of Marci's perky voice made Chester's eyes fly open. She hovered above him and on her face ... for a split second ... something ...

"Sir?"

"Water."

"Would you like lemon or lime with your water, Sir?"

"Ice."

"The other men?"

"Ask them." The words came out more forcefully than he'd intended.

"Ice water for all of us," Sean said, playing the peacemaker.

Head high, Marci swept toward the back of the helicopter. Chester shifted in his seat but couldn't relax now. It bothered him, that fleeting expression... so incongruous with her cheerful voice. Maybe Marci hated flying too. If so, she was in the wrong job. Sean wasn't looking so good, and they'd barely started their flight.

"Is everything set up?" Chester asked. Maybe he could distract Sean. "You know how picky Walter can get."

The corners of Sean's mouth slowly turned up and his wide eyes betrayed his shock. Everyone knew this was the pot calling the kettle black! Nobody was more detail-oriented than Chester. There were many times Chester's attention to details uncovered some plot or orchestration concocted to chisel, steal or assassinate them.

"Yes Chester" Sean replied with a smile, "Sanchez just texted me. Everything is set. They're all ready and waiting for us."

Marci returned and smiled toward Sean, "Is there anything else I can get for you gentlemen?" she asked. Nobody spoke so she walked back to her station Sean turned his head to watch her walk away. She looked very fit and her dress accentuated her physique. As she reached the rear, she half turned and gave Sean a small smile, indicating she noticed Sean's interest. He quickly turned back and slowly turned red. Chester noticed Sean's flirtation, but was preoccupied with thoughts of dread that for some reason kept surfacing.

Outside, the brown of the desert valley floor was giving way to lusher green vegetation as the copter climbed higher into the mountains. Shimmering in the morning light of daybreak, the green of the trees took on many different hues and the undergrowth between the trees, while mostly green,; was interspersed with a multitude of colour as alpine flowers were emerging from their winter dormancy. This soothing serenity was broken as Chester twisted in his seat and his elbow bumped the water glass that Marci must have placed there without him realizing it was there. The glass rolled and splashed onto the floor.

Just as Chester was bending down, the entire helicopter erupted with a cacophony of noise. Loud, but not ear-shattering. The sound was accompanied by a whizzing sound. Immediately, Chester recognised the sound of silenced gunfire. He turned his head to look behind, only for his face to be splattered with blood and brains from a bodyguard's head as it exploded right behind him. He wiped away the blood in time to see Sean's shoulder burst open as a bullet slammed into him. Chester, still in a prone position, was somewhat shielded. Peering behind him, he noticed another bodyguard slumped over.

Chester tried to roll onto the floor but he was being held by his seat belt. He wiped his eyes and saw Marci standing at the rear with an assault rifle. She was methodically spraying the cabin with gunfire. The carnage was everywhere - blood, bodies, chunks of leather, seat stuffing and shards of glass and plastic were flying everywhere in a blizzard of destruction. At that moment, Chester became aware of a burning ache coming from his left arm. As he looked; he saw the blood pooling on his white shirt. He had been hit. He realized it must not have been a significant injury as he still had full function of his arm. The adrenaline coursing through his body was camouflaging any pain he may have felt.

His years of dealing with life and death situations now served him well, instinctively he knew he had to remain calm. Dead people react; survivors remain in control and live.

He unbuckled his seat belt and deftly rolled to the floor as if in one continuous action. He saw Sean unconscious beside him with a gaping hole in his shoulder. He reached for Sean's holster and saw it was empty. He knew Sean had his beloved Glock with him as they entered the cabin, so it must have fallen somewhere. Suddenly, the helicopter seemed to dive and everything from the cabin fell forward like flotsam riding a tidal wave. Also riding this wave was none other than Marci. She had lost her footing as the helicopter lurched and she fell forward down the centre aisle, directly towards Chester. As she slid face first, Chester looked into her eyes. What he saw was a coldness and determination that could only come from a professional. She slammed into Chester. They wrestled on the floor in a death dance fueled by adrenaline and survival instincts. She regained control and pointed her gun towards Chester. An instant before she could pull the trigger, Chester swung his good arm towards her. His fist missed her but made full contact with her gun. She began firing haphazardly towards the front of the cabin. Chester's years of dodging body checks while playing hockey now were useful, as he quickly rolled so he was now positioned on top of her, almost sitting on her back. She matched his movement and rolled so she now faced him directly. Those cold eyes now inflamed with rage seemed to bore through Chester. The cabin was covered in blood, water, alcohol and shards of broken bottles and glass. Marci stood as she leveled her gun on Chester, who remained in a vulnerable position on the floor. He kicked so hard with his leg that he heard her bone snap and she lost her footing on the slippery floor. Instinctively, he rolled to free a space, then quick as a bolt of lightning he rolled back as she hit the floor. This time, he positioned himself securely on her back and with his good arm reached around until her head was in the crook of his arm. One quick snap and she became limp.

Chester quickly gathered his thoughts and looked out the window. The helicopter was dangerously close to the ground. Still sitting on Marci's lifeless corpse, he peered into the cockpit which was open to the cabin section. Inside, both pilots lay slumped over their controls. He knew there were mere seconds before the imminent crash. Running on adrenaline, he bolted into a seat and buckled the seat belt, just as the aircraft struck the ground.

Chapter Two

Twenty Years Earlier

It was a warm autumn day filled with brilliant sunshine, as Chester searched for a table. He carried a latte in one hand, while the other was occupied with a steaming morning glory muffin. He spotted an empty patio table among the sea of tables and chairs, then quickly scooted over to claim it before someone else did. He reclined into the chair on the patio of the café just outside the Granville Island market. Slowly he sipped his latte and savoured the warm muffin. Although the muffin was filled with all sorts of good things, like whole grains and seeds, Chester loved the taste. He was appreciating each nuance of the flavour and taking in the scene unfolding before him. He was admiring the view and watching the bustling docks as people mulled in and out of boats. Some on the little tourist ferries that ran around False Creek. Others were loading onto fishing boats and pleasure boats, heading out to the ocean to spend the day on the water. Chester was feeling a little envious and told himself, someday he would also own a big yacht and spend time out on the sea.

Chester looked across the small expanse of False Creek at the high rise downtown buildings framing the scene on the other side. Rising majestically above the buildings, the snow-capped North Shore mountains dominated the horizon with a blue sky hugging all below. He was young and had not experienced many other world class cities, however, he knew few places could possibly be more beautiful than where he was at this very moment. He yearned for success, but did not fail to stop and smell the roses around him.

Chester was a very smart, determined, young man and while he did not know what direction life would take him, he knew a couple of things. Firstly, he knew attending university and having a life as an educated professional, such as an engineer or lawyer, was definitely not in the cards for him. Secondly, a regular life did not excite him. He also knew deep down inside that whatever he did end up doing, he would most certainly be successful. For as long as he could remember, he knew he would attain success, that was his destiny. He also knew things happened for a reason and he knew he was the architect of his own destiny. Whatever situation he had to face, he knew he would create his own future. He was contemplating the opportunity before him and wondering whether he could pull this off ... or more so, whether he wanted to do this job. While ruminating over the moral implications, he did not notice someone had approached. The voice startled him a little as he was pulled back from his concentration.

"Hey chum, this chair taken?" Geoff exclaimed as he pulled out a chair and laughing, took a seat adjacent to Chester. "You looked a million miles away," he said, "what were you thinking about?"

"Nothing really," Chester replied. "Just caught up in my thoughts and enjoying this," he stretched his arms out to encompass the scene in front of them. "What a fantastic city we have."

"Truly a gorgeous city. I could sit here for hours just soaking it up. Particularly, some of those scantily clad lasses," Geoff stated as he lasciviously watched a young girl bouncing past them. "Lookeee there. I love summer," he added.

"Watch yourself buddy," Chester warned, nodding towards a guy, a body building type, in the direction the girl was headed, "your leering will get you into trouble." Geoff then noticed the fellow staring at him with daggers in his glare.

"I see your point. Thanks for the warning. I prefer not to have a scrap before my morning coffee. Not to mention the extra 40 kgs he has on me ... or the fact his biceps are the size of my waist!"

"Did you find any comfort last night? When I left the party, you seemed pretty occupied with that brunette in your arms."

"Beckie, yes, a real tiger!" Geoff laughed with a twinkle in his eye. "I noticed the little lady you were dancing with seemed to disappear about the same time as you?"

Chester laughed, "Yes, it was a good night all round."

"So, did we get any leads on any jobs?" Geoff asked, "My funds are running low and bills will soon pile up. If we don't find something soon, I may have to resort to a real job."

"Maybe", Chester moved forward in his chair "our friend from Club 81 has offered us a job, though I am not sure you will want to take it."

"How much?" Geoff quickly asked.

"40K split three ways."

Geoff whistled with astonishment, "that is not chump change, this must be a big one."

"Indeed. We will be crossing a line with this one," Chester looked serious for a moment, then relaxed a little. "We should wait for Sean before we discuss it."

"Yeah, I suppose, where the hell is he? Normally, he shows up before I do."

Chester nodded in the direction across the patio, "He showed up moments after you, but never made it much past the doors."

Geoff turned and saw Sean standing near the café entrance with a coffee and cinnamon roll in his hand, talking to a couple of pretty young ladies. While you couldn't make out their conversation, you could tell the young ladies were enraptured by it. They were staring up towards Sean, giving him flirty looks as they gently tossed their hair in an inviting manner. Sean was completely wrapped up in the conversation. He was very adept at speaking to women, and these two were completely enthralled with this dark-haired Adonis-like man and his disarming smile.

Geoff shook his head as he turned back towards Chester. "We might as well enjoy our coffee and sticky bun. I suspect Sean will be tied up for a while yet." Geoff was annoyed, but tried not to show it too much. "Doesn't he piss you off sometimes? No matter what happened the night before, he is always immaculately dressed and his slow impeccable Carey Grant-like enunciation seems to draw the babes right in. It definitely does piss me off." Geoff bit into his bun and mumbled "Some guys have all the luck."

Chester nodded in agreement, then continued, "Indeed I am envious, but look at him. Who could ever really get upset for long. He has 'good guy' written all over him."

"Yeah, I guess you're right. But seriously though – does he have to be so good looking too?

A few more minutes passed before Sean took his leave of the ladies and ambled over to the table. "Morning Gents," Sean said as he leisurely pulled out a chair and sat down, "who are we talking about?"

Startled by Sean's sudden appearance, Geoff replied "Nobody really, just some of the great looking girls here. You had quite a conversation over there. Did you get their numbers?"

Sean just smiled and tapped his pocket as he sat down.

Smiling, Geoff added, "You dog. On another note, Chester may have some work for us. Good timing bud."

"Good, I could use some cash." Then, turning to Chester, he nonchalantly asked, "So who do we have to kill?"

"Someone with a 40K price on his head," Chester replied, matter-of-factly.

This caught Sean by surprise and he momentarily choked on his coffee. After a couple of coughs, he cleared his throat and retorted, "Jesus man, I was just kidding. Are you for real?"

Chester lowered his voice now and nodding his head said, "Yes, we haven't accepted the job though. We need to decide if we want this, it is a whole new level. If we do this, it will open further doors for us but also commit us. Once we do this, there is no turning back ... it's murder man! I am not sure we want to go down that road. We certainly won't, unless we're all committed to it and in agreement to stay the course, come what may."

Both Sean and Geoff were now totally engrossed in what Chester was saying. Their eyes shone with both excitement and fear. It took a moment for the message to sink in, then Sean answered first, "I'm not sure ... that is a big step. What do you think Geoff?"

Geoff replied, "We need more information. Who? When?"

Chester had a small smirk on his face as he said, "Not now, this is too public. If you are interested, we can discuss this on the boat. The Irishman gave me the keys to his boat docked in the marina. We can take it out to the bay and discuss it out there."

They both nodded agreement and quickly drained their remaining coffee. The three of them stood up abruptly and attempted to casually walk towards the boat but their apprehension was noticeable in their gait, as they quickly walked to the marina, forcing small talk along the way.

Geoff was the only one licensed to operate a boat, so naturally he took charge. They all enjoyed the water and enjoyed the ride out to the bay. The Irishman was a friend who supervised the marina. For a small cash stipend, he would lend out one of the boats moored there. Many boats were owned by non-local people, and every so often they would have to take the boat out for a spin to make sure it was operational. If the spin happened to last a little longer, and the Irishman was able to profit from this endeavour – well that was just good business.

Today the Irishman had furnished them with a 40-foot cabin cruiser complete with drinks and snacks in the fridge. When they returned, Chester would pay for the fuel and what they consumed. They could comfortably spend the entire afternoon on the boat if they wanted. The three of them took positions on the top, and soaked up the warmth and the ride, without saying a word. As they passed under the Burrard Street Bridge and out into English Bay, Chester noticed all the people on the shore looking in their direction. He was too far away to see their faces but he knew their eyes were overflowing with jealousy. Their desire seemed to inflate his chest, as Geoff navigated the channel.

When they reached a spot between a couple of tankers anchored in the bay, queuing for their dock time, Geoff dropped anchor and turned off the engines after Chester gave him the okay . They each swiveled their chairs to face each other, curiosity evident on Sean and Geoff's faces. Trying to act cool and collected, Sean said, "okay, give us the scoop".

"Brown Jas is the target," Chester said and looked into their eyes. Neither seemed alarmed, so Chester continued, "this one, though, cannot be quietly removed. They want to make a statement, so this must be public."

"So why did your man choose us?" Geoff inquired.

Chester took a moment to answer, "I've thought about that too. He's a bright guy. I suspect there are two reasons. First, it is a test, if we can pull this off, they will give us more work. Second is a little more dire though, if we get caught there is nothing to tie us to them. If we go down, we go down alone … c'est la vie."

"Okay, that makes sense" Geoff replied. "Knowing you though, you have been thinking about this and I suspect you have a plan … right?"

Chester laughed and said, "still open to alterations and your input, but yes, I have the outline of a plan. But before that, we need to decide if we are going to accept this. If we don't accept it, that's okay. If we do accept it, we are committed, we must complete the job or there will be consequences. I don't mind saying I do have some reservations."

The question hung in the air. Sean then said, "C'mon guys, we have sold grass, stole, dealt with hot stuff. This is just the next step on the road. I am in."

Geoff reluctantly nodded his agreement, "Yes I'm in too."

Chester looked towards them both, "All for one, One for all. It's unanimous."

They spent the rest of the afternoon discussing the plan, making alterations and developing contingencies. They were so wrapped up in discussion they barely ate or drank anything. They were focused on work. By the time they returned to Granville Island, they had a firm plan and each knew their role.

* * *

Jasminder Gill was well known in the community as a leading drug dealer. He was known as Brown Jas and he had successfully developed the 'dial-a-dope' system. His clients had a number they called to place their order. On the surface, it appeared they were ordering a pizza, however, along with the pizza the client ordered a 'special topping'. For example, if you ordered a thin crust cheese pizza with extra mozzarella, you would receive your pizza along with a packet of cocaine in the corner. When your order arrived, you would pay your $20 for the pizza, but you also added a $100 gratuity. A simple plan that became so successful Brown Jas opened a dozen outlets spread out over Metro Vancouver.

Jas was the kind of guy who flaunted his wealth and his belligerence grew along with his bank account. He drew a lot of attention to himself, which was frowned upon. His biggest transgression occurred when he wanted to expand into areas Club 81 did not endorse. He became obstinate and just expanded anyway. This would not be tolerated and a message needed to be sent.

Brown Jas had a suite in the Spall Centre residences on Burrard Street downtown. Every Sunday evening, he would have dinner at the restaurant in his building. He would always sit at the table by the window in the far corner.

This table had the best view and the thick glass shielded the blanketing rain and accompanying cold that was normal Vancouver spring weather.

After surveying the site, Chester noted this table had a clean line of sight from the outside street. The street on that side of the building, Hornby Street, gradually sloped downward. Hornby was busy during the workday. There was a constant flow of business people and legal types who frequented the courthouse, adjacent to The Spall Centre. However, on Sunday evenings there was little traffic as most of the businesses were closed and there was very little residential housing in the area.

Inside the building, the restaurant was adjacent to the lounge in a large open area. They were also quiet on a Sunday evening as the hotel mostly serviced business travellers. The washrooms were located on the far side of the lounge area and immediately beside them was a room marked 'staff only'. Inside was a storage area equipped with four small windows that looked out towards the lounge. They were made of frosted glass to prevent patrons from looking inside. Conveniently, they opened in a sliding motion, not jutting out, so as to not draw attention when a window had opened. When opened slightly, one of these windows had a clear line of sight to Brown Jas's table.

They chose the following Sunday to make their move. The main challenge they faced was the need to make this assassination public. Club 81 needed to send a message. This public assassination added a risk of exposure. In order to avoid detection, they needed a distraction. Chester's plan called for impeccable precision. He would only trust people who he knew very well and could be counted on to not screw up.

They all knew collateral damage was not an option. No member of the public could be injured. Club 81 had very strict codes of conduct, one being that the public could not be threatened. They needed to keep matters internal and most importantly, there could be nothing to trace it back to the Club. Even though everyone would know who commissioned this hit, there could not be any direct evidence. So, every day, Chester, Sean and Geoff reviewed each step repeatedly, they started referring to Club 81 simply as 'The Club'.

* * *

At 7:00 PM, a man entered the north lobby. He had long grey hair tied in a ponytail, which stuck out the back of the large fedora he was wearing. He was wearing a tailored dark blue business suit with a paisley tie. His overcoat was large and longer than the current style. The overcoat didn't quite match the rest of his attire but it was clean and stylish. He had a neatly manicured, medium length grey beard. He walked over to the lounge and sat at an open table. He removed his hat and sat a little awkwardly, as if he had a stiff leg. He opened a laptop he was carrying and started tapping on the keyboard. This was Sunday evening and there were only two other people in the lounge, both of whom were occupied reading books. The hotel had skeleton staff on duty and after about five minutes the man behind the bar came out and collected orders. The old businessman ordered a soda with lime. When the bartender returned, the old man thanked him and took a drink. The bartender noticed the old man's hands had a weird appearance, they were wrinkled but something was a little odd, almost like his hands were wrinkled more than his face and he was definitely wearing too much fragrance.

In the meantime, Brown Jas was sitting at his regular table quaffing down his meal. He was chewing with an open mouth and when he called for the waiter you could see pieces of food being expelled from his mouth. Brown Jas was wealthy, but incredibly uncultured. People who knew him claimed he was the only man they knew who could wear a $5000 suit and make it look like a $49.95 Salvation Army special. Brown Jas was completely occupied with his meal, though reflexively he would look around him every few minutes scanning the surroundings for danger. He saw a homeless man across the street pushing his shopping cart, but otherwise not much was happening. He saw the elderly businessman in the lounge get up and go toward the restroom area, he also noticed he walked with a limp but he was nonthreatening.

As the old man got to the men's room door, he looked around to make sure he wasn't seen. Then, he quickly turned and entered the staff room instead. Inside, he threw off his overcoat and removed a small calibre rifle that was attached to his thigh. The rifle had a silencer attached and a small telescope. Slowly, he opened the window and looked out, he had a clear view of Brown Jas. He then removed a walkie talkie from around his waist and set it on a box beside him. He adjusted the box and placed another on top of it. Then he leaned on the top box as he placed the rifle out the window, with the silencer barely protruding. He took a couple of deep breaths, then lined up Brown Jas in the crosshairs. He reached over and tapped the talk button rapidly five times, then returned his focus to Brown Jas and quickly fired three times. Inside the room it sounded like three quick air puffs. Sitting at his table, Brown Jas's eyes opened in astonishment, just as a small trickle of blood appeared on his forehead. Metal jacketed bullets were discreet in their wounds and nearly as effective for their killing power if properly placed.

Outside, the homeless man removed a handgun and shot three times towards Brown Jas but too high to hit either Brown Jas or anyone in the vicinity. At the same time, car tires started squealing as a handgun emerged from the driver's window and there were three flashes but no sound. Several patrons were interrupted from their dinner and looked up. Nobody looked up in time to see the homeless man but they all noticed the red Charger speeding past and the three flashes from the gun. Brown Jas slumped forward and at first there was a stunned silence. Then, all hell broke loose when they realized what had happened. Diners were screaming and dropping to the floor to get out of the line of fire. Waiters joined them and staff started emerging from kitchens and backrooms. During the maelstrom of chaos, no one noticed as the old man slowly walked across the foyer and out the front doors.

The bartender did not notice the old man leave, but for a moment he thought he smelled gunpowder, soon overwhelmed by the odour of the old man's fragrance. He noticed the old man's computer was not sitting at the table top anymore but paid little notice with the cacophony of bedlam that was occurring.

Outside, the old man casually walked to the intersection and crossed the street towards St Paul's hospital. St Paul's, the only downtown hospital, was one of the busiest hospitals in the lower mainland and certainly had the busiest Emergency Room. Even on a Sunday night, there was a constant stream of ambulances with patients arriving with various serious ailments. Overdoses, cuts and bleeding, heart attack victims and other near fatal injuries. Doctors, nurses and attendants were busy dealing with triage and attending to the patients' care. As such, nobody really noticed the elderly businessman who walked through the waiting room and down one of the hallways. Once inside, he made his way downstairs to the garbage area and sliding behind a bin began removing the hairpiece and beard that obscured his face. He removed the overcoat and began peeling back clear latex gloves from his hands.

Chester knew the gloves were the ingenious piece of his disguise. These clear latex gloves made his skin wrinkle like an old man, a scattering of brown spots took on the disguise of liver spots and, best of all, they camouflaged his finger prints. After removing the latex gloves, he slipped on a pair of leather driving gloves he had in his pocket and proceeded to quickly disassemble the rifle he had concealed under his overcoat. He threw the pieces into the bin, making certain the bin he tossed these items into was medical waste, so all its contents would be incinerated after the bin was picked up. Since the hospital was very busy and space downtown was at a premium, the garbage trucks picked up their loads several times a day. The next truck would be arriving within the hour and with its departure any slim evidence pointing to Chester would be incinerated.

Chester then walked out of the open overhead doors and proceeded down the alley in the opposite direction from the hotel. In his pocket, he fumbled with the two remaining shells and decided against his instinct to throw them in a trash container as he had planned for their disposal, even though carrying these in his pocket exposed him to a slight danger if discovered. He walked north through the forest of high rise buildings towards Coal Harbour. Within ten minutes, he reached Canada Place and the docks where the cruise ships would dock. Since there were no cruise ships in harbour, he knew there would be very few people around and, as he expected, there was only a smattering of people in the vicinity. He leaned on the retaining fence over the water and looked out over Burrard inlet. After a moment, he reached into his pocket and removed the shells. Rubbing each of them in his gloved hands, he dropped them into the water.

Chester made his way towards the rendezvous, which was a small coffee shop in Gastown. When he entered, Sean and Geoff were already seated at a table in the far corner. Chester acknowledged them and made his way to the counter to place his order. With coffee in hand, he went over to the table and shook each of his accomplice's hands. "I think that went rather well," he said, "have you heard anything?"

"You're kidding, right?" Sean responded, "listen, all you hear are sirens and police swarming everywhere. The hit is on every radio and TV station. Not much is being released except for the police saying it was a targeted hit, the victim was known to police and the media is reporting that it looks like a professional job".

Geoff added, "apparently they're still working under the assumption the shots came from the vehicle driving past. From inside the restaurant, it looked like Brown Jas just leaned forward and collapsed into his plate. That was a great shot by the way and an amazing plan."

Chuckling slightly, Sean added, "I guess it's a good thing you grew up on a farm and shot lots of gophers."

They then reviewed each of their roles to make sure nothing was missed and all evidence was disposed of according to their plan. After they were certain everything came off perfectly, the atmosphere changed from business-like to celebratory. They laughed about nothing in particular and started to tell jokes and stories; making sure they never broached the subject of Brown Jas.

After half an hour or so, they decided they should part and reconvene in the morning. Sean was the first to leave, followed by Geoff. Chester hung back and ordered another coffee. He knew there was no way he was sleeping tonight anyway. With the adrenaline pulsing through him, another cup of coffee would have little effect.

Sitting with his hands wrapped around the steaming mug of coffee, Chester realized, tonight, he had indeed crossed a line. His days of innocence were behind him; he was now a fully-fledged, hard core criminal. He thought momentarily about Brown Jas. He felt remorse, though not so much for Brown Jas. More for the death of his own innocence. Brown Jas was a Troglodyte. He was an uncultured moron, who achieved a level of success far beyond his intellect. Chester slowly realized, while Sean and Geoff were accomplices - he had just killed a living, breathing person. It reminded him of his childhood when they would butcher an animal. The killing and butchering of an animal was just a means to an end. They needed food and the animal provided it. He didn't feel for the death of the animal.

He felt a little shudder, not an outward shudder but rather something deep inside. Not for the victim, but for the realization that he had transcended a barrier, he had become a murderer! It was like a small piece of his humanity just dried up and blew away with the wind. His eyes misted, but no tear was formed. Now, he thought, what was next? He lusted for more.

Chapter Three

With Brown Jas' assassination, the other factions came into line. They heeded the warning and the Club once again solidified their dominance of the criminal underworld. Every organization that ever existed needed structure, or chaos would soon follow. The world of drugs was no different. While at times it may have seemed as though chaos was gaining ground, behind the scenes Club 81 continued to enforce their rules and parameters, maintaining control.

As with all positions of power, when there is a vacancy, somebody rises to fill that vacuum. The leadership void left by Brown Jas' murder was soon filled with a splinter group from the remnants of Brown Jas' gang. This time, it was being led by a Caucasian guy. Like a Phoenix, Dael rose from the ashes and soon ascended to the leadership of the organization. Dael was tall, over six feet, and sort of looked a bit like an albino. His hair was bleached blonde. Closer to white really, with a slight hint of amber. His skin was pasty white, most certainly someone who had to avoid the sun or he would burn very quickly. He had blue eyes, which looked normal, though in fact they hid a most vicious, uncontrollable and violent temper. His look and name were truly indicative of his Norse heritage. He developed an appropriate nickname over time – Ghost.

Dael was a bad dude who did some contract work for Brown Jas. He loved indulging with the big three – drugs, women and guns. He was frequently characterised as being somewhat 'off his rocker', particularly when partaking in one of his major vices. His leadership style could best be classified as management by fear. Somewhere deep in his mind, he thought he was an American black gangsta rapper. He dressed in oversized clothing, his pants hung low, with the crotch almost low enough to be between his knees. He always wore a baseball cap askew, garish oversized gold chains and talked with a slang like 'boyz from the hood'. He had a bedazzled handgun, that was of course unregistered. He would only bring out 'his baby' when he was on business. He envied his counterparts in the US, where they could carry handguns quite openly. In Canada, handguns were effectively outlawed and you certainly could not carry weapons around.

Ghost took over leadership of the remnants of Brown Jas' crew, most critically, the lucrative dial a dope business. He asserted his leadership by force which resulted in a few of the suitors quietly disappearing. In the beginning,

Club 81 did not get involved in the power struggle. Their success partially came from their arm's length management style. Darwinian survival of the fittest served the organization very well over the years.

Ghost loved his nickname, as it made him sound wraithlike and mysterious. He also loved to party, and on more than one occasion somebody ended the evening being badly beaten and frequently, there were late night visits to the ER. Nobody ever 'ratted' on Ghost, as they knew the punishment for disobedience was far greater than a few bruises or broken bones.

After Chester's successful dispensation of Brown Jas, his status grew within the Club. This was eventually officially designated a cold case. The authorities found minor scraps of evidence, but nothing of any significance. There were no clues left behind to indicate who the culprits were. The police knew the drive-by shooting was a distraction and the kill shots came from the small storage room inside and adjacent to the washrooms. They picked up traces of gunpowder residue on some boxes around an open window. All indications pointed to the old man who was sitting in the lounge as the actual shooter, but, they could find no evidence or fingerprints anywhere and witness statements were useless as they were so contradictory, placing his age from late 30's to somewhere in his 80's. His height varied some eight inches, even the colour of his suit and overcoat varied. Unofficially, they believed Club 81 had sanctioned two 'professionals' to carry out this job and likely left the country within hours. That's how it was left, and the case became cold and remained as such.

Three weeks later, Chester was having a clandestine meeting with his contact from the Club. To maintain their anonymity, they always met in remote locations. On this occasion, they met at a park beside the Pitt River, outside the city. This location was so remote Chester had trouble finding it. The river cut through this small flood plain, and as a result, many roads ended abruptly when they reached the river. He did, however, prepare for this meeting by driving the route beforehand, and, after many false turns he mastered the route.

On the day of the meeting, as he arrived at his destination, he noticed a pickup truck parked at one end of the small parking lot. He believed he had arrived first, so he parked his new Ford Focus on the other side of the lot and decided to wait. He knew his contact had a preference for Jaguars, so he immediately discounted the truck. Once parked, he casually looked over towards the truck. He was shocked to see his contact sitting behind the wheel, casually waving at him.

Chester looked around to make sure nobody was around and walked over. As he walked, he thought to himself...of course he would use a truck, they were in farming country and more people drove trucks than cars here. His contact would not draw attention to himself if he blended in with the locals. He approached the truck from the passenger side and entered.

"I didn't recognise you at first," Chester said as he settled himself in the front seat of the truck

"As I am sure you know Chester, you never draw attention to yourself, always blend in," his contact replied then continued with a smirk. "If I could have found some horse shit, I would have loaded some in the back as well."

Chester laughed, "that may have worked until closer examination, your clothes would have given you away. I don't think many farmers in the area go to work in designer clothes."

"Quite right, I will remember that in the future." Then, becoming more businesslike, he changed the subject. "You performed exceptionally well with your last task. Thank you. While I was certain you could do the job, there is always a risk. From my point of view, I was also exposed. If you failed, I would have been held responsible as I was the one who recruited you."

Chester visibly relaxed. "I'm glad you're pleased with our work. I suspected there was an element of risk for you. I hope this means we can look forward to additional jobs in the future and that your faith in us will pay dividends in the long run."

"Well, now that you mention it Chester, a job has come up sooner than you may have anticipated. As you know, there is a bit of a battle for Brown Jas' replacement. We don't have a good handle on who will be victorious in the end, so we have an obligation to assist all parties until the end game becomes clearer."

Chester just nodded and said, "I understand. How can I be of assistance?"

"One of the combatants is a fellow called Ghost, he has removed one of his rivals and now has a body to be disposed of. That is where you come in. Would you accept this commission?"

Chester nodded in acknowledgement.

The man continued, "He is being kept on ice at the following address," as he passed a sheet of paper to Chester. "We want you to be thorough, but also quick. Can you complete this task within 48 hours?"

Chester rubbed his temple and nodded approval. "What's the signal when completed?"

"Go to the flower shop and order two dozen white roses to be delivered to the other address on that sheet of paper. They will have a package for you with 20K in it."

They shook hands and the deal was set. Chester left the truck and watched as the Club man drove down a small dirt road, raising a cloud of dust in his wake. Chester returned to his car and texted Sean and Geoff – meet at my place in one hour ...$$.

＊＊＊

When Chester arrived back to his apartment, Sean and Geoff were waiting out front and they all went up to his suite on the 20th floor together.

Upon entering, Sean immediately went to the fridge and pulled out three cold Peroni beer. Chester always had his fridge well stocked with interesting beer. After passing a beer to each of them, they sat in the living room and Chester outlined the job they were given. "The key to this job is to ensure there is no evidence left behind. So, we need to come up with a plan that will obliterate any record of the job at all."

For the next few minutes, they each made suggestions that were discounted for various failings. Finally, Sean came up with the best suggestion. He knew a guy who worked at a rendering plant in North Vancouver. This plant picked up leftover meat and other animal by-products from restaurants, butchers and slaughterhouses. They took this garbage to their plant, where they separated the products, then incinerated them to create fertilizer products such as bone meal, blood meal, etc. Sean's contact was a maintenance engineer who he met at the local pub. He had a young family and always complained about making ends meet. He worked the evening shift as it paid a premium. He was sure, for a couple of thousand, he would let them in and turn a blind eye.

It was agreed. Sean called his man, met with him and after the meeting reported back that his guy agreed to the plan and was working that evening. There were only two people working the overnight shift. When the other fellow went on his lunch break, he would signal to Sean and they could unload their cargo at the loading dock.

In the dark of night, Chester, Geoff and Sean arrived at the body pick up spot. It was in a storage building located in an industrial area, just east of downtown. At this time of evening, the streets were abandoned, and the only occupants seemed to be cats and dogs rummaging for food. At the front gate, Sean punched in the security code. The gates opened and once inside they slowly drove down to the loading area situated between two long rows of storage buildings, running the entire length of the lot. The area was not well lit, but the letters signifying the different buildings had a spotlight on them. They located the building easily and entered the entry code. Chester was never in doubt that all the instructions from his contact would be correct. The Club was very thorough. They were told there would be no security cameras in the compound. This was an additional precaution, as there would be no evidence a felony had ever been committed. When they rolled up the overhead door, all they saw was blackness, the lighting outside, while dim, was still much brighter than inside. Sean was searching for a light when Chester barked "do NOT turn on any lights!"

"Why?" Sean replied.

"Let's not draw any attention to us. If we wait a minute, our eyes will adjust." After a minute or so, the gloom began to draw back its veil of concealment and along the one wall, a freezer appeared. The almost imperceptible humming noise indicated it was working. Geoff walked over and noted this was a deep freezer that would be in most homes, not one of the large industrial varieties. He opened the top and inside was a wooden box, that appeared to be lined with some sort of plastic. The size was of proper dimensions to hold a body, if they twisted and broke limbs to form a compact square.

"Did anyone bring a hammer?" Geoff asked, "the lid appears to be tacked on and we need to be certain this is the correct cargo."

"Ahhh damn weaklings," Sean replied, "here, let me try to open the damn thing." Being the strongest of the three, he may be able to pry it open with shear muscle power. He grabbed the top and gave it a big, manly tug. The top came flying off quite easily, he lost balance and fell backwards, landing on some shelves behind him. The shelves collapsed and the erupting noise would surely draw attention if anyone was lurking. Everybody's senses became very keen and they looked around to see if anyone was alerted to their presence. After a couple minutes of total silence, they become confident nobody was around. Geoff walked over to the frozen box and peered inside. It contained the body! It was frozen in a contorted shape and unidentifiable.

"Got him," Geoff grunted.

Chester came over to examine the box and as he looked at the grotesquely twisted former person, he noted, "There is very little blood," then, after a brief pause, "I think this guy may just be broken and twisted, not dismembered."

Then, Sean spoke up from behind, "guys, I think you need to see this."

Chester and Geoff came over and looked at another body splayed out on the floor. There were empty eyes staring at them. Sean reached down and grabbing an arm he pulled his arm straight out.

"He's much fresher," Sean replied, "he's stiff, but still pliable." Sean bent down on his haunches and examined closer. "Judging by the marks on his neck, I would suggest this guy was strangled...maybe garrotted, as it is a thin line and there is a little blood where the skin was broken." Reaching for one of the cadaver's hands, he further mentioned, "there is a little blood on his fingers like he was trying to remove the garrotte."

"What the hell is this place?" Geoff replied, "it looks like a goddamned morgue. AND which one is ours?"

Sean and Chester both shook their heads, they didn't know. This was a chink in the armour they had not contemplated. Chester started to walk through the remaining enclosure searching for something. "What are you looking for?" Geoff asked.

"Checking to see what else may be hidden around here. I want to make sure there are no more bodies." Chester replied.

Soon, they were all looking through the boxes and racks strewn about. They found several things that may have had a nefarious background but fortunately, no more bodies. After about ten minutes, they gave up their reconnaissance and had to decide what to do with the two bodies. Chester knew this was very strange. The Club was normally very methodical in their preparations. Finding an extra carcass was not part of their modus operandi, something was amiss. What to do though? If they removed the wrong body, there may be a price to pay for screwing up. He was quite certain it was the fresh one, as his contact had told him time was of the essence. On the other hand, it may have been a few days between the killing and Chester receiving the commission, in which case the frozen one was his and the fresh corpse had been placed here recently. After examining the possible outcomes, Chester came to a decision. "Let's take them both."

Sean and Geoff mulled this over in their minds for a moment, then Geoff replied, "good decision. I don't see any other option. I just hope we are not sticking our necks in the noose."

Sean nodded his approval and they quickly loaded both bodies into the back of the unmarked cargo van, then quickly cleaned up the rack they had accidentally knocked over. They retraced their steps out of the compound and were soon heading for North Vancouver. At this hour there was little traffic, so the trip should be less than thirty minutes; during rush hour, this same trip could take two hours. After an uneventful ride, they parked the van about a block away and Sean sent a text advising his contact that they were poised.

Twenty minutes later, Sean's phone beeped. Sean read the message and said, "it's showtime boys".

They drove to the rear of the building at the loading dock and backed up their van. There was no security at this facility, as nobody would break in to steal decomposing garbage. One of the overhead doors opened and out came a man pushing a large metal vat with rubber wheels. Sean opened the rear door of the van and said, "hello Sanchez, is everything fine? Are we still good to go?"

"Yes," Sanchez responded, "but we must be quick, my partner will be back in fifteen minutes." They quickly dumped the frozen box and the fully wrapped body into the container. Slightly alarmed, Sanchez said, "you told me there was one package, now I see two."

Chester replied, "double the packages, double the price."

"More than adequate, let's move."

Chester and Sean went with Sanchez as they pushed their cargo into the open overhead door. Geoff remained behind to close the van doors and drive it out to the street and wait for his partners in crime.

Inside the building, Sanchez, Sean and Chester were quickly pushing the cart towards a large door. Chester said, "I grew up on a farm and cleaned a shitload of barns. This smell is way worse by far."

"Yes Meester," replied Sanchez with a pronounced Spanish accent. "I also know the smell of cow shit. Trust me though, it will get much worse," Sanchez motioned with his head towards the looming door. When they reached the door, he pushed a button, the large doors opened and inside was another set of doors, similar to an air lock on a spaceship. The smell hit them like a punch in the stomach, as Chester became sickeningly aware of the warning

Sanchez had just given them. Once inside, Sanchez again pushed a button and the door they just came through, descended.

Sanchez talked as he walked, "many people vomit. The smell is very intense. Please do not spew on the floors as we do not have enough time to clean it up." Then, Sanchez pushed another button and the inside door began to open. "Normally, we have a mask and air tanks if you were to spend any time inside. Of course, we do not have that luxury of time. Just be aware the smell will be very intense." As the door opened, the smell smacked them like a cloud of superheated pyroclastic flow from an erupting volcano. The effect was immediate. As the stench invaded every sense, Chester felt his stomach begin to pulsate and he doubled over. The air was completely forced from his lungs as his eyes watered, and he felt a loosening of his sphincter. As he tried to draw air, the foulness burnt each alveolus in his lungs, like he was trying to breathe the gas released from sulphuric acid. In a bent over position, he saw Sean beside him, he was also stooped over, and his normally dark complexion was white as snow.

They both wretched but did not puke. They regained their composure and stood upright. They quickly took their packages to an open oven; a large yawning steel hopper about eight feet across and six feet deep. They dumped the vat and both bodies rolled into the smelly cavern. Sanchez then pushed some buttons on the operating panel, the hopper rolled back, and they could hear a sizzle coming from the bodies. Sanchez then said, "there will be no flesh left in 15 minutes, the remaining bone will be fed down a conveyer to a large stone roller, where it will be ground down to a fine dust. Then, it will pass through a series of magnets that remove anything magnetic, and finally through a sieve that removes any larger pieces, like stones, that were accidentally placed in the vat. Finally, the mash is bagged and used as bone meal for fertilizer. Sanchez assured them he would clear the catch basins in both systems, in case any evidence got through. Then, they returned the vat to a stall among the other vats. Chester thought the lined up vats looked like shopping carts one would find at a grocery store. They left through a smaller set of air lock doors and briskly walked back to the loading dock.

As Sanchez opened the outside loading dock door, Sean said, "I'll buy you a beer at the pub tomorrow and deliver your package."

Sanchez nodded and said, "pleasure doing business with you gents, let me know if I can be of service in the future."

Chester and Sean quickly walked across the loading lot and Sean said, "that is the most disgusting thing I have ever done. I don't know if I will ever get that smell out of my nose."

Chester replied, "what is amazing, quite frankly, is that as intense as the smell was inside, you do not notice it outside. They must have incredible scrubbers that filter the air."

They spotted the van just outside on the street, they both jumped in quickly and closed the doors. Geoff's face curled up and he blurted out, "Holy Shit, you guys really stink! You better open the windows before I throw up."

Chester and Sean both laughed, and Sean said, "you should have smelled it inside, out here it smells like roses."

As they rolled the windows down, Geoff was still complaining of the smell and said, "for God's sake, it smells like somebody shit themselves." Once again, both Chester and Sean laughed. Sitting in the back seat, Sean surreptitiously adjusted himself so the smelly bit of goo he dropped in his pants didn't become more uncomfortable. He was not going to admit to anyone that he shat his drawers.

Chester barely noticed the foul smell. He was preoccupied with the thoughts of the two bodies. He was quite certain he did the right thing, but still an element of doubt lingered. He shifted in his seat uncomfortably at the thought. He knew no mistakes were permitted.

***

Two days later, Chester arrived at Garry Point park in southeast Richmond. While still in the city, this park overlooking Georgia Strait was infrequently visited except for weekends and mothers taking their preschool children for walks. Chester arrived at the small parking area at 9:50, ten minutes early. He wanted to arrive earlier, but heavy traffic delayed him. He wanted to show up for his meeting earlier than his contact this time. As he pulled in, he saw a black Jeep parked at the far side. Slowly, he entered the lot and he saw the Jeep's lights briefly flash so he proceeded close to it. He walked to the Jeep and entered the passenger's door.

"Good morning," the Clubman said, "come in."

"And top of the morning to you too," Chester replied, as he closed the door. Then, anxiously, he turned and said, "there was an additional package at the pick-up. We suspected the less frosty one was ours, but we couldn't be sure - so we picked them both up. I apologize if we overstepped the mark."

The other man just smiled and said, "no, no – you did not do anything wrong. As a matter of fact, you helped us out by picking them both up. The frosty one was prepared for you. The fresher one was not supposed to be there....unbeknownst to us, it was deposited there a few hours before. It was not pre-approved, and they broke the rules. You helped us out by picking up both, as it mitigated a separate trip." Then, he handed Chester a manila envelope that Chester was not expecting. He continued, "since you picked up two packages instead of just one, which you were charged for, there was one payment at the florists. Inside, you will find the fee for the additional work ... plus a bonus."

Chester did not look inside, rather he was feeling quite relieved. He was becoming more apprehensive about this meeting as it drew closer. "Thank you," he said, "the boys will be happy." After a brief pause, "and of course, so am I. I must admit I was a little shocked to find the additional package. Your protocol is usually very accurate, this did not fit with your normal directions."

"First, my friend, let me assure you this was not normal protocol. Second, in future, if ever in doubt always do more, rather than less. Something would be amiss if the plan was not exact, so you did very well. Finally, this leads to another commission for you."

Chester's enthusiasm was returning with the relief that not only had he had made the proper decision; he was being commended for his initiative. Now, he was being given additional work. "That's good, thank you. I look forward to the new job. What is it?"

"The same individual that provided the extra package for you ... Ghost! As you know, Ghost has eliminated his competitors and has effectively taken over for Brown Jas. He doesn't follow the rules though and presents a danger we cannot afford. Worse still, his haphazard actions cannot be condoned, as it leads others to believe they can operate without approval. This commission will be similar to Brown Jas, we need this to be visible and serve as a warning to others."

"What is the timeline?" Chester inquired.

"You need to take all the necessary precautions. We would like this completed within a month, but only if you are able to ensure you have done all preparations ... and we need this to be visible ... like Brown Jas''. The commission for this job is 75K."

Chester gulped, this was a large amount of money so, evidently, they wanted to send a message and were expecting something unmistakably obvious. Outwardly remaining calm, he replied, "that will be fine. We will advise should we require additional time, though I suspect this can be completed within a month as you have requested."

Chester's contact smiled and extended his hand, "then it's a deal."

Chester shook his hand and hoped his palms were not too sweaty to betray his trepidation. As he reached for the door, a thought suddenly struck him, and he paused as if pondering something. The Club man noticed this pause and said, "Is there something else, my friend?"

"I was just thinking ... with Ghost removed, there would be a vacuum with no likely candidate for ascension." Then, pausing briefly, Chester continued, "would your organization endorse us as the successor?"

"The quick answer is no ... with a caveat though."

Chester felt a little deflated but would not permit his disappointment to break his composure. "What would that caveat be?" Chester inquired.

"As you very well know Chester, there can only be one boss. We could never endorse 'your group', as outstanding as they are. However, if you were to change the question to 'would we endorse YOU', I would take the request back for consideration. Are you willing to alter your request?"

Chester mulled this over briefly. He had always operated with Sean and Geoff as equals, even though he made the final decisions and took the lead. He did not want his friends to feel he was deserting them. He then realized if his contact even posed the question, it probably meant he had anticipated the answer. He concluded the only way they would move forward would be with a designated 'boss'. He made direct eye contact and replied, "Yes, would your organization endorse ME?"

"I will take the request forward for consideration. You will receive your answer when a decision is rendered. In the meantime, though, you have a job to complete."

"Thanks," Chester replied, and this time he extended his hand. "Rest assured, you will be satisfied with our work. I will begin work on this immediately." After shaking hands, Chester exited the vehicle and watched the Jeep exit the parking lot. He sat behind the wheel of his car but did not start the engine. He just looked out at the expanse of blue water in front of him, with the Gulf Islands jutting out on the horizon. As he stared, he did not really take notice of the tranquil scene in front of him. Instead, he dreamed of the possibilities the future may hold. After a few minutes, he forced himself back to the reality in front of him and called both Sean and Geoff. They arranged to meet at Chester's place that afternoon. Chester started his car and drove downtown, he didn't even notice the stereo playing, he was concentrating on Ghost and trying to formulate a plan to complete the kill.

Upon returning to his apartment, Chester saw Sean and Geoff waiting out front of his building once more; Geoff using his waiting time to have a cigarette. Chester waved to them as he entered the secured garage and met them at the entrance. As they entered Chester's apartment, he tossed the envelope on the table and said, "Well boys, we did very well to remove the other body, they are very appreciative and have paid double."

Geoff opened the envelope and dumped the contents on the table. "Phew, more than double I would say. Looks like 30K, with the other 20K that makes 50K."

"They did say there was a bonus for our initiative. 10K is a nice bonus." Chester said, then continued, "let's give Sanchez a bonus as well, take 6 for him and divide the rest. Sean, I believe you are to meet with Sanchez this afternoon, do you think he will be happy with this?"

"Happy!" Sean exclaimed, "he will be ecstatic. I think I'll even make him buy the beer!"

"Great, at some point we may need his assistance again. In the meantime, they have also given us another commission."

"Holy crap!" Geoff replied, "this is becoming very lucrative ......so who do we have to whack now?"

"The same guy that made the mistake of giving us the additional body. It was not approved by the Club and they want him removed." Chester waited for this to sink in, then added, "Ghost."

Sean, in a matter-of-fact tone, then added, "looks like we may need Sanchez' services sooner rather than later."

Chester quickly responded, "No. They do not want him to disappear. This has to be public, as with Brown Jas, they want to send a message. This one is worth 75K." He saw Sean and Geoff's eyes open wider with shock. Chester waited for the message to sink in. Geoff whistled.

"With the successful completion of this job, I believe the doors will open for even bigger opportunities." Chester added, sounding like an afterthought, but of course it was calculated.

Enthusiastically, they began planning the hit. With every plan they devised, they encountered a downfall. Ghost was not like Brown Jas, who had a routine that was easy to dissect. While it needed to be public, they must make sure there would be no collateral damage and he was never routinely in an open spot to be picked off. After a couple of hours, they had still not reached a solid plan. They finally agreed to resume the following day, as Sean needed to head to the pub and meet with Sanchez.

For the next several days, they tried to ascertain some sort of routine. In conversations with various members of the community, they would ask casual questions about Ghost. These questions would of course be framed in such a way so as to not draw suspicion that they were actually engaging in reconnaissance. Randomly, they would also monitor his movements. This was difficult though, as they were well known to Ghost and his associates. They would have to accidentally run into each other at restaurants or on the street. One day, Geoff accidentally, on purpose, ran into Ghost at the Viennese Espresso coffee shop in Gastown. Ghost remarked, "I saw two of your compatriots earlier today. If I didn't know better, I would think you guys were casing me."

Geoff nonchalantly laughed while replying, "Ahh, c'mon Ghost, if we were going to do that, we would be much better at it. You wouldn't even see us." No better way to deflect than to tell a partial truth.

"True," Ghost replied. "Not to mention, it would be extremely hazardous to your health." They all laughed, "pull up a chair and let me buy you a coffee." Ghost was with three of his associates, one of them stood up to retrieve a chair from the adjoining table. "What can I get you?

"Thanks, I will have a latte." With that, Ghost's associate went to the counter and ordered a latte for him. He returned shortly and gave it to Geoff, the contempt on his face was hard to miss. He obviously did not like being a coffee server. Looking towards him, Geoff simply said, "Thanks," then turning towards Ghost continued, "I appreciate this, you didn't have to do this, but I appreciate the gesture."

Most everyone despised Ghost, not only did he dress like scum but the way he talked was annoying. He had a bit of a lisp that always made him elongate the pronunciation of the letter 's'. It sounded like how you would expect a snake to sound.

Ghost raised his glass, as if toasting him from across the table. After taking a drink, he continued, "so, what are you guys up to these days?"

"Not much," Geoff calmly replied, "a little this, a little that, you know, enough to pay the rent, buy some beer and enjoy the good things in life." After a brief pause, "I hear you are doing very well for yourself lately. Good for you." With that, Geoff raised his glass and said, "may the light of good fortune continue to shine on you."

Ghost raised his glass to accept the toast and continued, "You know, I could use people like you and your friends. I'm not sure how much coin you are making, but I can assure you if you came to work for me, you would need much larger pockets in those jeans."

Geoff smiled and tried to maintain his composure; however, it was evident he was excited. His facial expressions looked like a toddler who just received a favourite toy. Ghost understandably mistook this to mean he was excited about the prospect of working for him. In reality, there was no way he, or any of his group, would ever work for Ghost.

Chester often talked about Sun Tzu's Art of War, one of the principles of which was to keep your friends close but keep your enemies closer. Ghost didn't know it, but he was the enemy and he had inadvertently provided the basis for his demise.

"Interesting," Geoff replied, then he paused to give the effect he was considering the proposal before continuing, "you know we come as a group, we work together very well....and we are friends."

"Well, of course the offer was for you, Chester and Sean," Ghost replied, "I appreciate that you guys are friends, but you know sometimes friendship and business does not work together, business must always trump friendship."

Geoff nodded his agreement. They spent the next twenty minutes making small talk; various fishing trips, golfing expeditions and sports teams. It was a cordial exchange and as the meeting was drawing to a close, Ghost once again reverted to business. "If you give me your number, I will call you in a couple days and we can perhaps arrange another meeting with the rest of the gang?"

"That's a great idea," Geoff replied, and proceeded to recite his number as Ghost entered it into his phone. Then, Ghost stood up and extended his hand towards Geoff. Geoff casually wiped his sweaty palm on his jeans as he stood to shake Ghost's hand with a firm, friendly handshake. The rest of Ghost's entourage got up and Geoff gave a cursory handshake to each of them as they left.

After they left the building, Geoff sat back down and expelled the tension with an exhale that was loud enough it caused several patrons to look in his direction. He ordered another latte and pondered the information that had just fallen onto his lap. There is a solution to every quandary, you just have to keep searching until you find it. After several weeks of fruitless examination of Ghost's movements, the answer was laid out in front of him. Now, they had the rudimentary elements to develop the plan. He took out his phone and texted Chester and Sean - we need to meet. I have found the mouse for our elephant. After a couple of minutes, they both replied they could meet in an hour and they settled on meeting for lunch at Ricardo's in Coal Harbour.

During the slow walk to the restaurant, Geoff started putting pieces together for the plan. He arrived fifteen minutes early, which is what he was planning, he would then have a greater selection of seats and since it was a warm, sunny day, he chose a booth outside, just around the corner from the large patio. While this would not provide the best view, it would provide the privacy required.

Geoff sat there looking out over Burrard Inlet as it sparkled in the brilliant sunshine like sequins on a singer's gown. Sitting majestically overlooking the waters were 'The Lions'; two peaks on the North Shore Mountains. These peaks looked like a pair of male lions sitting on their haunches overlooking Vancouver. The Lions stood guard over the city and became part of Vancouver folklore. It was early summer and much of the snow had melted, what remained on the Lions' peaks wrapped around their necks and gave the appearance of their manes shining in the sunlight. As Geoff was contemplating the scenery and soaking up the beauty, the hostess came around the corner, followed by Chester. He also had the idea of showing up early to get a good table.

"You're early!" Geoff laughed.

"Great minds think alike," Chester replied, as he nestled into the bench seat opposite Geoff. At that moment, Geoff started laughing once more. Chester turned around to see why. He saw Sean standing there with a smirk on his face. After they all chuckled, Chester said, "I guess it's a good thing we didn't decide to meet at 11:45, as we would be here at 11:30 and the kitchen doesn't start up until noon. They all chuckled once again, as Sean sidled in beside Geoff.

As the hostess left, Sean quietly said, "so, tell us about the mouse?"

"What could have been a bad situation, turned into a most fortuitous one," Geoff replied. "While I was watching Ghost, I, accidentally on purpose, went into the same coffee shop he had entered. He said he had run into both of you earlier, and if he didn't know better, he would think we were following him. I, of course, laughed and replied if we were following him, we would not be spotted so easily. He seemed to buy the story and asked me to sit down. Then, he proceeded to propose we go to work for him."

Sean blurted loudly, "My God Geoff, you must have been shitting yourself". Fortunately, no other diners were present to overhear this uncharacteristic remark.

"I was," replied Geoff, "but then, it suddenly hit me. This is what we were looking for! An opportunity where we would know a time and place where Ghost would be exposed, and we could complete our job." He paused for effect, then, somewhat quieter, continued, "if we arranged a meeting, we would set the time and place. Voila, job done!"

"That's brilliant Geoff," Chester replied. Sean nodded his head in agreement.

The hostess reappeared with their drinks and they stopped talking. After taking their lunch orders, she left and the discourse continued. "I agree," Sean stated, then added, "I think we should reconvene in a more private location to develop the details."

Chester then said, "there is another opportunity we need to discuss. This opportunity, if we play our cards right, could blend together with Geoff's news very well."

"Okay, tell us," Sean asked.

"Well, the last time I met with the Clubman, I presented him with a proposal. Once Ghost is taken care of, would they endorse us to take over control of his operation?"

Geoff gave a short whistle, then in a long drawn out pronunciation said, "Nice!"

"There was a snag though?"

"What?" Sean retorted.

"They said no." Chester said and waited for the gravity of the news to sink in before continuing. "My man said, 'as you know, we never endorse a partnership to run an organization. There has to be a boss.' That is when he said they may endorse us IF I would take over as the boss."

Geoff replied, "That's a no brainer Chester, you have always been the leader. Of course you should be the boss." Enthusiastically, he reached over the table and extended his hand to Chester. "I love it - boss," then quickly added, "You will be a benevolent boss though, right?"

Chester chuckled and said, "nothing among us would change".

Then Sean chided in, "but of course it will change, Chester. You will now officially be the boss and we will work for you." He then reached over as well and after shaking his hand, raised his glass and toasting Chester said, "to the boss."

They then happily ate their meal. Chester was relieved to get that message off his chest and thought it went well. He couldn't help but be a little concerned about Sean though, 'of course it will change' kept running through his mind. While Sean outwardly appeared to be enjoying himself, Chester could not help but feel some tension. Sean was not completely comfortable with this. Perhaps he was reading too much into this. Still the seed of doubt, no matter how small, had been sown. Chester filed it away perhaps for another day ... perhaps not.

Chapter Four

Knowing they needed additional time to complete the mission, Chester had approached his contact with the Club and asked for an extension. He explained that while they had the plan in place, Ghost was very unpredictable, and they had to ensure he would be at a specified position and time. Additionally, it had to be public, this limited the opportunities. In fact, Chester had an ulterior motive as well, if he could shadow Ghost for a little while longer, he could get a better handle on his business and contacts.

One month later, the plan was in place. Since Chester and his crew now worked as independent contractors for Ghost, they were all very familiar with many of Ghost's contacts, distribution channel and of course, his entire crew. Unfortunately, Ghost's men were also very familiar with them. That meant they had to employ additional help to carry out the plan, as they needed people unknown to Ghost and his crew. Chester, Geoff and Sean would gather frequently at Chester's condo to develop, tweak and revise various details of the plan. One afternoon while deliberating at Chester's place, the choice of who to engage in the plan was obvious. Sanchez had proven to be reliable and loyal.

The Club was very impressed with their 'disposal' work. Since that evening when they first utilized Sanchez' services, they had been given several additional assignments and were quickly becoming the de facto main supplier for the Club's disposal business. This had grown into a lucrative business. Every week they had several charges to dispose of. At 10K each, this enterprise was growing substantially. There was an occasional pick up from a local location, mostly though, their charges arrived via refrigerated freight. There were a couple of trucking companies that were very discreet and could be counted on to deliver the goods from across the country. All the jobs they were given were domestic, never international. About a third of the packages arrived from southern Ontario, about a quarter from western Canada and the remainder from other parts of the country. Sanchez was very happy with this arrangement, his cut was 2K per delivery, and in a very short time his personal financial difficulties had been abated.

In an effort to assuage Sean's hurt feelings over Chester being in the position of being "the boss", Chester decided to assign Sean the responsibility of operating the disposal business. Chester hoped the additional 10% of the net proceeds would help to soothe the wound of Chester's rise to pre-eminence.

One evening, they invited Sanchez to attend the meeting at Chester's condo. When asked if he wanted in on the job, he enthusiastically accepted. While reviewing the plan, they determined they needed a driver and a shooter. Geoff could don a disguise to do the driving, little attention would be paid to the driver so his identity should be easily shadowed. The issue was they would need another person to act as the shooter. After a few minutes of vetting possible candidates, which were all discounted for one reason or another, Sanchez piped up, "Gentlemen, I may have an answer to your dilemma."

"We're all ears," Sean replied.

"I've known this person all my life and I can vouch for her loyalty and discretion. It is my sister Elena. Growing up in the Castillo neighbourhood of Medellin, from an early age, we were taught the need for discretion in order to survive. This was Escobar's playground and those who did not keep their mouths shut, were soon eliminated." Sanchez paused and looked around the room to see the reaction.

Sean replied, "Wow, Sanchez I didn't know you had a sister."

Then Geoff added, "I hope she is better looking than you."

They laughed and Sanchez continued, "fortunately, she takes after my mother who was very beautiful. I look more like my gruesome-featured father." This was evidently not true as Sanchez was an extremely handsome man. The room once again burst into laughter, then he continued, "Not only is she loyal and well acquainted with the darker side of business; she also works at the rendering plant and may be useful in the future as a back up to gain entry, should I be indisposed."

Chester suspected the taste of wealth had fueled Sanchez' aspirations for greater wealth by taking on a greater role within their ranks. It was understandable, since he couldn't possibly be happy working at that foul-smelling place and arriving home every night with the stench of decay oozing from his clothes.

Chester, however, caught this ploy immediately. He liked Sanchez, but the operation was running very smoothly, and he could not risk changing their procedures now. "I think you may have something here Sanchez, we need to vet Elena, but your endorsement means a lot. However, we cannot alter our procedures at this time, you are too valuable to us at your current capacity at the rendering plant. Sometime in the future, we may bring Elena onboard as our contact when the time warrants it." Sanchez was noticeably deflated, but still eager to proceed with the plan. He bid them good evening and departed on a high note.

Everyone was in a jovial mood, as they now had a reasonable plan going forward, Geoff peeped up, "we need to VET Elena? Really!" They all laughed. Geoff continued, "you know, of course, if we had the resources to complete a proper background check, we also wouldn't have had such difficulty finding another member of our team."

With a chortle, Chester answered, "of course you are right, but nevertheless, let's check the few resources we have." Everyone nodded in agreement. "It shouldn't take more than a day or two and make sure we do not talk to anyone with connections to Ghost."

Two days later, Sanchez arrived at Chester's condo with his little sister in tow. Chester punched in the access code on his phone, which permitted them to take the elevator to his floor. Sean and Geoff were already there, and they waited with anticipation, to meet this person whom their success and freedom would be reliant upon. A small knock on the door and in came Sanchez, followed by his sister. Almost in unison, their jaws dropped and their eyes bulged. Elena was not some frumpy Colombian girl; she was drop-dead gorgeous! She had dark brown Spanish eyes that seemed to ooze sensuality and stir every living man's chest with palpitations. Her pitch coloured hair framed dark skin, which shimmered with an iridescent glow. She was quite tall and had that lean lanky frame that screamed femininity.

After several awkward moments, the dumbfounded guys started to regain their composure. Sean jumped up first and offered her his hand. "Very pleased to meet you Elena, please sit in my spot on the sofa."

She smiled demurely in return, then in throaty, Spanish-accented English said, "thank you, that is very gentlemanly of you. Are you Chester?"

"No, I am Sean," he replied, with an ingratiating smile and pointed towards Geoff who had stood up a fraction of a second after Sean did. "That is Geoff," then pointing towards Chester, "that is Chester."

"Pleased to meet you Elena," Chester smiled, as he walked towards her with his hand extended. Geoff followed quickly thereafter. They stood for a few minutes exchanging small talk. Everyone in the room knew the barrage they had just suffered, and Geoff appeared to be shell shocked, as he barely uttered a word. If he had saliva running down his cheek, you could mistake him for Pavlov's dog. Stoically, Chester regained his composure, then said, "perhaps we should sit and start our meeting. Would you like anything to drink?"

"Sure," Elena replied, "a beer would be very nice." Comically, Sean and Geoff seemed to scramble over each other as they raced to serve Elena.

Sanchez sat down on the sofa beside his sister, while poorly masking a triumphant smile. Then, looking over his shoulder, he sarcastically said, "sure guys, I will have a beer too, thanks for the offer."

Chester sat down in an easy chair across from this gorgeous Spanish bombshell and he knew this would mean trouble. Their group was very tight and cohesive, as they were all friends and had similar beliefs and values. He knew Sean, however, was still harbouring animosity towards him. Now, the introduction of this enchantress would surely create further disruption, with Sean and Geoff tripping over themselves to serve her. Sanchez would surely become jealous, as he would feel responsible for protecting her virtue. Just then, he realized he too was smitten by her charm. He blushed with embarrassment, realizing his mouth was agape while unconsciously staring at her with a lascivious gaze. To break contact, he looked towards the kitchen and said, "would you mind bringing me a water from the fridge also?"

While he felt a premonition of impending trouble, he also knew they had little choice. They needed to complete their mission and there was no reasonable alternative. She would have to be the fifth member. If Sanchez vouched for her, he felt comfortable endorsing her also. He also knew time was running low; as they had already been granted one extension, asking for a further extension to recruit more people would display ineptitude and certainly result in an unfavourable assessment. This could jeopardize their endorsement to take over Ghost's business.

As the guys scrambled to compile the drinks, he thought of what the scene must look like to Elena. She was supposed to be meeting three rough and tough gangster guys. Instead, she had three guys that were awestruck and looked like pubescent teenagers with vacant expressions, and heat pulsing through their loins. Surely, they looked like cavemen when first introduced to fire. Wonder, bewilderment and desire pasted on their faces. With this realization, Chester once again felt his face starting to glow with a blush.

When the drinks were served and everyone was seated, they began to review the plan. Chester reviewed in detail the roles each of them were to play. In addition to the plan, he spent nearly as much time on how they were going to deal with the entire plan, not only the event itself, but the immediately preceding hours and days. After reviewing various contingencies, they realized they had all become hungry. Having spent the entire afternoon in Chester's condo, they did not want to order in. They went to a local pub and found an inconspicuous booth close to the rear. Sanchez and Elena entertained them with stories of their childhood growing up in Columbia.

The Columbia that was reported by the media was very little like the Columbia where Sanchez and Elena grew up. Understandably, they did not have some of the conveniences they enjoyed now. Nevertheless, it was a childhood filled with scraped knees, playgrounds, doting parents, and of course the fun and dread of school days. These stories reminded Chester of his own youthful days.

Throughout the dinner, Chester noticed Geoff and Elena seemed to have quickly formed a chemistry between them. There was the discreet smile and thoughtful gaze that could indicate the beginning of a romance. He took a mental note and decided to keep a careful eye on this situation. Should something develop, he may have to deal with it. Most certainly, a romance could jeopardize their future. His immediate concern was focused on Ghost.

After a couple more days, with a full complement of people, each had their assigned duties. Now they needed to wait for the opportunity. In the meantime, working in Ghost's organization had embedded them with Ghost's crew and also provided Chester with several insights. Ghost started his enterprise by assuming control of Brown Jas' distribution network. He later expanded as a wholesaler, mostly of cannabis, with a smattering of coke and crystal meth. One of Chester's insights was that while there were indeed additional profits to be made retailing, there was substantially greater risks. The more times you touch the product, the greater likelihood to be caught. Street level distribution has a lot of unreliable people, these guys are the people you read about in the news. They flaunt their newfound wealth with flashy cars, they dress like gangstas, and generally live for today with little thought for tomorrow. Chester called them Shooting Stars, they shine brightly but quickly burn up. Most end up dead or in prison.

Another insight Chester had was that Ghost was concerned about making money and buying nice things. He didn't focus any time on what to do with all that cash, once it starts showing up. Ghost kept reams of cash in closets. Chester would ensure they had a system in place to launder their cash and give the appearance of a successful business.

The last insight Chester was able to glean was where the challengers would come from once Ghost was dispatched. He knew there would be a fight for control. Chester decided he should have a brief meeting with his contact just before D-day (D-day is a well know abbreviation, but in this case; D stood for death).

***

They met at Marine Park in Burnaby. Pulling into the parking lot, Chester saw his contact sitting behind the wheel of a dark metallic Mercedes. He slid in the passenger door and they greeted each other. "The target date is within a week. I would like to be more specific, but Ghost keeps changing his pattern."

"Within a week is acceptable." The Clubman answered.

"Any news on our proposal after Ghost is eliminated?"

"Yes, as long as Ghost is terminated within a week, the club will endorse you to take over."

Chester was pleased with this anticipated news. Now though, he needed to plan things for when Ghost is eliminated. "Once Ghost is ...departed...there will be several factions fighting for control. In particular, some of his lieutenants. I would like permission to eliminate several threats."

The Clubman thought for a moment, then replied, "How many and who?"

Chester reviewed each individual and his reasons for eliminating them. The Clubman granted permission with one condition. "They must be eliminated quietly. I think you know how to do that my friend."

Chester nodded his head in agreement and slowly started to smile, "thank you for endorsing me. I won't let you down." They shook hands and left in different directions.

Chester's future now depended on Ghost's death. While he was confident with the plan, he needed to be certain Ghost would not survive. Unbeknownst to the others, Chester used his contact with the Club to introduce him to a fellow named Ellis. Ellis had developed a small, but extremely lucrative, business supplying guns and armaments to the underworld. His group of contacts were very small, and Chester doubted Ellis was even his real name.

Chester explained to Ellis he had a job to complete, and without naming targets explained the overview of the plan. Ellis thought for a moment and suggested instead of using a silenced gun for the actual attack, he could furnish them with a device that could easily be concealed inside the sleeve of an overcoat. Instead of a trigger, it would have to be activated by pushing the barrel of the weapon against the intended victim. If it was silenced properly, nobody would notice the sound with all the chaos happening. The downfall would be that it could only be equipped with one small calibre round. However, if positioned accurately, and using a hollow point bullet, it would be lethal. Chester agreed it was a great suggestion and ordered the device. Ellis said it would be ready the next day.

Ellis turned to Chester, "Have you ever heard of ricin?"

"It's a poison used by espionage agents for assassinations, I believe."

Ellis was smiling, "exactly! It's lethal, kills quickly and the best part is it's almost undetectable. If a pathologist is not looking for it, it will never show up in a postmortem."

Chester slowly rubbed his chin while thinking, and a smile started to cross his face. What better than to assassinate Ghost than with a weapon perfected by espionage agents during the Cold War to quietly assassinate enemies. "I love the concept, but how can it be administered?"

"To be most effective and achieve the fastest result, it needs to be injected. The good news is that only a very small dose is required, so the syringe can easily be disguised in an everyday device. The actual injection would feel like a mosquito sting. The victim will be incapacitated within five minutes and dead within fifteen. What do you think?" Ellis asked. Chester enthusiastically agreed. They discussed the various details over the next few minutes, Chester paid him and made arrangements to pick up the devices.

The next day, Geoff and Chester were visiting Ghost at his suite in the Spall Centre. They were discussing the arrival of a shipment, and while normally, Ghost would not assign this task to Chester, his crew would be busy with other tasks and unable to make the meeting. Chester indicated they would certainly be willing to accept the assignment. One of Ghost's Captains noted Chester was not wearing his Tag Heuer wristwatch and asked if he had lost it.

Chester replied, "No, I needed to replace the battery so I dropped it off earlier, it will be ready later today." What were the chances one of Ghost's goons would notice his missing watch, Chester thought to himself. These guys always dressed like gangsters' bums, oversized clothes, big neck chains and baseball caps always askew. Chester and his crew, on the other hand, always dressed business-like. They wore dress shirts, and most often suits with open collars. He believed these guys were envious and hence noticing the missing wristwatch.

Two days later was D-day. Ghost had asked Chester to arrange a meeting with another gang leader who ran a distribution network in North Vancouver. They agreed to meet for lunch at the Phoenix restaurant in the Hotel Vancouver at noon. Chester and Sean arrived at the Spall Centre to accompany Ghost to the hotel. The plan was that Chester would introduce them, then he and Sean would leave them to their discussions. The restaurant was three blocks away, so commuting on foot was much more expedient than taking a car. As they departed Ghost's condo, the entourage consisted of five people; Ghost and two of his captains, followed by Sean and Chester.

One of Ghost's captains was a thoroughly despicable man, named Dan, who had earlier questioned Chester's wristwatch. He was nicknamed 'Weasel' but was never called it directly to his face. He was reasonably intelligent but was completely lacking in empathy. He was the classic narcissist, who only rose to prominence because he could be counted on to always agree with Ghost, and had no issue eliminating people and dispensing beatings. The story was he liked to pulverize people with baseball bats. On more than one occasion when on a rampage, he would become increasingly deranged and batter his victim so severely he left them dead, instead of being taught a lesson. He would then stand over the disfigured pulp and laugh like a crazy person with blood, brains and entrails spewed everywhere. After Ghost's demise, he was most certainly the first who would need to 'disappear', he would be a definite challenger for leadership, simply because of his unhinged character.

Chester feigned the outward appearance of calm confidence; he knew Sean was also roiling with apprehension as they began their 'dead man walking' journey. They stood on the corner of Burrard Street waiting for the walk light to turn, when an old blind gentleman approached from the rear. Chester and Sean parted slightly to leave room for the elderly gentleman to position himself behind Ghost. Weasel Dan noticed this old fellow, but soon discharged him as a threat as he was elderly, and his white cane indicated he was blind. It was a normal busy day downtown and there were about thirty people waiting on the corner. Just before the walk light turned, a late model car turned the corner in front of them. Chester saw the rear window was lowered, with a gun barrel protruding. The old blind fellow was positioned right behind Ghost, while Chester was off the old man's right shoulder. Instantaneously, the car rounded the corner and fired twice. Nobody noticed Chester opening a small clasp on the inside of his wristwatch to reveal a small protruding needle.

Chester reached around Ghost to pull him back. As he did this, he wrapped his arm around Ghost and subtly injected Ghost with the small needle. Ghost was too busy looking at himself to see if he had been hit, he barely noticed something had pinched him. As if in one motion, Chester pulled Ghost down and onto the ground, over the old blind guy who happened to be in the wrong place at the wrong time. Chaos erupted! Bystanders started screaming and in the cacophony that ensued, nobody noticed the old guy that had fallen over Ghost. The old guy was awkwardly twisting his sleeve to clandestinely unveil a gun barrel. He placed the gun on Ghost's head and pushed the barrel into his temple. There was a brief phpht sound and some blood started to pool under Ghost's limp body. There was a smell of gunpowder in the air, but that was natural as somebody just took a shot at him as he rounded the corner.

Dan the Weasel reached inside his coat and pulled out a revolver. He blindly unleashed five shots in quick succession. Three shots missed the car, but two found their mark. The rear window of the offending vehicle shattered as the car continued speeding down the road. The old blind guy was now becoming extremely agitated, as he tried to untangle himself from the bleeding body he was entwined with. He stood up from the melee and starting cursing in Spanish as he disappeared into the crowd of spectators. Many people from the crowd were screaming and scrambling to safety. The old guy joined the fracas. With all the commotion, nobody noticed the old fellow walking away very briskly, without the use of his cane.

From the corner of his eye, Sean caught a glimpse of the old guy vacating the scene and the shadow of a smile went unnoticed by anyone. Sean yelled at Dan, "don't be an idiot! You can't shoot into a crowd!" Dan turned and his face was red with rage, then quickly the colour drained, when he realized what he had just done.

Chester took charge and yelled, "everyone back! Give us space." Then, he looked towards Sean and barked, "call 911." Sean grabbed his phone and while calling, he appraised the scene before him. Chester and a few other good Samaritans trying to stem the bleeding. Ghost was sprawled across the sidewalk, with a gaping wound in his head. Weasel Dan was just standing there, as if in a trance. He was too much of an idiot to even realize he should be running.

Dan walked over, and motioned towards Ghost and asked, "is he still alive?"

"Yes, I think so," Chester replied. Then quietly added to himself, but not for long.

A few minutes later, an ambulance and a couple of police cars came around the corner. The paramedics jumped out and took over administering first aid to Ghost. They were able to bind his head and stem the bleeding. After checking his vitals, they loaded him onto the gurney and rushed off to the hospital, which, fortunately, was only a couple of blocks away.

In the meantime, the police had cordoned off the area and were busy rounding up witnesses. Dan, realizing the precarious risk he had placed on himself, attempted to sidle away from the area. Sean accidentally, on purpose, noticed this and positioned Dan between himself and the police officers. To ensure the police noticed this, Sean accidentally stepped on somebody's foot and then yelled to draw the policeman's attention. One of the police officers took notice and detained Dan. What he did not notice was that Dan dropped his gun into the garbage receptacle behind his back, as he turned around.

Chester, by this time having replaced the clasp on his wristwatch, was feeling very pleased he had taken the insurance of the ricin, since Ghost was still breathing when he was carried away by the paramedics. Soon, the ricin would begin its deadly journey, as it traveled through Ghost's system and Ghost would cease to breathe. With a massive bullet wound in his head, a coroner would undoubtedly not look any further for the cause of death.

Chester was so keenly focused on his task he hadn't noticed until now, that just up the street, the police were attending to another scene and had set up a perimeter with police tape. There appeared to be two areas cordoned off. Then he remembered Dan blasting at the car racing away; he must have haphazardly struck a bystander – or perhaps two.

Chapter Five

Geoff and Elena waited in their red Ford Mustang on a side street just off Burrard. They were waiting for Sean's signal; a phone call he would make from his pocket. He would not speak, but Geoff would know they were in position.

Geoff had a fake moustache and beard and was wearing a black wig pulled into a ponytail at the back. Since Geoff was mostly bald, the disguise very effectively shielded his identity. Elena, sitting behind him, had her hair tied up under a fedora, and was wearing a man's dress shirt with a polo jacket. She had used makeup to darken her already dark complexion, so unless you paid careful attention, her femininity was completely concealed. To complete the look, she had pasted on a handlebar moustache. Geoff chuckled as he teased her, "you know, for a pretty girl you are looking very unattractive."

Elena laughed in the back seat, "well sonny boy, you are not looking very appealing either! At least my moustache makes me look more manly!"

They both laughed, then turning more serious, Geoff asked, "are you feeling nervous? Are you ready for this?"

Elena pointedly replied, "Yes, I am nervous and yes I am ready! It's not like I will actually be shooting someone, I'll just be firing blanks."

Geoff watched her in the rear-view mirror, as she slowly placed her big-rimmed sunglasses on her delicate turned up nose. Even wearing the dark glasses, he could see her brown eyes glinting back at him. She exuded femininity and Geoff lapped it up like a hungry dog. He realized he had been smitten. He wasn't sure though if it was just lust or the beginnings of true affection. He knew he would have a battle on his hands, as Sean was most certainly on the prowl and had her in his sights. Sean was bigger, stronger and generally better looking. Geoff, though, was known for his tenacity. Every time he looked at her, his heart seemed to skip a beat and involuntarily, a smile creased his face.

The past two days they'd spent a great deal of time together. They sourced a car, which of course had been recently stolen and repainted. They spent hours driving their escape route and ran through the disposal processes many times. The fact was, they both knew they reviewed these scenarios many more times than they needed to. What they really desired was to spend more time in each other's company. Their affection and passion for each other was slowly growing.

The first night, after finding the car, they had dinner together at one of those eclectic restaurants along Commercial Drive, the Punic Café. The food was excellent. They really appreciated the fact the meal was served slowly and they had the extra time to relax and get to know each other better.

"So, tell me Elena. How does a Columbian girl make her way to Vancouver?"

"Well, it's pretty much as you might expect" she smiled wistfully as if watching a retro film in her mind. "Our mother was an elementary school teacher and our father worked as a custodian at the school. That way, either one or the other was with us most days. Papa worked evenings and Momma worked days." She shifted slightly in her chair and crossed her legs. "In hindsight, I see it was a pretty rough neighbourhood but, we didn't know it at the time; it was just home to us. We laughed, played and pretty much had a normal childhood." Elena uncrossed her legs and leaned closer to Geoff. "One evening Papa witnessed a shooting outside the school. There was lots of gunfire and he became quite frightened, so he called the police." She paused for effect, "this was a mistake. Everyone knew this was Escobar's town. He ran the politicians, the police....he effectively ran the city. When the police eventually showed up, there were five people lying dead on the street. Worst of all, Papa was now earmarked as an informer."

Geoff was leaning forward and fully enthralled with the story. He found Elena's voice mesmerizing and he was so lost in her story he paid little attention to any of his surroundings. His food was getting cold and he had barely touched his wine. "So, what happened next?"

"Well, life became very difficult for us. Papa soon lost his job, and nobody would hire him, as he was blacklisted by the cartel. Soon after, Momma lost her job, and then apparently there were death threats. One afternoon, while sitting on the porch, somebody tried to shoot him. After that, we moved to Canada and were given political refugee status. I was very young you see, so Gabriel fills me in on some of the stories."

"Oh My God," Geoff responded. "Do you know I didn't know what his first name was? We always just referred to him as Sanchez."

Laughing, Elena responded, "that's okay, most people know him simply as Sanchez." She looked at Geoff with those big brown eyes, "do you know you haven't touched your food? And ... you were also staring."

Geoff smiled, "well the reason for both is this captivating woman I'm having dinner with."

Slightly blushing, Elena replied, "You smooth talker." She lowered her gaze, shifted slightly in her seat and then raised them again. "And you? What's your story?"

Geoff was coming back to himself, "not nearly as interesting as yours. I grew up in Richmond, just a few miles from here, as you know. It was a lot different back then. It was very English, and my father was a United Church minister. To most people, he was the beloved head of their congregation." Suddenly Geoff's face became hardened, "To me, he was a mean, unforgiving despotic ruler. Needless to say, we never got along very well. Then, when I was fourteen, my mother was diagnosed with cancer. In those days, that pretty much meant a death sentence. I was sixteen when we buried her. Shortly after I moved out, and I haven't seen my father since. I met Chester and Sean a couple of years later and they have been my family ever since." Geoff picked up his fork and started back into eating his dinner.

Elena smiled with genuine interest, "it's funny, you three seem to be very different but you still get along."

"Yes, we are the best of friends. I haven't really thought about it, but yes, we are quite different, aren't we?"

"Yes, for sure. Chester is the natural leader; he is the most serious. Sean is the handsome eye candy, but also extremely friendly and outgoing. You are funny and always making people laugh. She pauses then looked at him intently, "However, I think that's a mechanism you developed to hide your true feelings. You are one of the most sensitive, caring men I have ever met."

Geoff feigning laughter replied, "Ah shucks. You just want to get to know me better."

"There's that joking mechanism at work ... but yes, I would like to get to know you better."

Geoff's heart skipped a double beat! He fell deeper. The remainder of the evening was like a dream. They talked, they laughed, and they definitely drank too much wine. After dinner he called taxis for both of them, as Elena lived in North Van and he lived in south Vancouver. When the cabs arrived, he paid Elena's driver and she gently gave him a kiss. He sensed she really wanted more than a friendly kiss on the cheek and he very much wanted to spend the evening with her. However, he knew this was neither the time nor the place.

Riding in the taxi, Geoff could now understand what people meant when they said, 'love at first sight'. From the moment he first met her, he was fully engrossed in her. He needed to know if it was just infatuation that emanated from his burning loins or if it truly was love. He was certainly open to it being love ... even hoping things would escalate after the job was finished

* * *

Now, as he sat looking at her in his rear-view mirror smiling, his phone rang – it was Sean. He answered, but as prearranged, all he heard was static from pocket noise as the phone rubbed inside Sean's jacket. "Showtime," he declared, and casually easing the car into traffic, they arrived at the designated location in under a minute. As he approached the corner, he first spotted Sean

49

as he was the tallest, then the remainder of the entourage came into view with Dael perched closest to the road at the front. "Get ready," Geoff said, as he slowly turned the corner. He witnessed the scene unfold. Chester was reaching for Dael to pull him out of danger and Sanchez was dressed as an old blind man just behind Dael. He was staring straight ahead and slightly upward, as blind people usually do.

Just then, the car rocked with a blast of noise coming from the back seat. Even though Elena's gun was equipped with blanks, they needed to ensure everyone heard the shots, so they had Ellis load the blanks with 'extra bang'. This would ensure no bystanders were accidentally shot, but they also required them as witnesses and a distraction. As he was driving off, Geoff heard Elena expel a loud "Yes," and as he turned, he saw her accompanied fist punch to the sky. Elena's portion of the plan had gone precisely as planned, now Geoff needed to focus on getting the hell out, before the place was buzzing with cops. Through his rear-view mirror, he briefly glanced in the distance and saw Weasel Dan reaching into his jacket.

This section of Robson Street was busy with many pedestrians, and traffic usually crawled very slowly. Geoff, being in an understandable haste to leave the area, had focused his attention on the road in front of him. As the Vancouver Art Gallery came into focus on the left, there was another loud boom. The glass from the rear window shattered and shards of glass were flying through the air like shrapnel.

It took a moment for Geoff to realize what had happened and to regain his senses, while his ears were buzzing like he had just attended a Black Sabbath concert. His sole focus now was to get out of the area. He gunned the car and took a quick left on Hornby, then a right on Georgia. He slowed to road speed, so as not to draw attention. Elena was quiet in the rear seat and Geoff knew he could not be distracted, so he remained focused on the task ahead. Within minutes, they were across the Georgia Viaduct and into the Strathcona neighbourhood. Strathcona was one of the oldest areas of Vancouver and most of the homes had been designated as 'heritage', with many built in the 1940's. The area was mostly settled with Chinese immigrants and naturally, this area became known as 'Chinatown'. Earlier that week, Geoff and Elena had rented a big three-story house with a detached double garage in the rear.

Geoff pulled into the alley and pressed the clicker as he closed in on the garage. He swiftly pulled in then hit the remote to close the large overhead doors. Now, he felt slightly less on edge and the adrenaline running through his veins slowly subsided. He gradually became aware the back of his head felt wet and sticky. As he reached around, he felt wetness there. Pulling his arm back, he saw the red stain of blood. He suspected he'd caught some of the glass and his scalp was bleeding. H   e felt no pain so he was certain it was just a minor injury.

Then, like a wallop to the chest from a baseball bat, the fear suddenly hit him ... Elena! He looked around and saw her lying slouched over her knees.

"Elena," he called out, then in a much louder voice he barked, "Elena, Are you okay?" No response. He was hoping she too had only been hit with shrapnel and had fallen unconscious, though he feared the worst.

As the garage doors came to rest, he quickly opened his car door. He took several deep breaths before he approached the rear door. Looking through the rear door, he saw a pool of blood on the floor directly under Elena's head. Then he saw there was still blood dripping and adding to the growing pool on the floor. Shocked, he leaned in through the open window and checked for a pulse on her neck. Her carotid artery was no longer pumping, and he knew she was dead!

He collapsed beside the car and noticed tears were running down his cheek. After a moment of reflection, he screamed "NOOOOOOOOO". He sat weeping for several minutes. In a flash, his dreams had been dashed. This was the first woman he had met where he thought their relationship may develop into something more than sex. Through his despair, he remembered his own wound. Through his tears, he reached behind his head to examine the damage. At that moment, he remembered he was still in disguise and wearing the wig with a ponytail. As he was blindly checking, he felt something that seemed to be stuck in his ponytail.

The wig was attached with 2-sided tape and as he pulled the wig off, it ripped like Velcro being pulled apart. He brought the wig into view and in horror he just stared. Stuck to the hair was one of Elena's big, gorgeous brown eyes! Immediately he felt the vomit rising in this throat demanding to be released. After a few moments he crumpled like a rag doll with no skeletal structure. Lying on the floor in a sobbing pool of anguish.

Chapter Six

Chester and Sean had arrived at the house, having picked up Sean's Jeep that was parked in a parking lot adjacent to the Spall Centre. When they pulled up to the front of the house, they were surprised to see no lights on. "I guess we must be the first ones back," Sean said.

Suddenly, the jubilant mood changed. "I don't like this; something must have happened." Chester replied. "We should be the last ones to arrive. Geoff and Elena should have been the first ones back."

As they made their way up the front steps, they noticed how the wooden steps creaked with each step. They tried to be quiet, but the squeaking steps would certainly have given them away. Sean removed his keys and used one to unlock the front door. Gingerly, they stepped in and listened... no sound. Then, Sean said, "Hello," in a voice somewhat lower than normal conversational tone. Still no answer. After drawing all the curtains, they felt comfortable turning on the lights. They proceeded to search the house. Chester checked downstairs while Sean quickly ran up the stairs, two at a time.

After a brief search, Chester heard Sean, "I think I found them. Meet me in the kitchen."

Chester ran up the stairs and Sean was peeking through the blinds in the kitchen towards the garage. "Where are they?"

"In the garage – look there are lights on."

Peering through the blinds, Chester could see lights in the garage. As he turned, he saw Sean opening the rear door moving quickly towards the garage. Chester followed and entered the garage right behind Sean. They saw Geoff folded up on the floor next to the car with his arms wrapped around his knees. He looked up and immediately they knew something was terribly amiss. Chester quickly closed the door and Sean asked, "what's wrong?"

Geoff's eyes were red, he was clearly weeping, and slobber ran down his chin. He just motioned with his head towards the rear seat of the car. Afraid of what they might find, they tentatively approached. They could see the rear window was shattered and inside there were blood spatters. Then they saw Elena, hunched over and a pool of blood at her feet.

"Oh My God!" Chester exclaimed, as Sean reached in to check her pulse.

"It's too late Sean, I already did that, she's gone." Geoff sputtered, just prior to another spasm of weeping overtaking him. As he wept, he held up his wig. It took a moment to register that what they were looking at was an eyeball plastered to it.

"What happened?" Sean moved towards Geoff and put a consoling arm around him.

"That asshole Dan the Weasel, that's what happened!"

Then they heard Sanchez calling from the house. "Hey, are you guys out there?"

Sean looked at Chester. Chester said, "You go. Don't let him come out here."

Sean left and shortly after, from inside the house, they could hear wood splintering and glass breaking. Obviously, Sean had delivered the news. Chester knew there was no way they would be able to keep Sanchez away. He could though, at least, make her a little more presentable. He grabbed some paper towels and some wet rags. He wasn't going to clean the car, but he would clean her up. He laid her on the rear seat and began cleaning the blood and bits that were plastered on her face. He removed the disguise that she had worn and removed the man's jacket, leaving her with the shirt and trousers. The back of her head had a hole in it that was easy to cover, but the gaping hole that once contained her eye was very gruesome. He found a pair of sunglasses and placed them on her to cover up the wound.

He looked at his work and decided it was as good as he could make her look. Her beauty remained, but now her once glowing skin had taken on a pale, deathly pallor, and of course, if you removed her sunglasses the macabre cause of death was evident.

Leaving Geoff sitting there, Chester returned to the house. Inside, Sanchez had stopped screaming and breaking things, but he was barely controllable. He was pleading with Sean to let him see his sister.

"Sanchez, I am so sorry," Chester commiserated. "If you insist on seeing her, I must warn you it is not a pretty sight."

This seemed to calm Sanchez and he nodded agreement. "Yes, I would like to see her. I have seen dead bodies before, and I know it is not pretty."

Sean, putting his arm around Sanchez helped him to the garage. When he saw Elena, instead of losing it, he just stared blankly. He never spoke or cried – he just stared. After what seemed an eternity, Sanchez finally said, "Thanks for cleaning her up. I am fine now."

Seeing how Sanchez steeled his resolution, Geoff somehow gained control of himself. Together, the four of them trudged into the house without saying a word. Once inside, they talked about the events and what they needed to do. Chester and Sean assured Sanchez and Geoff they would look after things. Chester had a plan and if they all agreed he would proceed. Chester outlined the plan and while Geoff gulped when Chester discussed Elena, he agreed it was a good plan. Sanchez agreed as it would allow him to openly mourn his sister.

Chester left the room and made a phone call. Returning, he motioned Sean to come along and together they left. After several minutes, a car drove up the alley and two people got out. They went into the garage, and left carrying an oblong package wrapped in plastic and placed it in the trunk. Shortly after the first car departed, another one pulled up and one person got out. Chester shook his hand and opened the overhead garage doors. As the man got behind the wheel of the mustang, Chester said, "make sure there is nothing left."

As the car left and Sean returned to the house, Chester had a quick moment to reflect. Geoff took Elena's death very hard. Obviously, they grew much closer than he was aware of. What about Sanchez, what would this do to him? Would he unravel and go after the Weasel? Would this unhinge him? He knew too many secrets, if he could not be counted on…

The man drove the Mustang through back streets to the huge vacant parking lot at the Pacific National Exhibition grounds. The other car was waiting for him. Parking the Mustang, he retrieved a large phosphorus incendiary device and placed it in the back seat. They exited the parking lot and when they reached McGill Street, the driver pushed a button and immediately, the Mustang exploded into a large white flame.

✳✳✳

BRAZEN GANGLAND SHOOTING LEAVES 2 DEAD
VANCOUVER (BREAKING NEWS) –

Shortly before noon today, witnesses reported a drive-by shooting on the corner of Burrard and Robson. This brazen act occurred while the street corner was occupied by at least three dozen pedestrians. Police sources indicate it was likely a 'professional hit', as the shooter was able to identify and execute the victim from a moving car. The victim, who has not been identified, is known to police. He died shortly after arriving at the hospital from a single gunshot to the head, according to hospital sources.

Following the shooting, witnesses reported an alleged associate of the victim removed an illegal weapon he was carrying and began haphazardly firing at the vehicle as it sped away. At least two shots hit innocent bystanders. One victim died at the scene, while another is in critical condition at St. Paul's Hospital. Police have apprehended one suspect, identified as Dan LaCoq, also known as Weasel.

In an unrelated event, the body of a women in her mid 20's was discovered on East Georgia Street last evening. Police have not identified the victim, pending notification of her next of kin. Police sources indicate she wasnot known to them. They have not found any motivation for this heinous murder.

Chapter Seven

One Year Later

Chester had recently moved from his downtown condo and purchased a penthouse suite in Port Moody. Port Moody is a small suburb; a quaint little city nestled within the metro Vancouver area. His penthouse suite was in a new development called Newport Village which, when complete would become a small nearly self-sustaining community, furnished with restaurants, service businesses, grocery store and five twenty-five story high residential towers.

This location suited Chester much better. He had easy access to downtown, as well as the rest of metro Vancouver, plus it had a feeling of remoteness. Situated at the terminus of Burrard Inlet, there was plenty of greenspaces and parks that gave him the isolation he keenly desired at times, and yet within a few steps, he was back in the bustle of a metropolitan city.

At this moment, Chester was in one of his reflective moods. The top of Burnaby Mountain to the west and Mount Seymour to the northwest were shrouded in sparse, low clouds on an otherwise clear day. It was like the peaks of the mountains had a magnetic attraction that pulled the clouds towards them and wrapped around them like a blanket warming a sleeping child.

With a steaming cup of coffee in hand, he ventured out onto the large wraparound deck. He strode over towards the south eastern side of the deck where Mount Baker stood above the peaks of the Cascade mountain range. This was the granddaddy of mountains in the area; even though it was located in Washington state, inhabitants of Vancouver laid a claim to it, as it represented the south eastern edge of the Fraser Valley.

As he watched it while sipping steaming espresso, he thought he had seen a bloom of volcanic gases venting. Even though it hasn't erupted in hundreds of years, every once in a while, it liked to remind folks it is dangerous so it belches volcanic gases.

He was reminded of Elena, while watching Mount Baker; both were gorgeous and majestic with an element of danger lurking underneath. Geoff, while still reliable, never quite returned to his former self. He was still the joker, but in stolen moments you could find him very forlorn.

For Chester, the opportunity to get to know her more was torn away by that idiot Dan. Dan was indeed a weasel, he always found a way to extricate himself from situations where he should have taken the blame. Growing up on a farm in Saskatchewan, Chester recalled a saying, while a little crass, it perfectly suited Dan…'He could fall in a pile of shit and come out smelling like a rose.' That day, when the idiot Dan haphazardly fired at Elena's car, that mindless act killed three people. Elena, like the others, was an innocent victim. She deserved to live a full life.

Chester ruminated on how life could change the course of future events at a moment's notice. He realized if Elena had lived, her budding relationship with Geoff may have created a problem for the organization. In that respect, it may have been fortuitous. He quickly dismissed the thought as he didn't want to think of "what ifs" and he didn't want to acknowledge the brief feeling of shame threatening to sneak into his thoughts.

In Chester's eyes, Weasel Dan had effectively evaded justice once again. He was charged and convicted of manslaughter and would likely be released within 5-10 years, and once again come out smelling like the rose. Three of his fellow lieutenants, from Ghost's former gang, disappeared within a week of Ghost's death. The story on the street was, fearing for their lives, they left the country and were living undercover somewhere in Mexico or South America.

To maintain the gossip and deflect suspicion away from himself, Chester would feed the rumour mill with supposed sightings in various nefarious locales. He nearly laughed out loud when he recalled the story of how one of his lieutenants, Abdul, was sighted, training for ISIS in Chechnya and he was being prepared to fight in Syria. Most people are very gullible, and like sharks circling a wounded fish they devour a good story. They would be less fascinated with the true story. They simply disappeared and their remains were scattered as fertilizer in the gardens across metro Vancouver. Chester was reminded that in 5-10 years, with Dan's release, another disappearance would have to be scheduled.

Chester reminisced on his meeting with Sean and Geoff on the docks at Granville Island less than two years ago. At that time, they were young guys unsure which direction life would take them, let alone knowing where next month's rent would come from. They were happy and carefree.

Now, one year later, they had groomed a small narcotic distribution network they'd inherited from Ghost into a mid-level business and they were in the process of expanding into other business ventures. They were making more money than they ever imagined. This success came with a cost though. With greater success, there was a corresponding decrease in carefree happiness.

Their success brought satisfaction and an ever-increasing hunger for more. Success and wealth are an addiction, not significantly any different than a drug addict. The more you satiated your yearning, an ever-increasing quantity was needed to maintain the high.

Chester had finished his coffee and returned to his kitchen to refresh his cup. As he pushed the button to dispense another double shot of espresso, his phone rang. It was Sean. He had just arrived, and after parking he took the elevator up the twenty-five floors to the penthouse. Chester answered the door warmly, and after a greeting and a small hug asked Sean if he would like to refresh his coffee. Sean held a large take away cup in his hand and replied he still had almost a full cup. Chester grabbed his brew and invited Sean out to the deck.

"Every time I see this view, I am awed," Sean stated. Chester, having sat down indicated to Sean he could take the seat opposite.

"Thanks," Chester replied. "I was just sitting here thinking about how life has changed for us in a very short time. Can you believe some twenty months ago we were having coffee on Granville Island, discussing a proposition presented to us to get rid of Brown Jas." He paused for a moment as if reliving the day, "who would have thought that fateful decision would have led to where we are today?"

"Yeah," Sean replied, "two years ago, we didn't know where our next rent cheque was coming from," making a sweeping gesture with his hand. "Now … all this!"

They were comfortable in each other's presence and sat quietly for a few moments. Their reflective silence was broken with Chester's phone ringing; it was Geoff at the intercom.

After Geoff arrived, the three of them sat down outside enjoying the warmth of the late morning sun. They were laughing as they discussed what had transpired in their lives over the past couple of years. The mood changed abruptly when Sean brought up Elena. Chester observed Geoff wince at the mention of her name. While they all felt an intense pain with her loss, Chester knew Geoff suffered more than either he or Sean. Like a trooper though, he never mentioned it and held the pain inside.

Chester broke the mournful solemnity with, "Sanchez will join us later." Then he changed the subject, "but first I wanted the three of us to have a discussion. Sanchez has proved his loyalty and friendship, but the three of us, Tifflen, Favelle and Moehr are the original group, TFM. We represent the senior leadership of this organization."

They looked at each other and nodded in agreement. Chester continued, "We have grown quite large and while I know you are aware of that, I am not sure you fully understand the magnitude of our operation and some of the problems this success entails. We need to be much more organized than Ghost. He was focused on making loads of cash and then stashed it in his closet. We need a legitimate business front that can explain our wealth. The cops will be suspicious if we suddenly have loads of money … which, of course, we do. So, we must be smart and not draw attention to ourselves, until we can justify it." Looking around at his condo he added, "this was likely not a smart investment; however, millions of people have mortgages way beyond what they should have. I could be like many others with huge mortgage payments."

"Okay," Geoff replied, "I get it. 'What do you have in mind?"

Chester proceeded, "one of the strengths of our organization is that the three of us openly discuss proposals and almost always come to a conclusion that is better than the original proposed. After all, three heads are better than one - TFM. Every successful organization requires a division of roles and principals. I propose three basic principles:

One, do not draw attention to yourself or do something that would endanger the organization or any of its members. Two, no matter how large we become, we will always respect the fact that the Club is the ultimate authority and

three, we will only invest in ventures that are profitable unto themselves."

Sean replied, "sounds fine to me. Nice and simple."

Geoff added, "I agree also," as he nodded his agreement.

Geoff, being more business-oriented, suggested they set up an investment company, with Chester maintaining 51% ownership, and with Sean and Geoff holding 24.5 % each. Distribution of profits would be split evenly three ways. After setting up the company, they would open an office downtown and operate as a legitimate business, as well as looking after cleaning their illicitly-acquired money.

Chester noticed Sean agreeing reluctantly. The strain on his face indicated he wasn't entirely happy. Chester quietly wondered if this would be a problem down the road. Sean's demeanor lightened when Geoff suggested Sean should become a senior partner in the new business, while continuing to operate the disposal business, which had become extremely lucrative. This business division was vital to their future success and more importantly, endeared themselves to the Club. Sean would continue to take his commission and place the remainder of the funds into general revenue.

Chester then suggested Geoff should also become a senior partner and assume the role of CEO (Chief Executive Officer). He would effectively run the legitimate side of the business. They had so much money coming in that they needed to divest it into other businesses, and in doing so ensure the money was properly laundered.

While Geoff was always a willing participant in their nefarious endeavors, Chester felt that ever since Elena's death, some of Geoff's motivation towards their illegal activities died as well. Additionally, Geoff was perhaps the most intelligent member of their group. He loved dealing with money and investments.

Chester would become the Senior Managing Partner. He would officially be the boss, but his focus would be on the drug distribution business. Of course, Chester's other major value, was that he was the contact to the Club. They agreed to bring Sanchez on as a captain.

Their organization would take a page from military structure. Under Sanchez, there would be several lieutenants who were currently in place running their separate units. Under these lieutenants were the crew chiefs, who distributed to the independent field force that looked after sales on the streets.

This organization served several purposes. First, by employing independent dealers on the streets it naturally diversified the business. Should one or two dealers disappear, the business would barely feel the loss. Second, street dealers were the notorious 'bad asses', they were often flaunting their wealth, doing stupid things and drawing the attention of police. This system separated the street business from distribution. These 'filters' in the organization protected not only the leadership, but each level of the organization. Third, by employing independent dealers, it would enable the organization to expand more rapidly, since they didn't have a recruitment issue as the independent dealers recruited their own street dealers.

Before bringing Sanchez on board, one of the first issues they would need to address was the rendering company. At this point, Sean's business had only one means of disposal. Worse yet, they had no control over this company. The rendering business on the north shore was one facility in a larger multinational conglomerate. The company itself was privately owned and valued at several hundred million dollars. Even if they wished to acquire it, they could not afford to buy it.

They needed to diversify. They came up with a couple of additional disposal channels. First, they would acquire a fishing business. While the commercial fishery was not as lucrative as it had been in the past, it was still profitable if operated correctly, and this was in accordance with their last principle. They would only invest in ventures that were profitable unto themselves. Additionally, if they owned a fishing vessel they could travel up and down the coast without drawing attention. The deep ocean was a natural disposal arena for bodies that would never be seen again. The various critters that were indigenous to this habitat would effectively clear away all flesh and bone.

Years earlier, people would dump the bodies too close to shore. Now, it had become common for body parts to wash ashore. Most of the body parts were feet. They would encase their victims with cement shoes and dump them the in the Georgia Strait. After a few years, the bodies would be consumed by various sea creatures and only the feet remained. After further decomposition, the feet would be freed from their cement shoes and wash ashore. Worse still, they would not remove clothing and frequently, the feet would still have their shoes on. Depending on the type of shoe that re-appeared; while it may be difficult to identify the victim himself, the shoes themselves provided a substantial clue. The manufacturer could usually identify the model and year of production.

With their own operation, they would ensure all identifying elements were removed, including clothes, dental pieces and all teeth. Additionally, they had sourced an old x-ray machine where they could identify any implants (knees, hips, etc.); these were removed prior to disposal. Sean was very proud when he professed that his disposal process would leave no item to identify the victim. He was a professional through and through, and always looking for ways to make his process even more infallible. Aware that cocksure people usually overlooked something that led to their downfall, Sean suggested that in addition to the fishing trawler, they also invest in a hog farm. Sean was familiar with events a few years prior, where a pig farmer disposed of prostitutes he murdered by feeding them to his pigs.

Chester had quickly agreed. Growing up in rural Saskatchewan, he had worked on several farms. One farm in particular was a large hog farm. What most people don't realize is that hogs will eat nearly anything, and cannibalism is not beyond their appetite. While doing morning chores, he would often find remnants of hogs. They had died and the other pigs in the pen would feast on the carcass, many times very little remained.

The hog farm was a disgusting smelly putrid place to work and he was certain this experience would not provide any insight he could draw upon somewhere in his future. He was wrong though, for now he understood the beauty behind Sean's suggestion. Furthermore, things like bones and teeth often remained after being devoured by cannibal hogs. They had an incinerator in the yard where they would burn the remaining carcasses and their remnants.

Chester suggested that in addition to the hog farm they set up a proper incinerator, complete with scrubbers to filter the air. This, in itself, could become a revenue generator, as other farmers could bring their animal carcasses for incineration.

With the macabre discussion that had just taken place, nobody had an appetite for lunch, so they agreed to part and reschedule a follow-up meeting in a couple of days to determine the next steps. Geoff had excused himself and went to the bathroom. Upon returning, Chester noticed a distinct grey pallor had washed over his face. He suspected he had been sick to his stomach. While Geoff was always a willing participant, he was also the most susceptible to emotion. Chester now felt even more assured that removing Geoff from the more gruesome divisions of business had been a correct assignment.

Three days later, they reassembled at Chester's condo. Sean reported, "I have found a fishing trawler that should serve our needs very handily. The current owner, after years of little to no profit, has decided to sell. There is a downside though; there are three boats in the fleet and as a result three fishing permits. Boats without permits were useless as they could not fish commercially. These three vessels and their corresponding licences had decreased value substantially over the past five years, from a high of $2,000,000 to today's value of about $1,000,000. The owner is motivated, and we can likely get them for under 900K."

Geoff whistled, "that's a lot of moola!"

"Indeed," Chester added, "but if we keep all the cash in the business and forego any dividends for a while, we can pull it off."

Geoff then said, "we have another issue though."

"That is?" Chester inquired.

"We know nothing about fishing boats, who's going to run them?"

Sean smiled and cheekily added, "Oh, did I fail to mention I also found an operator. He is convinced he could turn a nice profit if they were run properly. His name is Seamus O'Malley, an Irishman, whose family spent centuries as fishermen back in the old country. He was educated in business from Queen's University in Belfast, but ran into troubles, like a lot of other Irishmen, with the political divide that swelled there. He emigrated a decade ago and best of all, he has no love for authorities."

Geoff laughed, "You cheeky bugger, you know they refer to those days as 'The Troubles,' right?"

"Of course," Sean laughed.

"How reliable will he be to not interfere with your disposal business?" Chester asked.

Sean replied, "I believe Seamus will readily keep quiet as long as his pockets are suitably lined. However, I am not sure he could be fully trusted with all the details. We will have to keep him in the dark. The upside is he should be able to turn this into a thriving business. If, on occasion, I took a boat for excursions, nudge-nudge, wink-wink; he would certainly turn a blind eye."

"That's fantastic Sean," Geoff replied. "Any news on the farm?"

"So far nothing. However, I did find a realtor who specializes in farm acquisitions. He is currently looking and feels confident we will find something shortly. There is a lot of demand for small hobby farms, where rich guys can build their monster homes. Actual working farms are also in quite high demand as they are very profitable these days."

Geoff then reported, "Well, I have been quite successful. The best piece of news is I found a legal firm whose specialty is organizing companies for high worth individuals ... and almost all of their clients attained their wealth by means not strictly legal."

"Nice," Chester replied.

"At our meeting, they suggested we set up several companies, many in offshore countries that cater to businesses that require the greatest confidentiality. The law firm is operated by two brothers, Stevenson and Nathaniel Ostranski. I have set up a meeting for tomorrow. If that works for you two?"

"Works for me." Sean replied.

"What time?" added Chester.

"I have it set for 10:00, but they are flexible."

"That will work," Chester confirmed.

Geoff then continued. "At the meeting, they will outline the set-up of the companies and how, through holding companies, they could purchase various legitimate businesses that authorities could not trace back. The fishing fleet would likely be a great business to funnel some additional profits through. I have taken the liberty of having them set up the holding company that will be the face of the organization. The name of the company I chose was LNa Investments."

Chester smiled and nodded his agreement. "Nice touch," he said.

Geoff smiled and replied, "I thought it would keep a bit of her alive, if only in a name."

Sean then blurted out, "Okay, now I get it. I didn't at first. It is a play on Elena's name."

Nine Months Later

Chester pulled into the underground parking lot at Bentali Centre downtown. As Chester rounded the corner, he saw Geoff's and Sean's vehicles were already parked. He pulled in beside them in a space marked 'Reserved for LNa'. His sparkling black Maserati Ghibli Q4 looked right at home beside Sean's Land Rover and Geoff's Maybach. He was thinking to himself that this was good. At his condo, his car stood out in the condo parking lot, which was a sea of Fords, Toyotas, Mazdas, and a spattering of entry level BMWs and Mercedes Benz. He knew his car was a vice that drew too much attention to him. This was contrary to the edict of not drawing too much attention to themselves. However, he loved driving it and believed a penthouse owner should be driving something more exclusive than a Ford or a Toyota.

Chester entered the elevator in the parking garage and pushed the ground floor button. For security reasons, the elevators from the garage floors could only go as high as the ground floor. This way, everyone entering the building had to go past the security desk. As Chester approached the desk for Bentali 5, the security guard looked up and said, "good morning Mr. Moehr, I will buzz you up".

"Thanks, and good morning to you also," Chester replied, and made his way to the elevators on the south side. The bank of elevators on the north went to floors 2-22. The south elevators went to floors above 22. On this side, there was no directory for the businesses on the higher floors. The elevator opened and Chester pushed 30. Upon reaching his level, the doors opened and unveiled a spacious reception area that gleamed with glass and shiny gunmetal accents. The diffused lighting cascaded down and gave the appearance of natural light. Chester exited the elevator, turned right and walked through large, frosted glass doors at the end of the hallway. The etching on the door indicated the number was 3005 and the occupants were LNa Investments.

Chester opened the door and the receptionist looked up from behind her desk with a warm smile and said, "Hi Chester, Sean is here already, and I believe he is in with Geoff."

"Thanks Nancy, we have a meeting today with our lawyers. When Sanchez arrives, please ring us to let us know. We will call him when we are ready."

"No problem Chester, and I will let you know when Stevenson and Nathaniel arrive."

Chester walked towards his office down the corridor, passing the corner office which had the name Geoff Favelle, Senior Partner, CEO, emblazoned on the door. He heard voices inside and stuck his head in through the half-opened door. Inside, Geoff was sitting behind his large mahogany desk and Sean was seated in one of the easy chairs across the room. "Good morning gents," Chester said.

"Morning Chester," they both replied.

"Did you see the game last night?" Sean asked.

Chester replied, "I saw most of it. The Canucks didn't play very well and unfortunately, the result was exactly what they deserved. Even though they are down, they still have a chance to pull it off." The Canucks were in the Stanley Cup Playoffs, and after last night's loss, they were down 3 games to 1 in the best of seven series. This was the main, and perhaps the only topic the entire city was talking about. Vancouver is a hockey town and everywhere you went you overheard conversations about the Sedins or some other significant player.

The streets and every business were plastered with posters of the Canucks, mostly encouraging them on to victory. Chester excused himself and continued down the hallway towards the office next to Geoff's. The sign on the door read Chester Moehr, Senior Partner. His office was adorned just as elegantly as Geoff`s, though it was slightly smaller, and he did not have quite as nice a view. Chester was perfectly happy with this arrangement, as Geoff was the finance guy. Chester, while being the boss, did not get involved in day to day business; his focus was their drug distribution business. Chester and Sean made the money, Geoff cleaned and invested it.

Some thirty minutes later, the phone rang, and Nancy announced the lawyers had arrived. "Great," Chester replied, "please show them to meeting room one, I will let Geoff and Sean know." Chester got up from behind the desk, pulled on his suit jacket and grabbed a couple of files from his desk. He walked to Geoff's office and informed him the lawyers had arrived, then proceeded to the office on the other side, where the sign on the door read Sean Tifflen, Senior Partner.

As he approached Sean's door, Sean boomed out from inside, "I heard you Chester, I will be along shortly." This caught Chester by surprise. Something was amiss, Sean is usually more jovial. He peered into Sean's office. Sean seated at his desk, curtly repeating "I said I'll be along shortly." Now, Chester knew something was wrong ... but what? This should be a happy day.

On entering the conference room, Chester exchanged greetings with Stevenson and Nathaniel, then invited them to help themselves to the refreshments and snacks that were placed on a long, modern-styled, glass table at the far end of the room. The room was very bright and spacious, with a spectacular view of Coal Harbour and the boat club on the shores of Stanley Park, immediately across the water. The area was a beehive of activity with rowers skirting about, departing and returning from the pier. Others were carrying boats to and fro, while a small group were busy maintaining their boats having them propped upside down on sawhorses. Gazing out at this, Chester remarked how this sight would not be seen in almost any other part of Canada, as the water would be iced over from the depths of winter.

Chester indicated Stevenson and Nathaniel should take their seats against the inside wall. This would furnish them with the view outside, while Chester and his team would be facing the inside wall, which was glass and provided a view of the hall outside; certainly not as interesting a view. Chester purposely positioned meetings this way for two reasons. Firstly, the group facing outside ran the danger of being distracted by the view and being disarmed they may say something unintentionally. Secondly, it helped him and his team focus on the task at hand without the distraction.

Geoff and Sean arrived. After greeting and helping themselves to coffee, they sat down with Geoff to Chester's right and Sean to his left. The Orstranskis outlined the process for investing in new property development projects. Through a series of holding companies and offshore accounts, they would effectively finance their projects with funds they derived from their illegal activities. This would efficiently launder the money and come out the other side squeaky clean. Best of all, the property development projects would also be very profitable. In this climate of rising real estate values, it was nearly impossible for a property to not appreciate in value. This appealed to Chester, as he was always looking to make a profit on every venture. He hated the idea that in order to clean his money, what came out would be less than what was put in. He was always looking for a positive return.

The Ostranskis had come prepared with several investment opportunities. In all cases, they would take a minority position. This way, they would collect the profits without becoming bogged down with the hassle of overseeing the development. After reviewing and agreeing to this new property development initiative and several projects which they felt would be the most lucrative, they began their review of the other investments. The agricultural business had grown nicely. In addition to being a splendid method for Sean's disposal business, they had replaced the small incinerator with a larger one complete with filters and scrubbers. They then offered incineration service to other farmers in the area. This service was readily accepted, as the closest incinerator was over five hundred kilometers away. Once again, this incineration centre had turned into a nice profit producer, in addition to the profit the farm itself derived.

Meanwhile, Sanchez had arrived at the LNa offices. He had the customary greeting with Nancy, and she called through to let Chester know he had arrived. He was antsy, obviously on pins and needles, since receiving the call from Chester asking him to join them at the office.

Nervously sitting on the sofa, the company logo caught his attention. On the wall behind Nancy was a silhouette on a large backlit glass. The glass was contoured so the shadows formed an image. He was shocked when he realized it formed an obscure outline of his dead sister.

In the conference room, Chester advised the Ostranskis that Sanchez was the partner they spoke about and checked with them to ensure the proper documents were prepared. They indicated they had all the papers prepared and required signatures before filing to make it official. As Chester left the room to retrieve Sanchez, Nathaniel removed several documents from his attaché case and placed them on the desk in front of him.

Chester returned with Sanchez in tow and introduced Sanchez to the Ostranskis. Completing the obligatory handshakes, Sanchez was invited to take a seat beside Sean. He was obviously uncomfortable as he sat down. Chester smiled at Sanchez, knowing he remained completely lost as to the reason for him being there. Everyone felt the trepidation Sanchez brought into the room. This should be celebratory, but Sanchez wasn't feeling it ... yet.

Chester began speaking, "Gabriel." Sanchez knew something important was up, nobody ever called him by his actual name. "I suspect you may be feeling a little intimidated and wondering what you are doing here?"

Sanchez' Spanish-accented voice cracked slightly when he replied, "absolutely right... on both counts, I might add."

"Well, as you know, the three of us," Chester pointed to Geoff and Sean, "are partners in our business ventures and we guard this very tightly. We do not want additional partners and have never entertained bringing anyone else on board." He then paused for effect. "You have been a true and loyal employee for a long time. We trust your judgment, friendship, and value your service to our organization." Chester then looked towards both Geoff and Sean, who had beaming smiles and nodded their acknowledgement. "Today, we are setting up another company, this one is going to focus on international shipping, and we would like to offer you a piece of the pie. Within a few years, this venture, according to projections; will be valued at over 50 million dollars. And we would like to offer you a 5% share. What do you think?"

The shock was written on Sanchez' face and after a moment he replied, "That is incredibly generous guys, but I am afraid I do not have the money to invest."

Sean just smiled and slapped Sanchez on his back, "How do you know ... you haven't heard what the price is." Inwardly, Chester was happy as Sean appeared to be back to his usual self.

Still somewhat shaken, Sanchez replied, "I thought you said it would be 5% of 50 million! I am not great with math, but I know that is a lot more than what I've got!"

They all laughed, and Chester replied, "That is what it WILL be worth, today it is just being set up. To establish the company, the share price will initially be valued at a dollar a share. Your 100 shares will cost you a hundred bucks and you can pay us later if you wish … perhaps with a round of drinks."

Somewhat dumbfounded, Sanchez timidly squeaked out, "How can I refuse?!"

They all laughed and shook hands to welcome him onboard. The lawyers then explained how the company would be purchased through a holding company based in Malta, with the ship being registered in Bermuda for tax purposes. Over the next hour, they all endorsed and completed several documents. After wrapping this up, the Ostranskis bid their goodbyes and left. Chester asked Sanchez to stick around, as they needed to discuss further details with him.

Chester proceeded to explain the organization of the newly formed shipping division to Sanchez. Along with having an ownership stake in this new company, Sanchez would receive a very healthy salary. While his direct report would be Geoff, who looked after all the legitimate businesses, he would continue to be his 'number two' with the drug distribution business. Chester then reiterated the principles the organization operated under; never draw attention to yourself, always be professional, protect the organization and structure, and perhaps the most important principle – 'omerta' – their code of silence. Sanchez acknowledged these principles, but you could see he was curious why Chester would repeat these principles that everyone knew very well.

Chester then said that Sanchez' first order of business would be searching for a shipping vessel and finding out how the shipping business worked. He suggested perhaps the best way to do this was to find reliable people, who could assist him with the details, in addition to purchasing, registering, insurance, hiring a crew, arranging contracts for cargo, etc. The next partner meeting would be in a week and he could report on progress then.

Sanchez nodded acknowledgement of the task as hand, "it looks like I have some work ahead of me."

Chester looked towards Sean and winked. Sean taking the queue, stood up and said, "how about you follow me Sanchez? I would like to show you something." Sean then left the conference room and turned down the hallway instead of walking towards reception. Sanchez followed him past Chester and Geoff's offices. Sanchez assumed they were heading for Sean's office which was next to Geoff's. Instead, they walked past to the office next to Sean. "What do you think?"

Standing at the doorway, Sanchez replied, 'It a very nice office, with an incredible view. Wow, that looks like the port in the distance. From here, I can see Simon Fraser University perched on Burnaby Mountain...and of course the entire port. I didn't think we were high enough to see that from here."

Sean walked into the office and said, "well, if you are going to be looking after our shipping interests, it is likely a good idea to keep an eye on the ships, don't you think?" Sanchez then noticed the sign on the door. It read Gabriel Sanchez, Senior Associate. His eyes widened and he opened his mouth to speak, but nothing came out. "Welcome to your new office," Sean remarked and extended his hand for a handshake.

"I don't know what to say," Sanchez exclaimed, "I have never had an office before." Chester and Geoff came around the corner and congratulated him with hearty handshakes as well.

"Why don't you take your seat behind the desk and take a few minutes to absorb it all." Sean added.

Sanchez walked around the desk and sat down. With misting eyes, he said "I can't believe this. Imagine a couple years ago I was in danger of losing my house and in a lot of debt. Then, out of the blue, you show up Sean and now..." His hands opened in a gesture that indicated, 'all this'. Sanchez had a proud smile on this face. The smile was so pronounced there may have been a danger of it causing permanent creases.

"I'll come and get you in a few minutes and we can go for our celebratory drink." Sean said, and they departed, leaving Sanchez in his glory to soak up his good fortune.

As they walked to their respective offices, Chester said, "Sean, I need to discuss a couple things with you." Then, looking towards Geoff, "why don't you take Sanchez, and we will meet up with you after we are done here."

"I don't think that is a good idea," Sean unexpectedly protested. "I brought him in, I think it is only fitting I escort him."

"No, this is a serious matter. It is regarding the Clubman and must take precedence." Chester's contact with 'the Club' had morphed into referring to him simply as Clubman.

Sean was visibly agitated, but he understood the necessity. Chester and Geoff both looked at him with perplexed gazes. This was very odd for Sean to be upset at such a minor inconvenience. "Of course," Sean replied, "Clubman takes priority. I will just make a quick phone call and meet you in your office."

As Sean entered his office, Geoff looked at Chester with a perplexed look and shrugged his shoulders. "That's fine Chester, I will grab Sanchez and we will meet you at the lounge."

As Chester sat down behind his desk, he was bemused at Sean's strange reaction. Perhaps he felt an allegiance to Sanchez that Chester had underestimated. By the time Sean arrived in his office, he was back to his normal self. His affinity towards Sanchez had been replaced with his business demeanor, interspersed with occasional jocular quips for which he was known for. They sat for several minutes discussing Sanchez' ascension and how he was the first person to be added to their quorum. While he wasn't a partner, he was the first to have an equity interest in the business. While Chester wanted to bring him onboard and was certain Sean felt the same way, deep down he had some reservations about opening their business to others. The discussion with Sean seemed to assuage these smouldering doubts.

Chester then brought up the topic at the centre of this meeting. Clubman had informed him there was an especially large shipment arriving from Montreal within two days. It was paramount these packages be removed as quickly and quietly as possible.

Sean's curiosity had now peaked and he was a little concerned as they had never previously received directions like this. "How large is this shipment?" he inquired.

Chester shrugged his shoulders, which served as a reply that he didn't know. "I know you are thinking the same as I am. Why take this unusual step beforehand? It must be something special. Do you anticipate any issues?"

"Who knows! The operation is very efficient, and we have handled up to half a dozen at a time – so I think we should be fine."

At that moment, a loud cacophony arose from outside the window at street level. There were screams and loud retorts that sounded like gunfire. Chester was alarmed and jumped towards the window to investigate. He saw Sean out of the corner of his eye and all colour had been washed from his face. With genuine concern, Chester gazed upon what was happening below. Sean had joined him. They both watched aghast as they recognised Geoff's car in the mayhem.

* * *

Geoff and Sanchez had left their office and stopped at the security desk to register Sanchez as a new associate for LNa. As Geoff said the company name out loud, both of them seemed to have that faraway look for a moment. For a fleeting moment, they both recalled Elena with pangs of remorse, and the realization of the vacuum she left in their lives. They then took the elevator to the parking garage. By the time the doors opened, their moment of reminiscence had been replaced with laughter. This was a momentous day and they had regained their jovial spirit.

They were in high spirits as they made their way to Geoff's Maybach. Geoff loved this car and always enjoyed driving it. Even when ensnarled in gridlock, he always maintained a smile on his face as this luxurious car seemed to instill relaxed comfort and simple enjoyment. As Sanchez eased himself into the passenger seat, Geoff noticed the car had a similar effect on him as a larger smile crossed his face. "Nice wheels," Sanchez said.

As Geoff started the engine, he looked at Sanchez and said, "You can have one too you know. As a registered employee, you are entitled to a company car as well." This surprised Sanchez, as he hadn't thought that far ahead. Geoff then added, "of course, you can choose something else if you wish, as you can see Chester, Sean and myself have all chosen different vehicles."

"I....I....I don't know," sputtered Sanchez.

"Lots of time to decide on that and of course we need to get an additional parking space," Geoff replied.

They maneuvered their way towards the exit. As they snaked through the maze of vehicles, and after passing the sign that indicated the exit, there was another sign overhead that read 'right', and on the other lane it read "left". Geoff eased his glistening obsidian black automobile onto the right ramp, and upon entering street level he slowed to check for traffic. Gazing to his left, he saw two men open their trench coats and swing out their assault rifles. Geoff reactively punched the accelerator, instinctively, the Maybach flew onto the street, fishtailing as his tires screamed their resistance. Instantaneously, a large Mercedes Benz SUV pulled up the ramp attempting to turn left. The two assailants unleashed havoc, bullets were flying towards Geoff, but the occupants of the SUV received the brunt of the fusillade which effectively shielded Geoff and Sanchez from the onslaught.

Perched well above them, Chester and Sean witnessed Geoff's vehicle pulling away from the building and speedily driving down the street.

They were safe! Chester released an explosion of breath.

Beside him, Sean still looked rigid with shock.

"It's okay. They're okay," Chester said. "But my god..."

Sean wiped perspiration from his forehead and bolted for the door.

Chester did not ponder this. Reflexively, he grabbed his suit jacket and followed Sean out the door, struggling to put on his jacket while quickly running towards the front desk. He stopped at reception and told Nancy, "Sean and I are leaving."

"Do you know what that noise was outside? It sounded like shots."

"You are correct, there were shots. It will soon be swarming outside with police."

"Oh, My God! Geoff and Sanchez just left...."

"They're okay, we saw Geoff's car driving down the street. I'm not sure how much of that they saw....if they did...they are likely frightened as hell."

Sean raced towards the front. Chester was already at the door. Waiting for the elevator, Chester could feel his heart stop racing, he glanced over at Sean – he had more colour in his face. Obviously, he had calmed down, "there are likely cops everywhere. We will never get out of the parking garage. Let's grab a cab up the street."

"Good idea."

A short time later, they arrived at the Seafood House in Kitsilano. Chester saw Geoff and Sanchez seated at a window table. They both had drinks in front of them and another round had just arrived. Without waiting for the hostess, they walked to the table.

Chester said, "what the hell was that? Did you guys get caught up in it?

Geoff, still visibly shaken replied, "Yes we did. I have no idea what the fuck happened! I saw the gunmen ... and just gunned it!"

Sanchez added, "I didn't see who was in the SUV ... with all those bullets flying... I'm sure nobody survived."

Shocked, Chester blurted, "You saw the gunmen?"

"At first, I thought they were after us ... I saw the Uzi's ... then the black SUV pulled up! I wasn't about to stick around ... I took a bullet in the back of my car. We saw a hole in the trunk." Geoff then took a big swig of Scotch.

"You don't think it was meant for you, do you?" Chester retorted.

Shaking his head, Geoff replied, "No, I don't think so." Then, in true Geoff fashion, he made light of it. "Who would want to kill us ... everybody loves us!"

"Thank God you guys are okay." Sean added. "I heard on a news report coming over that there were two people killed in the vehicle. They aren't releasing names, but they say the victims are 'known to police."

"Well let's find out who they were, I hate these meat heads screwing up business. The police will be on high alert for a while" Chester replied.

Chapter Eight

After having a couple of drinks, the tension subsided and soon they were eating an early dinner. They had forgotten about the shooting and high spirits ensued. With many toasts, they welcomed Sanchez to the team. As the evening wore on, the talk and laughter grew louder. Soon, Geoff was slurring slightly more than the rest. "I don't think I can drive home guys ... well maybe Sean could drive, my car and drop us off ... he hasn't been drinking like the rest of us."

"Naw, I can't drive either. I think we should all take cabs home." Sean said offhandedly.

Chester had noticed Sean wasn't drinking as much as the rest of them, but when Sean said, 'Naw", he knew Sean was also drunk. Mister elocutionist would never say 'Naw'. "You are, as always, absolutely correct Geoffrey, my friend. But ... no cabs. Let's get the waiter to line up some limos. It is, after all, a celebration!" Chester had only had a couple glasses of wine. He hated getting drunk and losing control.

After settling their tab and leaving an extremely generous tip, the waiter announced the limos had arrived.

As they were leaving, Chester pulled out his billfold and peeled off several hundred-dollar bills, then quietly stuffed them in Sanchez' pocket. "Just in case you don't have enough cash on you."

Sanchez smiled, "thanks."

***

Sean had his limo take him to their offices downtown. He slid behind the wheel of his Range Rover and after exiting the parking lot he made a hurried phone call. When the person on the other end answered, Sean was very short with him and barked, "we need to meet!" He was crossing the Georgia viaduct as he listened for the reply. After hanging up, he changed lanes then exited on Main Street and started his drive towards the valley. At the first stop light, he violently hit the steering wheel with both hands, while screaming with a loud angry voice, "Fuck, Fuck, Fuck!" As the light turned green, he noticed several people were staring at him as they witnessed his outburst. He regained his composure, then continued on his drive.

He listened to news reports as he drove. The report on the shooting indicated two people were killed on the scene. These two were known to police and were affiliated with a lower mainland drug gang. One of the reports indicated it was a couple that were shot, so likely a drug dealer and his girlfriend, Sean deduced. Fortunately, there was little pedestrian traffic so nobody else was inadvertently shot. Innocent bystanders being killed was a violation of the number one rule amongst gangsters. The two shooting suspects had left the scene by the time police arrived. IHIT had taken control and were conducting the investigation.

As he was travelling, Sean kept reliving the events as they happened. Starting with his reaction to Chester, when he suggested Geoff take Sanchez to the restaurant. Sean knew he overreacted, and this caused suspicion with both Chester and Geoff. Upon returning to his office, he regained his senses and texted his contact – ABORT, ABORT. He was worried Chester might have read something odd into Sean's reaction. Then, when all hell broke out, he wondered if Chester thought he had over-reacted to that too.

Traffic was heavy. He'd caught the tail end of rush hour traffic, normally this trip should take about forty-five minutes took much longer. Now, nearly ninety minutes later, he pulled into the parking lot of the Shark Club on 88th Ave. After parking, he purposefully walked very quickly to the entrance. He took the flight of stairs two at a time and as he approached the concierge, he thought to himself that he was grateful for all those hours in the gym, as most people would be out of breath. Upon seeing Sean, the concierge directed him to the back room where his party was waiting for him.

Bursting into the room, "WHAT THE FUCK!" Sean blurted towards Walter Dyck who was sitting at a table with three of his compatriots enjoying their cocktails and laughing.

"Whoa, slow down there, buddy boy," Walter scolded. "Take a seat and we'll order you a drink while we talk about this."

Sean was fuming, and not in a mood to socialize with the man who nearly got him killed. Understanding his hostility would not serve his purpose, he took a couple of deep breaths and calmly replied, "Okay, I will listen, but I am very upset!" Turning to one of the soldiers sitting with Walter, he said, "I'll have a double Glenlivet, neat." One of the men reluctantly got up and went to the bar to get his drink. "So, talk," Sean barked at Walter.

Walter Dyck had developed a distribution business based in the Fraser Valley. Unlike LNa though, he ran the wholesale and the retail business. His market was smaller, but by taking profit from both levels he made a great deal of money. His profit likely rivaled that of Sean's business. Unlike LNa, 'The Dyck' (as he was known to others, but never to his face), didn't expand his enterprise into other fields and he was not as discreet. In fact, Sean, Chester and Geoff took great pride in the fact that they were 'not known' to the police. The Dyck was known to every junior police officer and half of the general public.

"Our guys made a mistake," Walter said.

"A mistake!" Sean exclaimed, as he took a swig from the glass of scotch that had just been delivered. "I texted you the abort signal."

" ... And I picked it up, but not in time to call off the boys. We got lucky in the fact they took out that miserable Asian, The Bean."

"The Bean! That's who got whacked?"

Walter laughed and nodded his head. "What are the chances he would show up just as Chester was about to be whacked. Too bad they got his old lady too – but I hear she was a bit of a low-life anyway."

Sean turned very red and he blurted, "That wasn't Chester you idiot! That was Geoff and an associate! Chester and I watched it unfold from 30 floors up!"

This time, Walter had a look of shock pasted across his face, "not Chester?"

"No, don't those idiots know the difference between a Maybach and a Maserati?"

Walter was still digesting this news and merely shrugged his shoulders to indicate 'who knows'. "Get real, they're just country boys. Ask them to tell the difference between an F150 and a Silverado and they can likely do it with their eyes closed. But, between two luxury cars. I doubt it. As a matter of fact, I'm not sure I could tell the difference. Which one is worth more money?"

"What?"

"Which one is worth more? I may have to get one too."

The absurdity of the question helped Sean calm down and regain control. At first, he shrugged off the question, he then realized the brilliance. By making an absurd remark, it shocked him, and Walter was able to diffuse the situation. He then redirected the conversation back to the business at hand.

Sean went into repair mode. "So, tell me what happened to the idiot shooters?"

"They were just a couple of local guys from the valley. They are freelancers."

"Names?"

Walter provided Sean with the names. He knew he had just signed their death warrants. They were obviously expendable, or he wouldn't have handed over the names so easily. "So, where can I find them and what do they look like?"

The Dyck provided the details.

"Okay, for now just lay low," Sean replied, "I don't know at this point what the next steps are, or when we will get another opportunity. There is nothing tying you to this fiasco, so just keep your mouth shut." Then, coldly looking towards Walter's two associates, "How about these guys? Can they be trusted?"

The two soldiers simultaneously looked very shocked with Sean's death stare. The guy who brought Sean his drink nearly choked on his own saliva. "I can vouch for them," Walter said, "These guys are loyal."

"Good," Sean replied, then holding his empty glass towards the first associate said, "I'll have another ... please."

This time, the guys jumped up to get his drink. Walter then spoke, "you will let me know when we have another opportunity. This is good for both of us you understand. I put my neck out too, as this is not a sanctioned hit."

Nodding his head, Sean replied, "I know. This is what the Americans called the MAD strategy in the Cold War - Mutually Assured Destruction. If one of us goes down, the other will follow."

The Dyck's smirk disappeared momentarily ... Sean had once again wrestled control. After finishing his drink, Sean got up and shook hands with Walter and his two associates. Sean noticed both associates had a very wet and clammy handshake. Good, he thought to himself, I hope I frightened them enough to keep quiet.

As Sean left, he looked around the room to do a quick evaluation. Normally, he scanned every room he entered, but in this case, he was so upset he overlooked this tactic. The only fellow who was somewhat suspicious was the guy sitting along the one wall. He had long hair tied into a ponytail and was dressed rather casually like a mechanic or somebody who made his living by manual labour. It was odd though that his hands looked clean and without callouses. Sean decided he wanted to check him out a little closer, so he turned towards the bar and ordered a couple of Coors beers. He grabbed them and walked towards the guy sitting by himself. As Sean was approaching him, the guy got up and greeted two guys that had entered the pub. They shook hands and sat down.

Seeing this, Sean sat down at a table and feigned looking at his phone. The long- haired guy was watching him as Sean got up and walked over to him. "I see you have good taste. I just got called away and I haven't touched my beer. Would you like them?"

"Well that's very kind of you, most certainly I will. It's not every day a painter gets a free beer."

"Not a house painter I assume?" Sean retorted.

"No, how did you guess?" the guy asked.

"Most painters are wearing their whites after a day of work."

"Thanks again," the painter said raising his bottle as if toasting him.

Sean left and walked to his Range Rover. He noticed two guys sitting in a Ford pickup. In Vancouver, this would be unusual. Here, he thought to himself it would be unusual to see a couple of guys sitting in a sedan. Sean didn't notice the one fellow taking discreet photographs as he crossed the parking lot.

Inside the restaurant, a couple sitting by themselves were having dinner. She looked at the man and said, "You are always working, aren't you?"

"Crime works all hours, my love," he responded as his phone buzzed. He read the text – thanks boss got some good pics, no idea who this guy is. Likely a nobody.

The detectives were dejected as they watched Sean leave the parking lot. The fellow in the passenger seat with the camera said, "I guess it was fortunate we were not far away when the new boss called. I just hope nothing happened at the stakeout while we were gone."

"Yeah, not a good way to start. The new boss may have blown our cover, just to get a snap of a nobody. Want a coffee before we head back?"

Chapter Nine

On a farm on the Matsqui Prairie, just north of the rural city of Abbotsford, a strange series of events were playing out. At the entrance to the farm, there was a sign that read 'A.J. Moser Farms'. The farmyard was clean, the buildings had been recently painted bright red with a white trim, and the lawn was tidy and overwhelmed the yard with that smell of freshly cut grass. Behind the manicured yard, sat an austere 1960's farmhouse. There was a manicured and weeded vegetable garden that contained rows of assorted vegetables in perfectly straight lines. Lining the garden on three sides were rows of fruit trees. A small grove of assorted blueberry and raspberry bushes were blooming adjacent to the house. This setting gave the appearance of a conventional farm, where the occupants toiled throughout the day to provide for their family, and after decades of life and hard work the owners would live out their elderly years on the farm and die peacefully in their sleep. It was a quaint, serene setting. Everything was green with life. The Fraser River could be seen from the upper floors of the house and just beyond the river, the forest carpeted slopes of the Coastal mountain range were visible. Further still, the snow-capped peaks appeared to touch the sky.

What was missing in this scene were children playing outside, and the scurrying farm activity associated with an operating farm. Normalcy had been replaced with a scene that looked like something out of a disaster movie. At the entrance to the farm, a pickup truck was positioned and two sentries, dressed in white vests, stood guard outside. There was a logo on the vests and on the truck that read 'Agriculture Canada'. On the large sign posted across a makeshift gate that spanned the entrance, were the words – 'Agriculture Canada Hazard Containment Area – Entry Prohibited'. The entire farm had yellow tape surrounding it, much like what you would expect to see at a police crime scene.

Next to one of two large barns was a large 20-foot panel truck. People were standing around wearing white containment suits with the hoods pulled down, respirators askew and their faces exposed. The scene was reminiscent of a containment area where Ebola or some other deadly virus was found.

This general area of Abbotsford was intensively farmed. The farms were small compared to farms in most other parts of Canada. The average farm was under forty hectares, though extremely productive and profitable. Due to the smaller sizes of the farms, they were positioned very close to one another. AJ Moser Farm's main source of income came from those chicken barns currently the scene of intense scrutiny. Inside the large white truck was an on-site mobile laboratory. The technicians inside were running a series of tests with some very sophisticated diagnostic equipment. They had just confirmed the barn had been infected with an avian flu virus. The strain of H5N2 was new to this country, and an outbreak in the general public would overrun the health care industry. Current estimates were that this strain came with a mortality rate of nearly 15% within the human population. Additionally, the economy would be devastated as tourism was the number one industry in British Columbia.

The news that an infected barn was discovered on Matsqui Prairie spread amongst the farmers like a proverbial prairie wildfire. Farmers were all too aware of the devastation an outbreak like this would do to their livelihoods. The last time there was an outbreak, 90% of the chicken and turkey farms had their flocks destroyed. It took several years to rebuild the flocks and they never really recovered from the financial blow.

During the last episode, the farmers received compensation from Ag Canada for their euthanized flocks, and while the compensation was reasonable, it didn't fully cover all the costs. Many suppliers also endured a financial blow for which they did not receive compensation. In order to reconcile the losses, many had to increase their prices and like almost every other good – when the price goes up, they never come down.

A little over a year ago, Sean had begun his search for a hog farm. After months of futility, the realtor brought him to a medium-sized farm called 'GH Reed Hog Producers' The owner was an elderly gentleman named George Henry. George Henry loved the Canadian Football League, and when he incorporated his farm, he added the Reed in honour of his most revered CFL player – George Reed. George Henry had recently passed away and the estate was now trying to sell off the farm. The farm had a small amount of land that had been turned into a hay field, and a hog barn complete with a small incinerator. Sean made an offer that day and by the end of the day, the farm was theirs.

Bennie Rolheiser was understandably very apprehensive when he saw the Ag Canada truck pull into the yard. Bennie was the General Manager of GH Reed Hog Producers and had been hired by Geoff Favelle. Under his stewardship, the farm had grown from an operation that had a single 2000 herd barn, to a now extensive operation that had six barns, over 15,000 hogs and 200 employees. Unknown to people outside the management group, the single most profitable part of the operation was the incinerator Geoff had insisted they maintain. They refurbished the incinerator to ensure they would not run into emission issues. In fact, outside of the incinerator building, you could barely notice any odour. Bennie was sitting in his office at their small nondescript administration building. There was a simple sign over the outside door that read, 'Office'.

As the two gentlemen drove up to the office building, they seemed to sit for a couple minutes reading documents and looking towards the incinerator. When they finally emerged from the truck, they came directly to the office. They introduced themselves and asked Bennie if he had a couple of minutes for a discussion. After entering Bennies office, Bernie extended the normal pleasantries of offering coffee.

Taking a seat, the man who had introduced himself as Dr. White cleared his throat, "by now I am sure you know what has happened at the Moser farm."

Bennie nodded, "Yes I heard."

Smiling Dr. White continued, "rumours here spread faster than the virus. I am quite certain everyone knew about our presence within half an hour of us showing up on the site."

Congenially, Bennie nodded and added, "well, you know this is how we make a living. If there is another outbreak it affects all of us."

Dr. White then said, "but in your case, Mr. Rolheiser, instead of this being financially devastating, it could be a windfall." He then paused to gauge Bennie's reaction. Bennie had a puzzled look on his face that indicated he did not understand. "I understand, Mr. Rolheiser, that you have the only incinerator in the valley. With any outbreak, it is imperative we cull the flock and incinerate the carcasses."

Like a light switch suddenly being switched on, Bennie understood, "Ahh, you want me to burn your birds."

"We have to examine your incinerator to ensure it reaches a high enough temperature. We need to make certain the virus is destroyed. From our research, I do not think this will be an issue, but we need to confirm that. If it passes, we would like to contract you to incinerate any infected flocks. Of course, you will be compensated directly from AgCan."

Bennie smiled, and said, "of course we will help." Then added, "of course the compensation will have to be acceptable."

"First things first. Let's begin with checking out the incinerator. We have our gear with us, and we can do our tests the next time you fire it up."

"We will be firing it up this afternoon. I can get it started right after lunch if you like. It takes about an hour to reach maximum temperature."

"And what temperature would that be?"

"If we fire all the burners, we can get close to 1000 degrees."

"I assume you mean Celsius?"

"Yes, of course" Bennie laughed. Then in jest added, "less than that, you just get roast pig!"

That afternoon, they confirmed the temperature reached 990C and agreed to the fee. Normally, Bennie would charge his customers by weight. Instead of weight, AgCan wanted to pay a price per unit. During negotiations, Bennie completed simple calculations in his head, and once Dr. White and his associate left, Bennie quickly confirmed his calculations. The government was effectively paying ten times the regular rate! This windfall would make for a very nice year-end bonus.

Chapter Ten

As the first rays of the morning sun reached the apex of the window, the bright sunlight began pouring into the darkness. The spilling light's first victim was the large two-meter saltwater aquarium that filled much of the wall, next to the floor to ceiling glass windows. The invading sunlight caused the fish in the aquarium to begin darting about. As the frenzied fish swam, they created tiny ripples and wavelets on the surface of the water. The sunlight was refracted through these waves and showered the light in a cornucopia of colour across the ceiling and opposing wall. This symphony of colour danced and dazzled its way across the room in an incessant march towards Sean, who was lying asleep at the far side of the room.

Sean was lying in a twisted sort of foetal position, with the faintest hint of a smile at the corners of his slightly upturned mouth. He was being held deeply in the throes of his subconscious. Burrowing into his dream state, Sean had ascended to the position of 'the boss'. He was sitting in a big luxurious office, surrounded by several of his captains, suddenly the door burst open! Through the blazing light that poured through the door, he saw an ethereal figure standing there. With a startle, he realized it was Chester!

Sean's eyes popped open with fright as he was bombarded with the blazing morning light and immediately shocked awake. He felt a weight in his chest as he struggled for breath. This tortuous episode left his sheets drenched with perspiration. He threw off the sheets and sat up, he calmed himself and slowly the agitation drained from his body. He looked at the bedside clock. It was 7:00 AM.

He looked over at his new girlfriend, Ava, resting. Even with her shoulder length dark hair askew, she looked incredibly beautiful. Her flawless skin seemed to have a natural radiation about it that caused Sean to smile in amazement. He was so enthralled with watching her, he did not hear Ella. As she stealthily approached the bed, she jumped and landed full force on Sean's chest. He laughed and rolled with the Golden Retriever. Ava, awoken from her slumber, also started petting the dog and laughing.

Leaning over to give Ava a kiss, Sean said, "good morning, beautiful." Before his lips found hers though, Ella began licking and jumping once again, bringing on another round of laughter and frolicking.

Jumping up, unashamedly naked, Sean smiled, "want a coffee?"

"Absolutely ... .with cream,"

"Of course, I know that ... lots of cream!" Sean knew she was watching his bare derriere as he walked towards the kitchen. As he was making coffee, he thought about how his life had changed in the past couple of months since meeting Ava. They had an immediate connection, he felt comfortable with her ... perhaps for the first time in his life, he had a relationship with a lady that seemed unstrained. He felt a nuzzle on his leg, Ella, obviously wanted something to eat. Smiling, he rubbed her head.

After feeding Ella, when Sean returned to the bedroom with the cup of coffee, Ava sat up in the bed with a big smile.

"Now that's a sight for sore eyes," Sean said as he passed her the coffee. Then out of the corner of his eye, he noticed an envelope on his pillow. "What's this?" he said as he crawled into his side of the bed. He opened the envelope and inside was an anniversary card. Somewhat bewildered, he looked at Ava.

"It's our three-month anniversary, dummy!"

"Oh, I'm sorry ... I didn't get you anything." Sean said apologetically.

"That's okay – you can take me out to dinner tonight."

"I'm so sorry sweetie, I will be working late tonight. Can I take a rain check?"

"No problem. It will have to be in a couple weeks though. There is a new television series starting soon and we have to start preparing the set tomorrow. With these things, new setups and all the preps, we're never really sure how long it will take." Ava replied.

"I'm still getting used to your job. The movie business works strange hours."

Ava, with a shocked look on her face, replied "... and your hours are normal?"

Sean laughed, "touché."

"Anyhow, I have a few errands to run today, before we start work on the set tomorrow. I have to arrange sitters for Ella as neither of us will be around to take her for walks." She paused in reflection momentarily, "are you sure you're still okay with us living here? You not only got a girlfriend, but you also inherited a dog as part of the package, and I daresay, a dog who is seemingly even more demanding than a child."

Sean kissed her and said, "life has never been better."

They threw off the covers and made love. Spent, they rolled over. Immediately, they were pounced on by Ella again. Sean rubbed Ella's head and said, "I have to go to the gym ... even though I would much rather spend the day wrapped in your arms."

He got dressed, grabbed an apple juice and headed to the gym. He liked living in his condo and was glad he bought his condo on the north shore. He liked the gym in his condo, and with his erratic schedule he could work out whenever time permitted. Being a keen advocate for maintaining physical health, daily exercise was mandatory for him. It was a point of pride that he maintained a properly toned body. He was fit and energetic, not like the gangbangers that would spend hours every day in a gym and frequently with the aid of steroids, their muscles grew increasingly large and misshapen. He had a naturally large body type with large muscles that were evident with his large, chiseled biceps.

As he began his workout, he started formulating the report he would be giving to Chester and Geoff today. After the fiasco of those boneheads The Dyck hired, he knew the stage was set to easily deflect suspicion by simple coincidence. Geoff and Sanchez had simply been in the wrong place, at the wrong time. He also knew Chester would shelter some suspicion and want to find the shooters for interrogation. He unconsciously checked his phone to see if there were any messages. He knew it was too early, but it was still instinct to check.

Last night after leaving The Dyck, he texted Ressler and Poirier. These were associates he employed in his disposal operation. These two could be relied upon to quietly snatch the idiot gunmen. After completion, they would deliver them to the cold storage complex that now served as the basis for Sean's disposal business. It was a large complex they acquired and purchased through one of the offshore companies, so if somehow the operation was uncovered, they would not have the entire complex confiscated by police. He knew the first part of his cover-up was to apprehend and silence those two. Ressler and Poirier were efficient and good at their jobs. Unfortunately, they were also not gifted with great intelligence and had a propensity towards excessive cocaine use; which of course leads to the danger of loose lips.

After showering and having breakfast with Ava, Sean made his way to the office downtown. He was seldom the first one in, as Geoff almost always preceded him. Nancy was the early bird and was always the first to arrive. She was quiet, discreet and always pleasant and professional. Geoff certainly made a good hire when he brought her onboard. She would of course have some suspicions about the nature of their business, but she kept those thoughts to herself. She didn't want to know too much, just in case at some point it may impair her deniability.

"Morning Nancy," Sean greeted upon entering the office.

"Good Morning Sean. Chester called earlier and said he would like a senior partner meeting at 10:30. Will that work for you?"

"Yes, no problem. Is Geoff in his office?"

"He is, as well as our new senior associate, Mr. Sanchez."

"Thanks Nancy," Sean stated as he proceeded down the hall towards the offices. During all that transpired over the past day, he had forgotten they had brought Sanchez on as an equity partner. He smiled for perhaps the first time in the past 24 hours, when he thought about Sanchez.

"Morning Sanchez," he said, as he poked his head into his new office. Sanchez looked up from his desk and immediately, he beamed a big smile.

"Hi Sean. Just getting used to all this. I still can't believe my good fortune. I think I sat in all the chairs and the chesterfield in my office, just to try them out. They are all very comfy you know."

"Indeed, they are, and the chesterfield is long enough that you can stretch out on it if you need quick nap."

They both laughed then Sean continued on to his own office. After hanging up his jacket, he looked through his contact list and placed a call to Seamus O'Malley, who ran the fishing fleet He needed Seamus to check on which ships may be available for Sean to take on a trip with a couple of his buddies over the weekend.

Seamus, being a quintessential Irishman, was not only a good administrator but one that came furnished with many Irish quirks and superstitions.

Sean had little understanding of the commercial fishing business, and, as such, he gave Seamus a free hand in setting up the company. Including naming the company – 'Aos Si Limited'. Aos Si was the name of some sort of mythological supernatural race of beings.

Sean always pictured them as tiny leprechauns with funny hats and pointy-toed shoes. This mythological race, like every race, had good people interspersed with some bad ones. The original boat was named Abarta, which was a member of this race that was known as the doer of deeds. This was appropriate as this boat would be the foundation from which Seamus would build his fleet. He named the second and third ships: Sheevra – which meant 'spirit' to Seamus, and his fellow Ulstermen. Then finally, Sluagh Sidhe – which was 'fairy host'. Later, they added Abhartach – which was a 'magician', and Fachun – was the last and largest of the fleet. Fachun meant 'single eyed monster'.

Seamus told Sean that Abhartach was in dock and would be undertaking some routine maintenance while the crew was taking two weeks leave, before departing on an eight week tour up to Langara on the north end of Haida Gwai. They would be operating out of Prince Rupert for a faster turnaround. Since the maintenance was simple oiling and greasing, there would be no problem with him taking it for a few days.

Sean knew that Seamus was more than happy to have him use the boat for a few days. A boat sitting in dock was a boat not generating any revenue. Seamus was handsomely compensated for his work. The largest part of his compensation came from his bonus. When Sean or any member of the LNa team used a boat, Aos Si Limited would be paid $5000 per day, plus the consumables that were used, most of which was fuel. They didn't actually transfer funds, instead his profit target would be reduced by a corresponding amount. While Seamus understood the priority was to operate the business profitably, he was also well aware that he was an employee, and when Sean commissioned a boat, he was the boss.

* * *

Sean entered the conference room to find Chester and Geoff already there and helping themselves to coffee and snacks that Nancy had arranged. "Morning, Gents," Sean haughtily said, "how's everyone today?"

"I have to admit there were a few cobwebs this morning," Geoff replied.

Sitting down, Chester said, "morning to you as well. Any more details on the shooting?"

Sean replied, "still working the rumour mill, but all initial indications are that you guys," as he looked towards Geoff, "were just in the wrong place, at the wrong time. The intended victim was most certainly the Asian, known as 'The Bean'. He was an idiot gangbanger who flaunted his wealth and made many enemies. It looks like he was the target and his wife just happened to be along for the ride."

"Well I have to admit, even if we were not the intended victims, it scared the shit out of me! It took several rums last night before I could fall asleep." Geoff replied.

"And the shooters?" Chester asked.

"Still working on that. If, as rumoured, it was a couple of low-level coke heads, they may be long gone. I am sure I will know more over the next couple of days."

"Okay," Chester replied, while his body language seemed to indicate he wasn't completely convinced. Then, as if flipping a switch he continued, "Clubman indicated this morning their special shipment should arrive within a day. Are you prepared?"

"I am working on it today. I have two guys lined up to help with the processing at the storage unit. The largest issue is that we don't know how large the shipment is. I don't want to bring in more help unless we need it, trying to keep it on the QT as much as possible."

"Sounds good to me Sean," Chester added, "I would suggest, as a precaution, you line up some additional help. Don't tell them what the job is, just to be on call in case you need them."

"Good idea," Sean replied coolly. Chester sensed Sean was not as cautious as his response sounded.

"Sorry Sean if you think I am overstepping. It's just that this is an important commission. I know you know your business."

Sean replied, "I guess we are all a little edgy."

Geoff then added, "I had an interesting conversation with Sanchez yesterday after the shooting. I said something about the Club not being happy about open gunfire in the street. He said that within our organization people refer to us simply as 'the Clubmen'- funny don't you think?"

Chester shrugged his shoulders and Sean replied, "Well, I guess that's better than LNa Men ... I think I like the ring of that."

Getting back on subject, Chester said, "So, anything else we should add to the agenda?".

"Mostly routine stuff," Geoff spoke up. "However, this morning I had a call from Bennie on the farm. It appears there is another outbreak of the avian flu virus on poultry farms in the valley. At this point, they don't know how many flocks have been infected, but Ag Canada has commissioned Bennie to incinerate the carcasses at ten times the usual rate. We will be in for a bit of a windfall. It's a good thing we put in the new charcoal scrubbers last fall. If we get a lot of business, there would be a lot of smoke without them. We don't want neighbours, or environmental police down our backs."

"Alright then, thanks guys," Chester stated. "Let's make ourselves available over the next couple of days, in case our special shipment requires more attention. Also, I suspect Sanchez may be feeling a little overwhelmed with trying to set up the new shipping enterprise. Anything you can do to help him will be appreciated."

* * *

By midafternoon, Sean received a text from Ressler which read: 'the items you requested have been picked up and are being stored'.

Sean was smiling and replied – 'see you in 45'.

Sean arrived at the cold storage unit and entered the front office area. There was no need for full time staff to run this business, but they still required an office to file paperwork and have a place to meet, when renting units or for routine business. The office was dark and vacant when Sean arrived through the front door and left via the rear. As the door closed, the motion sensors activated and illuminated a hallway. The hallway was a vast ten feet in width and the ceilings vaulted twenty-five feet overhead. The concrete floors echoed as Sean walked down the stark hall. On either side were large roll-up doors, with a standard door beside it. The occupants could use the large doors to load or unload cargo or just enter their unit from the smaller pedestrian door. As he walked further, he activated another bank of light, revealing another section of continuous hall. The only thing distinguishing one unit from the next was a number above each pedestrian door. When Sean reached A6, he unlocked the door and entered. Inside, Ressler and Poirier were waiting for him, along with two pimply faced, long-haired kids who were tied to chairs with their hands and legs snugly secured.

Poirier then heinously started laughing, and said, "these two are very frightened. Look the blonde one has pissed himself."

Sean saw that they each looked petrified, with tears running down their faces and their faces devoid of any colour. "Did they say anything?"

85

"Just that they were given a job and they were sorry."

Sean looked at them, then walked around them towards a bench about two meters behind the chairs. The boys contorted their bodies in an effort to see what he was doing, but no matter how they tried they could not twist around enough to see. If they had, they would have seen Sean examining utensils neatly lined up on the bench, most of which looked like various knives and cleavers, interspersed with some odd-looking instruments. Sean picked up one which had a wooden handle and a long thin blade about eight inches long. He examined it for a minute, then picked up a second identical one. He walked over to the two terrified boys and drove the blade straight down into the top of the blonde boy's head. There was surprisingly little noise, as the small blade penetrated the full length of its spike after overcoming the initial crunching resistance from bone. His eyes bulged, but he did not say a word. Slowly, his head slumped forward. Leaving the blade in the boy's head, Sean turned to the second one, and ripping the tape off his mouth said, "who hired you?"

There was now the faint aroma of shit in the area. Between the second boy's legs, his jeans became darker and slowly the darkness smeared outwards. Stuttering, he now said "I don't know! Jeremy was the contact and, and....... and you just killed him!" Sean walked around behind the boy who just shit himself, then quickly inserted the second blade into the boy's head. Like the first, there was a quick bulging of his eyes, followed by blackness. Death for each was nearly instantaneous.

"Leave them here for an hour, that way the blood will coagulate, and it will be less messy."

Poirier and Ressler watched the scene unfold and each shuddered, as Sean calmly skewered each boy. Even though they had been involved in many killings, they were both awed and afraid at the same time with the callous way Sean dispatched both of these boys without any expression, neither remorse nor enjoyment, just work that needed to be done.

While waiting, they moved to the unit next door. This one was not refrigerated and much more comfortable. They grabbed a cold beer and sat down on the sofas. There was snack food in the fridge, but they did not eat. Sean wasn't hungry. Both Ressler and Poirier had lost any appetite they might have had. Their next step would involve running both boys through the portable X-ray machine to check if they had any metal implants. They would then remove their teeth, dismember them and place them in plastic-lined heavy cardboard boxes. When incinerated, all that would remain would be a small pile of dust.

Ressler and Poirier drank two beers in quick succession, then leisurely drew on another for the next hour. After some small talk about the Canucks and other local topics, they returned next door and began processing. They had become quite proficient, and within the next hour and a half both boys were processed, packaged and placed in the cold storage unit. Before they had an opportunity to leave, Sean received a text that a shipment was arriving. He directed them to drive around to the large loading door that this unit came equipped with.

When Sean opened the door, he saw a large ten-foot delivery truck outside. As per normal deliveries, the driver handed Sean the keys and quickly walked out through the front gate. He entered his code and made sure the gate was secured before leaving. Sean stepped up and into the driver's seat, and slowly backed the truck into the bay. Ressler closed the large overhead door and Sean went to the rear of the truck and lifted the roll up door. As they opened the door, they first noticed there was a lot of cargo. The truck was full. They then noticed the torpedo-shaped wrapped packages. My God! They were dumbfounded when the realization hit them that there were a lot of bodies. Sean did a quick calculation, there were well over thirty bodies.

After the magnitude of this delivery wore off, Sean simply said, "well, looks like we will be here all night. We might as well begin." As they removed the first body, they noticed it was cold and stiff but not frozen. That meant rigor mortis had set in. Since the bodies were cool, it would mean the timelines would be extended. Normally, rigor mortis dissipates after about 48 hours, the temperature may extend this for another day or so. Sean deduced these people had been killed less than 72 hours ago. As they removed the wrapping on the first individual, they noticed the leather biker vest; this guy looked like a biker. As they rolled him over, they saw the emblem for the Black Rebels. The Black Rebels were scrapping with the Club over a turf war in Montreal. Based on the bodies in front of him, Sean suspected the Black Rebels were losing.

They worked very efficiently, and by 6:00 AM the following morning, they had processed all of them. Due to the high volume, Sean realized he would have to use multiple methods to dispose of the bodies. He directed that six of the bodies be prepped for disposal at sea. For the first time, Sean sat back and started counting. There was a total of 38 bodies, plus the two boys from earlier, and three boxes of clothes, and a gallon can full of teeth and metal implants removed as they stripped the bodies.

Sean then said to Ressler and Poirier, "Great job guys. That was a lot of work. Once everything is completed, there is going to be a very substantial bonus for you. I can guarantee it will be larger than anything you have received before." Through their exhaustion, they both smiled as they knew Sean always looked after them generously.

"Why don't you guys go home and get some rest. I can take it from here. I will text you later, after I have made the arrangements for disposal. This lot will take several deliveries. I suspect we have a couple more late nights ahead of us." They removed their disposable aprons, one-piece coveralls and overshoes that they tossed into an open box, that was already filled with some of the victim's discarded clothes. As they left, they could see Sean prepping the pressurized canisters with bleach. These canisters were worn like backpacks and had a spray gun that thoroughly soaked the entire scene. Sean sprayed down the delivery truck, including the rear cargo area and the entire exterior. His final touch was to wipe the inside dash, steering wheel and door handles with disinfectant wipes.

After putting the canisters back and releasing the latent pressure still remaining in the tanks, Sean walked to the open box and cut the emblem from one of the vests. Since this was against his own rules, he waited until Ressler and Poirier had left. He rolled up the patch and stuffed it in his pocket. Then, he opened the outside doors and drove the truck out and parked it in the general parking area. He locked the doors, then reached under the front wheel and searched for something. He removed a small plastic case that had a magnet on one side. He clicked the case open, placed the keys inside and replaced the case under the wheel well. He then texted one word to a number – 'pickup'. He locked the compound and headed to a greasy spoon down the street for breakfast. He was famished, and this place always had huge servings. Today, he suspected he could eat the entire meal, and perhaps more.

The dimly lit restaurant was about half full. Most of the clientele were blue collar workers who worked at various businesses in the area. Most were regulars or semi-regulars who stopped in for breakfast and conversation before their shift began. You could smell frying in the air, mostly bacon, eggs and hash browns. There was, however, a distinct but not overpowering background odour of grease, oil and body odour.

Sean spied a table by the window that was unoccupied, so he ambled over and slid onto the bench seat. He knew the regulars claimed certain spots for breakfast, so as a courtesy when the waitress came over, he first asked if this booth was free. She replied it was and thanked him for asking. She had seen him before, but he was certainly not a regular. Sean ordered the standard Hungryman Canadian breakfast. The Hungryman came with three eggs, bacon, ham, hash browns, toast and coffee. A lot of food, but he was hungry. After taking his order, the waitress poured his coffee; having come prepared with a coffee pot in hand.

Sean sipped the coffee and as the hot elixir warmed his body, it seemed to give him a bump in energy. He nursed his coffee and began contemplating what had just happened. During the previous several hours, he was focused on his work. The only thing on his mind was processing those bodies as quickly as possible. He then realized he had never dispatched an order that size. He didn't know how many members the Black Rebels had, but he suspected its Club was effectively dissolved. Like a smack across the face, another realization suddenly hit him. There were no obvious signs of death. He tried to recall all the bodies and he could not remember any gunshot or stab wounds. All of the bodies were completely intact. There was a faint odour he couldn't quite identify, and the skin of the cadavers had a slight blue tinge to them.

The waitress brought his food and Sean began eagerly devouring it. Towards the end of his meal, he looked up and saw the delivery truck driving down the street. Sean recognised it instantly as the truck he just parked. These guys were good he thought to himself, it was maybe thirty minutes since he texted them that it was ready for pick up. He knew they would return to the shop and thoroughly wash, clean and disinfect the truck, including the cab, to make sure no evidence of its misadventures would ever be discovered.

As the truck passed from his view, he had an epiphany. The odd smell he couldn't identify was carbon monoxide from an exhaust. That also explained the blue tinge to the skin. These guys were gassed.

After finishing his breakfast, Sean decided he would stop by the office on his way home. Geoff was in his office, but Chester was not expected in that day. Upon entering Geoff's office, Sean flopped on his sofa. Geoff was reading some file and peered at Sean from over his glasses. "You look like shit. Something wrong?"

"No, it's been a very long night. I haven't made it home yet. Do you remember the special shipment that Clubman had arranged?"

Geoff suddenly looked a little uneasy. While he knew the business Sean was looking after, he never spoke directly to him about it. "Yes," he replied, "I recall Chester spoke of this at yesterday's meeting."

"Well, it arrived last night. A couple of guys and myself spent all night processing it. This is the largest shipment we've ever had. I will need to speak to Chester, but it doesn't have to be right away as it will take a few days to complete this procedure. In the meantime, can you get in touch with Bennie? We will need the incinerator for a couple of nights."

"Sure, no problem. In fact, the timing may be good, as he is processing some of the diseased birds and has had the incinerator running day and night. Processing your stuff should not raise any suspicions. When do you need it and for how long?"

"Tell Bennie we will be out at 10:00 tonight, we will need it for six to eight hours."

"I will let him know," Geoff gulped. A single body took two hours to completely incinerate. Each additional body took an additional thirty minutes. 6-8 hours would be between 7-11 bodies.

"Thanks," Sean said then added, "you can let him know we will need the same for the following three nights also." Geoff was shocked.

Sean texted Ressler and Poirier – 'meet tonight at 8:00'.

* * *

It had been a very long week. Saturday morning finally rolled around, the sun had not yet broken, but the halo cast across the eastern sky announced the impending sunrise. It was a cool humid morning that was quite normal when the temperatures rose to near summer highs. Sean had arrived at the Royal City Marina earlier. He had some difficulty locating the security code he needed to enter the docks. Seamus had arranged for the Abhartach to be docked there the day before. After finding the code, he found the mooring diagram that indicated where his boat was docked. He carried a large cooler with him that he rolled down the docks towards the boat. Once on board, he gave the boat a once over to make sure it was properly equipped.

Being an operating fishing vessel, it was not equipped with the accoutrements you would find on a recreational boat. The dock was coated with a non-slip coating directly onto the steel decking. Wet slimy decks can become very slippery and dangerous for the crew. It was clean, but a drab grey colour. Along the front of the vessel were several steel compartments. These would normally contain fishing gear and various apparatus the crew would need for their fishing tour. In one of the lockers, this equipment was replaced with many heavy steel chains. He made his way up to the captain's cockpit and checked fuel levels. Satisfied, he dragged his cooler down to the dining mess and set the cooler in a corner. He checked the fridge to ensure it was stocked with various drinks, water, and an assortment of juice and, most importantly, a massive supply of various beers and canned drinks. In the next fridge, was a huge quantity of food. Sean smiled; Seamus always overdid this. He could be out for weeks with this amount of grub. Better to oversupply than undersupply.

Satisfied, he dragged the cooler with him to the Captain's quarters and checked out his room. It was very comfortable but spartan. A practical room for a practical ship. He looked out the porthole and noticed the sky was brightening. He walked up to the dock and looked around. As the sun crested the horizon, he could see the streetlights turning off, as their illumination was no longer necessary. His phone rang and he answered. Ressler and Poirier had arrived and were waiting just outside the dock gates. Sean told them the code that opened the large security fence. They punched in the code and the chain link fence began to roll aside. Sean gave them directions and within a couple of minutes, he saw the large panel van lumbering down the dock towards him.

This dock was primarily used for business. There were several fishing trawlers, tugboats, pilot boats, various working barges and assorted commercial watercraft. A working dock, it would normally be buzzing with activity, however, on weekends people rested late so it would be after 9:00 before activity started to pick up. At present, there was nobody to be seen. Ressler and Poirier parked the van just outside the Abhartach. Sean joined them and they quickly removed six large boxes and hurriedly carried them down to the hold, which would normally be filled with freshly caught fish. After removing the cargo, Poirier drove the van back to the parking area and left the keys under the front drivers side wheel well, attached in a small magnetized box, as directed by Sean.

When Poirier returned to the Abhartach, Sean and Ressler were lounging on the deck. Ressler had cracked a beer and Sean was leisurely drinking an orange juice. Stepping onto the boat and pointing towards Ressler's beer, Poirier said, "I think I need one of those too. It's gotta be past noon somewhere."

They all laughed, and Ressler replied, "working all night this past week, this feels more like late evening than early morning."

When Poirier returned with a cracked beer in hand, Sean held up his juice and said "Gentlemen, to a job well done. By the time we return on Monday, we will have completed our consignment and a large bonus will be waiting for all of us. Even though we still have a little work to do, tonight let's just relax and enjoy. You deserve it."

Sean got up and moved to the Captain's deck. Starting the engine from the bridge, he shouted to Ressler and Poirier to cast off the mooring lines, and they slowly navigated their way through the maze of docks and entered the Fraser River to make their way to the ocean. Once entering Georgia Strait, they continued on through the Strait of Juan de Fuca and out to the open ocean. Next land mass- Japan.

Ressler and Poirier spent the morning and afternoon relaxing and soaking up the sun. After preparing some cold cuts and salads for dinner, they brought up the food to Sean who was still operating the boat. Since he was the only one who had a navigation certificate, technically, he was the only one who should be operating the boat.

The seas were calm with gentle five feet swells, so piloting the ship was easy and Sean took several breaks where the guys spelled him off. There was an autopilot but Sean always preferred operating manually. After dinner, Ressler and Poirier cleaned the dishes and returned to deck, just in time for Sean to direct them to start preparing for the chains and weights.

They opened the locker located at midship and started removing the chains. There were very large diameter links and they were very heavy, each six foot in length weighing 30 KG. The chains were set in one pile and the metal weights were on the other side at the rear of the ship, where gates could easily be removed for access to the diving platform. As the sun started setting, they went to the hold to begin retrieving the boxes. Inside each box was a body that had been prepared. All teeth and identifying objects, such as metal implants had been removed. Inserted in each body were several stainless-steel rods. One through the chest, one drilled through the hips and one which skewered each leg through both femurs. Onto each metal shaft, Poirier and Ressler attached chains and weights, which they secured by bolting the ends together.

Sean slowed the boat, so it was easier for the guys to work. After an hour, all six bodies were properly suited for their journey to Davy Jones' locker. Sean now stopped the main propeller and kept the boat steady with the thrusters. Poirier and Ressler removed the rear gate and dragged each body onto the platform, which was about a meter and a half wide, and ran nearly the entire width of the boat. They brought each body out, pushed them over the edge and they quickly disappeared. Various fish and creatures would soon leave very little evidence that this was once a person.

Just before dumping the body overboard, Poirier used a large knife to slash the torso of each victim. This would ensure that fish would come and feed before the body began to decompose, and the internal gas build up which could force them to the surface, similar to a person wearing a life preserver. It was next to impossible for the bodies to rise with the amount of weight attached to them, but as added security they performed this anyway. The last two that were dumped were the two boys Sean had callously murdered just four days ago.

They reinserted the rear gate and saw several additional links of chains and weights still remaining. Normally during these trips, they carry extra weight as a precaution, but this seemed like a significant miscalculation. Sean barked out at them to break down the boxes first, he didn't want any of them to accidentally get blown overboard. Sean re-engaged the main propeller after they had broken down the boxes. They were about to begin storing the extra chains when they saw Sean come up from below with a bottle of rum and three glasses. Sean had already cracked the seal and poured himself a tumbler. He set the other two glasses down and poured a generous amount into each. "A toast, gentlemen, job successfully completed." They clinked glasses and downed the contents.

"Thanks, Boss," Ressler said. Then added, "That tasted very nice! What kind of rum is that?"

"Only the best for my boys! Ron Zacapa XO. 20-year-old." Sean showed them the ornate, flask shaped bottle. "Want another?"

"You bet," they both exclaimed. Sean generously poured each another shot but passed over pouring one for himself.

"How about you Boss? You worked hard too." Ressler remarked.

"I can't, I am still driving. Once we stop for the night, I will have several. Now, we need to make our way to the bay where we will anchor for the evening." Then, passing the bottle to Ressler, he added, "You guys enjoy. We can store the chains later. Don't bother saving any for me, I have three more bottles in my room." Then noticing the can with teeth and metal implants, he added, "but before you drink too much, throw some weights in this and toss it overboard"

Sean went back to the bridge and disengaged the autopilot. He checked his screens and started heading east northeast towards Tofino. He then engaged the autopilot once more and sat back listening to Poirier and Ressler laughing and living it up on the deck. Their laughter and guffawing grew louder, as the remainder of the rum disappeared. After fifteen minutes, it became quiet. Sean looked out the door and saw both guys spread out across a couple of padded benches. The empty bottle of rum lying on its side and rocking with the ocean swales. After another fifteen minutes, Sean reduced the engines to dead slow, he checked his heading and once confident he was still heading towards Tofino, he got up and went to check on Poirier and Ressler. He approached them, grabbed the empty rum bottle and threw it overboard.

He then reached over towards Poirier and checked his pulse at his carotid artery on his neck, after about a minute, he did the same with Ressler.

He then reached into his top shirt pocket and removed a small ampule that was empty. He tossed this over the side as well and dragged Poirier to the rear of the boat. He removed his clothes and started attaching the chains that were remaining on the deck. After securing several chains, he dragged him to the platform and tossed him over. He did not slash his torso as they had done with the previous victims as this was merely a precaution. After repeating the action with Ressler, he disappeared underneath and returned with two backpacks Poirier and Ressler had brought onboard. He checked through the backpacks and removed their wallets and any other identifying pieces. Then, he stuffed the clothes he just removed from the two unfortunate souls and put the remaining weights inside them. After securing the last two chains on each backpack, he tossed these overboard as well. Bringing out the water hose, he washed down the deck as most people shortly after death evacuate their bowels and bladders. Poirier and Ressler were no exception. As Sean was washing down the deck, he smiled to himself. All loose ends had been covered, nothing left to tie him to the attack against Geoff. Except ... The Dyck.

The following morning, Sean texted a couple of friends in Tofino. He had previously arranged to meet them there. They would sail, fish and drink their way back to Vancouver. So they could all imbibe in drinking and relaxing, Sean had hired the first mate from the Abhartach to come along and drive them back. It was Sunday, and they would be back in New Westminster on Tuesday evening. The next three days were to be gorgeous and sunny. As his mates arrived, Sean toured them through the boat and showed them their quarters. They were very impressed with the beer fridge, as they shouted and whooped with delight. They were even more thrilled when Sean rolled out a cooler from his quarters and pulled out three bottles of very expensive rum and set them on the table. Then, he added another three bottles of very expensive scotch, and since one of his buddies loved vodka, he also produced three bottles of Crystal Head Vodka. While the guys were celebrating downstairs, the first mate had started the engine and was pulling anchor to start the run home.

Seamus had arranged for several easy chairs to be brought on board and Sean sat back, sipping his Ron Zacapa and enjoying the sunshine, laughing with his buddies. After an hour or so, he remembered that he forgot to text Chester. He grabbed his phone and texted: 'job completed, will return late Tuesday. Meeting on Wednesday?'

A few minutes later, Sean's phone beeped. Sean looked at the message, it read: 'nice work, as usual! Wednesday 11:00 AM?' Sean replied: 'affirmative.'

On Wednesday morning, Sean dragged himself out of bed. He didn't realize how much stress he was enduring the past couple weeks and during the trip back, he was pretty much in a constant state of mild to severe inebriation. After the boat docked, he realized neither himself, nor his buddies, were in any shape to drive, so he called the car service to arrange for a ride home for them. Waiting for the car just outside the security gates, Sean saw his Range Rover still parked where he left it, and the delivery van had been picked up as he had arranged prior to his departure. Sean arrived home late and Ava was asleep. The next morning, Sean had slept late and Ava had already left. There was a note on her pillow.

'Welcome home, my love. You must have had a good weekend as you were quite smashed last night. If you can make it, let's go for dinner tonight. Ella and I missed you.'

Sean had arranged the car service to pick him up at 9:30. He didn't have time to go to the gym, so he showered, dressed and poured himself an espresso. As he sat on his deck chair, his phone buzzed to let him know the car was waiting at the front entrance.

Sean arrived at the office and as usual, Nancy greeted him with a friendly smile. "Good Morning, Sean. You look like you got some sun."

"Good morning, to you too Nancy. Yes, I had a few days on the water. Lots of sun and even more drink."

Sean arrived at the conference room, just before Chester and Geoff bounded in while having an animated conversation. After a few minutes of small talk, Sean began, "That was quite the delivery the Clubman arranged. Did Geoff tell you how many?"

Chester nodded. "He said there were 38?"

"Yes, 38 plus several boxes of clothes. The avian outbreak was fortunate timing, as we had the burners going every night for four days. We disposed of the remainder offshore on the weekend."

In unison, Chester and Geoff both whistled a whew. Then Chester added, "I let the Clubman know the job had been completed. He was very grateful and provided a very substantial bonus."

"There's more," and Sean reached into his suit pocket and removed a patch that read 'Black Rebel' and tossed it on the table between Chester and Geoff.

Chester just stared, and said, "that explains a lot. You know it has been all over the news the past few days. They don't know what happened, but they suspect there was a mass murder and the Black Rebels seem to have just disappeared. The good news is the biker wars seem to have been settled. The media have termed it 'The New Extirpation Proclamation'."

"The what?" Geoff replied.

"Edward Cornwallis was a British general who after decimating the Jacobite rebellion in Scotland was assigned to take control and settle hostilities in the colonies. He was made Governor General of Nova Scotia. The British were fighting their perennial enemy the French. This time though, the French were operating through the Acadians and the local Micmac Indians. Cornwallis put a bounty on their heads. They called this The Extirpation Proclamation, which means local extinction. With the Black Rebels exterminated, the biker wars were naturally resolved."

"That is quite a tactic. Though it does appear to be very effective! We need to destroy this," Sean said, as he grabbed the patch and put it back in his pocket, "I know it is against the rules, but I needed to show you guys."

"Thanks again Sean, you did a fantastic job. Did anyone else see any of this endeavor? We need to be extremely discreet."

"Yes, I had Poirier and Ressler assist with the processing. As you can appreciate, it was much too large for me to handle by myself......but they will not be talking as they are currently becoming very familiar with the Pacific."

"How substantial was the bonus?" Geoff inquired.

Chester smiled, and turned to Sean, "well, let's say your cut off the top is 1.5 mil!"

Sean's eyes started popping, and Geoff interjected, "that means the bonus was 10 mil!"

"Yes, that's a lot of 'shut your mouth' money." Chester said. Then, changing topic while Sean and Geoff were still digesting this news, he asked, "Any news on The Bean's assassination?"

"It seems to be very quiet," Sean replied. "I suspect the shooters are long gone and one of The Bean's lieutenants has assumed control, so he is likely behind it. I have been a little preoccupied lately, so I haven't dug anymore."

Chester seemed satisfied, "that fine, thanks. The good news is that it hasn't interrupted our business, the new guy is moving as much product as Bean did." Turning towards Geoff, "anything new for you Geoff?"

"Yes. I have been working with Sanchez. The shipping industry is quite fascinating. Ships are nowhere near as expensive as I thought they would be. Also, the shipping companies almost never own the ships. They are normally leased through an outside financing firm. So, of course, we will do the leasing through one of our companies based in Malta, which is where we will also register the ship. We have sourced an experienced fellow to run the operation. He is a Greek guy, named Christophe. I can see how Onassis built an empire so quickly. You need a lot of operating capital, but not much to buy a ship."

"Great news. Let's be sure we dot all the 'I's and cross all the 'T's, This is looking very promising. Do you have an ETA on when we might be running our first shipment?"

"There is a lot of paperwork and legal requirements, the Ostrankis are loving the windfall, but I suspect 2-3 months and we will be ready to go."

* * *

WHERE DID THE BLACK REBELS GO? EXTIRPATION?

MONTREAL (Nathan Chevrefils) – Emergency rooms in every hospital are prepared for the next wave of victims in the ongoing Biker Wars affecting our city. People are afraid to venture outdoors, concerned they may become the latest victims. Surete du Quebec have been on high alert, waiting for a report of more carnage. The level of violence has ramped up in the past six months, as the two warring factions wrestle for control of the illicit drug business. Drive by shootings, or the discovery of some grisly murder scene, have become daily incidents.

However, for the past week it has grown eerily silent. Emergency room practitioners are toning their chess skills while passing time, firefighters' girths are bulging from larger meals and the Surete are scratching their heads in wonder. Where did the Black Rebels go? It is as if someone just turned the lights off and left town. The Black Rebels have just disappeared. One theory is that they are laying low, as they prepare for a larger all out push to catch their opponents off guard. They are mustering their forces for an all-out assault.

Another rumour making its rounds is that there has been a mass execution, of the magnitude Hitler or the Khmer Rouge would be proud of. This reporter has investigated multiple sources and unearthed a nefarious possibility. First, it is very strange that there has been no sightings of the Black Rebels. On the streets, all sources of the Black Rebels alleged drug distribution business has dried up. Drug users are looking for a high and there is a vast shortage. Junkies are going through DTs because they cannot find a 'fix'. Emergency rooms have seen a sharp spike in visits from habitual drug users suffering from withdrawal symptoms.

Reports indicate there was a gathering of the Black Rebels at an unknown location on the south shore towards the end of last week. Residents reported noise violations coming from quiet neighbourhoods as loud Harleys were spotted in the area. That was the last reported sighting of any Black Rebels. The theory is, that somewhere over the next several hours, when the Black Rebels were all gathered, they were systematically murdered, and all the evidence of this heinous event eliminated. On the streets, this is being called the New Extirpation Proclamation.

If The Black Rebels do not resurface, we may never know the truth behind this disappearance, but if no Black Rebels surface within the next week or so, one thing we can be certain of is that it involved mass murder of the most egregious sort.

✳ ✳ ✳

Chapter Eleven

Sitting behind their desks at RCMP headquarters in Surrey, Inspectors Bailey and Brine were reviewing the background information on the fellow that the new boss had them take a few photos of at the Shark Club. Tossing the report on his desk, Bailey said, "remember how pissed we were when he summoned us that night?"

Brine nodded his head, "Yeah, we had good intel and had just settled down for an evening of surveillance. I think you even paid for the joe."

"Yes, as it turned out nothing really happened, so not too much of an inconvenience. And yes, of course I paid for the coffee. I always have to pay since I'm the junior."

"By six months buddy boy," Brine quickly retorted, then with a twinkle in his eye added, "but I look at least a couple years younger than you. Not sure if it's because you look old or I look young."

"Up yours, old man!" Bailey blurted.

"I hate doing this stuff, we have been doing this job for fifteen years. The junior guys should be doing these background checks."

"Yeah, but after this many years, you develop a sixth sense. Something here just doesn't smell right to me. How about you?"

"Me too." Brine replied, "When does the old man want us up there?

Looking at his wristwatch, Bailey replied, "thirty minutes."

Inspector's Bailey and Brine were both 40 years old. While they weren't related, in many ways they were twins. Both were career policemen, both had failed marriages and most importantly, they were much better together than they were individually. Intuitively, they understood each other and knew when to speak and when to watch and listen.

Thirty minutes later, Bailey and Brine took the stairs up the second floor to Provincial Superintendent Robert Robinson's office. Announcing themselves to the secretary, she ushered them into his office. "Good morning, Superintendent," Bailey spoke first.

Looking up from a report, Robert Robinson said, "Morning guys. Just following up on those surveillance pictures you took the other night of that guy who was meeting with Walter Dyck at the Shark Club. Did you find anything out about him?"

"As we suspected," Brine spoke. "He is nobody we have heard about. His name is Sean Tifflen, and he owns part of a large conglomerate that has their fingers in many areas. Property development is their main concern, but they also own a large farm in the valley and have several fishing boats that operate out of Steveston. He's a rich guy who lives in a penthouse apartment in North Van."

"So, what is his connection with Walter Dyck?"

"We haven't been able to make any connection, perhaps there is something with Walter's son, William."

After a moment of stunned silence, Superintendent Robinson burst out laughing. Bailey and Brine were not really sure what was so funny but laughed cordially. Then Bailey with a quizzical look said, "Sorry Sir, did we say something funny?"

"Don't you get it?"

"Afraid not, Sir."

"What's with these people? If you have a last name of Dyck, don't you think you would be careful when naming your kids.... Willy Dyck!" He renewed his laughter, "I guess two penises are better than one!" He laughed again.

This time Brine and Bailey were also laughing. Brine replied "I knew a girl called Seema. I guess she should keep her last name if she married into the Dyck family." They all howled with laughter again.

Slowly, Superintendent Robinson regained his composure, and in a more serious tone said, "I think I needed that. Too many reports dry a guy out. But seriously, I think you should check into this guy a little further. Why would some rich property developer meet with Walter Dyck?" A smile crossed his face again.

"Sure thing," Brine said. "We don't have a lot going on at the moment, we can do a little more checking." Then they turned and started walking out.

Behind them they heard, "See Ma Dyck!" Followed by a renewed round of laughter.

The next day, Bailey and Brine arrived at the Bentali building, and after checking in with the security desk were given permission to proceed to the secure 30th floor. As they exited the elevator, they were thoroughly impressed with the grandeur and opulence of this place. They gave each other a look like this was a waste of time. They entered LNa's offices and asked to speak with Sean Tifflen. Nancy asked them to wait in the reception area, as she rang through to Sean's office. Settling into the reception area, Bailey looked at Brine and said, "This sofa is worth more than my entire living room furniture."

Brine smirking said, "that's because our exes got all our nice furniture."

A few moments later, Nancy looked up and said, "Mr. Tifflen can see you now. If you would like to come with me, I can show you to his office." She led them down the hallway and into Sean's office.

Showing their badges, Bailey said, "Thank you for taking the time to meet with us Mr. Tifflen. My name is Detective Bailey, and this is my partner Detective Brine. We are conducting a routine investigation and would like to ask you a few questions."

"Perfectly fine, gentlemen, anything I can do for the boys in blue. Can I get you a coffee or refreshment?"

"No that's fine, thanks for the offer though, we really don't want to take up too much of your time. A couple of weeks ago, it was reported you were seen in the company of a fellow named Walter Dyck at the Shark Club in Walnut Grove. What was that meeting regarding?"

Sean was practiced in the art of 'boardroom demeanor'. Simply, it meant you could not show any emotions, even if inside you were startled and burning up. If they had shocked him, neither Bailey nor Brine could tell. "Hmmm……… let me think," after a moment, he continued, "yes, I do recall…. it wasn't a very long meeting, maybe about half an hour. Part of our business is in property development. Mr. Dyck made some inquiries about investing in a residential tower we are building in Burnaby, around Metrotown." Sean paused for a moment then added, this questioning is very unusual, is there something I should know about Mr. Dyck?" Sean knew many times the best defence is offence.

"We are not at liberty to discuss our case, Mr. Tifflen. If I may ask – did Mr. Dyck invest in your development?"

"Undecided. We receive many requests to invest in our developments. Few of them make it through the process and are subsequently asked to invest. Based on this conversation, I suspect Mr. Dyck will not be offered a position."

Brine, who was being purposefully silent, just nodded. His role was as an observer. While Bailey asked the questions, Brine kept a close eye on the body language, in case Bailey missed something.

Bailey replied, "okay then, thank you, Mr. Tifflen, for taking the time to meet with us. I don't think we need to take up any more of your time."

As they stood up to leave, Brine interjected, "I am curious about one thing though, Mr. Tifflen. With an office like this, why would you meet Mr. Dyck at a mediocre restaurant in Walnut Grove?"

"If I recall correctly, Mr. Dyck had requested it. Something about his schedule was too full to make a trip downtown."

"Okay, thanks again," replied Brine and they cordially departed, making sure they said thanks to Nancy on the way out.

After the inspectors had departed, Sean closed his office door. He was visibly shaken. As he took a long draw from his coffee, that by now had turned tepid, he just stared out the window and took long deep breaths. Geoff suddenly knocked at the door.

"It's open," Sean said with a voice that was a few octaves higher than normal.

Opening the door, Geoff blurted, "What the hell was that all about? I don't think we have ever had cops in the office."

"Nothing really, apparently, at some function a while back I was spotted having a conversation with Walter Dyck. The cops certainly know who he is, and they were just making routine enquiries."

"Good, we certainly don't want the cops sniffing around our business," and with that remark, Geoff kept walking nonchalantly down the hall towards the coffee room.

While riding down in the elevator, Brine said, "So, what do you think?"

"As I suspected, there's nothing. He seems like an egotistical rich guy. His answers were logical and quite frankly, why would a guy like that have anything to do with a scumbag like The Dyck? What did you think?"

"I am mostly inclined to agree with you. The only thing I saw was a momentary look when you mentioned The Dyck. You shocked him a little. While his answer seemed logical, I suspect he is hiding something. Maybe he buys his dope from him, who knows, but I think we should dig a little deeper."

A couple of days later, Bailey was at his desk reading over a deeper background check on Sean Tifflen. As he closed the file and looked towards Brine, he said, "there were no surprises here. He seems to be a lucky guy who made a lot of money in real estate. Not unlike thousands of guys in this market. You didn't need a lot of money to speculate....at least that is what I have been told. I have this talkative neighbour who boasted about buying several condos with a small down payment, and the balance due in a couple years when the building was ready for occupancy. Before then, the value of the condo will have appreciated and he will sell the unit before he has to pay the balance, pocketing the difference."

"Phew, that sounds ... interesting," Brine replied. "That could turn into a lot of money. Property has been going through the roof recently."

"Yeah, my neighbour said he has made as much as a hundred grand on a ten grand down payment ... easy cash ... as long as prices keep going up. You can lose your shirt if they go down." Bailey took the file and tossed it onto Brine's desk. "Here's the file, there's not much there. Rich guy made money on real estate with two other partners, then grew the business to include farming, fishing and now they are expanding into the shipping business. Have a look for yourself."

"I think I will," Brine replied, "want Thai food for lunch?"

"Love to, I haven't had Thai for a couple weeks."

"It's nearly 11, want to go in an hour?"

"You bet."

Brine then opened the file and started reading. The important details in a file is not what the file contains, you must read between the lines to see what is not in the report. These tidbits of missing information sometimes gleam insights you may miss. Shortly before noon, Bailey stood up from his desk and grabbed his coat. "Ready to go for lunch?"

A few blocks south on King George Highway, was a small mall that had a great little Thai restaurant. Like most Asian places, this one was nothing special to look at, but the food was excellent. The hostess showed them to their table and brought menus. After ordering their lunch, while they waited Bailey said, "Did you finish the file?"

Brine nodded and said, "Yes, I read it. You were right, not much there."

"Yeah, we have enough bad guys to deal with, without trying to find something on regular schmoes."

The waitress returned with their bowls of Pho, and as he began eating Brine said, "Just one thing though, I see these guys made money in real estate, that is not very unusual these days. The one detail that keeps nagging at me is – where did they get the money to begin with? Three young guys, not knowing where next month's rent was coming from, suddenly have enough money to invest in real estate. Where did the original stake come from?"

Bailey looked at him, and with a quizzical look said, "interesting."

Returning to headquarters, they began doing more research on LNa and all the principals. This was slow tedious police work. The old idiom was that when conducting an investigation, a good cop used a great deal of shoe leather. If you turn over enough rocks and ask enough questions, something is eventually unearthed. Today, that saying should actually be eyesight instead of shoe leather, as most of the work is done on a computer, reading files.

By the end of the day, they had little to show for their progress. Since LNa was not a public company, little corporate information existed outside of routine things like officers, employees, etc. Nothing about how much money they made, and only an estimate of the value of the company. Experience taught most people that estimates were wildly inaccurate.

As the new Superintendent was leaving at the end of the day, he passed the detectives room and noticed Bailey and Brine still at their desks. He walked over to their desks and said, "burning the late-night oil, gentlemen?"

Looking up, Bailey replied, "just some routine background checks, Sir."

"Anything I should know about?"

Police are notoriously private and do not like sharing intelligence on cases they are working on. This lack of sharing information was the driving force behind the creation of the IHIT force. Cops and police departments not sharing information permitted several criminals to operate much longer than they should have. Despite this, all police detectives still harboured distrust of their superiors. They felt politics swayed their decisions more than good police work.

"Nothing much, sir," Brine replied.

Robert Robinson was not going to drop it so quickly. "Anything on the property developer we saw with The Dyck?"

"We went to see him today," Bailey responded. "It all seems above board, he claimed The Dyck was looking at investing in a property development project in Metrotown but something just doesn't quite smell right. Everything seems to check out but, there's a lingering fishy smell."

Robinson laughed, "when have you ever met a rich guy that didn't have something to hide? There's always something not completely upright. Don't spend too much time on this. You have a lot of other cases to solve. Including that young girl that was killed out at UBC."

"Sure boss, we won't?" Brine replied. As Robinson exited, he looked towards Bailey. "Why does the brass always stick their noses where they don't belong?"

Bailey shrugged his shoulders, "yeah ... well the good news is he is a 'shooting star' (using air quotes) and will not be here long, this is just a brief stopover before heading to Ottawa."

"I don't think we really have any choice now, we have to put this on the back burner. But I don't want to drop it. You still have that contact in forensic accounting. Let's see if he can help us out as a side project. I still don't see where they got their original money to start their first property development project. I suggest we keep the file open and work on it when we have time. Agreed?"

"Agreed. My friend in accounting owes me a favour," replied Bailey. "Let's call it a night. Want a beer?"

"Your turn to buy."

"It's always my turn, Old Man." Bailey laughed.

Chapter Twelve

In the five years that passed, business continued to prosper. The GH Reed Hog Producers grew substantially, not only did they add several more barns for hog production, they also expanded into the berry market. They now had over 1000 hectares devoted to blueberry and raspberry production. They were currently looking at acquiring a winery in the Okanagan. This would not only be another profit centre, but it would justify their frequent road trips to the interior. British Columbian's referred to most of the areas in southern BC, east of the coastal area, as 'the interior'. Frequent trips to the interior were due to the growth of their drug distribution business. With the endorsement of the Club, Chester took over distribution throughout BC, with the exception of the Fraser Valley, which remained under the protected domain of Walter Dyck. A couple of years ago, they took over distribution on the Island (another colloquialism BC residents use to refer to Vancouver Island). Then a few months ago, with the unfortunate demise of the local drug kingpin, the Club offered the interior to Chester as well.

The Okanagan kingpin was a very unfortunate fellow, whose fall from grace was both swift and decisive. While being a generally repugnant individual, it was discovered he had a proclivity for prepubescent children. A militant group, called the Creep Catchers, was formed several years ago, comprising community members who took it upon themselves to uncover these individuals that the police were ineffective in uncovering. They would set a trap (or sting, as they preferred to call it), where they could catch these paedophiles and miscreants. Then, they would publicly chastise them using social media. Once a person was uncovered and his name was plastered across social media sites, he became a targeted man. One evening while dining at a steak house in Kelowna, the kingpin excused himself and went to the washroom. Somehow, while standing in front of a urinal relieving himself, he accidentally garroted himself with his dick still in his hand. He then proceeded to accidentally impale himself several times with a butcher knife, that just happened to be in the bathroom. While this was not the official version, the fact was the local constabulary only gave the scene a quick once over, this is what the general public was hinting. The city was better off without him.

The cannabis business was extremely lucrative and a steady source of income. However, the real money came from cocaine, methamphetamine, heroin and a plethora of derivative opioid products. LNa were now producing literally pallet loads of cash every week. Most of this was washed through the real estate arm of their conglomerate. Several years ago, LNa expanded into the international shipping business. Chester believed this could be used to ship the cash to offshore banks where they could launder the money. As it turned out, this was not required and they could launder money locally, which is always preferable. When they moved funds to their offshore banks, the money was already cleaned. They needed the offshore banks to shield the money from tax authorities. The banks they employed were particularly adept at hiding money.

Geoff, Sean and Chester grew exceedingly wealthy. The Ostranskis now worked exclusively for LNa, and they themselves had become very wealthy off the proceeds of LNa's business. They were very appreciative and often mentioned that they were very fortunate to work for a firm where every owner is a multi-millionaire. Of course, they only mentioned this when meeting with the LNa partners. All the partners had purchased their own private enclaves outside the city. Chester found a property in the small hamlet of Anmore. While the property was technically in Anmore, it was effectively located 'above' Anmore, as it was on the top of a mountain. It overlooked Anmore on one side, and down the slope on the other you could see Belcarra and Indian Arm. On a cool clear night, you could see across the water of Burrard Inlet, the lights coruscating off the reflective rippling water. The estate was massive and contained fifteen hectares of buildings and woods that were completely surrounded by a three-meter rock wall.

Outside the wall, at its base, wild blackberry bushes were planted. Blackberries are devilishly insidious plants. While the ripened fruit is delicious and sweet, the plants themselves are armed with sharp, steely thorns. These thorns can easily reach a centimeter or more in length and are as sharp as a knife's edge. When attempting to reach the succulent berries, you would often see blood running down your arm as the thorns gashed and poked your skin. These bushes also grew exceedingly fast. It was not unusual for vines to grow one or two meters in a growing season. These bushes provided a greater deterrent than razor wire.

Chester loved the old castles in Europe, and this served as the inspiration for designing his new home. There were several buildings, besides the main house which itself was a massive 28 room rock fortress complete with balustrades, corniced roofs and of course, turrets and spires. No gargoyles though, as Chester believed they were creepy.

Chester made a purposeful decision when he began his career, that family would be detrimental to his success, not to mention a weakness his enemies could exploit. The result was he had many casual acquaintances, and passionate dalliances. But he never allowed himself to fall in love with anyone. As a result, he had quite a shock when one of these casual flings advised him she was going to be having his child. Chester was torn between his heart and his head. He knew he could not have a family, but he also knew he could never let his child's life be terminated. He was quite surprised at how the prospect of fatherhood brought out a nurturing part of his psyche he didn't know existed.

Anne was about to become the mother of his child; this caused a further transformation Chester was not expecting. He grew exceedingly fond of her, in fact, he suspected he was beginning to love her. Not in the passionate way Geoff seemed to have loved Elena, or in the incredibly comfortable easy manner that Sean loved Ava. Instead, it was a love built on circumstance and one day, while they were parted, he found himself missing her.

While in her second trimester, Anne agreed to Chester's suggestion that she move onto the estate. Rather than moving into the big house with Chester though, she moved into the opulent carriage house that was referred to as the guest cottage. After the birth of their son, they named the house Clarence Hall, after their newborn, Clarence. Chester was concerned about his son having his family name and agreed Clarence should adopt his mother's name. Having the name Moehr could bring danger … that was a condition of his business.

Clarence Tetley (just like the tea) lived in Clarence Hall with his mother. Clarence had the run of the estate and his laughter brightened up every corner of the estate. All the guards, housekeepers, gardeners loved little Clarie. Chester himself spent much of his free time with him. He loved teasing and tickling him. His giggles were infectious and soon everyone was laughing with Clarie.

Clarie's room was filled with stuffed animals he loved. The amazing thing was, he knew each one by name. He could even tell the difference between the dozens of Dalmations. Clarie especially loved Barney. Barney was a purple dinosaur puppet who was featured on a morning television program.

One morning, Clarie and Anne were coming over for a prearranged breakfast. Arriving through the front door, the attendant informed them that Chester was waiting for them on the outside patio. Holding hands, they walked to the patio and Clarie said, "I hope Daddy arranged for pancakes. I love pancakes."

Smiling, Anne said, "I am sure that will not be a problem, my darling. Everyone knows your love of pancakes."

As they rounded the door and stepped out to the patio, they saw a table and chairs set up under the glass pagoda, but no Chester. Anne felt a tug on her arm and looking down, Clarie was staring out on the lawn with a look of complete amazement. His mouth opened to speak, but nothing came out at first. Then he screamed, "Barrrrrneeeeeey".

Out on the lawn, a man-sized Barney was casually darting across the grass. Clarie was screaming with joy, as he ran down the dozen stone steps to the lawn. It was only when he was on his way down, that Anne realized it could be dangerous if he fell, so she scampered after him. Once reaching the lawn, Clarie made a direct line to Barney. Anne was losing the race trying to catch him. As he reached Barney, he opened his arms and gave him a giant hug. Barney was leaning down to pick him up.

"Barney, I love you!"

In return, Barney gave Clarie a bigger hug and started to laugh. Clarie's eyes grew wider with recognition. "Daddy?" he queried.

Still laughing, Chester removed the head from his life-sized Barney costume. "Yes, my son, it is. Do you like my outfit?"

"Yes, I love it! Thank you, Daddy."

Anne joined them and the three of them laughed and hugged each other. After a couple of minutes, Chester said, "Let's go have breakfast, this suit is very hot, and I suspect I may have sweated off a couple of pounds."

Clarie reached up to grab his Mom and Dad's hands. The three of them walked back to the patio. Standing just outside the door were several members of the house staff smiling and clapping, as Mom, Clarie and Barney walked up the stairs. At breakfast that morning, there was an abundance of laughter, smiling and of course pancakes. Clarie asked what his Dad was going to do with the Barney outfit. Chester laughed and said, "Well son, I thought it might look good in your room with all the stuffies. What do you think?"

Enthusiastically, Clarie replied, "Yes, yes, thanks Daddy."

"But first we need to get it cleaned, it is very warm and a little stinky." Chester responded.

"Okay," then as an afterthought Clarie added, "Dad stink isn't so bad?"

Another round of laughter. Chester said, "we will take it to the cleaner and have it back in a couple days."

Somewhat dejected, Clarie answered, "Welllll okay……. When it comes back, we may have to rearrange my buds. Mom, can we do that tomorrow?"

Anne replied, "we can't do that tomorrow. You remember what tomorrow is, right?"

"Yes, I remember … Uncle Sean's and Auntie Ava's wedding……I'm going to be the ring bear"

"Bearer," Anne corrected him.

After breakfast, Chester and Clarie were walking to the playground on the estate when Chester's phone buzzed, letting him know he had a text. There were no words, just a simple picture.

Others would not know what this meant – Chester did. He needed to call the Clubman to arrange a meeting. Many years ago when meeting with the Clubman, Chester mentioned that his partners referred to him as 'Clubman', just a single word. The Clubman laughed and in order to maintain discretion he started signalling Chester with a simple picture.

Chester texted a meeting location and time on his Blackberry. They had begun using Blackberries for business purposes when they learned that many government officials and politicians still used Blackberries. They were preferred because their messages were processed on Research In Motion's internal computer system. In doing this, messages could not be traced. Very handy for a politician who wanted to maintain secrecy. Also good for drug traffickers.

A few years earlier, Sean and Ava, had purchased an estate in the British Properties. This was a gorgeous example of modern architecture, complete with resplendent views of English Bay and the vast array of ships anchored, awaiting their line in the queue to enter the harbour and load or offload their cargo. Today, Sean smiled as he caught a glimpse of one of their ships. His jocundity was soon smashed with the crashing of an arbour the workers were installing in the back yard.

Preparations for the wedding were very intrusive, with workers running hither and yore, preparing for Sean and Ava's upcoming nuptials. Ava had insisted they host their wedding at their home. They had a colossal home on a two hectare estate complete with trees, streams and several rock faces, that on occasion Sean would scale. The buffer created by the estate should effectively shield their neighbours from any noise. However, they also invited all their neighbours as a precaution.

The wedding service would occur outdoors in the English garden. There were several shipping containers partially hidden off to one side. One contained the various elements and sound system the workers installed. In another was a large white tent, that could be erected fairly quickly should the weather take a turn toward rain. The party would happen inside. Workers had removed the floor to ceiling windows in solarium area of the house. The solarium was a vast open space and the vaulted ceilings provide excellent acoustics. The space was at least 10 meters long, but only about 4 meters wide. Removing the windows allowed workers to expand the room another 25 meters and install temporary glass walls and ceiling outside on the patio, effectively creating a large ballroom.

Sean saw Ava outside in the English garden directing the workers. He strolled over and gave her a kiss on the cheek. "You know I am the luckiest man in the world."

"Ahh, you're just saying that because you love me."

"Can't deny that."

"Well that is a lucky coincidence," Ava smirked. "Cause I love you too."

Sean interjected quickly, "hey I have an idea, how about we tie the knot."

"Not so fast Buster, we have only been living together for five years. What if we don't get along."

"I'm willing to chance it."

"Me too!"

They laughed and embraced. "If you don't need me for anything, I have a little work to do." Sean stated.

"No, go ahead. I think we are under control here."

Sean went to the garage and dismissed the driver stating he wanted to drive himself. He took the BMW 5 series. Arriving at the storage unit, he parked at the front and went through the office, making his way to their unit. On entering the unit, he saw two of his workers sitting on a sofa, having a couple of beers and eating pizza. "Afternoon, gents."

"Hiya boss," the shorter blonde one replied. "I didn't think we would see you, after all you have a busy day tomorrow."

Sean chortled, "Yes indeed, but until tomorrow, I am not really needed. I think I just get in the way."

Raising his beer bottle, the older dark-haired fellow said, "we hear ya. Want a beer?"

Sean walked to the fridge, pulled out a beer and sat in the easy chair, opposite the other two. "So are our charges processed?"

The older fellow replied, "just got finished, we had two today. They are in the freezer. Tonight, we will take them to the farm."

"That's great guys, thanks." Reaching into his pocket, he pulled out an envelope and tossed it on the coffee table between them, "here's your payment. Anything for me?"

The older man grabbed the envelope and opened the flap. Inside was a stack of $50 bills. "Thanks for this boss. We have a can over there with some teeth and a new hip. I don't think our guy will be needing it anymore," he said with a sneering laugh."

Standing up, Sean said, "okay guys, thanks. I should get going as I want to miss traffic."

The blonde man went to retrieve the empty gallon paint can and set it on the coffee table. "There you go boss ... and congratulations on your hitchin'."

Sean left the room with his paint can rattling, likely from the metal hip. As the guys sat down, the older man said, "you notice he never takes more than two swigs from a beer."

"Yes, but then again ... he can afford it."

Sean left the storage unit and on reaching his car, he went to the trunk and located a screwdriver from the toolbox and opened the can. He then tore off reams of paper towels and stuffed them inside. After closing the lid, he shook the can. It no longer rattled. Pulling into the parking lot in Steveston, he grabbed the can and walked down the pier to a fishing boat, Bean Nighe. This name meant 'washer woman', which was appropriate as it would wash away evidence. The captain came out on dock. Handing him the can, Sean said, "how long have you been waiting for me?"

"Not long," the captain replied, "The usual?"

"Yes," Sean replied. "Your bonus will be waiting for you when you return. Where are you off to now?"

"Back up to Haida Gwaii. Early runs of Coho are arriving. Should be about two weeks."

"Happy fishing," Sean replied, as he shook the captain's hand.

***

The following afternoon, about 100 guests were seated in the English Garden at Sean and Ava's home. Sean was standing at the front with the minister, Chester and Geoff beside as his groomsmen. On a small patio, beside a water feature, a four-piece chamber ensemble was playing Pachelbel. After receiving notification, the tune changed. Everyone turned around and from the house, you could see the bridal group start down the steps toward the reception. Ava looked radiant with a long gown and a tiara that sparkled in the sunlight like stars in a pitch-black night sky.

Leading the entourage were Clarie, along with Ava's young niece. The niece was a little distracted, but Clarie smiled straight ahead carrying a pillow that had wedding rings attached. When Clarie reached the front, he waved to his Dad standing beside Sean. Chester broke out into an even bigger smile and waved back. He went to Uncle Geoff and gave him the pillow with the rings. Anne was sitting in the front and Clarie took his seat beside his Mom.

The service was splendid and after the service they moved to the Japanese garden area where they mingled and had cocktails. After cocktails they returned to the English garden, where the dinner tables were set up. There were the usual speeches, where Geoff had the congregation rolling with laughter as he roasted Sean. After the toasts, Sean and Ava stood and with microphone in hand, Ava thanked everyone for making this day so special for them. Sean then grabbed the microphone and speaking to the audience said, "As I am sure you all know, all of this organization is courtesy of my wife. With no malice towards any of the guys here, I must say that today ... I am the luckiest man in the world. I have just married my best friend ... my soul mate." He leaned over and kissed Ava. "The only thing I insisted upon arranging this evening was the entertainment. My darling Ava has a very eclectic taste in music ... but she does have some favourites. So, ladies and gentlemen, please join my wife and I as we make our way back to the newly expanded conservatory, where tonight we have a special treat ... a band called the E street band." Then, looking into Ava's eyes, "My love, this is the one and only ... THE BOSS!"

As the group reached the patio doors, booming out of the conservatory came ... Born in the USA ..."

Arriving inside, Clarie was pulling on his Mom's hand. "It's really loud, Mommy." They found a spot as far away from the band as they could. One of the attendants noticing Clarie's agitation, produced a set of portable ear plugs that when inserted, Clarie said sounded like wool but his ears didn't hurt. He was looking at his Dad when he said, "Daddy are you okay?"

Chester had a look on his face that instantly changed from shock white to enraged red. He stood up and stared at the man that just entered the conservatory. It was the Dyck! What the hell was he doing here? Did Sean invite that piece of shit!

Sean, having been alerted by Chester's aggressive standing while pushing his chair over, looked towards the entrance and saw what caused Chester's aggravation. He immediately walked over to the entrance. Most of the people felt the tension and were watching as Sean approached this stranger. Sean spoke to him for a few moments. When Ava arrived, the Dyck shook her hand and spoke a few words. He then reached into his jacket pocket and pulled out an envelope that he gave to Sean and Ava. He then turned and walked back out ... but not before turning and smiling towards Chester.

Chester was fuming, as Sean approached him. Geoff arrived at the same time. "What is that bastard doing here?" he barked. "I can't believe you invited that asshole!"

Sean replied, "I didn't invite him Chester! He showed up on his own ... as you saw, I asked him to leave and he did."

"How does that fucker even know where you live?" Chester blurted. Just then, he felt a little tug on his arm. He looked down and he saw Clarie with a mortified look on his face. Anne was shocked as she stared at Chester with one of those looks that said he overstepped.

"D ... D ... Daddy?" Clarie spoke.

Chester immediately calmed down and felt like a heel. Leaning down and grabbing his son, he said, "Oh My God, Clarie ... I am so sorry."

Clarie looked at his Mom and said, "Can we go home, Mommy?"

On their way home, Chester tried unsuccessfully to mend the hurt he caused Clarie. He kissed both Clarie and Anne goodnight, then he went to his study and closed the door. He opened his liquor cabinet and poured himself a whisky that he gulped down. He topped off his glass as he fell into the big easy chair. He wondered if Clarie would ever forgive him?

Then it hit him like a ton of bricks ... what was the Dyck doing there? Is there something going on between him and Sean?

Chapter Thirteen

Sean worked odd hours and soon Ava became bored. She had given up her work with set design, as this also called for long unscheduled hours. With Sean, she did not need the income. Without her working, she had the flexibility to leave at a moment's notice when Sean's schedule permitted. She loved her luxurious life of excess, but aimlessly traipsing throughout the estate looking for something to occupy her time became tedious. Even Ella became less of a distraction.

Eventually, she started doing volunteer work and met several ladies there who had similar stories. Their successful husbands worked long hours and they were left to fill this void of time. Ava meshed with these ladies very well and soon they became a close network of friends

Despite the fact they were very wealthy, Ava soon discovered there was a hierarchy in Vancouver society. People who lived the opulent lifestyle on the north shore were frowned upon by the gentry that lived on the west side of Vancouver. Shaughnessy trumped the British Properties. This was the home to the 'old money' families, the people in the British Properties were the Nouveau Riche and didn't have the lineage to be considered equal with the older families. In an attempt to raise their stature, Ava and several of her new girlfriends decided to start a charity organization of their own. They all had a passion for their animals. In particular, they doted over their dogs. After mulling over several possible names for their new group, they decided on the 'Golden Retriever Club'.

The Golden Retriever club became ingrained in many local and national charities. Their wealth enabled them to cajole, promote and generally become very successful in raising funds for their handpicked charities. One of these charity dinners was being held in the Grand Ballroom of the Hotel Vancouver. Ava had convinced Sean to book two tables for this function. Most other attendees only booked one and Ava needed to outclass her contemporaries. There were eight place settings at every table and the price was $1500 per plate. Sean had persuaded Chester, Geoff and Sanchez to join them with accompanying escorts.

The entrance of the hotel appeared to be a back alley entrance. In fact, it was the main entrance and much more elaborate with banks of lights that would not look out of place in Las Vegas. It also had the added benefit of being covered, the roof, which was inlaid with thousands of small spotlights, kept the patrons protected from the harshness of the weather. It was Vancouver and it frequently rained during all seasons and even more so over the winter. As the guests arrived, the men looked dapper in their tuxedos and the women were decorated in designer gowns, fully adorned with jewels and expensive accoutrements. They must have spent the entire day having their hair and make-up prepared. Until they arrived inside the ballroom, they lived with the fear that a rogue drop of rain may soil their gowns, or a blast of wind would dislocate a strand of hair.

Chester's Bentley pulled up and the doorman opened his door before the driver could attend to it. Anne accompanied him this evening and she shone like some divine being; her smile made every man adore her. The diamond necklace and earrings she wore sparkled like a thousand shimmering beams of light cascading on a dew-covered meadow. When Chester and Anne arrived in the ballroom, they were astounded. The room was decorated with thousands of flowers, which made Chester wonder if any flower shop in Vancouver had any inventory remaining to serve other clients. Between the pillars of this gold gilded room were gigantic posters of Golden Retrievers.

The concierge escorted Chester and Anne to their table. Sanchez was already there with his new girlfriend (he and his wife had a nasty divorce that just recently concluded with Sanchez paying through his nose). Sean and Ava were near the front mingling with other patrons who were in attendance.

After dinner, a guest speaker from the Canadian Cancer Society talked about the new discoveries being made in the fight against Cancer. Then, the chairwomen of the Golden Retriever Club introduced the six founding members, who all stood and were cordially applauded when their names were called. Finally, she thanked the sponsors who generously underwrote the costs for the evening. As she called out the names on the giant screen behind her, company logos and/or faces appeared, depending on whether it was an individual or a company. Chester's eyes widened when the gold level sponsor was announced, and on the screen appeared a picture of Ashton Boyle.

After the dinner concluded, the guests mingled and amongst the small talk several substantial business arrangements were either started or completed. Chester was speaking with another property developer when, from the corner of his eye, he saw Ashton Boyle approaching. As he approached, Chester turned and Ashton held out his hand, and with a friendly smile simply said, "Chester."

Chester took his hand and replied, "Ashton."

Ashton smiled, "Ash to friends, Chester." Then, turning to his wife, "and this is my wife, Tanya."

Taking Tanya's hand, Chester replied, "you are a lucky man, Ash ... and may I introduce you to Anne."

Ashton took her hand and gently kissed it. "I would say we are both very fortunate Chester."

After a brief exchange of pleasantries, Ashton and Tanya were about to move on when Chester nodded towards Ashton and with a smirk said, "You two put on a great party, thank you. I hope to see you again."

Chester noticed Sean and Ava were speaking with another couple. Sean, though, was not paying attention to their conversation, instead he was looking in Chester's direction.

As the evening drew to a close their table's occupants were standing together at the entrance to the ballroom. Sean looked at Ava and said "that was a wonderful night honey. I hope you raised a boatload of money."

Ava smiled radiantly, "it was a great evening, thanks to all of you for coming." Then, looking directly at Sean, " ... and most of all, thank you sweetie for generously booking two tables." Then she stood on her tip toes and gave Sean a peck on the cheek.

"Your welcome my darling. It was fun." Turning towards the rest of the group, "I hope you enjoyed yourselves as well." Everyone nodded that they had, then looking toward Chester, "I saw that you met Ashton Boyle. He is a very private person and I was surprised to see his picture on the screen." Sean paused for effect. "His wife is one of the original members, and she must have used all her charms to get him to do that. He is someone we should get to know better as he has many connections with the film industry. Have you met him before?"

Chester didn't like the direction this conversation was going, but replied, "I met him before at some function or other – just casual acquaintances."

Then Anne added, "C'mon Chester, I think more than casual. He did ask you to call him Ash."

Shit! Chester thought to himself. Quickly though he rebutted, "they do when they are trying to make friends." Sean looked at Chester. He wasn't buying it. There was something Chester was not telling them.

Chapter Fourteen

Chester had called for the car. Throughout the estate, everyone jumped to Chester's requests. Not that he was an evil dictator, in fact he was very benevolent, he would always provide time off when requested, or even small things like remembering birthdays and anniversaries. However, he was the boss, and everyone respected that he paid their wages. When he called for a car, his driver naturally assumed he would be driving Chester somewhere. He started the Rolls and drove it up to the front entrance of the main house. He then proceeded to the kitchen, where he grabbed a small cooler and raided the refrigerator for snacks, various drinks and ice. Finally, he grabbed his thermos and filled it with coffee. Chester was notorious for never indicating where they were going or how long they would be away. The driver had spent many long hours waiting at some rather remote location, slowly having thirst and hunger pangs overwhelm him. If their destination was an urban location, he could easily locate a coffee shop to pass the time. He would not take a chance though as they could end up in some rural location.

As he returned to his car, he spotted a couple of Chester's associates (bodyguards) had parked their Suburban in the drive as well. This was entirely expected as Chester seldom ventured anywhere without an entourage. They were clustered together between the vehicles carrying on some sort of small talk, when Chester's private secretary came out. He informed them that today Chester wanted the Toyota Camry and he would drive himself. They would not be required to accompany him. This was very unusual, but not entirely unprecedented. On occasion, he would venture out by himself, one of the rumours among the staff was that he needed some 'alone time', it was reported that he would go to some public beach and just spend a few hours reading on a beach. His bodyguards were not happy with this, as it would leave him unguarded and exposed. They, however, knew he was the boss.

The driver returned the Rolls to the garage, and a few minutes later left driving a dark metallic grey Camry up to the driveway where Chester would take up the driver's seat. The bodyguards remained standing and waiting and when

Chester emerged, they questioned Chester once again – "Are you certain to want to leave without any guards, boss?"

"Most definitely. I should be four hours or so, and I am well prepared," Chester replied, as he held up a large thermos and a backpack that likely had books and snacks inside. He crawled in behind the wheel and waving goodbye, he approached the gates just as they were retracting. He looked over his shoulder and he saw Clarie in the bay window at Clarence Hall, waving manically towards him. Chester's heart warmed and he lovingly returned a wave towards his precious boy.

Through the gates, Chester started snaking his car down the mountain side. He exhaled exaggeratedly and as the air escaped his body, it seemed to release tension. Interesting, he thought, as he did not know he felt any stress.

He started to look around and took in the greenery from the forest. The greenery screamed of life, in sharp but glorious contrast to the bare rock faces that had been cut in the mountains to build this stretch of road. Chester was thinking to himself, that while he loved the luxurious things in his life, it was amazing how sometimes the simple things provided the greatest pleasures, like popcorn at a movie or a stale overcooked hot dog at a ball game. Mostly though, it was simply an enthusiastic smile from his son that would lighten up even his darkest days.

He thought of a saying he had read. 'To the world you are but one … But to one you are the world'. This was Clarie. Though Chester may not mean the world to him; that was more the domain of his mother, to Chester, Clarie meant the world.

For the next hour, he contentedly drove towards Cates Park in Deep Cove. As he was driving across the Second Narrows Bridge, now renamed the Iron Workers' Memorial Bridge, he realized he'd been lost in thought for the past 20 minutes. He had navigated his way through Port Moody, along Barnet Highway and through Burnaby, without really taking any notice of his surroundings. While he paid attention to his driving, it was like second nature … it wasn't in the forefront of his mind.

After crossing the bridge, he turned onto Dollarton Highway that snaked along the north shore of the Burrard Inlet. Deep Cove was a quiet little alcove, which while part of metropolitan Vancouver, somehow seemed remote and separate. It is nestled on the curve as Burrard inlet splits off to form Indian Arm to the north, while the rest of the inlet proceeds further east toward Port Moody.

As Chester pulled into Cates Park, he found the parking area was vacant. Seldom did he arrive at a meeting with the Clubman arriving before him. He parked and looked out across Indian Arm towards Belcarra on the other side. Just beyond Belcarra, the mountain rose to the peak where Chester could clearly see the turrets and walls of his estate. From Deep Cove to Chester's home was less than three kilometers. With Indian Arm separating them though, you had to traverse across Burrard Inlet to reach it. He knew he could have arranged for a boat to pick him up at Belcarra marina, which would have resulted in a commute of less than ten minutes. However, that would have required letting more people know his plans, which would have defeated the purpose of a clandestine meeting.

Chester reached across and retrieved his thermos to pour himself a cup of coffee. Not as good as stopping at a coffee shop for a take-out, but once again, that would open up the possibility of someone recognizing him and exposing his secret meeting. As he took a draw of his steaming cup of java, a dark Ford SUV pulled in about three spaces away from him. Chester recognised the Clubman and looking around to be certain they were not being watched, he walked over and got in the passenger side door. Warmly, the Clubman extended a hand and said, "Chester, good to see you."

"Thanks Ash, the same to you." Since their accidental meeting at the Golden Retriever dinner, formalities were dropped as they were now known to each other. Their relationship, while still discreet had grown quite friendly. For many years now, Chester had provided him with a great deal of money, in return Chester also grew incredibly wealthy. They both understood their long-term success would depend on maintaining this veil of secrecy that shrouded their lives from authorities. All that being said, they had developed a friendship and the resulting candor.

"So, I doubt if you arranged this to recruit me as an investor for one of your films."

Laughing, Ash replied, "no, indeed I didn't. We have a bit of a situation I am hoping you can help us with. This situation would be very lucrative … for all of us."

Chester laughed in return and said, "you know how to get my attention, tell me more. How are we going to make boatloads of money?"

Ashton explained how their system of importing product from Central and South America was in danger of being compromised. With the recent rise of the Asian gangs, there was an elevation of gang violence. The accompanying public outcry had motivated the authorities to become ever more diligent. During a recent board meeting, it was suggested perhaps Chester could be used for importing cocaine. They would of course maintain their own internal channels but augment them with Chester. This was a big step as they had never outsourced importing product. They decided to make this offer to Chester, and one other group that Ash was not at liberty to divulge the identity of.

"I know this is a big step for you Chester and you need to discuss this with your partners. We can give you a week for your decision. If you choose to pursue this endeavor, we can assist you with introductions and logistical information as required. One last thing, you would look after distribution. We would receive a 20% royalty, but all other profits and expenses would be yours."

"That sounds very promising, but as you said, I need to confer with my partners. I have a question. What sort of volume would we be looking at?"

"4-5 Mil," Ash replied, then added, "per week."

Chester whistled, "at 80% gross profit that would be up to 3 mil profit per week." Then, regaining his composure, he added, "and I assume the growth potential would be substantially more?"

Ash laughed. Some might term this as greed, Ash understood it was just good business. "You are always looking for more aren't you ... yes indeed, the sky is the limit."

"I will let you know within a week......but I think you already know our answer."

They were both jubilant as they parted ways. The Clubman was happy as this would provide them with further separation of drug business and protection for the Club. Chester was of course happy as they would make another fortune!

Chester returned to his car and watched the Clubman depart from his rear-view mirror. Chester grabbed the coffee he had poured just before the Clubman arrived, and noticed it was cold. Opening the door, he tossed the coffee, grabbed the thermos and his backpack which had snacks and went to sit at a picnic table in the park. He sat on the top of the table with his feet perched on the bench. He poured a coffee and retrieved a can of nuts from his backpack. As he sat there, he was reminded of his adolescence on the farm. The fall was harvest season and he recalled many meals similar to this out in the field. The farmer's wife would prepare meals and drive them out to the field. Mostly sitting on the open end gate of a pickup truck, they would eat. Food always tasted so good in those days! The smell of grain chaff hung in the air and those warm sunny days somehow made the food taste better. Sort of like a hamburger at a hockey game. The burgers always tasted better there....and It always had fried onions with mustard and relish.

Reminiscing was soon replaced with the news he had just received from the Clubman. This was an incredible opportunity and they could make an astronomical amount of money. They could grow into the moniker Sanchez had mentioned long ago ... they could become the Clubmen.

As Chester sat there, he began to wonder if it was worth it. Right now, he had more money than he could possibly spend in one lifetime. He was making scads of money from his legitimate businesses. The real estate development, agriculture, fishing and shipping businesses would individually make a fortune for them. Combined, it ensured the wealth would also be enjoyed for all his children and grandchildren. Getting involved in importing coke was a whole new ball game. There were tremendous gains, but also huge risks. This would bring in the international authorities. The Federal RCMP divisions, Interpol, the DEA from the US, plus the nasty dealings with cartels. In an effort to instill fear, the cartels had recently started beheading people. Nothing scares people into towing the line better than seeing decapitated heads rolling across your floor. A Tijuana Haircut was the euphemism people used to describe this type of barbarous execution.

There were two issues with turning down this offer. The first issue was the Club didn't make 'offers' that could be turned down. It was a forgone conclusion that it was more of an order than an offer. It was the proverbial 'offer you couldn't refuse'. The second issue was that, while Chester was already wealthy, he had an insatiable hunger for more. A billion was better than a million, two billion was better than one billion, and so on and so on. Some strange internal measuring gauge told him he always needed more.

His brief flirtation with declining the offer soon turned to the logistics of how to pull this off. Chester pulled out his phone. He texted Geoff and Sean the following message: 'Senior management meeting tomorrow at 10AM. Does this work?' Chester quickly turned around, as he thought he heard something rustle in the small grove of bushes on the far side of the vacant parking lot behind him. As he watched, he saw some birds fly off. He must be a little jittery, he thought to himself. His phone buzzed, first from Geoff, then shortly after from Sean. They would both be available tomorrow.

Chester leisurely finished off his coffee and packed up to leave. As he left the park, he noticed a vehicle parked in another lot. It was parked in the shade behind the grove of trees he noticed earlier. Chester thought it was funny that he missed it when he arrived. Then, he recalled being startled and thought perhaps it was when this car entered. They likely parked close to the trees to avoid the car getting too hot in the sunshine. He slowly exited the parking lot and started to make his way back home. He checked his watch, it was 2:45 PM. Crap he thought to himself, I will probably get stuck in traffic going across the Second Narrows Bridge. This bridge had become notorious for being the most congested choke point in the entire area. Chester realized he would catch the start of rush hour but that was okay as he had lots of thinking to do on the way back home.

Then he thought of Clarie and once more he was flooded with joy. It had taken a long time for Clarie to forgive him for his outburst at Sean and Ava's wedding. For the longest time he seemed to avoid Chester, but eventually the smiles and hugs returned. Children are very resilient and forgiving. Clarie's substantial inheritance was about to grow to a level that should firmly establish wealth for Clarie and the many generations that followed.

✳✳✳

Sean was sitting in his rental car at Cates Park. Earlier in the day, quite by accident, one of Chester's bodyguards let slip that Chester would be going out on his own. Immediately, Sean went to rent a car and see what he was up to. Chester did not notice the Ford Escape that was following him and when he entered Cates Park, Sean parked in the adjoining parking lot, directly behind a thicket of bushes and small trees. After parking his vehicle, he thought to himself it was one of the few times he was thankful Blackberry bushes grew into a tall gnarly tangle. From Chester's vantage point, he would not be able to see Sean.

Sean parked the vehicle and waded through a small opening in the blackberry bramble and into the small thicket of gangly trees just beyond, finding a spot that would offer concealment if he sat on his haunches. It also offered a clear view of Chester across the parking lot. He saw Chester sitting in his car, he appeared to be pouring himself something from a thermos. Then, another SUV pulled up a few spaces away from Chester. He witnessed Chester exiting his vehicle and looking around before he made his way to the other vehicle and entered the passenger side. He could see two people talking, but he couldn't make out the identity of the mystery person. After fifteen minutes, though to Sean it seemed more like an hour as his thighs were burning, but he dared not stand up to relieve the strain, Chester emerged, and the SUV drove off. As the SUV passed, Sean caught a glimpse of Ashton Boyle.

I knew there was something between those two! Sean thought. While he still didn't know what the nature of their relationship was, he knew Chester was hiding something from him ... again! He knew he couldn't leave while Chester was lollygagging at the park, so he just remained quiet at his perch in the woods. He was trying to deduce the nature of Chester and Ashton's relationship in an effort to take his mind off his searing legs. He leaned forward in a kneeling manner to reduce the tension. What he forgot was that this bramble was filled with Blackberry vines, and the sharp thorns pierced his trousers and embedded themselves in his knees. It hurt like hell, and he could feel the blood starting to seep out and coat his pants. Suddenly, his phone rang – dammit, he thought! He had a special ringtone for Chester, that sounded a little like a death march. He quickly hit silent mode, but not before Chester turned around and was looking in his direction. Afraid to move, he remained motionless, like a crocodile about to pounce on its prey. His thighs burned and the pain from the blackberry thorns became more excruciating as they embedded deeper into his knees. Thankfully, Chester eventually turned around and continued to drink his coffee. His heart was pounding, only then did he realize that he had been holding his breath. Taking deep breaths, his heartbeat began to slow down, and he regained his composure.

Damn phone! He looked and saw a text from Chester. He requested a meeting tomorrow. This could be interesting he thought, as he confirmed his attendance.

Eventually, Chester left, and Sean remained seated for several minutes. After what seemed like an appropriate amount of time, he gingerly stepped out of the blackberry quagmire on Chester's side, as it was the closest. He walked around the bushes, on what he was certain looked like peg legs. As the blood slowly started returning to his legs, he noticed the knees of his pants were glued to his kneecaps with patches of partly dried blood.

Looking at his wristwatch, he realized traffic was going to be horrific. Without a doubt, he would run into congestion. He called Ava to let her know he would be a little late, as they had dinner reservations at CinCin, and they were planning on going for cocktails beforehand. They would now have to go directly to the restaurant.

Even with Chester leaving several minutes ahead of him, he realized they could conceivably run into each other while at the entrance to the Second Narrows Bridge. Sean would not be going over the bridge, instead he would just drive straight past and enter the upper levels highway towards his house, which was in the opposite direction. He checked his wristwatch, and after some quick calculations decided he would wait another half an hour. The last thing he wanted to risk was running into Chester, another half hour and he would be long gone.

* * *

Meanwhile, after leaving Cates Park, Chester decided since he was going to be stuck in traffic anyway, he had a fancy for a latte and a JJ Beans cinnamon roll. He had passed a JJ Beans on Dollarton Highway on his drive to meet Ash. Chester saw the coffee shop up ahead and pulled into the parking lot. It was a busy place at this time of the afternoon, and after traversing the parking lot in front of the store, he located a spot around the side of the building. There was a long queue to place his order and he was beginning to think his need for a cinnamon roll fix was not that great and perhaps he should just leave, when he looked up and saw it was his turn. He took a seat on the front veranda overlooking Dollarton Highway. Enjoying the last remnants of his latte, and having satiated his cinnamon roll desire, he was preparing to leave just as Sean drove past in a Ford Escape. Chester was not one to believe in coincidences and this started his mind wondering. It was particularly strange that Sean was driving a Ford Escape, not his preferred Range Rover.

Strange ... had he somehow seen his meeting with Ashton? And if so, would he conclude that Ashton was the Clubman? ... and what the hell was he doing driving a Ford Escape?

The next day at the office, Chester attempted to gently steer the conversation in a direction that may nudge Sean into explaining his presence in that area yesterday. He asked many leading questions. He could not ask him directly; this would lead to the natural reciprocal question of why he was there. He, of course, could not divulge the meeting he had with the Clubman. Chester didn't know if Sean was being coy, or if he just wasn't buying into the line of questions and volunteering any information that may have seemed inconsequential to him but would prove most valuable to Chester.

Just before 10:00, Geoff asked if they could delay the meeting for 15 minutes. He had a small piece of business to take care of. Of course, they all agreed, and when Geoff arrived at the conference room, Chester and Sean were already seated and were making small talk. Geoff grabbed a coffee and a muffin, then sat down. He then said, "I have some good news guys. That's why I was a little late. I was attending a teleconference with Sanchez and Christophe."

"Great," Chester replied, "I have good news also, but I think you should go first."

"Well, we are going to be buying another boat!"

"Nice," Sean interjected.

"This is a big one. Ever since the oil spill in Prince William Sound, all oil tankers have a reputation of being just slightly more repugnant than Satan himself. A lot of oil shipping firms have shied away from growing their fleets, and many oil companies have started outsourcing more of their shipping. They are shying away from owning their own fleets as the association with oil tankers is detrimental to their public perception. The result is the price of the resale market for oil tankers has dropped and there is currently a premium being charged for shipping …. at least in North America. We can make a lot of money on this."

"Fantastic news Geoff," Chester replied, "great work on seizing an opportunity." After waiting for a round of congratulations and allowing Geoff to deservedly glow in the spotlight for a while, Chester added, "speaking of opportunities …"

He then proceeded to outline the proposal the Clubman had presented. Sean was immediately on board, and enthusiastically endorsed their business expansion. Geoff, as was the normal protocol, did not as readily agree. He pointed out many of the dangers and downfalls. After a few minutes of enthusiastic discussion, Chester interjected with a suggestion. Even though it was against their rules to leave behind any paper trail with their drug business, Chester suggested they brainstorm all the dangers and systematically approach each item independently. After several hours of discussion, they started growing hungry as they worked through lunch. Chester paged Nancy and she came in with menus from several restaurants in the complex. If they were going to work right through lunch, they needed fuel to keep their synapses firing.

They continued for the next several hours, and by 3:30 they sat back and looked at what they had accomplished. There were many obstacles to overcome, but by tackling them one at a time they had either solutions or next steps for each item. Sean then said, "I guess we have agreed to move forward on this then?"

Geoff replied, "I don't think we actually had any choice. If they offer, we have to accept. We just need to be sure we do this professionally and by being smart we can make a lot of money with minimizing the danger."

Chester agreed, "I will advise the Clubman, but I will ask him for some time to sort through the details. Agreed?"

They each gave their assent and they divided the responsibilities on the next steps.

Chester noticed Sean had a thoughtful look which slowly changed into a smirk, as if he had just discovered something ... what is it? ... suddenly it hit him. Sean had put it together and deduced that Ashton Boyle was the Clubman. All these years of deception and subterfuge had been uncovered. Now that the mystique was shattered, what would it mean? No matter how hard he tried to discount this revelation as being dangerous ... he couldn't shake the feeling this was bad.

Chapter Fifteen

It was a cold grey November morning. The misting rain created a multi-coloured rainbow-like effect encapsulating the homeless vagrants just waking from their slumber. They were wrapped in filthy sleeping bags that had an unkempt build-up of grime. Effluence from both humans and animals, combined with grease stains from many slobbered meals, left their marks on their threadbare clothing. The only semi-positive aspect to this encrusting filth was it served as a partial barrier from the incessant rain.

Dan was looking out the window rendered partially opaque with an accumulation of grime. Peering at the vagrants, the mist created a halo effect, almost like they were God's people. "As if they could be God's children," Dan said with disgust and spat at the window. As the spittle slowly crept down the window it left tracks, the wetting effect rendered it more transparent. Through this somewhat cleaner splodge, Dan saw a homeless person who appeared to be caressing and petting a small animal. Dan concentrated his gaze to make out what it was … shit! It was a pet rat!

Dan LeCoq had been released from prison, having served his full term. The length of his incarceration was nearly unheard of. Most convicts were released after serving somewhere between a third and a half of their sentence. Dan's lawyers ran into a stone wall every time they made a petition for early release. The judicial system knew Dan 'the weasel' was truly a cruel, vile person. He was convicted on a lesser charge of manslaughter, even though everyone knew he had committed many more sinister crimes, but he 'weaseled' his way out of those. Much like Al Capone, everyone knew he was an abhorrent gangster but was convicted on a lesser charge. In an attempt to provide a little more justice, the authorities made sure there was no early release.

Instead of reforming, Dan took advantage of the system and became a more adept crook. To the general public, prison was a place where criminals served their penalty to society, and in the process learned a skill that, upon release, would provide them with a basis for a life of a law-abiding citizen.

In fact, prison served as an institution of higher learning, for the criminal element. Much like a person wishing to become more adept at accounting would attend university and gain a degree. Prisoners did not necessarily choose this incarceration, but they learned a great deal about criminal endeavors from a multitude of tempered mentors.

Inside, Dan was not well liked. Even among criminals there was a code. Being a weasel was detested. He kept to himself and had few friends. In the quiet times though he did overhear many conversations. He had a keen sense of hearing, as long as he kept his cool and focused. Dan was becoming a more proficient gangster. However, his derangement also found new depths.

As the years wore on, he became more unhinged. His savage unpredictability could frighten the most hardened criminal with an evil smirk. Mostly it was those glazed over crazy eyes, reminiscent of Charles Manson, that would give people the heebie-jeebies. When in this state, everyone, including the guards, gave him a wide berth.

Now this twisted, deranged convict was living in a flea bag hotel on the downtown eastside, courtesy of a small allowance from the Justice department to assist convicts begin a new life. Convicts that are paroled have to report to their parole officer and complete several programs before they are granted their complete freedom. The upside for The Weasel having served his full term was he did not have to complete any of these programs. He was free to enter society without any of these safeguards. Without treatment, Dan's depravity deepened.

After being convicted, Dan saw Chester's ascendency to drug lord. He knew this could never have happened without being sanctioned by Club 81. Through the fog of his demented mind, he eventually deduced it must have been Chester who was the architect of his former and deceased boss Dael's demise. During his incarceration, his obsession with Chester grew. While inside, the grapevine was very effective on reporting what was happening outside. With each report on Chester, his anger grew. It reached a point during the last few years that other inmates would only share a report on Chester when Dan was securely within the confines of his cell. As the messenger, you often became the object of his fury. It was safer to tell him when he could only harm himself. This also happened on several occasions.

Dan was called The Weasel for a reason, in addition to an insidious temperament, he was bestowed with a narcissistic spirit. Only he was important. Nobody trusted him, with the exception of Dael, and Dael only trusted him because

Dael was an idiot. Dan was not a good-looking man. He was short and squat and looked sort of like a bratwurst sausage. Pale and rounded with an enlarged girth. Prior to prison, his face was pale with a clustering of veins around his nose and cheeks. Much like someone who drank too much or had a fisherman's face weathered with years of salt spray. After spending the past decade in prison, he had become even paler. His hair that was once thinning and looked a little like down on a plucked goose, was replaced with a small amount of fluff, mostly concentrated on the sides.

Even though he now lived in this mangy apartment, he still tried to keep a certain degree of self-worth by maintaining a reasonably clean appearance. He shaved everyday, even though his pale skin pronounced his sallow veneer. Dan dressed and went to the local food kitchen for breakfast. While he had some money, he didn't want to spend it on things like accommodation and food, he needed to save his resources to get back in the game. He was narcophilic. This was the term they used inside to describe someone attracted to the narcotics business.

Most of his closest contacts had disappeared shortly after Dael's assassination. It didn't take long for him to ascertain that Chester had eliminated his competition. He needed to get back into business, but he needed to develop new contacts and cash. He was fully aware he was still being watched. On several occasions, he had overheard the cops. They had taken to calling him The Cock! This pissed off Dan incredibly. His name was LaCoq. Pronounced La Coke, as you would say coq et vin. Even though he had a French name, he was brought up English and English society had bastardized his name, and they anglicized it to La Cock.

He recalled one of the few conversations he had with Chester years ago, he was one of the few people who pronounced his name correctly. Growing up in Saskatchewan, Chester recalled a small community in southern Saskatchewan called Bean Fate. Years later, Chester drove through the town and when he saw the actual spelling was Bienfait, which was anglicized to Bean Fate. Dan realized it was one of the few times he and Chester actually shared a laugh. Didn't matter though, he was still going to kill him, and he needed to suck up these disparaging remarks from the cops, in order to achieve that goal.

***

Sean was sitting in his office. Staring into space as if in deep thought. In front of him, his computer screen was open to an email that said The Weasel was to be released from prison in a few days. The Weasel was the one that got away. After eliminating Dael, the remainder of Dael's crew quietly disappeared. The few that were not loyal to Dael were recruited and became the basis for their drug empire. Since the Weasel's incarceration, LNa had been monitoring him, biding their time until his release in order to eliminate that last straw. It has been ten years and the world had changed drastically. Their collective focus had been on developing their business. Sean was now contemplating what to do about The Weasel. He would be easy enough to eliminate. A quick text and within a couple of days, Dan LeCoq would become a guest at GH Reed's incinerator.

Sean was pondering this decision. Wondering if Dan may actually serve a purpose yet. After a few minutes, he sent a text. Instead of asking his associates to apprehend Dan, he simply asked them to monitor him and report back. He had a few days before he needed to make a decision. He was being cautious.

In the past couple of months, he had managed to nurture a relationship with Ashton Boyle, and despite the fact that he could now comfortably pick up a phone and place a call to him, there remained a barrier. He'd seen this sort of situation before, mostly it had to do with religion. He had many Muslim friends, some of whom he'd become quite close to over the years. However, there was a point he just could never pass because he did not share their religion. There was a door that was closed to him. Catholics, Jews were much the same way, not to mention the smaller, more fanatical religions like the Mormons or Jehovah Witnesses. The basis of this barrier, while usually religion, in some cases was also culture – Russians, Germans, Scots, Irish, etc... If you did not have this heritage in your background, you were not permitted full access.

Sean's relationship with Ashton was similar. They enjoyed many expensive dinners together and met quite regularly at social events. When Sean discovered Ashton's love of English Premier League football, he even started to learn all he could in order to get closer. Ashton was a Chelsea supporter. Sean chose Manchester City as his favourite to provide jocularity. All to no avail though, as he could not break through that wall. Ashton would not fully drop his guard.

On the domestic front, he and Ava had separated.... again. They had a relationship built on passion. Their friends referred to them as having an Elizabeth Taylor – Richard Burton marriage. They loved each other immensely but fought when together. Ava remained at their British Properties estate. Sean returned to high-rise living. He took over the entire top floor on one of their developments. He had Ava assist with the designing and furnishing, since they were still very friendly, and on occasion even shared the same bed. Ava loved celebrity and enjoyed being in the public eye. On the other hand, Sean wanted, and needed to maintain secrecy.

Sean and Ava realized they loved each other. It is was simply that their lifestyles were like oil and water. They still spent a lot of time together and Sean would show up whenever he liked to visit with Ella. Ava became very involved in the SPCA and on occasion, Sean would meet her there and they would spend hours playing with the animals. When some sick animal needed rescuing, Sean could always be counted on to fund the treatment if it was beyond the facilities' means.

They still attended the symphony together and took in many functions as each other's escort. One day, Sean called Ava and asked if she had any plans for the weekend. "No," she replied, "it's only Thursday though Sean....what do you have planned?"

"Pack your bags my love. Can you arrange a sitter for Ella? We will be back early next week. Trust me you will love it."

"I love the intrigue. When should I arrange for Ella's sitter?"

"Today. I will be there around noon. We can drop Ella off on the way."

Ava was giddy with excitement, "Okay, sounds like fun. What should I pack?"

Sean was not going to fall for this ploy. He wasn't about to give it away. "Just your overnight bag....we can buy what we need there ... oh and bring a jacket we are going to be flying."

Sean arrived at noon with Chester's Bentley and driver. Ava was waiting with a small suitcase and a big hug and kiss. Ella was jumping all over Sean with excitement. After a few minutes, she obediently got in her travel case and off they went to the sitters. After dropping off Ella, they went straight to the south terminal at YVR, where a private Lear jet was waiting for them. Ava had a smile that stretched from ear to ear, as soon as they took off, she said, "Okay, I have been patient long enough. Where are we going?"

Laughing, Sean said, "I can't believe you waited this long, my darling. I know you have been dying to see Andrea Bocelli. We have tickets to his concert on Saturday night."

"Oh My God," she cried that's incredible – thank you." Then, a moment of reflection and she said, "but I didn't pack anything for the concert............and where is it?"

Smiling, Sean said, "La Scala."

Shocked, Ava replied, "La Scala ... as in Milan?"

"Yes indeed, I think they may have a shop or two where we can pick up clothes for the festivities."

They arrived at noon the following day, where a car picked them up and took them to the Bulgari Hotel Milano. They cleaned up and went shopping. Sean splurged on Ava, plus picked up several outfits for their weekend as well. The next evening, they had box seats at La Scala and attended the after-dinner reception. On Sunday, the hotel arranged for a private tour of Milan in a Rolls Royce sedan, complete with private tour guide.

When they arrived back in Vancouver, Ava was stunned as Sean filled out his custom's declaration. He had spent over €200K on clothes and gifts. That, of course, included several pieces of jewelry he adorned her with. "Thank you for an incredible experience, my love, even though we can't seem to live together, you know I will always love you."

Sean smiled, "I will always love you too, my darling."

"Do you think we should try it again?"

Sean grabbed her and said, "I have been thinking the same thing, my love."

On the drive home, they were like young kids exploring each other in giddy excitement.

***

On the economic front, business was exploding. In addition to the growth and ever-growing profits derived from their legitimate businesses, their drug distribution business continued to flourish. This generated a huge amount of cash that they were able to route through their assorted businesses. Their biggest windfall over the last year was their cocaine importing business. Through their shipping business, they were able to discreetly import vast quantities of cocaine. South American countries continued to be the manufacturing hub. The difficulty was moving it from South America to Vancouver.

LNa hired several chemists, technicians and generally extremely smart, creative people, at their privately funded laboratory, under the guise of conducting leading edge carbon capture and plastic mollification research. This endeavor was funded by private firms in the hopes their research would lead to economically feasible businesses. In fact, all the private firms were owned by LNa. One of the breakthroughs the scientists discovered was the ability to imbed cocaine within plastic. When coated properly, it would be undetectable even by sniffer dogs with the most sensitive noses. Once reaching its destination, the plastic could be broken down with a system of heat, solvent wash and finally immersed in a weak acid bath. All that remained was the pure cocaine.

Christophe Ibrahim, who was the President of Hellenic Shipping Lines (HSL), now had a fleet of 15 ships to manage. The CEO of HSL was Gabriel Sanchez, who left the operating of the fleet to Christophe. Occasionally, one of their ships would take on cargo in Tumaco, Columbia. When picking up special containers, they would travel from Tumaco to the Philippines. Customs and border patrol agents could easily be bribed. Graft was such a common practise, that frequently cargo that did not have proper documentation was released. As long as enough palm greasing was applied.

The special cargo, once offloaded, would be sent to a facility outside Manilla where the cocaine would be embedded into plastic that was imported from China. The term they used for cocaine loaded plastic was Snow Plastic. Snow Plastic would then be sent to factories that had plastic extruding equipment to form various items such as car parts, children's toys and equipment. Once dried and packaged, it would be imported through the Port of Vancouver and taken to a separate facility where the extraction process would take place. This was so clean and efficient that after a while, the authorities began to wonder where the cocaine was coming from. Realizing the cops would keep digging until they found a source, Chester decided they needed to offer some sacrificial lambs. He worked out an arrangement with Ashton and the suppliers in Columbia, where they would occasionally send a shipment that would easily be confiscated. All three would share in the costs for the loss. Never, though, would any of LNa's companies be used for these dummy loads. They needed to keep their reputation clean. They could always find some idiot gangbanger who wants to make a huge profit and bring in a load of drugs. They never knew they were actually ritual slaughter.

The import business had become so lucrative that the volume of money they needed to clean overwhelmed their ability to launder it. Financial authorities were constantly looking for abnormalities with extraordinary profits. So rather than jeopardize some of their existing enterprises, it was decided they would need to run cash through some offshore banks. They were looking at several possible locations for this business venture. After the Ostranskis narrowed down the list of possible banks, it was decided Chester should appraise each bank in a personal visit. After stops in Belize, Panama and Grand Cayman, Chester arrived in Cyprus. There, he met with the bank manager of Nicosia Bank, who also happened to be one of the owners. Mr. Stavros was eager to work with Chester and after negotiating, a fee of 3.5% for cash transactions greater than 10M CDN$ was agreed upon.

The plan was to evaluate four more locations. After his meeting in Cyprus though, Chester decided to forgo the remaining locations. The original plan was to conceal this working vacation under the guise of a family vacation. Outside of short 3-4 day trips, Clarie had never had an extended family vacation. Chester had chartered a private 100-foot yacht that met him in Cyprus. This would form his transportation to the remaining locations, as they leisurely cruised through the Mediterranean. After concluding his business with Mr. Stavros the following morning, he departed for Crete, where he would meet up with Clarie and Anne.

Chester loved the Mediterranean, he was fascinated with the history and culture that exploded in this region. In Canada, outside of some small remnants of the Vikings on the East coast, and a smattering of first nations burial sites, the oldest cultural edifices were a few hundred years ago. Quebec City is the oldest city in what was then termed the 'new world', slightly over 400 years old. In western Canada, the oldest non-native inhabited cities were less than 200 years old. In the Mediterranean, cultures reached back thousands of years – Ancient Egypt was some 5000 years ago!

Chester loved this and wanted his son to be exposed to these ancient cultures. When they arrived in Crete and docked, Chester looked over the side of the ship as the port inspectors cleared their vessel. Excitedly jumping up on the dock was Clarie and his Mom. Chester had promised to take Clarie on a trip for his fifth birthday. In five days, he would celebrate his birthday. Chester was watching Clarie from the rear of the ship and the huge smile that crossed Clarie`s face was enough to brighten the darkest recesses of his heart. After a few minutes, Chester could tell Clarie was getting upset with the waiting. His Dad was only 30 meters away and he was not allowed to go see him. He didn't care about port authorities and immigration procedures, he wanted to see his Dad. To Clarie, the wait must have felt like cruel and unusual punishment. The guard at the gangway finally removed the rope with a sign that said, 'NO ENTRY'. Clarie ran up and gave his father a giant hug.

"This is a big boat Daddy," Clarie proclaimed.

Anne added, "Ship ... Clarie ... remember some people do not like it being called a boat."

Chester showed Anne and Clarie around the ship. He could tell Anne was very impressed with their luxurious surroundings. "I thought the hotel we were staying at was magnificent ... this is even better. Thank you Chester."

Clarie was not as impressed with the yacht, he had other activities on his mind. "Mom said we could go exploring today, but we had to wait for you. Can we go now?"

"Of course, son, first let me show you your rooms and I will arrange for a car to come and pick us up. Is that okay."

Clarie nodded.

They packed up some gear and went exploring through the streets of Heraklion. Clarie was interested in seeing the Palace of Knossos, though in truth, he was more impressed with the gelato they purchased in a stinky market, than with the Minoans. The market was quite dirty and smelled like rotting fish and slaughtered animals. The gelato was a huge hit and tasted even better because of the stinky market they just vacated.

After a few hours, Clarie was starting to lose his battle with drowsiness. Eventually, he could not supress his yawns anymore. They made their way back to the dock and as they boarded the ship, Clarie fell asleep in Chester's arms. Chester laid Clarie in his bed. As he covered up his son and gave him a gentle kiss on his forehead, he just stood and smiled at his Clarie. How he loved this boy. Perhaps for the first time in his life, there was something that took precedence over his own need for self-fulfillment.

That evening, they decided to dine onboard as several days of traveling and today's tour resulted in Clarie sleeping for three hours. When he woke up, he played shuffleboard with Chester. Clarie questioned the rule changes a few times. In the end though, he was okay with it as it always seemed to benefit him. He howled and hooted with victory after beating Chester. In very short order, he had endeared himself to the entire staff on the ship.

While in port, the ship's captain, officers and engineers would perform maintenance on the vessel. However, they also had lots of free time and Chester encouraged them to use whatever ship facilities they wanted to. During the shuffleboard match, there were several ship personnel cheering Clarie on and when he proved victorious, they applauded. Clarie was having a blast! So was Chester.

When the chef inquired what he would like for dinner, Clarie told him he liked seafood. Being on the Mediterranean, there was an ample supply of fresh seafood. As they sat down for dinner that evening, Clarie sort of poked at his food. The first dish was something called calamari, Clarie started chewing on his first piece and quickly decided he didn't like it. When Chester asked him what he thought, he replied, "I don't like it. It tastes like a balloon, very chewy!" Everyone laughed, as Clarie picked at the sauce it was served with. The next dish had a fish with the head still on it. Clarie immediately knew he would not like this. "Why wouldn't they cut the head off, it's looking at me!" Clarie balked. Everyone laughed.

Still giggling, Chester replied, "Would you like them to remove the head?"

"It's looking at me, Dad!"

The waiter removed Clarie's dish and returned a few minutes later with the same fish. This time the head was removed. Reluctantly, he took a small mouthful. The revulsion on his face was obvious as he took the offending fish and spit it into his napkin. Once again, everyone laughed. By now, the chef had appeared and said, "I thought you said you like seafood Clarie?"

Clarie looked at him with a disgusted look, "Fish and Chips is seafood, you know!"

This time there was a general uproar. Chester was laughing so hard he had tears running down his face. When Clarie saw this, he became more upset and gave Chester the dirty eye look. This caused Chester to laugh even harder. Chefs are normally very particular about the food they have prepared and are easily offended. In this case though, the chef was also laughing as he reached down and removed Clarie's dish. He reappeared a few minutes later with something resembling fish sticks and French-fries. As he placed this dish in front of Clarie, a smile crossed Clarie's face and he blurted, "that's better – that's real seafood!"

Reaching into his apron, he pulled out a bottle of ketchup. "I suspect you may want this as a garnishment, Master Clarie?"

"Yup," as Clarie dove into his proper dinner, he leaned over towards his Mom and quietly said, "being in a foreign country, I guess I will have to be clearer with my directions." He smiled then added, "I wonder what would have happened if I ordered hamburger ... maybe a piece of ham."

After dinner, they sat at the rear of the ship and watched the sunset while drinking evening cocktails. Clarie took great delight in ordering a Caesar. Chester knew Clarie loved these, so he had a few cases of Clamato juice sent over. He knew nobody outside of Canada had any idea what a Caesar was. Clarie's was of course without the vodka and no tabasco sauce, but he did have a couple of shrimps, grasping the lightly salted rim.

Chester's relationship with Anne was slightly more complicated. Actually, it wasn't that complicated. Anne was a tall, vivacious brunette. She was very striking, and Chester liked her, but his affection certainly did not deepen into love. Chester was very comfortable with her, but they didn't share the passion that was so obvious with Sean and Ava. They both loved the product of their union ... Clarie. Frequently, they would spend the evenings together and they would release their basic instincts in uninhibited lovemaking. They each had other partners and while Anne would frequently date other men, she could never find anyone who stole her heart. To Clarie, this was normal, sometimes Mom and Dad would spend the evening together and he would sleep in his room in Dad's house. Other nights, he would sleep in his bed in his Mom's house. On occasion, other men would spend the evening with his Mom.

Therefore, it seemed perfectly natural when Clarie woke the following morning and looking into his Dad's room, he saw his Mom and Dad sleeping together. It was still quite early, and normally Clarie had no trouble sleeping later. His Mom told him he was suffering from something called jet lag. He wasn't sure what that was, but he knew it made him wake earlier than normal. With his circadian rhythm out of kilter, he went upstairs to the main deck. There were two people busy doing a multitude of chores. Clarie wished both of them a good morning and they smiled back at him. As he walked towards the front of the ship, the chef was just coming up from his galley with a steaming espresso in his hand. He sat on one of the chairs and lit a cigarette. Clarie approached and said good morning.

"Ah bonjour Clarie," he said in a French accent, "Did you sleep well?"

To Clarie, the chef spoke funny. He was a nice guy though and Clarie liked him. Even if he now questioned his cooking skills. "Bon jour," he replied, accentuating both syllables. Then, repeating the chef's broken English, "I sleep very good. How about you Fran cois?" again accentuating both syllables of Francois' name.

Francois laughed a hearty Frenchman's laugh and said, "very fine Clarie – very fine indeed. Would you care for some breakfast?"

This sounded like a good idea as he was quite hungry. His reply was a cross between a wish and a request. "Bacon and eggs?"

"Certainement, Clarie. Eggs and bacon coming up."

Clarie obviously recalling the seafood fiasco last night, quickly added, "chicken's eggs and pig's bacon," then with a quizzical look he added, "right?"

Francois burst out laughing, he nearly choked on his coffee as a fine mist of espresso spewed from his mouth like a volcano erupting. He wiped his mouth with the apron he was wearing and took one last drag from his cigarette before tapping it out in the ashtray. Still laughing, he started down to his galley and turned to Clarie, "Do you want to eat in the kitchen, or should I bring it up here?"

Francois' laughing surprised Clarie. Why would he laugh so hard, he was the one who screwed up his seafood, after all. Regardless, Francois seemed like fun, "I'll come with you, if that's okay. There is nobody here to talk with. You will eat as well, right?"

"Indeed, Clarie, it would be my pleasure."

After a short period of time, Chester appeared in the galley. Clarie and Francois were eating at the breakfast nook beside the galley. "Good morning, you two."

Clarie burst into a huge smile and said, "good morning, sleepy bones Daddy"

"Good Morning Monsieur, would you care for some breakfast as well?"

"Just a coffee, thanks Francois. I see you are eating so please you just sit; I can get my own coffee." Chester left and returned in a couple minutes with a double espresso. He sat beside Clarie and said, "I heard you guys talking and laughing – what did I miss?"

Francois replied, "you have quite a boy there, monsieur. He made a special request for chicken's eggs and pig's bacon."

It took a moment for this to sink in, then Chester also burst out laughing and said, "I think I will have some of those too."

"Monsieur, young Clarie has a lot of questions. I believe my ears may be starting to swell with listening so much."

"But Dad, on boats they say things differently. Big boats are called ships. The kitchen is called a galley. And instead of left and right, they say port and starboard. Did you know that?"

"As a matter of fact, I did Clarie, but I always get port and starboard mixed up."

"That's okay Dad, I do too." As he reached over, he gave Chester a hug.

Over the next week, they visited several Greek Islands. Santorini, Ios, Milos, then spent three days in Athens. Walking up the Acropolis, Chester felt a tingling sensation running through his feet. It was a sensation similar to the feeling he would get when standing on a roof and looking over the edge. This time though it was not a tingle of fear. This was a tingle of realization. He was walking in the same footsteps as Plato and Socrates. As he approached the Parthenon, he felt slightly lightheaded, quickly though, Clarie brought his feet back down to the ground. As he looked at the Parthenon, Clarie noted the building was broken. "They should just knock it down and rebuild it, Daddy." Chester laughed and he started to explain the history and how old it was when he realized anything more than five years old would have just been really old to Clarie. 30 years old or 3000, they were both just really old to him.

Clarie liked the changing of the guard at the Parliament, he thought their outfits looked a little goofy and could not understand how they could walk in those silly looking pointed shoes. They found a nice restaurant in an open courtyard, not far from the Parliament for dinner. Unfortunately for Clarie though, Chester decided to try the local sardines. When they brought the dish with a dozen dressed sardines, Clarie was repulsed when he saw the heads were still on. Clarie was now more convinced than ever that these foreign people always ate fish with their heads on. With a great deal of abhorrence, Clarie whispered in his Dad's ear, "they took the guts out, didn't they?" Laughing, Chester nodded yes.

For Clarie's birthday, they took him for a ride on the Athens Happy Train, then took a mythology tour which Clarie found rather boring, but he was fascinated by the girl with snakes for hair. Afterward, they walked through the national gardens. Clarie liked it but grew bored with all the trees. He had trees at home, and they were bigger. He liked the petting zoo though and loved the funny looking ducks with the fat bellies.

It was truly a trip with a lifetime of memories. They laughed, played and much to Chester's amazement, he grew even closer to Clarie. Clarie seemed to have completely forgotten about the incident at Sean and Ava's wedding, where Chester lost it when he saw Walter Dyck.

By the time they pulled into Valletta harbour, Chester had almost forgotten about his life back home. He was totally immersed in family life with Clarie. Valletta was a marvelous city. Like many Mediterranean cities, the buildings were mostly stone and brick. They were all various shades of tan. Back home, buildings had colour and seemed somehow livelier. Here, they were all a natural tan colour, but even with the lack of colour they spoke a language of history and natural beauty. Chester had been to Malta twice before and he loved the small island. One of the endearing features is that in a sea of foreign languages, English was the predominant language in Malta. Just like most other European countries, the locals spoke many other languages, but English was the main one. Perhaps it was the language, but for some reason Chester felt like Malta was his home away from home.

After docking, they had to wait for a couple hours while the port authorities inspected their vessel and made sure all proper papers had been completed. They had lunch on the ship, then disembarked. Clarie was quite sad as they were leaving the ship and would be staying at a villa in the Fort St. Elmo area. The porters were removing their luggage and taking them to the villa. As Clarie, Chester and Anne bid their farewells to the crew and started walking down the dock, Clarie's disappointment was soon overshadowed by what he saw waiting at the edge of the dock. There was a horse and carriage. Chester had arranged for a horse drawn carriage to tour the city and take them to their new lodgings. They likely could have walked to their new home in about 15 minutes. The tour, however, took about an hour before they arrived.

A great vacation Chester thought, as they ascended the front steps into the opened front door.

Chapter Sixteen

The sun was streaming through the window as Chester awoke. It was one of those intense beams of sunlight that highlights the dust floating in an otherwise clean room. Chester walked over to the window and saw his first historical edifice to start the day. Fort St. Elmo looked majestic with the early morning light highlighting its many hues. Looking at Fort St. Elmo, he saw a sweeper truck driving down the street, sweeping up bits of paper and waste people had discarded on the street over the previous day. The front of the sweeper was spraying a mist of water from a nozzle underneath the machine. This water was being swept with another set of brushes. Effectively cleaning the garbage and scrubbing the street with a single pass. On his side of the street, a truck was picking up garbage that was bagged and sitting on the front sidewalk.

As Chester made his way down to the main floor, the house staff were already bustling about preparing for the day. He greeted several people on his way to the kitchen. There, he was greeted with a cold glass of orange juice, presented to him by a young man working in the kitchen. "Good morning, Mr. Moehr. I have taken the liberty of pouring your orange juice, can I get anything else for you?"

Chester smiled, "You guys are thorough, aren't you. You even know I like a glass of orange juice first thing in the morning. I suspect during your research you also found out what I am going to ask for next?"

"Perhaps a double espresso, straight up without sugar?"

Chester laughed, "you got it. If you could bring it out to the veranda, I will drink it there."

Chester walked down the small hallway that led to the dining area, but deviated to the left just before the dining room, and led to the inner compound. He sat in a large ornate metal chair with a small table similarly fashioned sitting beside it. The villa was more like a townhouse as they shared walls on two sides of the building with neighbouring villas. The rear of the house wrapped around to form a square with an open courtyard in the middle. This villa was the former residence of a Duke of Malta. This fellow was apparently the last

Duke in his family. Malta, at the time, was a protectorate of Italy, ruled by some noble out of Calabria. When the Italian aristocracy were overthrown, the royal families maintained titles, but little power. This particular Duke was infamous for saving many Maltese citizens during the Nazi occupation.

In the courtyard was a set of old stairs, these stairs went down to the cistern, where the family stored its water. There were actually 2 cisterns, this first one was about 10 meters in diameter with a 2-meter ceiling. The second one now had a tunnel going to it. The second tunnel was four times the size. During the Nazi and Allied bombardment, the Duke invited citizens to take refuge in his cisterns. After the Nazis first occupied the city, they began rounding up the Maltese citizens. They found 40 or 50 souls hidden in the first cistern. They did not notice (at the time) the small connecting porthole to the larger cistern that held hundreds more.

Chester sat there for awhile think about this and gazing at the tastefully manicured gardens. There were birds chirping their morning melodies to add to the peaceful morning splendor. That peace was soon interrupted with rustle and bustle, that seemed to be emanating from an upstairs window. As Chester looked up, he saw Clarie peering out the window and enthusiastically waving at him. "Hi Daddy," he shouted. As always, Chester's heart skipped a beat, he was enjoying his peace and quiet, but who could not be happy with that smiling face?

"Good morning, son," Chester waved back.

A couple minutes later, Clarie came bouncing out the doors into the courtyard. He ran towards his Dad and gave him a good morning kiss and hug. "What are we going to do today, Daddy?"

"I'm sorry son, I have some business to take care of. You get to spend the day with your Mom today."

The expressions on Clarie's face never left any doubt as to what he was feeling. On this occasion, Clarie's giant smile turned into a dour frown and the sadness he displayed would make the most cold-hearted villain feel a moment of remorse. "I'm sorry son, but I will be home tonight. I know your Mom wants to spend some time with you too. I have taken up a lot of your time over the past couple of weeks."

Dejectedly, he replied, "Yeah – I guess."

They ate breakfast and enjoyed a bit of small talk and then it was time for Chester to attend to business.

* * *

Chester showered, shaved and dressed for his business meeting. As he was putting on his suit, he realized he hadn't worn a suit since his meeting at the Cypriot bank. It was nice to dress casually while vacationing, but now he was back to business, donning his suit he felt somehow more serious. He had arranged for a car service for the next three days. When the driver wasn't busy with Chester, he would take Clarie and Anne on their excursions.

Arriving at the Danske Banque Of Malta, Chester's driver opened his door and as Chester ascended the steps a doorman opened the door for him. While Chester had several accounts with this branch of the Danske Banque for many years, this was the first time he had actually been there in person. All the previous arrangements had been made through the Ostranskis. As he entered through the large glass doors, Chester noted the doors were incredibly thick. The glass in the doors was at least ten centimeters thick, thick enough to stop any significant explosion. The sides of the door had large metal pieces that, when locked, fitted into the slots in the door paneling- sort of like tongue and grove wood paneling. The interior was very cavernous and grandiose. The high ornate, domed ceiling perfectly matched the stone and carved wood walls. The columns were topped with splendidly carved cornices and a balcony ran along three sides of the building. Obviously, this was where the senior officers conducted their business. Unlike traditional banks, this one did not have traditional teller booths, but there were several clerks working behind exquisitely carved desks. Chester did not know the type of wood it was, but it looked incredibly rich, sort of like walnut. They were polished to a glimmer and the chairs and sparse furnishings were elegant and suited the surroundings impeccably.

As Chester approached what appeared to be the reception desk, a well-dressed middle-aged lady looked up. "Hello, I am Chester Moehr, I have an appointment with Mr. Rickman."

Chester noticed the pupils of her eyes enlarge slightly. This was the only response he could read on her. "Yes, Mr. Moehr, we have been expecting you. I believe this is the first time you have graced our bank?"

"Yes," looking around Chester said, "this is a magnificent building, I am very happy to be here now."

"I will call Mr. Rickman immediately, he is expecting you." She picked up her phone, and in less than a minute one of the big ornate doors on the second floor opened and out came a middle-aged man with grey hair, wearing an exquisitely tailored suit. He was slightly plump but walked with a slight jump to his step. As he descended the steps, a large smile crossed his face and warmly, he walked towards Chester with his hand extended.

"Very nice to meet you, Mr. Moehr. You are a most valued customer and I am pleased to finally meet you." Chester detected a slight accent, it sounded somewhat German.

Shaking hands, Chester replied, "and very nice to meet you also, Mr. Rickman, you have a splendid building here."

"Thank you, yes we are proud of it. This is one of the few buildings the bombs of the Second World War missed somehow. Many buildings were damaged when the Nazis came, but more were destroyed when the allies liberated our little island. But please do call me Alain."

"And you must call me Chester."

Alain led Chester up the stairs and into his office. There were no nameplates on the doors, but the fact that this was the only double door upstairs, Chester could tell he was the boss. Inside, Alain's office was huge, it was bigger than Chester's first apartment. It had to be at least 100 square meters. In keeping with the entrance, it was decorated with very rich tapestries and paintings. While Chester could not be certain, a couple appeared to be some of the lost Picassos the Nazis confiscated during the war. Chester thought it could be possible, as several Swiss banks had been suspected of working with the Nazis hoarding their plunder of gold, precious gems and art. While this bank was fully chartered as a Maltese bank, it was also known that it was owned by one of the large Swiss banking families. Likely in a similar fashion to the way Chester owned many companies by hiding its true ownership through foreign holdings and subsidiary companies.

Instead of going to Alain's lavish baroque style desk, Chester was shown to the conference table at the side of the office. This table was very elaborately carved, and Chester felt it was a little too ostentatious. Chester did like this touch though, instead of sitting behind his desk Alain chose to sit beside Chester as equals. This guy knows how to charm, Chester thought to himself. Chester proceeded to explain that he would be depositing funds into a bank in Cyprus and he would like Alain to move these funds through several different bank accounts and deposit them equally across four accounts he would open in Malta. The first three accounts would be under the names Sean Tifflen, Geoff Favelle, one in his name and the final one for a numbered company, for which he had the incorporation papers with him.

Chester spent the remaining morning with Alain, as he outlined how the money would be transferred and reviewed the required papers. LNa currently had over twenty accounts with the Danske Banque Of Malta. They were of course under several subsidiaries, as well as LNa itself. After signing various documents, Alain took Chester out for lunch. They went to a small local restaurant close to the Is-Suq Tal-Belt market. Is-Suq Tal-Belt simply means 'City market', but it sounds much more exotic in Turkish. After a delightful meal, Chester insisted on picking up a 'pastizzi' on the short walk back to the bank. Pastizzi was a Maltese treat he loved. It was a flaky pastry stuffed with various ingredients such as cheese and mashed peas. Chester liked the ricotta cheese-stuffed pastizzi.

After returning to the bank, Alain reviewed the security measures they utilized to ensure the safety of their client's investments. Many of the procedures were computer programs and firewalls. As an independent country, they had a very small population on a very small island in the middle of the Mediterranean with little natural resources. After gaining independence from the British, they also lost the transfer payments that came from the UK. The banking industry grew from this need to feed and employ its people.

By extending discretion and not participating in normal disclosure of transactions with foreign countries, their banking industry flourished. Much like the Swiss banking industry was spawned from people needing a safe haven for their funds, Malta grew quickly over the past several decades.

By the time 4:00 PM rolled around, Chester was more convinced than ever that their funds were secure with this bank. Alain dealt with many high-worth individuals from around the world. American and European families that wished to hide their wealth from taxation. Chinese, Russian and Eastern European Oligarchs who wanted to move their wealth out of their country, to ensure their lifestyle could be maintained no matter what happened to them domestically. Danske Banque Of Malta had many clients that had substantial deposits with them. For Alain to devote most of his day to Chester certainly made Chester feel welcomed and special.

Alain extended an invitation for dinner that evening. While tempted, Chester declined stating part of his trip was a vacation with his son, so he wanted to spend the evening with him. He also declined the invitation for a car to drive him back to his villa. It was a gorgeous sunny day with temperatures in the high 20's. After spending all day reviewing numbers and sitting, a walk home would be therapeutic. Exchanging goodbyes to Alain and his staff, Chester slung his computer case over his shoulder and walked home. He smiled, imagining Clarie's warm smile and hug that were sure to greet him.

Chapter Seventeen

Clarie woke very early, it was nice to be sleeping in his own bed. He loved his vacation but liked the comfort of his own bed. Clarie looked out his window, he saw the sun was rising and the sky was sculpted with sparse clouds covered with red. Just like sunset, but on the other side of the sky. He felt very wide awake, his Mom had told him he was once again suffering from that jet lag thing. Staring out his window, he twisted his head towards the main house. In what was his Dad's study, he could see some movement. Perhaps his Dad was also suffering from jet lag.

Chester had gone to bed at a reasonable hour and after a brief period of sleep, he found himself wide awake. His body's circadian time clock was all screwed up. He would frequently take a nap in the afternoon on many days. He found a 15-minute nap would refresh him for the remainder of the day. Now though, he was certain his body had mistaken his afternoon nap for his evening sleep. He was thinking this was amusing since he did not keep a regular sleep pattern. Most days, he would be in bed somewhere between midnight and 1:00. However, frequently in his line of work, there were activities that required the cloak of darkness to complete. On many days, he would witness sunrise before going to bed.

Ah Hell, he was awake now! So, he decided to get up and get some work done. He stopped in the kitchen, made himself a latte, and then proceeded to his office. He loved his office; it was richly decorated with heavy brocaded tapestries and curtains. The rich smell of leather and rare woods permeated the air. As he sat behind his desk, he looked around. After visiting Alain Rickman's office, he had to admit some of his love for his own office had waned. Alain's office was much more sophisticated and cultured. Chester realized he was slightly jealous. Perhaps he would get his office redecorated.

Chester came back to the present and turned on his laptop. While he was away, he could still keep in touch with his business back home. The remarkable thing about technology is you can be connected to your business from nearly every corner of the world. Despite the fact nearly all communications and documents that were exchanged electronically were scrambled, disguised, then decoded and reassembled, Chester still felt uncomfortable about sharing too much information over these devices. Even with many assurances that it was extremely secure, something niggled at him deep in his mind. He frequently told people – it might be secure now but, with new technology, who knows if it will be in the future.

Nancy prepared a brief every day that she sent to him. Geoff, Sean, and occasionally Sanchez would send him emails to keep him on top of what was happening with their businesses. Frequently, regular business documents were sent that he would need to sign and return, either electronically or couriered from the next port. A couple of hours a day and he kept on top of his business.

Some topics were always taboo and never sent though. Anything relating to illegal activities was never sent. These documents were stored on a jump drive and sent to pre-arranged locations. These locations were always banks, through which they were doing business. Banks in Cyprus, Athens and of course Malta all received packages for Chester, he would retrieve them when he arrived. This jump drive was encrypted and had a self-destruct scrambling mechanism. After two attempts to enter the passcodes, all information would be scrambled and completely useless. Chester took the further measure of burning the jump drives after reading them. Some thought he was paranoid – he felt he was just being cautious.

Business continued to thrive, the drug importing business was generating profits of some $20M per month. Even with payments to the Club and funding dummy shipments that were destined to be confiscated by authorities, they still netted well over $100M per annum. Chester found the surprising part was that a quarter of the dummy shipments actually made it through. The profits from those shipments offset most of the losses from the ones which were apprehended. The police were happy as they were making arrests and received great publicity on their war on drugs and Chester was happy as he was making boatloads of money. Literally!

One of the notices he read stated Dan LeCoq had been released, it was hard to believe that 10 years had passed. It was like another lifetime ago and things had changed so much. The Weasel was a loose string that needed to be snipped off. He was the only one remaining who could place Chester at the scene of Dael's assassination. He also knew Sean would have received a report on The Weasel's release too. There was a standing order to remove him when he was released, he didn't give it much more thought as Sean would take care of it. Sean was excellent in taking care of business, ever since the disappearance of the Black Rebels, Chester thought Sean had proven he could be counted on.

Now back at his home office, Chester was excited to get back to work. He polished off reading the various reports he had missed while away. He spent several hours walking the grounds which was his `thinking time`. During the course of a normal day, he would spend at least an hour just thinking. It was during these times he developed new ideas. He would roll these ideas over in his mind and mentally evaluate the pros and cons. Most of his ideas were discarded but, occasionally, something evolved from one of these `thinking times`. During these times, he also evaluated his existing team, strengths and weaknesses as well as lurking dangers. Somehow, he always came back to thinking about Sean.

While the three of them were still close and the original founders of their organization - TFM, Chester had an inkling that while Geoff was straightforward, Sean held his cards close to his chest and there was something about Sean that made his senses tingle ... he couldn't quite put his finger on it, but nevertheless, it existed.

After a couple of hours reading reports, his eyes started to cross, and every report started sounding like the last one. He heard some movement in the kitchen and decided the house was starting to come to life. Turning off his computer, he returned to his bedroom. After a refreshing shower, he felt like he was ready to tackle the day. He got dressed and went downstairs for breakfast. He decided to have his breakfast served on the deck behind the house, overlooking Indian Arm. He proceeded outside and as he waited for his breakfast to arrive, he saw something in the bay. After a short while a couple of boats appeared, and as his breakfast arrived, he asked for a pair of binoculars. After watching for a short time, he saw a large black fin break the water. The Orcas had returned. Years ago, killer whales would frequently be spotted in Indian Arm, as they ventured in from the open ocean for a feed of salmon or seals. The past 10-20 years they were never spotted, now in the past few years, they had returned.

Chester heard a commotion and turned to see Clarie jumping and pointing towards the bay. As he noticed Chester having breakfast, he ran over, "Daddy, did you see them? I think they are whales!"

"Yes indeed, killer whales, my son. Here, have a look through the binoculars you can see them better."

"Wow they are so close." Clarie exclaimed, as he watched them through the binoculars.

"Would you care to have breakfast with me?"

"Yeah. Pancakes with syrup please." After the mix up with seafood while they were on vacation, Clarie was afraid to order anything other than chicken eggs and pig bacon. He dearly wanted pancakes a couple times but decided against it. They got the bacon and eggs right, no sense in risking the order of a new meal they could screw up.

They leisurely ate their breakfast while they watched the killer whales dancing and preening below. Chester knew their dance was carefully choreographed to isolate seals and salmon for a feeding frenzy, but he told Clarie they were merely putting on a show for them. After breakfast, they laughed as they recalled some of their adventures on vacation. When the discussion turned to fish being served with their heads on, Clarie turned up his nose with disgust, once more this brought about a new round of laughter from Chester. Much to Clarie's dismay, after a bit, Chester insisted he had to go to the office, but he would leave Clarie with the binoculars.

Chester actually enjoyed the drive to the office. Normally, he didn't like the traffic and the fact a 35-minute drive could take up to 90 minutes. Having a driver helped ease the tedium on a normal day. Today, he actually spent time looking out the windows and appreciated the scenery unfolding before him. Even though he could see much of the scenery from his house, by driving on the south shore of the inlet he gained a different perspective. Perhaps, he had a different perspective because he was happy, he thought. Even though he did not have the traditional nuclear family, he did have a family! His affection for Anne had grown and his love for Clarie grew each day.

Before reaching the office, he had the driver stop by a flower shop and Chester picked up an arrangement of flowers for Nancy.

When he arrived at the office, Nancy gave Chester a big warm smile to welcome him back. Chester presented Nancy with the flowers and thanked her for the extra work she did for him while he was away. The office was now substantially busier as they had employed ten additional people working in various disciplines and support personnel. Nancy, of course, not only looked after reception, but she took on the added responsibility of office manager. During his walk-through, Chester said good morning to everyone, and they in turn said it was good to have him back. Geoff and Sean had not arrived yet, but Sanchez was in the office. After dropping off his jacket and computer satchel, he returned to Sanchez' office.

"Good morning, Sanchez"

"Chester! You are back. It's good to see you." Sanchez excitedly replied.

"It's good to be back Gabriel. I had a great holiday, but it's always nice to come home. Somebody told me a long time ago that traveling is great because you get to see new places and have experiences. It also makes you appreciate coming home too. They were right. " He paused for a moment and straightened his already straightened tie. "How's everything going?"

"Just great Chester."

"Well, if you have the time I would love to catch up."

"Certainly, I have time, please have a seat. I never knew the shipping business would be so much fun, and quite frankly so profitable. I love it when some left-wing environmental group protests against that nasty oil and how it's destroying the planet. Every time they make a headline, our bottom line gets a little fatter because more and more companies are getting out of oil shipping. Less competition means greater profit and what those idiots do not realize is our entire economy is based on oil."

Chester had a small laugh and said, "Yes, that is a certainty and how is Christophe working out?"

"He's fantastic. He is a Greek and sometimes that Greek stubbornness results in the occasional outburst but, he is a mariner after all, and all mariners are a bit gruff. He runs a tight ship though and has taught me a lot."

They proceeded to talk about their shipping business. As Chester was getting up to leave, Sanchez added, "I will always remember what you did for me Chester, I am thankful every day and you know if you ever need anything, I will always be there for you."

Chester nodded and said, "thanks Sanchez, you earned it," then turned and left the room. He heard a noise coming from down the hallway and he knew Sean had arrived and he suspected Geoff would be in by now as well. He quickly searched them out and wished them both good morning but didn't linger for small talk, as they had their senior partners meeting shortly and they would be talking about his vacation then.

After Geoff, Sean and Chester had assembled and they had their discussion about the vacation, Chester proceeded to explain to them the details of the trip. He outlined the arrangement where cash would be delivered to the Nicosia Bank in Cyprus, the funds would then be moved several times by the Danske Banque Of Malta and finally, fully cleaned, the money would be deposited equally into four accounts; Chester's, Sean's and Geoff's. The fourth account, a numbered account, would be used for investment purposes. Geoff replied that shipments greater than $10M would be easy to attain. Then, he added that this was the first time they had individual accounts. Chester brought up the fact that the cash from the importing business was in excess of anything they needed for normal operation. So, they might as well divide it up immediately. The fourth account would likely prove to be unnecessary and occasionally they may disperse some of those funds into their individual accounts as well. But should an opportunity arise, they would have the funds to invest.

Early that afternoon, the Ostranskis would be arriving with documents for Geoff and Sean to sign, to complete the setup of their accounts. Chester then advised them it would be wise to move the money around into accounts set up in other banking locations. If they wished to set up additional accounts in Cayman Islands, Switzerland, Panama or wherever, the Ostranskis would assist them and bill the business accordingly. Geoff indicated the process was to divide the money into plain non-descript suitcases. A normal sized suitcase that could fit as carry-on baggage contained $1 million. They put 1 million into each suitcase, and at this time they had several pallet loads of suitcases being stored. Geoff would arrange for them to be loaded onto a container and they would take care of shipping through various ports before the shipment arrived in Cyprus. When he had a better timeline, he would advise.

They proceeded to review other business over the next couple of hours. While Sean was providing his updates during his session, Chester noted an item Sean did not mention - Dan LeCoq. He knew Sean would have seen a report that The Weasel was released. What was he up to?

Over the course of conversation, Chester did not broach the subject directly, but did provide ample opportunity for Sean to approach the topic. After Geoff had reviewed the financials on their various businesses, it was almost lunchtime, Chester said, "Well, it looks like everything is running very smoothly, you guys did a great job of keeping tabs on things while I was away. Unless there is something else we should discuss," then he paused, "substantial or small," another pause, "with any other part of our business" pause, "I will buy you lunch."

Geoff and Sean were both thinking and shook their heads to indicate nothing. Then Geoff, being the thorough man he was remarked, "well, there is one thing. The Weasel was released a few weeks ago."

Aha, Chester thought to himself. Good old Geoff!

Sean suspected Chester already knew this as he asked too many leading questions, but Sean was not going to take the bait. Quickly thinking, Sean replied, "Oh yes, six weeks ago actually. I am sorry I forgot to mention it. He has been living in some fleabag hotel in the downtown eastside. He is not doing too well, and the cops have been keeping an annoyingly close watch on him. This has prevented us from picking him up. Perhaps an opportunity will present itself soon."

Chester thought to himself – good one Sean. You were always bright and could think quickly on your feet … but why fail to mention this? . Once again, Chester felt that tingle of danger. "I assume he still suspects us for the Dael hit."

"I suspect he does, but I cannot confirm that. As I said, if surveillance eases off more and opportunity should present itself, we will snatch him. I don't think we want to do this haphazardly and risk exposure." Sean was maintaining his composure, however, Chester sensed an uneasiness.

"We have eyes on him at all times, right?" Chester replied.

"Definitely."

"Ok, maintain surveillance and let me think about this one," after a brief pause, "now what do you want to eat? Remind me to tell you about Clarie's experience with seafood over lunch." With that, Chester dropped the subject and moved on. He gleaned two insights from this meeting. First, he would have to deal with Dan LeCoq himself. Second, Sean was up to something.

Chapter Eighteen

Chester was in his office reviewing a building report on a new residential/retail development complex they had invested in at Metrotown in Burnaby. He was reviewing the sales figures and based on what he was reading, they should have most units sold within the next month and they could begin construction shortly thereafter. They had a 30% equity stake in the project which effectively made them the largest investor. The beauty behind the project is that they had arranged construction financing for the entire project through an offshore subsidiary. Not only would they make millions on the development project itself, they'd also make a nice profit on the financing side, not to mention the millions of dollars they could funnel through the project to launder their drug money.

Geoff stepped into Chester's office wearing a giant smile and sat on the easy chair in front of his desk.

Chester returned the smile, "Okay, I'll bite, what's the good news?"

Geoff tried the innocent look, which of course he could not pull off, as the smile he was sporting seemed to be unerasable. "Why do you think it is good news?"

Chester started to laugh and said, "remind me to play poker with you! Your beaming face can be seen for 10 city blocks!"

"Okay, I do have good news. The shipment is set to arrive in Cyprus tomorrow. Here is the shipping manifest. Now it's over to you. Can you let the bankers know so they can retrieve it?"

"Most certainly. What is the size of the shipment?"

"Three pallets, 66 cases"

Chester whistled. "I will let them know."

After Geoff left, Chester logged onto a secure website Mr. Stavros had set up. Chester typed – 'shipment arriving June 7, manifest papers arriving later today via Ostranski Legal Services.'

Chester then picked up the phone and called Nathaniel Ostranski. Chester asked if he could stop by his office to drop off some papers that needed to be forwarded. "Of course," Nathaniel replied, "I am free anytime. If you would prefer, I could come to your office?"

"No, that's fine. I would like to get out for a while, I should be there within half an hour."

"Okay, see you in a little while then," Nathaniel replied.

Chester logged off his laptop, then put the manifest documents into his satchel and told Nancy on his way out that he would return after lunch. As he arrived in the lobby, he texted Sanchez - want to meet for lunch? Just you and me, I need a favour.

As he walked towards the Ostranskis, his phone beeped in his pocket. It was Sanchez – 'certainly when and where?'

Chester replied – 'Chamber on Beatty, 12:30 – great mussels.'

He arrived at Ostranski Legal Services and was immediately shown into Nathaniel's office. Chester explained to Nathaniel that they had cargo being shipped to the Nicosia Bank in Cyprus. The shipment was due to arrive tomorrow and he needed Nathaniel to send the following manifest papers to Mr. Stavros, so they could retrieve the cargo which consisted of three pallets. Nathaniel replied, "certainly Chester, I will do this right away. Should we tell them how much is on those three pallets?"

"No, their business is built on their discretion and accuracy. If they cheated one of their clients, word would quickly get around and their business would be destroyed."

"You are right. It is nearly lunch. Would you let me buy you lunch?"

"Thanks Nathaniel, but no. Can I have a rain check? I have made arrangements already."

"Okay, I understand. If you wait here for a moment, I will get this sent off via secure communication immediately." With that, Nathaniel left his office and returned five minutes later. "The documents have been sent and we have confirmation they were received. Would you like the confirmation number?"

"No, that's fine, thanks anyway though." Chester replied, knowing the confirmation number would also have been sent to him via the secure channel Mr. Stavros had set up. He felt the phone in his pocket vibrate, which likely meant the documents had been received. "Thanks for this, Nathaniel. As for lunch, how about tomorrow?"

"Sure, say noon? Would you like the Hawksby?"

"Sounds great, see you then." Chester left and started his walk towards the Chamber. It was a nice walk through downtown and Chester enjoyed the fresh air. As he walked, he checked his phone and saw a notification that a message was waiting for him on the SWIFT network. The Society for Worldwide Interbank Financial Telecommunication was a network set up for secure communication within the banking industry. Chester had several accounts on this network, individual accounts for each bank he dealt with. He could not confirm this message was from Mr. Stavros, until he got back to the office and logged onto the secure network, but he was almost certain it was.

He arrived at Chamber before Sanchez; he was happy about that. He proceeded to get a secluded table towards the rear of the restaurant. It normally sat 4 people, so Chester assured them his tip would more than make up for the 2 missing diners. Shortly after being seated, Chester saw Sanchez arrive at the entrance. He stood up to let Sanchez know where he was, and Sanchez strolled over to his table.

"Thanks for asking me to lunch, Chester, your message sounded very ....mysterious."

"It is a rather large favour, so I thought the least I could do is buy you a nice lunch."

"Sounds great. I have never been here before. Just so you know, I do not like mussels."

Chester laughed. "Its okay, all the food is great here. If you like lamb, they have the best lamb chops in the city."

"I love lamb!"

"Good, and I know you like red wine as well – correct?"

"Oh Yes!"

Chester waved the waiter over and they placed their orders, along with a very nice red wine. Montoya Cabernet Reserve 2006. After giving the customary congratulations on an excellent choice, the waiter left and placed the order.

"So, I'm curious Chester what is this favour?"

"Okay, remember this is between you and me only, okay?"

"Sure thing"

"Do you remember Dan LeCoq?"

"How could I ever forget that rat-faced weasel. He's the idiot that killed my sister, you remember?"

"Of course, I remember, we will never forget her."

Sanchez immediately took on a sad demeanor. He had that look like a puppy dog that just lost his master. "What would you like me to do with him, hopefully it involves cruel torturous dismemberment."

"Nothing would make me happier, but it is not the right time."

The waiter brought the wine and asked Chester to do the tasting. Chester insisted Sanchez do the honours. Instead of sipping and nosing the wine, an agitated Sanchez just downed it and said, "That's fine, please pour a large glass for me." Chester only had a half glass, as he was not known for drinking, and seldom did he ever have a drink at lunch. This was a special occasion though.

After the waiter left, Chester continued, "He is out and living in the downtown eastside. The cops are keeping a very close eye on him. I would like you to arrange for one of the boys to set him up as a street agent. Once the cops nab him for selling dope, they will put him away again. Once back inside, we will arrange for him to have an accident and never make it back out. It's not as fulfilling as him being hung, drawn and quartered, but the end result is the same."

"Yeah, I can do that. I would be lying though if I didn't admit a certain disappointment."

"Thanks Gabriel. Most importantly, we must keep this between ourselves. Nobody else can be brought into the loop. Not even Geoff or Sean. Okay?"

Sanchez nodded in agreement, then proceeded to take another drink of wine. "This wine is fantastic."

"It should be, they will likely rape me for over a thousand dollars for it."

Sanchez whistled and had another drink. They had a great lunch and for the first time, perhaps ever, Sanchez and Chester spent a long time alone and discussed their childhoods. Sanchez noted the price of the bottle of wine would be enough to feed the neighbourhood he grew up in for a month. His parents struggled to earn a living and they were fortunate as the area they lived in had electricity, thanks to Pablo Escobar. When they were forced to emigrate, his parents were happy that Canada granted them asylum. They found regular work, sadly, both died in a freak car accident when Elena was 17. Sanchez, being two years older started looking after his younger sister.

Sanchez did not know that Chester grew up in a small farming town in Saskatchewan. Chester added that while they always had plenty to eat, they were by no means wealthy. Farming at that time was a struggle, but like Sanchez, they didn't know there was another life; such as the life they currently lived. Separately, they both returned to the office and were happy they had the chance to get to know each other a little better. Chester was very pleased his plan for The Weasel was coming together before he could do any damage.

* * *

At the senior partners meeting the following Monday, Chester congratulated both Sean and Geoff as their individual bank accounts at the Danske Banque of Malta had grown handsomely and now had a balance of $15,922,500. Sean was rather stoic, Geoff, on the other hand, just started laughing. They were already very wealthy; this was sort of like additional play money. They were each drawing a salary of $1.2M and their individual year end bonuses were at least $20M. Additionally, LNa had assets on paper of almost $500M, plus another $600M in offshore companies and accounts.

While this was happening, Sanchez was meeting with one of the street distributors. The street guys never received a visit from 'head office'. In fact, the street guys didn't even know who was in head office or where head office was. Their dealings were only with the captains. The captains ran a group of street guys they referred to as a platoon. The captains reported to their Colonel. Nobody knew who the colonels reported too. Nobody even knew how many captains and colonels there were. It was always kept very confidential and the only information shared was on a need to know basis – and of course, nobody needed to know anything outside their own world.

When Andy received word from his Colonel that one of the bosses from head office wanted to meet with him, at first, he was understandably very concerned. What did they want with him? Was he in trouble? After thinking about this for a while, he realized this was doubtful. If he was in trouble, a head office man wouldn't bother to meet with him. His Colonel would deal with it. He could not think of any reason for the meeting. His territory was in the downtown eastside, while there were a lot of drug users in his area, it was certainly not an extremely lucrative territory as it was also extremely poor. Andy was often embarrassed at the condition of the money he turned over to his Colonel, as it was frequently extremely soiled and who knows what sort of koodies were on it.

Andy knew he was supposed to meet this fellow at Salty Dawg Café on Carrall Street. Andy would approach him; all he knew was this guy would be wearing a lapel pin with a Canadian flag on it. Andy had put on his cleanest clothes. He even shaved and combed his hair. When he entered the coffee shop, he noticed a smartly dressed guy sitting at a corner table with a Canadian flag lapel pin. This guy was wearing casual clothes, but Andy could tell they were very expensive. Andy ordered his coffee and then went over to the table. Sanchez saw Andy coming in as he had read a dossier on this guy and he knew what he looked like. As he approached the table, Sanchez took a drink from his bottle of water and pushed a chair out with his foot. As Andy sat down, Sanchez could plainly see this guy was scared.

"Hi, I'm Andy. I hear you want to talk to me."

"Yes, this will be the only time you and I will meet. I suggest you forget my face as soon as we leave this place."

"I can barely remember what you look like already."

Sanchez pushed a photo towards Andy, "Do you know this guy?"

"Yes, he was just released from prison. He is a bit of a whacko. His name is Dan, I believe, but down here he is known simply as Cock."

"Correct," Sanchez replied, "Before he went to prison, he was involved in the business. Now, he is struggling as all his contacts have disappeared while he was away. We want you to help him out by setting him up as a distributor. Nothing too large, but enough for him to earn a few bucks. The first order will be on credit."

"He has the cops watching him all the time."

"Then you must be very careful when you make contact."

"Okay, I can do that. Anything else?"

"Just one thing, after you have made your first delivery to him, I need you to call this number," Sanchez pushed a sheet of paper towards him with a number typed on it. "Once he is set up, you can take your cut as you would with any other distributor."

"Sure thing. Consider it done." Andy was feeling much more relaxed now. This was an easy job and could be his way to moving up in the organization and getting out of this shithole.

Sanchez then got up and said, "thanks Andy. I will be grateful." Then, as Sanchez started to walk out, he stopped abruptly then returned to the table to grab the bottle of water he was drinking. No sense in leaving any evidence of his presence. Sitting on the street out the front of the café was a homeless guy begging for money. Sanchez, being a Good Samaritan, dropped a handful of coins into the hat sitting in front of him.

Sanchez had picked up a burner phone the previous day and he carried it in his pocket. Two days later, it buzzed to let him know there was a message. When he retrieved the message from Andy, it simply said – "first shipment delivered."

Corporal Romero of the Vancouver PD was working undercover in the downtown eastside, as part of the integrated drug enforcement squad. When he noticed Andy, a known drug pusher, meeting with a well-dressed guy at a café, he sat down on the street with his blanket and started begging for money. When the guy came out from the café, he dropped a handful of change into his hat. Romero knew immediately this guy wasn't from the area, as he dropped several loonies and toonies in his hat. He said thanks to the guy after he dropped the coins, the guy turned around and didn't notice Romero had concealed a smart phone under his grungy blanket and snapped a picture.

A few days later having identified the guy as a senior associate with a property development company, Romero thought this guy must have just been slumming it or had some distant connection with Andy. When a request came in from the RCMP for information on Andy, Detective Romero thought it was strange and called Detective Bailey directly. Apparently, Andy was seen making contact with a guy the RCMP were keeping an eye on. Romero gave Detective Bailey Andy's background and during the conversation he mentioned that Andy had a very unusual visitor a couple days ago, a fellow from a property development company called LNa.

Detective Bailey perked up when he heard this, "it wouldn't happen to be a fellow called Sean Tifflen?"

"No, it was a guy called Gabriel Sanchez, he is a senior associate with LNa. I have no idea who Sean Tifflen is. Should I?"

"No, likely just a coincidence, we ran into him a while back and thought it would be a coincidence if it happened to be the same guy. Thanks though."

"No problem," Romero replied, "let me know if there is anything else you need from me."

Bailey hung up the phone and sat back, reflecting on the information he just received. He got up and went over to Brine's desk. Sitting down, he said, "I just had an interesting conversation. It may be nothing more than a coincidence, but as you always say – there is often substance behind coincidences."

Brine's interest was piqued, "so tell me about it."

"Remember, Sean Tifflen?"

"Yes, I remember, we haven't had a chance to do much work on that file."

"Well, we just ran into another coincidence. A low-level drug pusher having a meeting with another high-ranking guy from the LNa – the same company Tifflen works for."

"Interesting, tell me more."

Bailey went on to explain his phone call with Officer Romero and the connection between Gabriel Sanchez, Andy the pusher and Dan LeCoq. "There are just too many coincidences, don't you think?"

"I don't know – what I do know though is there are too many coincidences to not do a little more digging." Brine replied. He was rubbing his chin and had that faraway look, like he was trying to piece together a puzzle.

After a few days of investigating, they could find no common threads to tie Sanchez, Andy and Dan LeCoq together. They read several reports, and if anything, it pointed to no connection at all. Perhaps it was strictly a coincidence. Bailey threw another report on his desk and exasperated said, "I think it's a dead end. We can't find anything."

"I am inclined to agree with you. However, let's make one more trip to the LNa offices and see if something smells fishy."

Shortly after lunch, they arrived at the LNa offices and remembered the routine to gain access to LNa's secure floor. After checking in with security and getting cleared by Nancy, they arrived at the reception desk.

Flashing their badges Bailey said, "Hi, I'm not sure if you remember us but we were here a while back?"

"I certainly do," Nancy replied, "You were the first and only policemen to ever visit our office. What can I do for you today?"

"We would like to see Mr. Sanchez." Years of experience had trained Bailey to never ask for permission, but to simply state the request in such a way that it sounded more like a demand.

"I am sorry, Mr. Sanchez is not in today."

Brine replied, "Mr. Tifflen?"

"Sorry, the only senior partner in today is Mr. Moehr, he is our senior partner." Nancy replied.

To her surprise, Brine replied, "Ok. We'll see Mr. Moehr."

Okay, please take a seat, gentlemen, I will see if Mr. Moehr can meet with you?"

Chester knew that in his line of work, contact with police was certainly a likely outcome at some point. That being said though, after all these years he was very apprehensive. "Give me ten minutes Nancy, then show them to my office please." Chester took a drink from his water glass at his desk and swiveled his chair around to face the harbour. He willed himself to lower his heart rate and remain calm. He had no idea what they wanted and while it was likely nothing, he would be careful to not give anything away. He knew they mostly worked as a team so one could ask the questions while the other observed. The quiet one would be the one to be concerned with, he would be adept at picking up inflections and nuances that indicated stress.

Calmed now, Chester swung his chair around and checked his desk and computer screen to make sure nothing untoward was noticeable. There was a file on the Metrotown development sitting on his desk. He closed the folder but left it remain sitting there. He thought about putting on his suit jacket, then decided against it – his shirt and tie would look more casual.

Nancy came down the hall and gave a quick knock on the open door, peering in she said, "Mr. Moehr, these are the police officers I spoke about." As Bailey and Brine entered the room Chester stood up from his desk and extended his hand towards them. Nancy motioned to them separately, "this is Detective Bailey," and then gesturing towards the other, "This is Detective Brine." Nancy smiled casually and left the room.

"Gentlemen, please, have a seat. What can I do for you today?"

Sitting, Bailey replied, "thanks for seeing us, we are just following up on a routine inquiry. It is likely nothing, but nevertheless it is something we need to do in order to close our file."

"Certainly, go ahead and ask away."

Brine was watching Chester carefully. He knew Chester had to be nervous, who wouldn't be with cops coming to their office. Chester, though, gave no outward indication that he was uneasy. No wonder this guy is successful, Brine thought. He is the type that always maintains his cool even in stressful negotiations.

Bailey then opened his case notes and stated, "we are working on a case and one of your corporate officers was seen at a café meeting with a fellow who is known to be in the drug business. Mr. Sanchez was seen meeting this fellow a few days ago. What would Mr. Sanchez want with this guy?"

Chester was a little shocked but maintained his composure, "I really have no idea - you would have to ask Mr. Sanchez." Chester was not going to give anything away. He could make some excuse about Sanchez being Columbian, and how many Columbians are not necessarily the most upstanding citizens, but he chose to give away as little as possible.

"It's just that this is the second time your company has come up into our investigations, and ... quite frankly, that is unusual."

Now Chester was curious ... "Second time?"

"Yes, a while back another of your associates, Mr. Tifflen, was seen meeting with another fellow we know is in the drug business." Bailey was flipping through the pages on his case notes, "Yes, here we are on April 16. Mr. Tifflen met with Mr. Dyck."

Chester was floored! He tried to maintain his demeanor, but he was certain Brine had picked up on Chester's reaction. "Once again, I have no idea. Did Mr. Tifflen answer your inquiries?"

"Oh yes indeed, apparently he was interested in an investment with a development project around Metrotown."

"Well, I do not personally know all the people we deal with in our various businesses, but that name does not sound familiar to me. However, as you can see by the folder on my desk, we are indeed investing in a development in the Metrotown area."

Bailey and Brine both took note of the name on the tab from the folder as Chester lifted it up. "Well, thanks for meeting with us Mr. Moehr. We won't be taking up any more of your time." Bailey and Brine shook hands with Chester and left. Riding down on the elevator, Bailey looked towards Brine and said, "well?"

"He is one cool cucumber that boy. One thing though, he certainly didn't know we met with Sean Tifflen earlier. That got a reaction. I suspect he is a bit of a control freak and didn't like the fact something happened that he didn't know about."

"You think there is anything worth following up on?"

"Nope, I suspect this case is closed."

***

Chester was fuming. He felt like throwing something out the window. What the hell was Sean up to? He knew there was something going on, he sensed something strange about him; but now! It's not so much that he met with The Dyck without his knowledge, which was bad enough. No, it was more so, why the hell meet with him on the day Geoff and Sanchez were caught in the crossfire that killed the Bean? He needed time to think. He knew if he left the building right away, people would know something was up, so he decided he needed to wait for a while. And those detectives may have someone on surveillance to see if and where her went. Chester realized he must be careful in all he did concerning this new turn of events.

He went to the coffee room and made himself a double espresso, then returned to his office. Instead of sitting at his desk, he sat on the chesterfield and began to think about what had just transpired. After an hour, he texted his driver and said he would be leaving early.

A few minutes later, his phone vibrated with a message from his driver – 'sure boss, I am about 20 minutes away. Will that work?' Chester replied that he would be leaving in about half an hour, so no need to rush. He needed to ensure nobody at the office had picked up on how unhinged he had become with the visit from the cops.

He then called Nancy, "Hi Nancy, I'll be leaving early today. I don't have any appointments for the rest of the day, so I am going to take advantage of it and perhaps spend some time with Clarie."

"That's great Chester, you enjoy your time with him."

Chester left 45 minutes later, and during the drive home he was deep in thought. He had not put everything together yet. On one hand, Sean's meeting with The Dyck may have been that he was investigating the shooting. That didn't seem too viable, as they were together the entire afternoon and there was no time for him to connect the shooters with Walter Dyck. The second alternative cried of conspiracy. Were Sean and the Dyck working together for some purpose? Perhaps to eliminate Chester? Was this shooting truly meant for The Bean, or was it just a fortuitous coincidence?

After much thought, he suspected he could not inherently trust Sean. There was something he was hiding. He did not believe their partnership had come to its end ... but perhaps, the beginning of the end ... could he fully trust Sean? Sean was one of his closest friends and allies. They grew the business together and this in itself made Chester feel Sean deserved his trust, but Chester knew feelings couldn't always be trusted.

One thing he was absolutely certain of ... his sixth sense was tingling. Danger was lurking!

Chapter Nineteen

Dan LeCoq had set up his operation in the alley behind and across from the popular Blackstone pub. Dan picked the location because it was easy to find, had plenty of traffic and the name Blood Alley most likely appealed to his perverse nature. The cops seemed to have lost interest in him so he could comfortably resume work, but he had to be extremely diligent. Business was brisk and after a few days, he found he ran out of supply long before he ran out of customers.

At his next resupply with Andy, he asked to increase his order because business was good. He still didn't know who was responsible for getting him started, since he did not have the money to pay for initial supply. Andy indicated Dan's guardian angel had already paid for the initial allotment, but from that point forward, he would have to pay in advance for his supply. Since Dan was motivated to develop a nest egg, he continued to eat in the soup kitchen, stayed at the fleabag hotel and pocketed his profits.

One day while conducting his business, a homeless guy that Dan had seen many times scavenging and panning for money; came up to him and placed an order for some coke. Dan explained that he was short today but would have a new supply tomorrow, all he had left today was a couple of rocks of meth. The homeless guy wanted coke and would wait. Dan told him to be around at 11:00, he would be fully stocked by then. At 11:00, the homeless guy showed up and bought $25 worth of coke. As soon as the transaction took place, a couple of plain clothes cops came around the corner and arrested Dan. The homeless guy, seeing them, left the scene very quickly and the cops missed out on apprehending him.

Officer Romero knew he would have to testify at the trial, but he needed to get away from the arrest very quickly, so his cover wasn't blown. He had carefully developed his cover over several months and was a little perturbed when his Sargent told him the plan to apprehend LeCoq. He knew he was putting his cover in danger for a small street pusher and he didn't like it. He ran from the alley and as soon as he was around the corner, he spread his blanket and immediately sat, placing his hat on the ground. He was pretty sure nobody had seen him in the alley so his cover should still be intact. After a short while, a lady passed by and tossed a few coins in his hat. One of the coins missed the hat and started rolling. She reached down to grab the coin and placed it in his hat this time. As she was doing so, the vagrant passed her the package he had just purchased. He waited for a while, then packed his gear and started off down the street.

When the arresting officers turned the street corner, Dan saw the vagrant scooting down the alley. Dan offered no resistance and while the handcuffs were being slapped on him, he had a goofy smirk. "Hello, officers," he stated, "I've been expecting you."

The two arresting officers looked at each other and one said, "did you really think you would get away with this, Le Cock?"

"Lead away officers." Dan replied, as one grabbed Dan's backpack.

Arriving at the local police station, the officers roughly pushed Dan into the processing room. The police sergeant was perched on a high chair behind the processing desk. The arresting officer read out the charge and pushed Dan's backpack under the cage towards the sergeant. He opened the backpack and saw five small cellophane packages that contained white powder. Opening the first package, he noticed a medicated smell. He reached a finger into the package and rubbed the powder between his fingers. He had a concerned look on his face and looked up at the arresting cops. They now looked concerned as well. At that moment, an evil laugh erupted from the room. Dan LeCoq was bent over laughing

"What. Just in case you catch a diaper rash, this will help." Dan spat out between fits of laughing.

"What the fuck!" One of the cops said as he reached for the package. He didn't bother putting on his latex gloves in his haste and smelled the baby powder in the bag. Just then, the lady who picked up a package from Officer Romero appeared behind the sergeant and with a look of horror, she opened her package ... it was baby powder too.

The Weasel had managed to weasel out once again. He was heinously laughing as he walked out the front of the community Police station. He went for lunch at the soup kitchen than walked back to his station in Blood Alley. He spotted Officer Romero sitting on his blanket down a side street. "Fucking Pig!" He spat out as he kicked him in the stomach. Then, reaching down, he picked up the dirty backpack Officer Romero had tucked in behind him.

With satisfaction, The Weasel rounded the corner to his station and placed the backpack on top of the small brick wall that served as a tabletop. He then unzipped the backpack to examine the contents. Inside were clean clothes, a pair of shoes and a jacket. He shouted to a vagrant walking past, "Hey you scumbag, come here." He gave him the clothes and he whistled as he walked away. On the rear of the small retaining wall underneath the backpack was a small opening in the bricks, he reached into this opening and felt around. His stash was safe. He laughed again.

***

Officer Romero slowly straightened out. That idiot, Le Cock, had kicked him in his rib cage. Not only did he wind him, but he suspected a couple of ribs may have been broken. Worse, as he painfully looked up, he could see several street people pointing towards him and talking. "That Fucking Le Cock," he spat out in a loud voice. He knew his cover had been blown. Painfully, he stood up and walked to the community police centre. No sense in being discreet now, within the next hour everyone in the downtown eastside would know he was a cop.

As the sergeant explained the reason why Dan LeCoq was still on the streets, Officer Romero became more and more incensed. He was well known in the force for having a short fuse. He surprised nearly everyone by maintaining his cover for the past three years. Now that was behind him, and after kicking a few chairs and hurting his foot kicking at a wall, he started to slowly calm down. "That bastard," he exclaimed, "this assignment cost me three years and a marriage. What the fuck am I going to do now?"

"Well, you will get another assignment. First though, you should go get those ribs looked at ... and maybe your foot," the sergeant replied, with a muffled grin. Dejectedly, Romero walked out. After a couple of hours, he found himself at the Blackstone Pub. For the next several hours, he consoled himself with pints of Guinness. In the shadows of Blood Alley across the street, he could see Dan LeCoq making several transactions. Darkness descended and his intoxication grew. His anger became more intense, as he watched the slimy bastard in the shadows across the street.

The next morning, fighting a massive hangover, Officer Romero checked into the medical clinic. He was diagnosed with three broken ribs and a badly strained right ankle. He was given a walking boot and crutches. As he hobbled his way back home, he stopped at a refuse bin and opening his backpack, removed a black plastic bag and tossed it inside. Then, he continued on his way.

Meanwhile the police officers that arrested Dan LeCoq the day before were making their rounds. They turned down the street towards Blood Alley and were shocked to see the streets were completely empty. This was not usual, people should be everywhere, sitting on the street, bustling back and forth. As the officers reached Blood Alley, they understood why.

Hanging in front of them was Dan LeCoq. He was spread eagled, with his hands attached to the brick wall behind. His entrails spilled from his torso through a gapping hole across his stomach. He had a look of horror on his face, but with a weird grin. Upon closer inspection, the cause of the grin became obvious. Dangling from the corner of his mouth were several packets of cocaine, as well as his penis and testicles. Both officers involuntarily wretched.

***

The next day, Sanchez received a text from Chester requesting they have lunch together that day. Sanchez thought this was strange, since they were sitting a few offices apart at the time. He realized it was likely to do with the favour Chester had asked of him. Sanchez had heard that morning that Dan LeCoq was found dead in a back alley, so he suspected this was something to do with that. He texted back – 'Yes'. A few moments later his phone buzzed; 'Fortis – noon', came the reply.

Chester arrived at the restaurant. Sanchez was already there and had a table on the rooftop patio. As Chester arrived at the table, he said to Sanchez while sitting down, "this is one of the best rooftop patios in the city. Thanks for getting here early and for picking a great table. I suspect my text sounded a little cloak and dagger like?"

"Yes, it did, but of course I am pretty sure I know the topic of discussion and your desire for secrecy."

"Well, as you know, that little matter I asked you to deal with has been taken care of. I have to ask … were you directly involved?"

Sanchez eagerly replied, "No, though I wish I was. Apparently, it was a pretty gruesome scene."

"I understand he was disemboweled," then with a sly smirk, "and his balls were inserted in his mouth."

Quickly Sanchez replied, "I know I said that is what I wanted to do … but Chester you have to believe me … it wasn't me!"

Chester replied, "I don't think it was you. Apparently, he was picked up earlier in the day for possession of coke. When they checked the evidence, it was talcum powder, so he weaseled out of that one. I hear the police suspect it may be one of their own that did the deed."

"Good … good that you don't think it was me, .and good that bastard finally got his!"

"We have a small snag."

"Snag? Curious. What is this snag?"

"I am certain you did everything to cover your tracks, but unfortunately, you were seen meeting with Andy at the coffee shop."

The colour drained from Sanchez' face as the shock of what he just heard set in. "I was so careful," He somewhat stuttered, "I was positive nobody saw me."

"It's okay, sometimes the streets themselves have eyes. The important thing is that your contact has now become a liability. He could ID you if they bring him in."

"I understand," replied Sanchez as he started collecting himself. Then, it dawned on him what he must do next, "I will resolve that loose thread."

"Thanks, Gabriel"

***

Later that evening during the wee hours, Andy was just finishing up his delivery route. It had been a decent day, but there was a loss of revenue from Dan LeCoq. He was a bit of a maniac, but in a short period of time he had become a reasonable producer. Now, he would have to find a replacement since the idiot got himself killed. The cops obviously hated this guy, as the street says it was a cop that did him in. This would mean the cops wouldn't investigate too deeply, as they wouldn't want to pin this on one of their own. This was a good thing, as he didn't want to get pulled in for questioning. Slowly walking down East Cordova Street, a thought suddenly hit him. Perhaps this was a set up to begin with! Maybe that boss man actually wanted that idiot put away. Too many things did not make sense about this entire situation. First, the boss man making contact with him, that sort of thing never happens. Second, giving him his initial supply with no charge. Once again, unheard of. Finally, word on the street was that Le Cock was under constant surveillance, so it was just a matter of time. The more Andy thought about this, the more he believed it must have been a set up.

Suddenly, like a drop kick from Bruce Lee into the solar plexus, it hit him. If this was a set up, he may also be in danger. Then, he became aware he was walking down a deserted street. He looked up and down the street and he could see nobody lurking, in fact there was no one in sight. During the day, this place is usually buzzing with activity. He normally felt very secure and comfortable walking these streets at night. His business required this, but now he was apprehensive. He thought it was fortunate he was walking towards Pigeon Park, as there was certain to be more people and with people came security. Then the more he thought about it, he realized the irony. He realized he might be the pigeon! Picking up his pace, he heard a rustling from a doorway he passed. Anxiously, he turned to see a homeless guy sleeping off a drunken stupor under his cardboard box. He passed Oppenheimer Park and started to feel a little more relaxed as there were several people standing around just talking and drinking. On the next block, he saw an addict further up ahead, just staring into space with that comatose look that indicated he was having a great trip.

Further ahead was a small alley between a couple of non-descript brown brick buildings. The darkened alley was quite narrow, as it was referred to as a pedestrian precinct, simply meaning pedestrians only. On the other end of the alley, a streetlamp cast an indirect light. This dim light turned the alley into a forest of shadows. Close to the street, Andy saw a lone figure was standing. In the subdued light, he could not identify him. However, his silhouette betrayed some features. He was wearing an overcoat several sizes too large. The coat hung well below his knees and the shadow it created looked similar to a priest wearing a cassock. The wide-brimmed hat he was wearing could not contain the mass of long frizzy hair that burst out under the rim. The look was finished off with a huge scraggy beard, creating a look like a mountain man wearing a coat and hat.

Andy stopped to look down the alley. The skulking figure receded in the shadows. After a moment, he assessed there was no danger. He turned to continue walking. The lurking guy grabbed Andy by wrapping his arm around his neck and pulling him into the darkened alleyway. Before Andy had a chance to say anything, he had a warm wet feeling around his neck. He started to say something, but all that came out was a gurgling noise that seemed to erupt from his neck. Quickly, he understood he was about to die. From his periphery, the blackness began to close in upon him until his vision darkened. Painlessly, he drifted away.

The assassin gently set Andy onto the ground, almost like laying him down for a night's sleep. Then quickly, he removed the dark overcoat he had picked up that afternoon at the Salvation Army Thrift Store in Coquitlam. He dropped the overcoat to cover Andy and noticed a few drops of blood on his shoes. With the gloves he was still wearing. He rubbed his shoes and stepped out onto the street. Briskly, he walked up to Hastings and into the downtown core. As he passed Victory Square, he dropped his gloves and hat into the garbage container on the street. A couple of blocks further down, he removed the beard and wig he was wearing and tossed them in another bin. He walked several more deserted blocks towards the harbour waterfront. He casually walked through the front doors of the Fairmont Pacific Rim Hotel. At this time of night, the lobby was vacant, the only people were the clerks behind the front desk. They were preoccupied with some sort of game on their computer and did not notice the patron that walked towards the bank of elevators. Entering the elevator, he pushed the floor for his room. Nothing happened. He then remembered the security feature as he retrieved the credit card sized key from his pocket and tapped it on the reading device. The elevator ascended to his floor, and using his key card, he entered his room.

In the morning, Sanchez had breakfast and checked out of the hotel, after settling his bill with cash. He strolled out the front doors and down the street pulling his suitcase. He walked the four blocks towards LNa's offices. He went up to his office and passing Chester's office, he stuck his head in. "Good Morning, Chester," as Chester looked up from his desk, Sanchez added, "no more loose threads," and walked to his office.

Chapter Twenty

Chester remained suspicious of Sean, however, over the past several months he had not been able to piece any assumptions or evidence together. There were dubious elements but nothing concrete. He remembered how he was uncharacteristically short just prior to Geoff and Sanchez being shot at. Was the Bean truly the target? Or was it a remarkably convenient accident. Also, what role did The Dyck play? Why did he appear at Sean and Ava's wedding? And why did Sean visit him the day of the shooting?

While Chester kept a close watch on Sean, he fully trusted Geoff, and everyday, Sanchez was becoming more of a very valuable confidante. Still gnawing away inside, like a constantly queasy stomach, was a feeling that he needed to be cautious. Quietly, he was able to recruit additional bodyguards. These bodyguards began to become frequent companions. Every day Chester came into the office, one or two of the bodyguards also came in with him. Only on those rare days when Chester required confidential meetings would you see him without his bodyguards. They had become known as Chester's Brigade. They did not carry guns or knives as this was an illegal practise; however, they could inflict a lot of damage with a Billy club.

Despite Chester's concerns, the business kept churning out more and more money. Hellenic shipping added another oil tanker. GH Reed Hog Producers had expanded with a processing facility to handle the blueberries they now grew. Even the commercial fishing fleet was still maintaining profitability. Most significantly, the property development business was exploding. Every day there were more and more projects. The profits from property development rivaled the drug distribution business (the importing business excluded). The biggest difference was that property development was taxable. They even expanded into commercial property. Through a separate property management company, they owned several different complexes throughout Canada, and without drawing attention to themselves, they had become one of the largest, privately owned landlords in the country.

One day, he received a text message from Ashton requesting a meeting. Chester and Ashton were both members of the Royal Vancouver

Yacht Club and as such, they were entitled to attend the Wigwam Inn, a facility at the end of Indian Arm. It was reserved strictly for VYC members only. This resort is over 100 years old and throughout its history has boasted of hosting dignitaries such as JD Rockefeller, John Astor, Al Capone and many members of European royalty included Kaiser Wilhelm. The best part of this facility is the fact it is only accessible by water.

Independently, both Chester and Ashton reserved rooms for the next weekend. After Ashton made his reservation, Chester booked his, making certain they overlapped only one day – Saturday.

Since Chester would not be traveling far, he just packed a suitcase and rode to the Inn on his 30-foot, exquisitely maintained, vintage 'cigarette boat'. This was always moored at Belcarra and sometimes Chester used this to commute to the office. 20 minutes via the inlet and he was downtown. Today, he had the driver take him and his suitcase to the Wigwam Inn. Fifteen minutes after passing the last vestiges of any civilization, the Wigwam Inn came into view, nestled in a little cove.

This bucolic facility is surrounded with nothing but forest, mountains and water. It is not an elaborate place, but functional, nicely decorated and extremely remote. As they pulled up to the dock, the attendants checked Chester's credentials and after Chester disembarked, they indicated to the driver where he could moor the boat. Chester informed them the boat would not be staying, just him. Chester started down the dock and turned to see his boat heading back towards Belcarra, with its distinctive rooster tail spray towering over the crest of the boat's cockpit. He loved this boat, despite its chequered past as a smuggling boat. Actually, when he thought about it, he likely loved it more because of its history.

Chester checked in and by the time he reached his room his luggage had already arrived. The remoteness of this place was part of its charm. If the stories are to be believed, decades ago, wealthy industrialists and developers would spend the day here fishing, playing cards, smoking expensive cigars and drinking fine whiskey. Their wives were home looking after the home front while the men were away. In the evening, boatloads of young ladies arrived for the patron's enjoyment. These were termed the ladies of the evening. Now, while it cannot be confirmed that this is where the term started, it nevertheless is a great story.

One recorded historical fact is that during one of these retreats, the RCMP raided the facility and while no individuals were arrested, the facility was charged with illegal gambling. With today`s technology, you were never out of contact and the first thing Chester did when arriving at his room was unpack his computer and set up the satellite network communications provided by the Inn.

For several hours, Chester reviewed some development projects LNa was entertaining. He then changed into more rugged hiking clothes and went for a walk along a path, naturally carved into the rocks along the shoreline. He returned to the Inn after working up an appetite and had an exquisite meal of wild halibut, with Fanny Bay Oysters. After dinner, he sat outside on the veranda and watched the stars. On evenings like this he realized he missed those dark prairie evenings on the farm where the skies sparkled with starlight. Light pollution from urban living shrouded the stars. Remote areas like this were able to majestically showcase Mother Nature's bounty.

Chester recalled growing up in Saskatchewan and how you took this fulgurating light show for granted. His appreciation for this simple pleasure didn't materialize, until his world was devoid of it.

After a while, he retired to his room and he crawled into the crisply pressed cotton sheets. The smell could only be described as very clean. The fragrant sheets complemented the soft compliant mattress as it seemed to wrap around his body in a gentle hug and ease him into a deep restful slumber.

***

The following morning was Saturday. Chester slept late and felt completely refreshed and alive. He could not remember the last time he slept so soundly; or so late. After he showered, dressed and had breakfast it was past 10:00.

It was a warm sunny morning and he decided to go for a hike on a hiking route that took him towards the mouth of the river that fed into the inlet, the river was appropriately called Indian River. Since he would be out for several hours, he asked the kitchen staff to prepare a lunch and water that he could take in a backpack. By the time he was ready to leave, they had prepared a lunch for him of several salads, smoked salmon, cold ham, a couple of bottles of water and a thermos of coffee, all stored in a backpack they provided. They also provided a map of the hiking routes and GPS coordinates at various points, should he get lost or require retrieval.

Chester thoroughly enjoyed his hike along the trail. The path was easily navigable, but there were several sections where you needed to pay special attention to your footwork. Many areas on the map indicated viewpoints or places of interest.

One particular location mentioned a rockslide area, this also happened to be an area that required attention to your footing. At a couple of different viewpoints, he stopped to look at the landslide area. The size of the rocks that came down from the mountainside was incredible. Much of the debris was overgrown with trees and other vegetation, but careful observation revealed chaotic placement of huge stones and at one vantage point Chester could see the deep scar that remained from where a mountainside once was. He had walked for about an hour, and checking his map he saw he was approaching an observation point that had a picnic area.

Arriving at the picnic area, he offloaded his backpack and after taking a long gulp of water, he removed the thermos and poured a steaming cup of coffee. The coffee tasted fantastic! Chester knew it was because of the spectacular outdoor setting, but that didn't matter, it still tasted great. He sat on the top of the table with his legs dangling over the side, just sipping his coffee and admiring the mouth of the river as it spilled into the bay. There, the fresh water intermingled with the salt water to form the brackish water the inlet was known for.

He was becoming mesmerized with the view and was startled when he heard a noise coming from down the path. He looked towards the entrance of the path and saw a man coming towards him.

"Now, that's a very impressive view," the man said.

"Indeed it is, I have seen this before, but never really saw it – if you know what I mean," Chester replied.

"I certainly do."

"I gotta give it to you, Ash, you pick some pretty incredible locations for meetings."

"Well, after Sean seeing us the last time, I thought we needed a place even more ….discreet."

"I can't say for certain he saw us in Deep Cove although I am definitely inclined to believe he did."

"He most definitely did. Since that day, Sean has been trying very hard to befriend me. His sycophantic charm is a dead giveaway."

"It has been a long time since that day. What's up?"

"Well, there is good news and also something I believe you will have a bit of a tough time swallowing. First, the good news. We would like you to expand the importing business, initially double but eventually maybe triple or more."

Chester was somewhat shocked and of course pleased. "That's great news. As you know, the systems we have in place are capable of handling substantially more volume than we currently process. So, what's the news I am not going to like?"

"As you know, every good investment strategy involves spreading the risk. Diversification enables us to not put all our eggs in a single basket – even if it is a good solid, proven basket. In this case, we are bringing another group into the fold to begin importing product for us. We are growing your business, but also bringing on Walter Dyck."

"The Dyck! Seriously?"

"I know you don't like his methods, I'm not sure I do either, but you can't argue the fact that he has been successful."

"Successful, yes, but he is not discreet. Now I know full well that the decision has already been made and that you are doing me a favour by letting me know in person. While I do not like it, I know it is not my position to argue, so let me just say – thank you for letting me know. I really do appreciate it."

"You are an honourable person, Chester, and you are reacting professionally, just as I expected you would. I have another request though; I would like you to work with Walter to ensure both streams of importation remain intact. I am not asking you to share your routes or even practices, but I will ask you to maintain contact with each other and assist. Though not at the expense of risking your individual businesses."

Chester was quiet for a moment of reflection, then said, "I will make contact and assist him where I can."

"Thanks Chester, I know it is tough to swallow, but don't forget you are getting a much bigger share of the pie too."

"I know and I am grateful. Thanks Ash."

They chatted for a few more minutes then Ashton shook hands and departed. As he left, he asked, "are you sticking around here for long?"

"Yes, I have a lunch prepared and I thought I would work my way up the river for a bit before I turned back. Why do you ask?"

"Because even though I love this view, I am not a hiking sort of guy. I will walk back about 10 minutes to the next retrieval point and ask the Inn to send a boat to pick me up. I don't want our paths to cross when they arrive."

"No danger Ash, I am heading the other way. I hope you enjoyed your vacation at the Inn."

Chester had plenty of time to think over the next several hours, as he continued his hike. He tried to focus on the growth of the business. This would mean clearing $10-15M per week. However, every time he tried to focus on the money his hatred of the Dyck poured back in his mind and he became upset. When Ash made his request, he was certain he wasn't aware of this twist, that somehow, The Dyck was in cahoots with Sean ... and now he would have to help the guy who may be plotting against him!

After returning that evening, Chester thought about leaving early. He decided against it though as it would look suspicious. A weekend in a luxurious remote lodge where he had plenty of time to wander, think and catch up on some paperwork should be a welcomed relaxation. It wasn't though, as the prospect of working with The Dyck haunted him. The blissful sleep he had enjoyed the previous evening eluded him tonight.

After tossing and rolling for several hours he decided to get some fresh air. He dressed and walked along the elevated promenade built along the water's edge and perched above the dock below. The dock had activity which sort of surprised Chester. The barge at the dock had a large tank on it, a fuel supply barge. This made sense, the facility obviously needed fuel to keep it operating. Just like oil tankers, they usually left and arrived under the guise of darkness. People in Vancouver didn't like to be reminded they needed fuel to maintain their lifestyle.

After his evening stroll, he returned to his room and struggled through a fitful sleep. He awoke early, as normal, and got dressed. On his way to breakfast, he wandered through the building that was outfitted with pictures and artifacts from its history. It was a bit like strolling through a museum.

Indian Arm was a fiord fed by the glacial runoff from the Coastal Mountain Range. In the late 18th Century, a Spanish Explorer- Jose Maria Narvaez, met a group of aboriginal natives. They explained that further up the Inlet was a fiord they called 'Sasamat', which was a derivative of their word for 'cool place,' in their native Tsaatsmat language. Since they were given direction from the native Indians, they named this arm after them, and hence the term Indian Arm was first coined.

Chester loved history. He found, in most cases, history today was distorted. History had a tendency to turn people into heroes or villains. The true fact in most cases was they were a combination of both, the difference between the two extremes is that the individual when faced with certain situations had more good than evil or vice versa. For example, Winston Churchill was a hero of WWII and led Britain and the free world from the tyranny of the fascists. In many peoples' opinions, this is true, however, if you asked the millions of starving people in colonial India, you might get a different answer. Churchill refused to send relief rations and in fact demanded they produce more food. They were not of the same importance as the Brits in his estimation. History frequently creates a dichotomy and you either end up as good or bad. So, it depends on your perspective. After wandering through the halls and soaking up the history of this place, he noted that some people who were chastised as hoodlums and crooks in their day, were now revered as the founders of this facility. His thoughts returned to the present as he approached the breakfast area.

After breakfast, he returned to his room and packed his bags, then texted for his boat to return and pick him up. The cigarette boat operator replied he would be there within an hour. Enough time to sign his bill and have a coffee on the dock.

The sun was warming him as he drank his coffee. In the distance, he saw the distinctive rooster tail from the cigarette boat. Chester didn't like the name 'cigarette boat', he preferred the name 'rum runners'. Effectively, both the same boat, used for transporting illegal rum and cigarettes early in the 20th century. Over the more recent past, they were known for doing drug runs in the southern US. They had a shallow draft, long and elongated hull resembling a torpedo (or cigarette) and they were very fast. Chester was polishing off the last of his double espresso just as his boat pulled up to the dock.

✳ ✳ ✳

The following day, Chester arrived at the office. Despite his instincts to hold a meeting immediately to let Sean and Geoff in on his meeting over the weekend, he decided to wait for a couple of days before making the announcement. He wanted to conceal his meeting as much as possible. If Sean happened to uncover the fact that both Ashton and he had gone to the Wigwam

Inn over the weekend, it would confirm his suspicions of Chester's contact. So, he acted nonchalant as if this was just another regular day. He went for a walk that afternoon to a cell phone shop in the Pacific Centre Mall. This was the only location he could find Blackberry phones he could buy preloaded with time. Everyone purchased burner phones that operated on Android and a few on Apple but rarely did anyone want a Blackberry. The Blackberries didn't have the features other phones had, but they had something that was very important in Chester's line of work. Secure networks. It was easy for the police to tap into networks these days and trace your calls. Blackberries were still secure. Likely because nobody really used them anymore. The result was this shop charged an exorbitant price for them. Chester didn't care, he bought two.

Noting the numbers, he took one of the phones and had it packaged up and sent via regular parcel post to Walter Dyck. This would take 3-4 days to arrive, even though it was less than 100 kilometres away. No wonder the postal service floundered for so many years. Thank goodness for online shopping to breathe new life into that dying business. He pulled out a business card and wrote, 'I will call,' on the back of it, then stuffed it under the lip of the box and had the fellow wrap and send it off. Chester grabbed his other cellphone, tucked it under his arm and returned to work.

On Wednesday evening, Chester texted Sean and Geoff that he would like a partners meeting on Thursday if they were available. The following day, Chester outlined his meeting with the Clubman and let them know they would be ramping up their importing business with the Club.

Doing some quick math in his head, Geoff whistled, "that's a lot of dough."

"Can we handle that volume?" Sean asked.

"No problem, with the systems we have in place, we could easily handle 10 times our current volume." Geoff continued, "we are looking at several additional methods for bringing in product, one that looks promising involves submarines. Pretty cool, eh!"

"So, there may be a problem with the plastic system?" Sean asked, somewhat startled.

"No, No, we are just developing contingencies in case something happens."

Chester then chimed in, "that is a nice lead into the next topic." He had their attention. "The Club is also granting a license to another importer. As you said Geoff – contingencies."

"Who?" Sean asked.

"Walter Dyck."

"The Dyck is an asshole," Geoff exclaimed, "Why did they pick him?"

"Well, first of all they didn't ask for our opinion. I agree he is an asshole, but quite frankly he is also successful. I do not like his methods, but you cannot argue with his success. The Club also wants contingencies."

"So, why did they tell us who it is?" Sean asked.

"Because they want us to help him. Nothing that would jeopardize our business, but to act like a consultant when asked." Chester was having trouble maintaining an even keel. He was afraid his hatred of the Dyck was coming through. The other piece of information he gleaned in this exchange was that Geoff was pissed. Sean was much cooler....did he know what was coming?

Over the next couple of weeks, they made preparations for the increased volume of product. Chester had contacted the Dyck, and as he suspected, Walter Dyck did not really want any assistance. Chester told him he would keep his new phone charged and if Walter wanted anything, he could contact him through that number. Walter thanked him and said he would contact him if something came up, he might need advice or help with.

The increased volume was handled without a hiccup. The only difference was the cash shipments to Cyprus were sent twice as often. A shipment arrived now twice a month, instead of once a month, as previously happened. With the growth of their legitimate businesses, it was possible they could launder more cash through them. Chester, however, preferred to keep the system in place through Cyprus. It was processed efficiently, and their cash balances were growing substantially.

****

Business was thriving and Ashton, true to his word, had increased the volume of business with LNa; they were now doing four times the volume they were doing a year ago when Chester met with him at the Wigwam Inn. Clarie had grown and Chester's affection for his son grew with each passing day. He was now in Grade One, and would shortly be off for his summer vacation. Clarie loved his trip to the Mediterranean and frequently mentioned it to his Dad. Chester decided to spend the summer with Clarie, reliving what was without a doubt, one of the most enjoyable times in Chester's life.

Instead of renting another yacht, Chester purchased one that would be christened "The Clarie"; by none other than Clarie himself. After school was out, they would travel to Athens, where the ship was still receiving final touches before its maiden voyage. Chester had made several trips to Athens over the past year while the ship was being outfitted and to hire a crew. Chester found, over the years, he really loved sailing and his business could be managed remotely most of the time. If an occasion arose that required a personal meeting, the yacht was equipped with a helicopter that could fly him to the nearest airport and he could easily return to Vancouver.

****

They had a fantastic summer, Clarie was overjoyed to christen the ship after his name. He thought it was super cool. Their entourage that summer included Clarie's Mom, Anne and their chef, who had developed a keen understanding of what food they liked – also, he was very, very good. Chester was pleased that he enthusiastically agreed to go with them for the summer. It really wasn't that much of a hardship after all - a summer cruise on the Mediterranean. The entourage also included two bodyguards who spent a great deal of time sunning themselves on one of the several decks or spending hours working out in the gym. Other than that, the rest of the crew on board came with the ship.

There were several highlights that summer. Chester loved the excursion when they docked in Cairo to visit the Great Pyramids at Giza. Clarie was perplexed at the Sphinx, was it a lion or a man? One thing for certain, it was very old and needed to be fixed, a lot of the stones were broken and falling down. It was really hot and dry, and the sand kept making his eyes water. He told his Mom he preferred visiting some of the Greek Islands, they were much prettier and did not constantly throw sand in your eyes. He remembered Malta as the highlight. Clarie reminisced with his Mom about visiting markets, museums or just spending time on the beach eating ice cream. Even though they called it gelato, he knew it was ice cream!

The previous year, Clarie started attending a private school called Thurston Academy. One of the original lumber barons in the area was a gentleman named Robert Thurston. He founded and built the original Academy. After his death, he bequeathed 50 acres of land to the Academy surrounding the existing structure. They renamed the school in his honour. The land was mostly second growth forest with several streams running through it. The academy itself was constructed of wood supplied through Thurston's sawmill. The exterior walls were constructed from large uncut timbers, stacked and fitted together snugly. Over the years, this timber structure was in constant need of repair. The Academy administrator was in a constant battle. Splitting the funding between repairs to the building or funding academic supplies.

One evening at dinner, Anne advised Chester that she had received an email from the school administrator stating they needed to raise funds to keep the school open. They had 140 children registered for the upcoming year and those tuition fees were not enough to fund the school. Chester and Anne discussed this topic over dinner and Chester assured her the school would not close if he could help it. The next morning, he sent a message to Nathaniel Ostranski and told him he wanted to assist in funding this school. He asked Nathaniel if he would contact the administrator and see what the school needed to get back on solid economic grounds. Not just for the next year but investigate what it would need to ensure its long-term survivability.

Nathaniel investigated the school and visited with the administrator to review their books and ask for suggestions on long term success. It was a fairly simple solution but would require substantial funding to get the operation moving. Together, Nathaniel and the school administrator developed a plan. The plan consisted of several points. After completing the plan, he sent it in an email to Chester. Chester then asked Nathaniel if he could set up a meeting later that week, he would fly back for that meeting. The meeting was planned for Thursday at 10:00 AM. This gave Chester two days to make arrangements.

After lunch on Wednesday, Chester told Clarie he had to leave for a couple days to attend a meeting, but he would be back on Friday. They were in the eastern Mediterranean, so Chester boarded his helicopter for a quick trip to Tel Aviv. In Tel Aviv, a Bombardier Challenger was fueled and waiting to leave for Vancouver. Because of the distance, they had to stop to refuel in Helsinki, before continuing on the polar route to Vancouver. With the time difference, Chester would arrive in time for dinner and be able to sleep in his own bed that night.

The next morning after a restless sleep, Chester showered and went down for breakfast. Since the house was operating on skeleton staff for the summer, there weren't many people around. By the time he got downstairs, Nathaniel was already there. Eating his breakfast at the kitchen table that the assistant chef prepared for him, Chester pulled out a chair and joined Nathaniel at the table. Nathaniel reviewed the plan as they ate their breakfast. After eating, they left together in Chester's Rolls for the meeting with the administrator.

Entering the school compound, Chester was shocked by the emptiness. Every time he had visited this place it was a beehive of activity. Children scampering about, teachers shouting some instruction, and almost always some child crying in the distance. Today, not a soul could be seen. They parked in front of the school and entered. They were greeted by the administrator and escorted to her office. After exchanging the customary greetings, Chester said, "I suspect you know why we are here. I would like to assist with keeping this school open. You know my son, Clarie, is a student here and he loves his school. I am willing to underwrite costs to get this school operating in a sustainable fashion. Based on your discussions with Mr. Ostranski, we have put together a plan we would like to run past you."

The administrator nodded her head, "Yes, after meeting with Mr. Ostranski, I was hoping you could help us."

"First, in order to make the school viable you need much higher revenue from tuition. Since the tuition is on the high end right now, there really isn't room to increase it, so our only other option is to bring in more students.

Second, the school is quite remote – which by the way is part of the beauty of this place. We need to develop a residence to house students from further away.

Third, to attract students we will need to have exceptional academic standards.

So, I propose to first underwrite the costs necessary to keep the doors open this year. We will hire engineers and architects to develop and build our residence building, while also expanding the school to focus on academic excellence in science and technology. This will require additional computers and science labs for our bright young students. In order to achieve this academic excellence, I will grant scholarships to the 20 brightest and most gifted students from around the world. I will develop a foundation which will fund all these endeavors in perpetuity. According to our calculations, once the school has achieved at least 300 students, it will be generating enough revenue to keep the doors open. What do you think?"

"Oh My God! I am stunned. I was hoping for a few thousand dollars to help out with the upcoming school year! This is unbelievable."

Chester didn't say a word, he just quizzically looked at her for an answer.

"Yes, Yes, of course! We can't rename the school, but I suggest we name the residence after you?"

"There is another condition. I do not want any recognition. In fact, apart from you and perhaps, on a need to know basis, a few senior people, I wish to remain anonymous."

Now, the administrator had a questioning look on her face – "Really?"

"Definitely, without anonymity the plan is off."

"Nobody will know how generous you are, Mr. Moehr."

"Fine. My lawyer has prepared a letter of intent. Once we have the projections for the buildings, scholarships and future needs, I will create a foundation to secure your funding. One more condition please"

"Okay."

"No special favours for my son, he is to be treated no better or worse than any other student."

They signed the papers and after they got back into Chester's car, Nathaniel looked at Chester and said, "You know this will be many, many millions of dollars?"

Chester nodded, "I have been very fortunate, time to give some back."

"You really are a good man, Chester."

With a sly look, Chester replied, "Don't let that get out, charity may be bad for business!" They both laughed.

As they got into the car, Chester asked Nathaniel if he wanted to be dropped off back at the house or at the office. He said he was going to the office for some meetings and Nathaniel's office was along the way. Nathaniel chose the house as his car was there.

As Chester had prearranged, before he left the Mediterranean, LNa was going to have a senior partners meeting that afternoon. Arriving at the office, Nancy said, "I was surprised to hear from you yesterday, I thought you were still on your ship?"

"I am, I had some details to attend to. I am flying back tonight."

Laughing, she replied, "well, I guess the upside is you won't be here long enough for the jet lag to catch up on you. Geoff and Sanchez are here, Sean said he will be here within an hour."

"Thanks Nancy, you are the best."

An hour later, Geoff, Sean, Sanchez and Chester were in the conference room reviewing their business. All their businesses were running very smoothly and as Sanchez was providing his update, Geoff began to wonder why Chester had returned for this routine meeting. He knew Chester must have something else he wanted to discuss.

"Thank you for this update Sanchez, you are running your business like a true pro."

"Thanks Chester. Is there anything else? If not, I have a couple of pressing issues I need to deal with."

"No, thanks again. We can take it from here."

As Sanchez closed the door, Geoff piped up, "so what's up, Chester?"

"Welllll," Chester drew it out, "there is one other item to discuss." Then, lowering his voice, he continued, "as you know, The Dyck has been importing product for the Club for some time now. He hates being number two and no doubt has thought about eliminating us to take over as number one."

"So, what are you thinking?" Geoff replied.

"I think we should prepare ourselves."

"How so?" Sean replied.

"We need to find out more about him and his business. We need to keep this between us only. Geoff, I would like you to find out what you can about his business. Sean, you need to find out about his people and their weaknesses. I will contact The Dyck directly and see what I can ferret out."

"So, how does this information protect us?" Sean inquired.

Chester smiled, "I'm not exactly sure … yet. The more intelligence we can develop about these guys, the more we will uncover regarding their weaknesses and leverage. What that is … I don't know at this point."

"Okay, I will get started on this." Geoff stated.

"One other thing," Chester added, "we must keep this between ourselves. Nobody can know we are investigating him. Not even our own people. This has to be between us three. By dividing the tasks between the three of us, we can keep it tight."

"Agreed," Sean replied. "We are after all- the Club Men," he said with a snigger.

Geoff added, "Yup, TFM."

While Chester knew investigating competitors was fairly standard protocol, he also knew the Club may frown upon this endeavor, as they were both key players for them. Returning to his office, he sent a text to the Clubman asking for a meeting. He added there was nothing urgent, just some information he wanted to pass along.

Within a few minutes, a reply came back. Ashton was out of the country. He knew Chester was in the Mediterranean with his family, so he proposed meeting in Alexandria in a week. He was scheduled to be on the filming location for a movie he was producing. He suggested Clarie may want to visit as well, as several Hollywood stars would be there.

***

On Friday afternoon, Clarie was playing on the top deck of the ship with his Mom, when a noise in the distance caught his attention. He recognised the thumping noise from helicopter rotors and looked off in the distance to see a helicopter approaching the yacht. "Daddy's home."

***

The following morning at the breakfast table, Clarie was munching down on a heaping portion of pancakes smothered in maple syrup, Chester was enjoying some smoked fish with stewed eggplant and humus, Anne was picking away at her toast with her nose stuck in her tablet reading something. Suddenly, she looked up and said to Chester, "I think I know where you were yesterday?" and turned her tablet for Chester to read the email she just received.

From the Thurston Academy Administrator- 'It is with great pleasure that I would like to inform you an anonymous benefactor has agreed to cover the shortfall in our funding. Additionally, he will fund a substantial expansion and enhancement to the school to ensure the viability of our school long into the future. We thank our anonymous benefactor who has only agreed to fund the program if his anonymity is maintained. We therefore request you make no further enquiries as to this person's identification, as it will not be forthcoming. Sincerely, Gillian'

Chester smiled and winked at Anne.

They slowly cruised towards Alexandria and docked at the port Wednesday evening. On Thursday, Anne was going to go shopping. Chester and Clarie were going to visit a friend at a movie set. They split up the bodyguards, with one going along with Anne, the other traveling with Chester and Clarie.

At breakfast the following morning, Clarie was very excited. "Are we going to see a real movie being filmed Daddy? Do you think there will be any stars there?"

"Yes, my son. It will be a real movie set. I do not know who is in the film, or even if they will be there when we are. Filming movies is sometimes very boring. Most of the time, they are setting up scenes and the actors are in their trailers."

"What kind of a movie is it ... Superheroes?"

"Again, my son. I don't know. We'll find out when we get there."

Shortly after, their vehicles arrived, and they began their journey. It was about a one-hour drive to the filming location outside of the city. As they left the urban cityscape behind, the barren land was a sea of sand. The paved road turned into a dirt path. The road was quite rough and now the fact that they were riding in a large Jeep-like vehicle made sense. A car would not be able to traverse these roads. There was the odd sparse bush, but mostly sand. The gentle wind grabbed the smaller particles and blew them across the vast openness, much like snow drifting on the vast open fields in Saskatchewan.

They turned off the main road and to Chester's amazement, the roads became even worse. Eventually they arrived at the set, the landscape transformed into a small village of trailers and transportable buildings, sort of resembling a circus coming to town and setting up their tents and trailers. After passing through security, they were given instructions on where to park. Ashton would meet them there.

Clarie was mesmerized as they drove past sets with WW II tanks and 1940's trucks and war vehicles. There were large transportable guns and several people scurrying around. In the shade of large tarpaulins were soldiers dressed in full gear, some wore Allied helmets, and others were obviously German Nazi's. "Do you think those big guns are real Dad?"

"No Clarie, I'm sure they are only for show. However, I think we can deduce this film is a World War II movie."

Ashton was waiting in the parking lot as they pulled up. "Welcome, Chester, so glad you could make it to the set." Then bending down and extending a hand towards Clarie, "and you must be young Master Clarence."

Frowning Clarie replied, "Nobody calls me Clarence ... well maybe teachers and doctors ... you can just call be Clarie. I am very pleased to meet you too, Mr. Boyle."

Ashton laughed in reply, and said, "... and Clarie, please call me Ash," then added, "it has been a long journey for you and the desert makes one thirsty – would you care for a bottle of water? I don't know how much time you have, but if you can spare some time, I would love to show you around. They are between takes so we shouldn't be disturbing anyone."

Clarie's eyes bulged with excitement, and seeing this, Chester laughed, "we have lots of time Ash, Thanks, that would be great ... besides, I think we have someone very eager here."

They grabbed water and started walking through the set. Ashton pointed out the various tents and trailers, then explained the storyline. As they approached the set that was being prepared, he explained there was going to be a battle and several soldiers were going to be killed, that is why there are bodies lying on one side of the set. This was going to be the scene after the battle. The area was filled with craters from exploding shells and bodies and body parts strewn about. Clarie just said, "Yuck."

Quickly, they moved through this carnage and into a large tent beside the set. Ashton showed them a clip from the scene they just shot on a large screen. Inside they met an assistant who Ashton had arranged to tour Clarie through the rest of the set. Ashton and Chester had some business to discuss and they would meet up again later with Clarie at the food tent.

As they left the tent and casually walked towards a coffee truck, Ashton said, "So, what's up Chester?"

"As I said, nothing that pressing, but nonetheless something I needed to talk to you about."

"Okay, I'm all ears."

"Over the past while, several strange things have occurred. While it may be nothing ... as you always practice ... it is better to be safe than sorry."

Ashton nodded, "continue."

"No matter how much I try to justify these incidents...something just doesn't feel right. All of these incidents are dealing with Walter Dyck!" Chester quickly added, "now, before you say anything, please hear me out. As I said, I have nothing concrete, mostly just a feeling. I know I do not have to ask for permission to investigate a competitor, but because of the relationship between you, Walter Dyck and myself, I wanted to get your permission."

"As you said Chester, you do not need my permission to investigate a competitor. I will add though, should you uncover anything you cannot act without permission. Furthermore, please be extremely discreet, as if there is any interruption to our business, we will be forced to act on it." He paused briefly to let those words sink in, then added, "Finally, as a friend, I will tell you my intuition has saved me many times. Trust your intuition but act on facts."

"Thanks, Ash."

"Is there anything else?"

"No." Chester wanted to let Ashton in on his suspicion of Sean. However, he knew this would open up a much bigger bag of worms. The last thing he wanted Ash to doubt was Chester's ability to run his empire.

They sat at a table by the coffee truck. Chester wanted a coffee, but he was already starting to perspire in the 30-degree weather. Instead, they both ordered the local iced tea. They drank their tea as Ashton told Chester about the process and costs in making a movie. Chester realized this was in case somebody overheard their conversation; this way he could justify Chester's visit saying he was a potential investor.

After a while, they saw Clarie approaching with his entourage. The bodyguard and driver were both straggling behind, fully clothed in dark suits, the sweat was dripping off of them. As Clarie reached them, a beeping sound came over the loudspeaker system. Ashton turned towards Chester and said, "they are beginning to film."

The bodyguard was obviously distressed with the heat and did not hear or at least recognise the beeping sound. Seconds later, the air was filled with the sound of bullets whizzing, followed by shells exploding. The bodyguard reactively threw Clarie to the ground and running towards Chester he drew the gun he had holstered. Clarie instinctively shrieked, as the bodyguard turned to see Clarie, he tripped over the driver who had squatted down. Falling, he inadvertently pulled the trigger and another shot rang out.

As if mortally wounded, Clarie started screaming. Everyone turned to see an ashen-faced Clarie staring at the bodyguard and his gun. Somehow, he found an elevated level to his torturous caterwauling as he pointed beyond the fallen bodyguard. Sitting beside Chester was a pale faced Ashton. The blood that should have normally been running through his veins now erupted in a gusher of blood erupting from his neck. Reacting, Chester lunged over the table towards Ashton. A quick triage told him the bullet had hit his carotid artery as he could see the pulsating bursts of blood. He pinched his neck to stem the bleeding. Within moments, first aid attendants were on the scene and relieved him.

Seeing Clarie was still distraught, Chester went to wrap his arms around him and console him. Clarie started punching Chester and yelled, "You said the guns weren't real! You said! … you said … you … " wrapping his arms around Clarie, eventually he started calming down.

Having stabilized Ashton, the attendants moved him to a shaded tent and minutes later, a helicopter appeared. Upon landing, the helicopter had to be turned off, as the rotors bombarded everything with such a torrent of sand that it was unsafe to bring Ashton onboard until it settled. As the helicopter left, the Egyptian police arrived. They immediately handcuffed the bodyguard and threw him in the back of the police car. This car was not equipped with air conditioning. The bodyguard was profusely sweating, whether from the heat or from fear.

The assistant that had earlier toured Clarie had located a change of clothing for Chester. Ashton's blood was soaked all over Chester's clothes and in this heat, it had already passed through the sticky stage and was cracking as it dried. After being interviewed by the police, they were permitted to return to their boat. They said they would have follow-up questions later, and Chester should not leave the port until given permission.

The drive back to the ship was extremely quiet. Clarie and Chester were sitting in the back seat and Clarie had positioned himself as far away from Chester as he could. Chester tried to console him, but this just brought about renewed rounds of sobbing. Chester grew more and more upset. It was as if Clarie somehow blamed him for Ashton being shot. Then he thought … what will this do to his relationship with Ashton?

Pulling onto the pier where their yacht was docked, they saw Anne standing on the gangway. She had been alerted and returned home immediately. Clarie jumped out and ran into her arms and began another round of sobbing. She hugged him tightly and as Chester approached, he elevated his cries again. Chester backed off.

Stroking his head, Anne said, "it's okay my love, Mom's here……what happened."

Through whimpering sobs, Clarie said, "one of Dad's soldiers shot that nice man … Dad said the guns weren't real … but they were … there was blood everywhere … then … then … then, Dad jumped on him and … and … and tried to strangle him!"

Chester was stunned! He hadn't thought Clarie would have misunderstood that he was trying to save Ash! Clarie was traumatized and not thinking logically. However, this revelation hit Chester very hard. In the pit of his very being, he felt gutted. The pain he felt was greater than being disemboweled, like that idiot Dan LeCoq. Chester could not approach his darling little boy to explain. He would only scream louder. Anne tried to explain that Chester was helping the man, but Clarie was having none of it. Clarie thought his Dad was a murderer!

Distraught, Chester went to the bar and poured himself a large tumbler of whiskey. After a moment, he regained his senses. He picked up his phone and called the hospital to check on Ash. This was futile, as he could not speak the language and the hospital staff could not speak English. He then called the captain and asked if anyone onboard could translate for him. Within a few minutes, one of the ship's stewards appeared and said he could assist Chester.

He called the hospital, and after a brief conversation explained to Chester that Ashton had lost quite a bit of blood. Thanks to the quick first aid he received he was now resting comfortable and out of danger.

Chester than asked if he could visit. The steward relayed the message and shook his head. "They say he needs his rest; we should call tomorrow and check again."

"Thanks," Chester said. "Can you travel with me tomorrow if we are allowed to visit him?"

"Yes, most certainly, Mr. Moehr."

Realizing he was still wearing his replacement clothes, Chester suddenly felt dirty. He had a long shower and after putting on clean clothes felt better. He went to his office and just sat behind his desk thinking. Anne showed up a short while later. "How is he?" Chester asked.

"He's very upset, he sat on my lap in his room, and after calming down he fell asleep. I laid him down. Sleep is likely the best medicine for him at this point."

"Just so you know, I didn't try to strangle Ashton. That idiot bodyguard accidentally shot him and nicked his carotid artery. I pinched it closed until help arrived. If I hadn't, he may have bled to death."

"I tried to explain that to him, but he wasn't buying it, maybe after a sleep he will be more rational." Anne explained, then continued, "Ashton Boyle? I didn't know you even knew him that well. What is he doing in Egypt?"

"He is in Egypt for the production of a movie. I was meeting with him about a possible investment. I hope you're right about Clarie. I am still flabbergasted he thought I was trying to strangle Ashton."

"Have you heard how Ashton is doing? Oh My God, has anyone told Tanya?"

"We just spoke with the hospital; he is resting comfortably. I don't know if anyone contacted Tanya, perhaps you should give her a call."

"Good idea, I will. Don't worry about Clarie, I'm sure he will come around." Anne gave Chester a tender kiss on the cheek and left to go call

Tanya. Chester found talking with Anne to be soothing. He was beginning to feel better about Clarie.

The following day, Clarie remained very cool towards Chester. Chester decided to go to the hospital and visit Ashton. When he arrived in his room, he was propped up on some pillows, heavily medicated but cognizant of Chester. He couldn't speak but Chester could tell he did not hold Chester responsible, it was an accident and he was grateful to Chester for helping to save his life. When Chester said he would return the following day Ashton shook his head. In a weak voice he squeaked "not a good idea, I'll see you when I get back home."

Chester could tell this was very hard for him, and replied, "I understand, you take care my friend."

After leaving the hospital, they stopped in at the police station where the bodyguard was being held. Chester spoke to the arresting officers the previous evening, when they stopped at the yacht. They informed him the case was pretty clear, and he did not have to stay in the country after he stopped in at their station to sign a few papers. Chester wanted to leave Egypt behind, so he eagerly agreed.

At the station, the officers explained through the translator the papers Chester was signing. Before they left, one of the officers asked Chester if he wanted to know what the bodyguard was facing. Chester replied with venom in his tone, "Let him rot!"

The last vestiges of their summer vacation came to a close without Chester fully repairing his relationship with Clarie.

* * *

Back home now, Clarie was preparing for school. One of the changes that occurred over the summer was this year they would now be wearing standardized school uniforms. Anne received notice that Clarie would have to come into the school for a fitting for the new uniforms.

When Clarie and his Mom arrived, they noticed a new metal gate had been installed as you entered the school compound. Above the gates, cascading over the top and connecting the two halves in large metal letters was the name, Thurston Academy. This was new and Clarie thought it looked very nice. Over the front door of the school was also a new carving, this time it was in wood and looked like the sort of piece that local native people would carve. It looked somewhat like the carving on a Totem Pole. Clarie did not understand the words 'Consecutionem Excellentiae', which were carved into it, but he still liked it.

On entering, Anne asked one of the attendants about the new nameplate over the door. She explained it meant 'Achievement of Excellence' in Latin. It was the school's new motto. Clarie's new uniform looked very sharp, and on the right pocket, Thurston Academy was monogrammed, on the left

Consecutionem Excellentiae. Clarie was mostly excited about the fact that some of his schoolmates were there to play with. Anne was pleased, Clarie had seemed very tense and dour since that day in Egypt. After running, getting dirty, scraping knees, interspersed with the occasional tears from scrapes and bruises, the boys grew bored with playing. Besides, Clarie was getting hungry. The driver took them to Buntzen Lake and when they arrived, they saw several household staff had arrived earlier and prepared a picnic for them on the beach.

Clarie loved picnics and excitedly, he told his Mom his mates said there were big changes coming to the school. It was going to get bigger with more kids and some of the kids were going to be staying at the school. They were going to build a place to house the kids that didn't live in the area. They spent most of the afternoon playing on the beach and they even went for a hike around part of the lake. The old Clarie seemed to have returned – at least partially. His melancholy had been mostly replaced with that charming, smiling, little boy

.***

Meanwhile, Sean had once again separated from Ava. This time though, it seemed a little different to Chester. Perhaps their 'on again – off again' relationship had finally run its course. If nothing else, their 'off again' plateau had reached a new height. This time, they were actually talking about divorce. Prior to this, it was only separation. Sean was in the doldrums and when Geoff suggested they take him out for an afternoon of golf, Chester agreed. Perhaps some sunshine, beers and male companionship would help ease his pain.

Chester arranged the golf and the transportation back to his estate for a barbeque and drinks after. Sean, Geoff and Sanchez joined Chester to make the foursome. They had a great afternoon and Sean seemed to enjoy himself. Being the best athlete in the group and most avid golfer, Sean naturally won.

They had plenty to drink at Chester's that evening. The chef had the barbeque fired up on the rear deck and the boys were sitting in easy chairs, slowly quaffing their beer. The smoke from the wood barbeque permeated the air. When Anne and Clarie returned from their afternoon at Buntzen Lake, they immediately caught the scent of the smoke. This wonderful smell that would set Pavlov's dog salivating most certainly attracted a small boy.

Running around the house, Clarie saw his Dad and Uncles. Sanchez was the first to notice Clarie, and he said, "Hello Clarie."

"Hi, Uncle Gabriel."

"I haven't seen you all summer Clarie. You have really grown." Sean remarked.

"Thanks, Uncle Sean, yes, I had to get bigger shoes the other day as mine were too small." Clarie proudly stated. "What are you barbequing Dad?"

Everyone laughed and Chester replied, "we have lots of stuff. Would you and your Mom like to join us?"

"Yes, yes, please."

The chef came around from behind the smoking grill and asked Clarie and Anne what they would like for dinner. Clarie talked with his Uncle Geoff for a while, then went and sat on Uncle Sean's lap. They talked about school and how the school was going to be getting bigger and have more kids attending it.

Sitting back, Chester was slightly jealous that Sean seemed to be getting more of his son's affection than him. Clarie was much better, but Chester felt that he somehow still blamed him for Ashton's accidental shooting. It dawned on him that Sean hadn't asked about the incident. With Ava and Tanya being close friends, it is highly unlikely Sean would not have heard about it. Even if he and Ava seldom talked. Interesting, he thought … I wonder why?

Clarie's laughter brought him back as Sean was tickling him and Clarie loved it. They had a wonderful evening and after Clarie and Anne returned to Clarence House, the boys sat out until the wee hours talking and laughing. Chester offered each a bed if they wanted to stay over, He had at least a dozen spare rooms. They all had something to do the following day, so Chester arranged with his staff to drive each home.

Chapter Twenty-One

As the lazy excitement of the summer rolled into the busy routine of the fall, Clarie was once again back in school. This year, he was in grade two and therefore had to work a little harder. Last year was more about fun and a little learning – this year more learning and less playing. After a few weeks back at school, the newness had worn off and it became routine. Clarie seemed to be spending more time with his Dad lately.

Back to school meant that once again the various flu bugs would start traveling through the schools. Sniffles, fevers, congestion and coughs were commonplace in any household with children. This is the bodies defence mechanism – as the body is exposed to various viruses, it develops antibodies and these antibodies protect against similar viruses for the rest of a person's life. That is why it is important for little boys to eat dirt and play with slimy creepy crawly things. Growing up in an environment that is too sterile and hygienic, prevents a child's body from developing these protective antibodies. Like any normal little boy, Clarie had frequent bouts with dripping noses, running eyes and stomach aches. When he developed a bit of a cough in late October, he was fed a dose of vitamin C, Echinacea and over the counter pain medications.

The cough worsened over the next couple of days, and by the third day, he was experiencing more bouts of coughing. Sometimes he would have coughing spasms so bad that he had trouble regaining his breath. Chester and Anne both became worried and by the fourth day, he became very lethargic and just wanted to stay in bed. He complained that everything hurt, worse still, he had developed a sort of wheeze between coughing spells. Rather than letting this flu bug run its course, they decided to take him in to see a physician. After his medical appointment, the Doctor admitted Clarie into hospital. The Doctor explained that at this point, it is precautionary until they can run further tests. Right now, they can put him in a bed with a sort of tent covering him, where they can treat him with aromatic medications that help ease his coughing spasms.

Immediately following his admission, Chester and Anne were at the bedside attending to Clarie. They had arranged a private room so Clarie could rest more comfortably. A few hours later, an attending nurse came into Clarie's room and informed Chester and Anne that the doctor would like to meet with them. He was in a consulting room in a separate wing. They were both weighed down with concern as they quietly walked down the hallways to the meeting. What was wrong with their little boy?

The doctor began, "so we have received the test results on your son. I am afraid he has developed Pertussis."

"Isn't that whooping cough?" Chester asked.

"Yes, and I am afraid it is very contagious. I am sorry to tell you that he will have to be placed into isolation and we will have to inform anyone who has come in contact with Clarie over the past week and they will be placed in quarantine. We have to inform the local health department and they will investigate to ensure the outbreak is contained."

Anxiously, Anne asked, "How long will he be sick?" then quickly added, "Oh My God, he will recover, won't he?"

"It will take several weeks for the virus to run its course, but almost for certain he will recover. While it is a dangerous disease, it is extremely rare there are any long-term complications."

"But --- he's had his immunizations. Aren't they supposed to prevent this from happening?" Chester asked.

"Normally yes, however, immunizations are not 100% effective. That is why it is important for everyone to get their shots. If everyone is immunized, the disease is effectively eradicated."

The realization struck Chester, "you mean that somebody who didn't get their vaccinations may have given my son this disease?"

"Well, I wouldn't put it quite that way – but the disease was eradicated for several decades, in recent years, we have begun to see a re-emergence."

"Anti-vaxxers!" Chester spat out, more as a statement and less of a question.

"Not definitive, but yes, likely. That is why we need to inform the local health authority; they will track this down and ensure it is contained. Do you have any idea where he may have caught this?"

Anne responded that there were several children at school with runny noses and some cases of the flu, but she was unaware of anyone who had whooping cough.

Chester said, "I do not know of anyone with it. I have very little contact with Clarie's friends, most of my contact is with adults."

"Adults can catch it too you know," the Dr. continue, "the symptoms are usually much less severe in adults."

Chester thought for a moment and then said, "how do you mean less severe?"

"In some cases, adults may think it is a flu bug. They may not show symptoms such as the wheezing cough."

With sudden recognition, Chester said, "so if a 40-year-old guy developed a flu, it may actually be whooping cough?"

"Yes, do you know of somebody?"

"Perhaps."

"Please tell me – I will pass along his or her name to the health authorities. They will test him or her."

"Him," Chester replied. "He was visiting this past weekend and was horsing around with Clarie. I work with him and he has been at home sick this week."

Within a couple of hours, a North Vancouver health nurse arrived at Sean's condo and after explaining why she was there, Sean agreed to be tested. He was obviously very sick and had not left his condo for several days. She asked about vaccinations he had received.

"When I was a child, my Mom somehow believed vaccinations were bad for children. I believe I had the original round of vaccinations, but nothing else."

"So, you don't know if you have had the vaccination for pertussis?"

Sean shook his head, "No I don't know. Can you tell me who is sick?"

"I'm sorry I cannot divulge that information at this time." The nurse replied. She proceeded to collect her samples. Before leaving, she asked for a phone number where he could be reached. They will be in contact within a day with the results.

***

Sean, having tested positive, had to undergo a thorough review to determine people he may have come in contact with. This was all done as he was transported to Lions Gate Hospital and placed in isolation. His queries of who he may have infected continued to be met with either 'we cannot comment' or 'we do not have that information'. His frustration was growing and when he wasn't allowed his cell phone, he became very agitated. In an effort to keep him calm, a nurse brought in a telephone that looked ancient. She plugged it into a telephone outlet and weaved the cord and phone through his isolation tent.

"My God," Sean replied, "I haven't seen one of those in ages."

The twentysomething nurse laughed and replied, "When I first saw it in the closet, I had to ask what it was. However, it still works and will allow you to make phone calls."

"Thanks." Sean said, as he lifted the handle and heard a dial tone. He stopped and added, "you wouldn't happen to have a phone book, would you? I have no idea what the numbers are."

She laughed, removed her phone from her pocket and said, "I will google a number for you....who do you want?"

A few minutes later, Ava answered her phone tentatively, as the caller ID read Lions Gate Hospital, "hello."

"Ava, it's me, Sean."

"Sean ... is everything okay?" She had genuine concern in her voice.

"It's a long story, but yes."

"Thank goodness ... you don't want to die before our divorce comes through," she sniggered. Even though they were divorcing, they were still friendly and could tease each other.

"Believe it or not, I have whooping cough and I'm in isolation at the hospital. I'll be okay but they don't want me infecting anyone else, so until I am no longer contagious, I have to stay here."

"Infect someone else! You mean you have infected someone?"

"Yes, but I don't know who. They took away my phone and have given me an old fashioned, plug in the wall phone. Unfortunately, I don't know any phone numbers. Could I get you to look a few up for me?"

"Sure, why don't I come over to the hospital and I can give them to you then?"

"I don't think they will allow you to see me ... isolation, remember?. Once I am no longer contagious, I will let you know. In the meantime, can you look up a couple numbers for me?"

At Eagle Ridge hospital in Port Moody, Chester was becoming very angry, some idiot infected his son. He had no use for stupid people – now one of those stupid people who didn't believe in vaccinations had infected an innocent victim. Caught up in his growing tirade he said, "Anti-vaxxers! Even though vaccinations are credited with saving more lives than any other advancement in society today, some idiots choose to believe discredited doctors and reactionaries rather than medical professionals!"

As Chester's ire continued to rise, he looked over at Anne, she was crying. He reached over to console her and somehow her tears washed away some of Chester's fury. Poor Clarie, Chester thought – his marvellous boy was going to suffer a great ordeal and there was nothing Chester could do to make it easier – he was on his own. Sitting there with his arm around Anne, he felt his phone vibrate. He saw it was Lions Gate Hospital and chose to ignore it. They can leave a message. At this moment, Anne was his priority.

Several hours later, he remembered the phone call. He went outside to check on his messages. Listening to Sean's message, he wasn't sure what to think. It wasn't some idiot from school who transmitted the virus to Clarie. It was his friend! Sean was certainly not an idiot ... so why would he not get his vaccinations? He called the number Sean had left on the message.

"Hello," a groggy Sean answered.

Chester wasn't sure what he was going to say. Upon hearing Sean's voice though, bile rose, and he suddenly understood he was pissed. "So, it was you!" He spat out.

In a much clearer voice, Sean responded, "Oh My God Chester ... I'm sorry ... I knew I passed this on to somebody ... but not whom. Is it you?"

"No, Clarie."

"Wasn't he vaccinated?"

"You know I can ask you the same question! You know not having your vaccinations is like walking around with a loaded gun with the safety off. Yes, Clarie was vaccinated, but the doctor said sometimes it doesn't take"

"My mother didn't believe in vaccinations; I know it's stupid. Quite frankly, as I got older, I just didn't think about it. I'm so sorry, how is Clarie doing?"

"He's a very sick boy ... at least now we know where it came from." Chester was controlling his anger and was glad he was talking to Sean on the phone. In person his anger would be blatantly evident.

Over the next days, they had several visitors. Several people from the office, Geoff and Sanchez stopped in daily. One day, while Chester was there by himself, resting in a sort of semi-comatose state, a figure showed up at the door. Chester did not recognise Ashton at first. Suddenly he stood up, and exclaimed, "Ash."

Ashton smiled, and said, "Yes, I am so sorry to hear about Clarie. I brought some flowers, but the nurses said I could not bring them into his room, something about pollen not being good for his breathing."

"This is certainly an unexpected visit ... how are you doing?"

"Fine....the doctors tell me there will be no lasting damage ... I will have a scar though, once they remove the rest of the bandages."

"I am so sorry; I cannot apologise enough ... that idiot is apparently still in an Egyptian jail."

"No need to apologise my friend, in fact it is I that need to thank you for my life. You saved me with your quick actions ... and that bodyguard had an unfortunate run in with some Egyptian Brotherhood. So how is Clarie?"

"The Doctors say the worse is likely still to come," then looking towards Clarie, "he should be fine, the worst part is he must be very scared when he can't catch his breath, so being unconscious is likely the best."

"Well when he gets better, I will arrange for a visit to a movie set." After a pause, he added, "I must be going."

"Yes, I understand, thanks for stopping in Ash, it is very thoughtful."

When Ashton reached the door, he turned around and said, "oh, one more thing...Walter Dyck knows you are investigating him." He then turned and walked out.

Chester was gobsmacked! He had set the stage and now one of his closest allies had turned on him. He would need to confirm who it was ... even though he almost certainly knew who the Judas was. Just then, Clarie started one of his coughing spells and drew Chester's attention.

Anne and Chester maintained vigil over Clarie. There was always one of them present by his bed, both of them most of the time. When one of them went home to rest, the other was always present. Clarie was nearly comatose, he would occasionally open an eye and seeing his parents gave them a brief smile, he would return to a subconscious state. Over his bed, a clear tent was draped that was pumping in medication along with oxygen and humidity. The tent was so humid that beads of water would form on the tent and run down the side to a collection container at the side of his bed. He would occasionally start coughing violently. During these spasms, you could read on the monitors that his heart rate spiked, and his oxygenation levels declined precipitously.

Over the first couple of days, they were interviewed several times by public health officials. They were pleased to find out that Clarie didn't appear to have caused a further outbreak. There was, however, another small cluster in downtown Vancouver. The nurse indicated that patient zero had an office downtown and he must have accidentally infected someone in the downtown eastside. There were public notices given out but because of the large incubation period they wouldn't know for several weeks, or even months, if it had been fully contained. Chester said he knew patient zero as they were partners in business. He was certainly concerned about the general public's health, however, Clarie weighed much heavier on his mind.

Chester had arranged to have a cot brought into Clarie's room. That way, when needed by either Chester or Anne, they could take a nap in the room without returning home. They were never able to sleep for long as Clarie's wheezing and coughing spells would wake them. To pass the days, they would read stories to Clarie. Most of the time, they weren't sure if he was awake enough to understand, but regardless, they were certain their voices alone were comforting. They had worked their way through many of the books from home. They now progressed to children's novels. Chester and Anne had just completed Treasure Island and on occasion, Clarie would sit up a little to listen to them.

In the early hours of the morning on the fifth day, Chester was sitting with Clarie while Anne had returned home for a break. Chester's eyes began to get heavy and he decided to lie down on the cot for a brief rest. He dozed off, and instead of being woke up by one of Clarie's coughing fits, he woke up to alarms buzzing. This was followed by several nurses rushing into the room. They quickly removed the draping curtain and began working on Clarie. One of the attendants grabbed Chester and rushed him outside, he said they needed the room to attend to Clarie. Despite Chester's protestations and inquiries as to what was happening, he agreed to leave and let them do what they needed to do. On his way out he caught sight of Clarie, and his skin face was beet red and seemed to have a blue tinge.

Chester soon became very worried, as he suspected something dreadfully serious was happening. As his mind started to think of the worst, he consciously pushed the negativity back and forced himself to focus logically ... this is a curable disease. Shortly after, Anne returned and wrapped in each other's arms, they provided some consolation.

People were rushing in and out of the room bring trays and pieces of equipment.   Suddenly, the beehive of activity seemed to slow. Chester immediately felt somewhat relieved. The furor was over and this could only mean they had Clarie stabilized. The door slowly opened and out came an attending physician. He had his stethoscope wrapped around his neck and a very dour look on his perspiring face.

Inside, Chester quietly said, "No, No," then his denials started ramping up, "NO NO NO."

The doctor just looked at him, and said, "I'm sorry".

Chester could not remember the last time he cried. Even as a child when friends, family and even his father died, he could not remember crying. Suddenly, as if all those tears were dammed up over the years, they all came flooding out. He was inconsolable, as he just dropped to the floor and sobbed. How could this happen? Not Clarie. As he wept, the walls began closing in and the veil of darkness overtook him.

He had fainted. Dear God, he never fainted. He was lying in the waiting room trying to make sense of what just happened. Then, Clarie came racing back to his consciousness and he began crying once more. He noticed Anne was also in the room and as he sat up, she came over and they both wept, wrapping each other in their arms.

The following few days were just a blur. Clarie's funeral was a blur. Geoff and Sean, who had been released from isolation, were tremendously supportive when Chester needed them most. They made the necessary arrangements for the funeral and burial, as Chester was barely able to look after himself. He had maintained control for most of the funeral service, but at the graveside he lost it again and had to be helped back to the car.

Sitting on the seat, beside Chester, Anne was staring straight ahead. While Chester openly wept, Anne took on a cadaverous appearance. She looked like all colour had been drained from her and her body seemed to go through the motions, but her soul was absent. After the service, there was a luncheon at the estate. Chester just sat in a chair and stared out the window, lost in his grief. Geoff approached and sat next to him. He placed his arms around Chester and asked if he needed anything.

"Whiskey," Chester replied.

He was obviously distraught. Geoff went to the bar area and poured a large tumbler of single malt scotch. Returning, he handed it to Chester and said, "TFM".

Chester drained the tumbler and with a weak voice squeaked out, "TFM … another."

Somehow, the alcohol seemed to brush away the web of despair and for the first time in several days, Chester felt something other than melancholy. As Geoff returned with his second tumbler, Chester noted Sean was standing close by. The crystal tumbler shattered as he threw it on the floor, in one motion he was up and threw himself at Sean. "You bastard! You killed him!" Sean was bigger and stronger, but he did not fight back as Chester unloaded his fury. A blow caught Sean full in the face, and his nose immediately started gushing as he fell to his knees. Quickly, Geoff and several bystanders were pulling Chester off Sean. Chester continued screaming, "Bastard. Bastard ... he was the most precious thing in my life!"

Chester seemed to be exorcising some inner demons as he berated Sean. Sean was profusely bleeding, and you could see he was seething. He stood up, threw over a table and stomped out. Geoff ran after him, when outside of earshot he protested, "Sean, Sean ... wait a minute ... you know that's not Chester. He needed to lash out at somebody, he doesn't really blame you."

Geoff's pleadings seemed to have worked, as Sean stopped and they talked for several minutes, then together they went to a washroom. A few minutes later, they emerged, and Sean was somewhat cleaned up. Rather than re-entering the reception room though, Sean left through the front door, where his car and driver were waiting for him.

Entering the reception area Geoff went over to Chester and he barked, "Has that bastard left?"

"Yes." Geoff replied.

Chester seemed to withdraw once more, and within a few moments, he was sitting in his chair. A solitary figure staring out the window but seeing nothing.

Winston Churchill talked about the days when the Black Dog took up residence. The Black Dog had certainly taken up residence with Chester. In fact, the Black Dog brought his entire family and decided to settle down for an extended stay. Chester was distraught and utterly empty. He had no desire to emerge from his bottomless depression.

Since Clarie's passing, Chester's days passed very slowly. Sometimes, he would not shower or change his clothes for days. Geoff frequently visited, but Sean avoided him. No matter what Geoff tried, he could not pull him out of the state of despair where he currently resided. After a month of wallowing, Chester awoke one morning and had an epiphany. He realized he had two choices. He either pulled himself up and got on with life, or he would slowly rot away in sloth, until a shadow of his former self would just not wake one morning. He knew it would be tough, but he also knew he wasn't ready to call it over just yet. He still wanted to live.

He gathered his resolve and with a gargantuan effort, he sat up in bed. He slowly made his way over to the bathroom where he showered, shaved and got dressed. With the black dog nipping at his heels, he went downstairs for breakfast. Seeing Chester descending the stairs, the staff were shocked and pleased.

The chef quickly prepared a double espresso and brought it in to Chester, as he made his way into the dining room. "Breakfast, sir?"

"Yes please. Bacon and eggs with toast please – also would you please let the driver know I will be going into the office today. One more thing; could you get an appointment at the barbers for me today. I am looking quite shaggy."

"With pleasure, sir" the chef replied, and quickly went to his kitchen to prepare Chester's breakfast.

Before Chester arrived at the office, he stopped at the barber shop in Newport Village to have his shaggy mane trimmed and groomed. Everyone at LNa was pleased to see him, instead of offering their condolences they were given advance notice from Geoff they should avoid the topic. Since Chester was struggling with Clarie's death, this may only send him back into despair. Nancy could not resist though and when Chester arrived, she walked out from behind her desk, gave him a big hug and said, "great to see you Chester."

Chester went to his office and got back to work. Occasionally throughout the day, he would find himself staring blankly out the window or at some inanimate object, but he would realize what he was doing and pull himself back. As he eased himself back into work over the next few weeks, he found his ambition was not what it once was, perhaps it was enough....maybe he should relax and enjoy life. He came to the realization the most enjoyment he had was when he was on his ship. Business was good, Geoff and Sean were running things. His leadership was not what it once was.

A couple weeks passed, nobody spoke about the altercation between Sean and Chester. There was a tension seething just below the surface, like the build-up of magma that everyone knew would blow one day....just not which day. Chester knew he could ease the tension by apologizing for his outburst. The issue was he could not forgive Sean. He would always blame him for the death of his son.

During one of their partner meetings, Sean brought up the fact that The Dyck wanted to meet with Chester. Chester was concerned. The Dyck had never contacted him from that day when they spoke on the phones Chester had purchased. Before agreeing to the meeting, Chester said, "the timing is interesting. We should talk about what our investigation has uncovered. Geoff, what have you uncovered?"

Geoff relayed the information he had, which was nothing very enlightening beyond what they currently knew. Sean added his piece, which unveiled little beyond unearthing a few associates that were mostly irrelevant.

Chester was thinking, after a couple moments he added ,"Most importantly, are you certain this investigation was not leaked? You kept it to yourself?"

"Definitely," Sean replied.

"Absolutely ... this is a very sensitive topic. The Dyck would be pissed if he knew we were checking on his affairs." Geoff added.

"Perhaps he knows, and that is why he wants the meeting." Chester proposed.

"I don't think he would have found out." Replied Sean.

Geoff continued, "if he did, I doubt he would want a meeting somewhere down the road – he's a hothead and would react very quickly. Likely sending a hit squad after us."

Chester knew The Dyck was well aware of their investigation from his conversation with Ashton ... but who told him? It was likely Sean, but he could not get a read on him to determine if he was actually lying. Geoff was a possible candidate too but very unlikely. Or perhaps one of them inadvertently shared the information with someone else, who relayed the information to The Dyck. He knew he would have to let this play out. He had previously promised the Clubman he would assist The Dyck. He suspected he may be walking into a trap, so he had to be cautious.

Knowing he had little choice, he said, "Okay, I will agree to the meeting....but it must be in a remote location where nobody could possibly see them. The Dyck was certainly known to the police and they kept a close watch on his every move. We don't want those nosey Detectives to become further suspicious, by having an open meeting with The Dyck."

Sean replied, "Okay, I will contact him and arrange a location ... are you okay with that?"

"Yes, please do, but be sure to give us a couple days to prepare."

Sean arrived at the office the next day and informed Chester they would be meeting at a remote campground in the Okanagan, at a location close to Chute Lake. This was LNa's turf, but The Dyck capitulated as it was remote. The campground had a large clear area ideal for landing a helicopter. Occasionally over the summer, a camper or two might stay there, at this time of the year though there would be nobody around. Chester agreed but added he wanted an advance party to be there before they arrived, The Dyck would likely want the same. Chester also wanted Sanchez to head up his advance party. Sean agreed and said he would let Sanchez know. Chester replied that he would talk to Sanchez himself directly.

They all left Chester's office. Geoff and Sean returned to their respective offices. Chester kept going until he reached Sanchez' office. He stopped at the doorway and said "Hello, Sanchez"

Sanchez looked up from his desk and said, "Hi, boss."

"You are looking hungry. How about I buy you lunch?"

Sanchez was about to decline when he saw Chester give him a wink. "Sure boss, can you give me 10 minutes. I will meet you in your office."

"Perfect. See you in 10," and Chester returned to his office.

***

As they sat down at the restaurant table for lunch, Sanchez looked at Chester and said, "So, what's happening boss?"

Chester replied, "Once again, my friend, I must ask another favour of you."

"Sure thing, what is it?"

"I am to have a meeting with Walter Dyck next week and I need someone to check things out beforehand, and make sure it is all as it should be. I would like you to head up the crew on the ground?"

"Of course, Chester, I thought it was going to be more difficult."

"It is. I need you to again keep this next bit just between you and me – nobody else – not even Sean or Geoff."

"My lips are sealed."

"At this meeting, I suspect there will be an attempt on my life. I can't go into details as to why, but let's just say I will have my life in your hands. That is why I need you to be very discreet. We are meeting at some remote campground in the Okanagan. We will be arriving by helicopter, so I need you to check out possible locations for snipers and any other possible means of taking me out."

Phew, Sanchez whistled. "Are you sure?"

"No, as I said I suspect! I hope nothing comes of it but just in case I need you on my side."

"I'm there."

"Okay, this afternoon, get the details from Sean, we are meeting in one week. Please scout out the location and after your visit, let's meet again to review our game plan and develop contingencies."

"Agreed," then, after a brief pause, Sanchez added, "I know this sounds weird, but thanks for trusting me with this boss."

"Chester – please, my friend."

"Chester," Sanchez replied.

Three days later, Sanchez met Chester in his office. They discussed the meeting and reviewed several possible locations where they could attempt an assassination. The one wild card Sanchez could not cover was the trip to the meeting. He suggested Chester minimize his travel time in the helicopter, where he may be more exposed. They should drive to Penticton, then travel by helicopter from there.

"One final piece," Chester added, "should they be successful, I know one of the conspirators will be Walter Dyck. I would like you to contact Ellis, you remember he is the fellow who devised that arm gun we used to dispose of Ghost?"

"Yes, I remember him"

"Find some device to bring down his helicopter, in case he gets to me first. Make sure it is undetectable."

"Don't think that way Chester."

"We need to cover all contingencies."

Chapter Twenty-Two

Present Day

Looking around the helicopter, there was carnage everywhere. Marci was sprawled on the floor with her head unnaturally ajar. Looking through the front windshield, the forest floor was approaching fast, as Chester instinctively jumped into his seat and latched the seatbelt moments before impact.

Everything was strewn about and they began to roll, this time there were also chucks of trees, rock and metal shards, that had obviously been broken off from some part of their aircraft. Chester was savagely swung about, but he did not lose consciousness. They came to a stop with the remnants of their aircraft positioned right-side up, feet to the ground.

After a few moments, Chester began to survey their situation, as he unbuckled himself and attempted to stand up. His left leg immediately collapsed, and he fell back into his seat. He looked and saw a piece of metal partially embedded into his thigh. As he touched the shard, a sharp piercing pain shot through his leg. This was going to be troublesome he thought, just as his peripheral vision started closing in and slowly faded to black.

***

The air was filled with dust and smoke. The acrid smell of gunpowder was mixed with the metallic smell of blood and death. Chester was caught in that state, somewhere between awake and unconscious. He thought how it was interesting how death had a smell, it was as distinct as fresh baked apple pie, though not as enjoyable. The smell of death was hard to describe; it was sort of the smell of vacancy, distinct and cold.

Slowly, he climbed from this semi-conscious state to a waking state. As the bombardment of thoughts began to clear, he began to appraise his current predicament. He wasn't sure how long he had been unconscious, but he thought it wasn't more than a couple minutes. He gauged the carnage and destruction around him, and he immediately recalled what had just happened.

Rather than react with panic as most people would, Chester remained calm and calculating. He had taught himself to remain calm over many years, he knew this attribute had saved his life many times over.

First thing to determine was whether his leg was operational at all. As he slowly started putting weight on it, the pain shot through him again. He found his suit jacket laying on the floor beside him and wrapped it around his leg like a field tourniquet, slowly, he tested it again and this time the pain while still intense was not debilitating. Next was an assessment to determine who was still alive.

He moved over to Sean and saw a large gaping wound on his shoulder, it was still oozing with blood, which was a good sign, as it likely meant his heart was still beating. He checked his pulse on his carotid artery in his neck, there was still a pulse. He tore the remnants of Sean's shirt to reveal the wound. He rolled these pieces into a grapefruit-sized ball and pressed it against the bleeding wound. He found another article of clothing laying in the cabin and tied it around his shoulder to stop the bleeding. He stumbled over Marci's corpse, as he worked his way through to the cockpit. She was getting revenge from the grave, Chester thought to himself.

After checking everyone over within a few minutes, he ascertained that the co-pilot, Sean, and he were the only survivors of this attempted assassination. The co-pilot slowly started to regain consciousness and once fully awake just looked at Chester and said, "what the hell happened? Everything was routine then all hell broke out. How many are alive?"

"Just you, Sean here, and myself," Chester replied, "the others were not so lucky. I don't think it is very safe for us to remain in what is left of this helicopter. I smell the distinct odour of kerosene, so there is jet fuel leaking somewhere. Can you give me a hand with Sean here?"

The co-pilot carefully picked his way to the cabin. Chester had unbuckled Sean and together they dragged him outside. They rested Sean next to a large tree, and Chester began to survey their surroundings. There was no immediate natural danger, like falling off a cliff, or obvious rocks or trees falling.

They were surrounded by trees, so they could not able to tell where they were. There was black, caustic smoke rising from the wreckage, so he knew somebody would be able to spot them and send rescue. Chester saw the co-pilot with his cell phone in hand checking on coverage. "We're in a dead zone," he said, "not even one bar."

"The smoke will certainly draw somebody's attention and we were only a few minutes out, so soon our party will know something is wrong and begin a search" Chester replied. Just then, Sean began to meekly groan and seemed to be regaining consciousness. Chester looked at Sean's field dressing to ensure it was still effectively stemming the bleeding.

Chester looked up at the co-pilot and said, "well, it looks like we'll have a story to tell." He extended his hand towards the co-pilot and said, "My name is Chester and this chap here is Sean, what is your name?"

"Peter," he replied and shook Chester's hand.

"Sorry about the pilot," Chester said, "have you known him long?"

"Not long, I just met him this morning. He seemed like a nice guy though, I believe he was married but no children."

"That's strange, I thought crews worked together all the time?"

Peter seemed somewhat evasive and just shrugged. "We didn't," he replied. Looking towards Chester's thigh, Peter continued, "That looks nasty. Must hurt like a bugger."

With all the activity, Chester had not checked his own wound. A rather large piece of metal protruded four inches out of his leg; no way to know how deep the shard had penetrated. "Yeah. I'm not getting far in this condition."

Peter looked at the remains of the helicopter. "Maybe the radio in the copter is still working. I'm going to go and check it out."

"Not sure that's a good idea, Peter," Chester replied. "There's still a lot of smoke and gas fumes."

"I'll be careful," Peter said, walking towards the debris. He entered the cabin and came back shortly after shaking his head. "Nope the radio is dead too." Chester noticed Peter seemed to be carrying something that he was hiding from him. As Peter got within a couple steps of Chester, behind him, propped up beside a tree, Sean made a groan. As Peter turned to look at Sean, Chester saw what he was concealing. It was Sean's missing handgun!

With Sean once again returning to his slumber, Peter turned towards Chester. "Somebody really wants you dead," he said matter-of-factly, "you may have thought you were one lucky bastard to survive the crash, in fact you just delayed the inevitable. Marci wasn't the only one you needed to be concerned with. I'm not sure how you evaded Marci, regardless, you will not escape me as well."

Chester coolly began to assess the situation and make a determination on a plan of action....what he needed right now was time. He knew he had to engage Peter in conversation to give him time to shape a plan for his getaway. "Well Peter, it looks like I made a mistake in saving you. My people are very good, so you must be exceptional at your job in order to evade their detection," Chester replied slowly, "Can you at least let me know which of my adversaries finally got me?"

"Well you know it is not very professional to let you know that, however since you won't be able to tell anyone ... sure. Not sure what you did to the valley boys, but they really don't like you. Trying to take you out is very dangerous. You would have to be a real dick, to put a bounty on your head."

"How large?" Chester casually replied. He knew his survival would depend on his ability to keep Peter the assassin talking.

"Let's say more than double my usual rate, now with Marci gone I will be able to collect the entire amount," Peter replied, followed with, "I know you're trying to delay me, I also know by now your people will be searching for you."

Just then, they could hear a helicopter not far away. "I think your guests have decided to leave." Peter smirked. While this discussion was taking place, Chester was also busy surveying his surroundings, not much to use as a weapon. The rocks were either too big to be handled or too small to inflict any damage.

Sean was propped up next to a tree, and slowly the veil of unconsciousness began to lift. He was stirring a little and he seemed to partially open an eye. Chester continued to engage Peter, talking as he evaluated the various options available to himself. Every tactic he devised ended badly for Chester as he had little time. About six feet separated Peter and himself and worse still, he was wounded, and his skewered leg would be of limited use.

Suddenly, from a seeming unconscious state, Sean stood up. Peter turned quickly and saw Sean standing erect, instinctively, he leveled his gun towards him and quickly unloaded two shots into Sean's torso. Chester realized this was his opportunity and with adrenaline pumping through his veins, he rose and pounced on Peter, like a predator about to make his kill. In a single motion as he flew through the air, his hand grabbed the metal shard piercing his thigh. The pain was nearly unbearable as he yanked the metal out. Quick as a leopard mounting its prey, Chester landed on Peter and quickly stabbed him in his exposed neck. Four quick blows and they both fell to the ground. Peter had a startled surprised look, as he reached for his neck with the blood gushing through his finger, his life pulsing away.

Chester had exhausted all his energy. He was overcome with the pain and exertion of the last few moments. He wanted to ensure Peter was dead but could not resist anymore. Like a sun setting on the ocean, one moment it was light and the next it was dark. Just as the last piercing rays of consciousness began to fade, through the fog and pain, Chester faintly heard an explosion.

* * *

Walter Dyck was waiting at the clearing for Chester to arrive when a loud explosion arose from the direction of the valley. Everyone immediately looked towards the noise. Sanchez looked concerned as he looked towards Dyck and said, "something is wrong, I don't like this. You wait here, while we go and see what has happened."

A small smile appeared on Walter Dyck's face. Quickly, his smile dissipated, and he put on an air of concern. "Yes, you should go and check things out, but it is not a good idea for us to hang out here – we will leave. If there is anything we can do, just radio us and we will arrange for help for you." With that, he and his entourage loaded on their awaiting helicopter.

Sanchez and his partner scrambled onto their own helicopter and he barked at their flight crew, "take off now! Something bad has happened, we need to find them quickly!"

Dyck's helicopter rose and eclipsed the tree line with Sanchez and his rescue mission close behind. As they ascended, they noticed a column of smoke rising in a more southerly direction. He directed the pilot towards the smoke only a kilometre or two away. Sanchez noticed Walker Dyck's helicopter must have also spotted the smoke and were headed in the same direction, instead of Northwest towards Kelowna where they came from.

Dyck's helicopter made a wide arching turn around the smoke, they seemed to hover for a moment, then headed off towards the north. As Sanchez' rescue helicopter approached the crash scene, he saw Dyck's helicopter just a short distance away retreating towards the northwest. Then, almost as if in slow motion, it seemed to stall in midair, and small plume of smoke arose from the tail rotor. It then appeared to begin breaking apart, as it spun wildly and quickly plunged into the forest below.

While everyone from the rescue helicopter watched in awe at what was unfolding, Sanchez had a fleeting smile of satisfaction that nobody took note of, as he pocketed a small device that looked similar to a cigarette lighter. As his helicopter hovered above the rising smoke from Chester's crash site, they witnessed Chester fly towards a man holding a gun and, in an instant, blood was being sprayed from the man's neck. Both men collapsed, Sean was lying next to them. They lowered the helicopter to just above the treetops, and from about thirty feet, a ladder emerged and several people scrambled down.

Sanchez was the first one on the ladder, as he got to the last five feet, he jumped, rolled and sprang to his feet all in one motion. Reaching the scene, he found Sean conscious but gravely injured. "Are you okay?"

"I am fine, take care of Chester, he is bleeding badly."

Chester was sprawled next to the dead pilot. The gash in his leg was pulsing blood, quickly Sanchez removed the belt from his waist and made a tourniquet to stem the flow of life. By then, others had shown up on the scene and they attended to Sean. After the triage, Sanchez assessed the situation and decided while Sean may survive, Chester was in a grave situation and needed an immediate extraction. He pulled his radio from his jacket and called the helicopter hovering just overhead.

"Do you have a winch and an extraction basket on board?" he asked hurriedly.

"We have a carrying basket, but no winch. There is a clearing about 100 meters to the west, where we may be able land," the pilot replied.

"Okay, can you lower the basket and we will carry him over to the clearing."

***

With the basket down, they nestled Chester into it and attached the harnesses to ensure he didn't move. While Sanchez was doing this, another of the group was wrapping Sean's shoulder and preparing him for the evacuation. Sean was conscious but barely. He groaned and complained anytime somebody touched his shoulder. After getting their patients ready, the crew made their way to the clearing where the helicopter had positioned itself.

They scrambled over branches and rocks; the uneven terrain was difficult to navigate. With every misstep and bump, Sean would agonize, and his complexion appeared to be turning from white to grey. Sean was struggling, but despite the pain he got to the clearing just behind Sanchez, who was carrying Chester. Upon entering the clearing, Chester and Sean were quickly loaded and secured. Sanchez had two of his accompanying crew jump in alongside him to facilitate first aid on the brief ride to Kelowna. Sanchez remained behind to clean up. More importantly, he needed to investigate

The rotors began cutting through the air and they ascended, with both Chester and Sean on board. As they passed over the remnants of Walker Dyck's helicopter, they noticed among the smoking carnage some movement, there were likely survivors. Identification was impossible though, as the smoke obscured the crash site.

Chapter Twenty-Three

Chester felt comfortably warm and content in a surreal, unworldly world. He was adrift in a hazy dreamland traveling through a foggy mist then suddenly, he was in elementary school, and he was ten years old once again. The school had these wooden banisters running beside the stairs to prevent the kids from falling down several floors when horsing around on the stairs. Of course, kids being kids, they would slide down the banisters when the teachers were not watching. The rails were varnished and further polished with repeated slides from mischievous children. As a rule of thumb, the standard scene would play out like this; slide, teacher catch you, receive a scolding, slide again on next opportunity. Hundreds, if not thousands of kids, had slid down these banisters.

Chester seemed to be somehow hovering above himself watching himself as a schoolboy gleefully sliding down the bannister from the second to the first floor, he felt a stabbing pain in his right butt cheek. Upon reaching the destination, the aching in his bottom escalated. He gingerly jumped off just in front of the teacher, who was poised to give him hell. Instead of dishing out a reprimand though, the teacher just looked curiously at him. At that point, Chester's right cheek started to really burn, with a searing, piercing ache. He looked behind and saw a spear of wood sticking out of his pants. This shard was at least a foot long and looked much like a matador's lance having stuck a bull. Quickly, he realized he had been impaled right in the ass! He reached behind and yanked the offending piece from his skewered bottom.

Of course, it didn't come out cleanly and snapped off right at the puncture point. The embarrassment was so extreme that he needed to shrug this off and nonchalantly walked to his next class, while the teacher and several classmates watched with their jaws agape. He was certain nobody would notice the limp in his gait and the agony each successive step brought. Somehow, he struggled through the next class, which fortunately was the last of the day. As the final bell rang, his ass was pulsating, like someone beating a large percussion drum in his much more private sensitive area. He could feel the impaled shard driving deeper with every step.

He thought he had suffered the greatest embarrassment when he explained to his Mom what happened. Nope, it got worse, he had to suffer the indignation of having his Mom see his butt as she tried to extricate the shard. You could call it a sliver, but a sliver implies small; this piece was more like an arrowhead firmly implanted in his derriere and it hurt. As his Mom rummaged around, he maintained stoicism even though he was quite concerned she may hit a major artery and result in his bleeding to death. This was more like surgery than a minor sliver removal! After what seemed like several hours (likely about 20 minutes), she finally admitted defeat, while she removed some of it, there was still a piece deeply imbedded and she could not remove it. So now, he had the further humiliation of having to go to the doctor and explain how he was innocently skewered in the ass by a piece of wood.

***

As slowly as the light begins to lighten the darkened sky at daybreak, Chester slowly began to realize he was no longer a ten-year-old boy and the pain in his butt migrated to his leg.

Unlike a daybreak that unveils a bright start to a new day, Chester remained foggy. Like heavy fog that hangs between mountain peaks, with the sun trying to pierce through the morning mists, Chester knew it was light but the details surrounding him remained shrouded in a haze. Chester knew he felt a sharp stabbing pain in his leg, but somehow, he remained detached.

Gradually, he began to be able to concentrate a bit and recognise his surroundings. The veil of unconsciousness lifted and through the fog, he heard a voice. The voice was familiar, but he could not identify who it was.

"Chester. Chester," he heard and gradually realized the voice was his partner, Geoff. He recognised Geoff's voice, but he did not recognise his surroundings.

"Chester, are you coming back to us buddy,"? Geoff repeated.

Chester groggily replied, "yeah, where the hell am I, and what are you doing here?"

What Geoff heard was, "yaaah, whaaa," and the rest was indecipherable, a sort of mumbling, warbling grunt. Like waking with a hangover from an evening of drink, slowly the cobwebs that permeated Chester's mind evaporated and the pain emerged. The pain was not in his head though, it was throughout his body, but mostly in his right leg.

"Can you repeat that buddy?" Geoff said.

Chester felt like his mouth was stuffed with cotton balls and tasted slimy and sticky, but this time his words were recognizable, "I said ... where the hell am I? And how the hell did I get here"?

"You are one lucky bastard," Geoff replied, then continued, "or maybe I should say tough bastard and too stubborn to die".

The memory of the crash and attack by the co-pilot started coming back, "the last I remember, I was scrapping with the co-pilot as he tried to kill me," Chester replied.

"Well, it's a long story … but the bottom line is you survived, and the co-pilot did not. We didn't think you would survive either. The doctor said the odds of you surviving were not much better than winning a lottery." Geoff continued, "but of course he didn't know you and how much fight you had in you. You have been in a coma while you recovered. They induced the coma to give you time to heal. Awake you may have caused irreversible damage if you had attempted to move."

With great effort, Chester sputtered, "How long?"

"It's been eight weeks! You lost so much blood you were nearly drained empty! The doctors said they have never seen anyone come back from that amount of blood loss." Geoff replied. Then in a joking fashion said, "I think you were down to your last quart."

Chester managed a hint of a smile, then remembered Sean. "How about Sean? Did he make it?" he asked.

"Yes, he was conscious when they got to you. Despite his shoulder being half ripped off, Sanchez said he still directed all of them. Then, when they got to the hospital, he wouldn't let them look at his wounds until you were being taken care of. His shoulder will never be the same and the bullets missed any major organs, but he is alive and started flirting with the nurses while still in recovery."

"Where exactly am I? Are we back in Vancouver?" Chester asked.

"No, we are in Kelowna. They brought you to Kelowna, as it was the closest and time was the enemy. They have a good trauma department here and obviously it was the right decision. It was touch and go for several weeks; the doctors felt moving you would have created more stress than you could handle. Remember, they didn't give you much of a chance anyway." Geoff lowered his voice to speak directly into Chester's ear then quietly said, "there are several things we need to talk about, but they can wait for a more private setting. The cops will be in shortly to ask about your version of what happened in the woods. Nathaniel Ostranski advised you just say you do not remember. The doctors have already warned them you would likely have no recollection of the event, hazy fragments at best."

At that point, Chester became aware there were other people in the room. He looked around and noticed two other ladies, likely a doctor and nurse. There was a lot of equipment attached to him - measuring, beeping and generally making a distracting noise. With the noise distraction, Chester felt quite sure his response would not be overheard. However, to be certain, he just gave Geoff a wink of acknowledgement.

The door of his room then opened and in walked two suits. Chester smiled to himself. Even if he hadn't been warned about their presence, Chester could pick out these cops at a hundred meters. They were those nuisance detectives Bailey and Brine. They both pulled out badges and introduced themselves as Detectives Bailey and Brine from the IHIT department.

Chester looked at them for minute, then said, "I know you. I seem to recall speaking to you at my office one day. I cannot recall what we talked about though." This was a fabrication, designed to show them his memory had not completely returned. He knew very well they had questioned him about Sanchez.

"Yes, that's right. Though at the time, we were not assigned to the IHIT department," Brine replied.

Detectives Bailey and Brine were very anxious to hear what Chester had to say about what happened in the forest. They had been able to piece together much of the scene. They were quite certain someone tried to assassinate Chester on the helicopter and that the pilot and several members of Chester's crew were killed. This led to the helicopter crashing and between the gunfire and the crash, all had been killed except for the three survivors. They were further able to determine that either Chester or Sean slashed the co-pilot, Peter Miller's throat. They were quite certain it was Chester but could not find any evidence linking either of them directly. With all the blood scattered over the scene, blood analysis was useless, fingerprints had conveniently disappeared and the fact that both were almost completely incapacitated further cast a doubt on the scene.

"Mr. Moehr, we have a few questions we would like to ask you," Detective Bailey began. "First, we need to talk about the day of the crash. What do you remember?"

Chester took a moment, as if he was processing the question and searching his memories for an answer. Weakly, he replied, "I am sorry officers, what crash"?

"On the day in question, you boarded a chartered helicopter from the Penticton airport at around 6:30 AM. May we ask where you were going?" Detective Brine asked.

Once again, Chester feigned he was processing the question and replied, "Once again I apologize, I do not recall that. Everything is rather foggy. I do not recall boarding a helicopter".

"What is the last thing you do recall, Mr. Moehr"? Detective Brine replied.

Chester thought for a moment, then responded, "I recall having dinner at DC Steak house, I was with Sean and a couple of the guys. I do not remember driving home though. Perhaps I had too much to drink".

Detectives Bailey and Brine now knew they were being played. Chester Moehr, they had discovered, was a cold-hearted gangster. Not just the fortunate businessman everyone perceived. He was also extremely smart and calculating. He would never have so much to drink that he blacked out. He needed to maintain control and would never succumb to drink. Just as they were both coming to the conclusion they were being played, Chester added,

"No, I don't think that would be true, while I love a nice Claret, I cannot remember the last time I was drunk. But for the life of me, I cannot recall leaving the restaurant".

The detectives exchanged guarded glances. "What can you tell us about Walter Dyck?" Detective Bailey continued.

"I don't know a great deal about the man. He wanted to make an investment in one of our property development projects a few years ago. After completing some rudimentary background checks we do with all our potential investors, we discovered he is not a nice man, he is mean and cruel even though he pretends to be a regular church-going Christian. Quite frankly, I don't like his kind."

"When was the last time you saw him?" Bailey retorted.

"Hmmm, I'm not sure," Chester pondered the question, "I believe I saw him a couple of weeks ago at the Chamber of Commerce luncheon, when Stephen Harper gave a speech."

"And you haven't seen him since then?" Bailey replied.

"No, I don't think so," Chester's brow furrowed, as if trying to think. After a brief pause, "Yes, I am quite certain that was the last time I saw him. However, I just found out I have been in a coma for the past eight weeks, so my memory is not in top form at the moment." Never answer a question with a straight yes or no, Chester always said. Always leave some 'wiggle room' so you can't be boxed in. Today he was definitely heeding his own advice.

"Ok," Bailey said with a bit of exasperation, then turning to the doctor he said, "When will more of his memory return?"

"Not an easy question to answer," Doctor Jessie replied, "sometimes memories return in a couple days or weeks. Other times they never return, or just fragments return. I am sorry ... it is not an exact science."

The Detectives knew they were unlikely to get anything from Chester today, and perhaps never. Bailey thought he would try one more tactic and watch for Chester's reaction. "Walter Dyck died on the same day as the crash, his helicopter crashed close to your crash site. Do you know what happened?"

Feigning surprise, Chester replied, "Oh My God, I didn't like the guy, but it's sad he died," careful not to say 'killed', as that would indicate he knew something. He continued, "what was he doing in the same area?" Both detectives saw Chester's reaction of surprise.

"That is an interesting question, Mr. Moehr. Hopefully, you can shed some light on that in a couple of days." The detectives then thanked the doctor and nurse and left the room.

Chester motioned Geoff to get closer and whispered in his ear, "The Dyck is dead?"

* * *

Spying the smile on The Dyck's face as they circled, Sanchez removed the control device from his pocket then remotely activated the charge. After ensuring Chester and Sean were off on their rescue helicopter, Sanchez turned to the other two guards and told them to wait behind for the emergency people. He was going to The Dyck's crash site to check for survivors. He turned and scampered through the forest floor, coming to a small incline he could see smoke rising from the crest. He hustled up the rise and saw a fellow. He was bloodied, with torn, mottled clothes and obviously in distress, but still alive. Sanchez ran towards him and said, "Hey, are you okay?"

The guy turned and said, "I'll live."

"Is there anyone else alive?"

"Yes, there's a chap over there who is pretty banged up, but he was alive when I checked." He turned towards the smoldering helicopter remains and said, "not sure over there, I haven't …"

As the guy turned towards the helicopter, Sanchez quickly darted behind him, and quick as a cheetah reached underneath the guys chin to grab the opposing jaw, then placing another hand on the top of his head gave a quick twist. You could hear the bones crunching as he dropped, like a 25-kilo bag of potatoes.

He checked each body for a pulse. He found a guard that was incapacitated but still alive. A quick twist of the neck and he joined his buddy. He then made his way to the helicopter where he found another guard alive, once more a quick twist and he died. Then he found Walter Dyck. The Dyck was badly injured but remained alive and unconscious. Sanchez stood over him, looked down at his face and tried to wake him. Groggily, Walter Dyck's eyes opened and after a moment, his eyes widened with the realization of his predicament. He knew his fate was sealed.

Sanchez found a sharp scrap of steel that would act like a rudimentary blade, and slowly opened The Dick's abdomen. More of a tearing action than a cutting. The Dyck just gagged as he saw his intestines begin to unravel from where his belly button once was. He had a look of horror as he fumbled in vain to hold his entrails in place. Sanchez then flipped him over, grabbed his hair and dragged him across the floor towards the door. As he dragged The Dyck across the floor, pieces of metal and other protrusions snagged his guts and they splayed across the floor leaving a foul-smelling trail of excrement and digestive fluids as his intestines ripped open. The Dick could only manage a gurgling groan through the excruciating pain knowing death would soon envelope him.

As they approached the door, Sanchez surveyed his handiwork and thought the scene sort of looked like a squid with its tentacles dragging behind it. He checked The Dyck's pulse and was shocked to discover he remained alive. While Sanchez knew he could never recover from his wounds, he needed to ensure his demise. Once at the door, he noticed a protruding piece of metal from what had once been the door with a rubber seal. Now the rubber hung loose, with the sharp edge exposed. He slowly dragged The Dick's neck over the edge, severing his carotid artery and his life pulsed away.

Before leaving the forest scene, Sanchez double-checked and removed all evidence of anyone having been there. With the site cleaned up, there was no evidence to indicate it was or wasn't entirely an accident. Complete with The Dyck slowly dragging himself across the floor and passing out at the door which had slit his throat. He suspected the investigators would not believe it wasn't intentional, but without any evidence to the contrary, they would have to list it as an accident.

The last thing Sanchez did was check to see that the magnetic device was still in place. It worked as advertised and there was no sign of any nefarious acts. The small explosion caused the device to blow off and would be scattered somewhere in the forest, likely in several pieces.

Chapter Twenty-Four

After a few more days of recuperation, Chester was feeling stronger. The doctors seemed to take great pleasure in reminding him how fortunate he was to survive this ordeal. Chester had asked Geoff to arrange for transportation back to his estate in Anmore. For the next several weeks, his recovery would consist of rest. Being home would be more restful than sitting in some hospital room.

Geoff made the arrangements, including a personal care nurse who would stay with Chester during his recovery. Sean was also confined to his home. Geoff indicated he was staying at his house with Ava. Then, with a shy grin, he said, "I think it's an on-again stage."

The following day, Chester checked himself out of the hospital and was wheeled out the front doors to his waiting Rolls. Chester loved the Rolls and was always extremely comfortable being wrapped in its sumptuous Italian leather seats. Today though, he was a little apprehensive about the drive back to Anmore. He would be sitting for a prolonged period and despite the luxurious surroundings, the pain of sitting in a prone position may eventually overwhelm him. Geoff, walking beside him, noted the look of concern on Chester's face. He laughed and said, "Don't worry Chester, we are not driving all the way back. The car is only taking us to the airport." Chester laughed in reply, though it was more a laugh of relief, rather than a laugh of amusement.

LNa had a contract with Air Charter Services and Chester had flown with them many times over the past few years. Today, they arrived at the airport and drove straight to a hanger outside the main terminal. Sitting there was a … helicopter! Chester once again balked a little and Geoff replied, "We can take you right to your front doorstep with this. If we used a jet, we would have to land at an airport, and you would then have to drive back home from there. I know your last helicopter trip ended badly but remember … when your horse bucks you off, you need to get right back on."

"You're right of course, no sense in shying away from a helicopter just because I was nearly killed in one?" Chester replied, while giving Geoff a sly and slightly sarcastic smile.

***

Less than 90 minutes later, Chester was in his own bed with his nurse in attendance. She gave him a couple of pills and explained it would help him sleep. Even though he had mostly slept for the past several weeks, he found the trip had indeed tired him out. He took his pills and quietly drifted off to that tender place, where he dreamt about Clarie. Instead of being haunted by Clarie's death, he only dreamt about his laughing and the joy he brought to Chester's life. At one point, he thought he had laughed out loud when he dreamt of Clarie and the seafood incident during their Mediterranean trip.

A few hours later he awoke and, as the grogginess dissipated, he realized he was in his own bed and the sun was still shining. Sitting in the corner was his personal care nurse, she smiled at him, and said, "good morning Mr. Moehr. I think you had a good rest."

"Yes, I did, I feel quite rested."

"I think you had some good dreams; at one point you were laughing in your sleep."

"I did indeed."

***

Over the three weeks that followed, Chester began to feel more energetic and physically had much less pain. Tomorrow he was scheduled to start physiotherapy. The Physiotherapist would arrive at 10:00 and he would begin with a one-hour session, adding 15 minutes every second day, as long as he could tolerate the routine. His home gym had been modified with stretching equipment to facilitate his recovery. One particular apparatus, which Chester nicknamed 'the rack,' resembled a medieval torture device where they slowly ripped their victim's appendages off. While it likely didn't get too many accurate confessions, it certainly would have caused a great deal of pain. Likewise, this stretching device would inflict a great deal of pain while stretching Chester's limbs.

Detectives Bailey and Brine made several visits to Chester's estate, unfortunately for them, Chester could not remember any of the events between leaving the Penticton airport and awaking in the hospital. They didn't seem to like his answers, but they could not force him to remember. In reality, Chester recalled each and every event in detail; from Marci turning into an assassin, to Peter trying to kill him after Chester rescued him from the wreckage of the helicopter. Furthermore, he definitely knew who was behind the assassination attempt. Luckily, the pilot had seen what was happening and veered the helicopter off balance. If not, Marci may have succeeded. Instead, she lost her footing and scattered shot throughout the fuselage, accidentally catching Sean in his shoulder.

The Ostranskis came by once a week with various documents to sign. They assured Chester that, while the authorities suspected Chester was responsible for the death of the co-pilot, they had no evidence to prove it with all the carnage strewn about. They could not get any fingerprints on the metal shard that was embedded in the co-pilot's neck. By this time, Chester had passed out, but he was quite certain he owed his freedom to Sanchez. He likely wiped Chester's fingerprints off the metal before the police arrived.

Geoff visited at least twice a week. On one of his visits earlier this week, he brought Sean with him. He said his doctor had told him it was finally okay for him to travel. On another of Geoff's visits when he was alone, he brought up the conversation Chester had with Sean before the crash. He asked if it was true that Chester had suggested he step back and let Sean take control of the organization.

"I was certainly contemplating it." Chester paused then continued, "with all that has happened these past couple of months, though I need to re-evaluate. Neither Sean nor I are in any shape to properly run the business right now. Thank God for you." Chester paused again and cleared his throat, "what would you think about letting Sean have control?"

"TFM," Geoff replied, "we are a team and as you constantly have reminded us over the years, we are stronger as a team. That being said, you know I love Sean, but I am just not sure he is cut out for the job."

"How about you?"

Geoff laughed, "I have thought about it, but no, I like my current position. I am not sure I could make some of the difficult decisions both you and Sean can make. I like where I am. We need you Chester. You can step back a bit, but we need you at the helm. Sorry, I'm not sure that's what you wanted to hear, but it is the truth."

"Thanks for the vote of confidence my friend."

Chester never mentioned stepping down again. His resolve had returned, and more than ever he wanted to run the company. He liked the idea of stepping back a bit as he would love to spend more time on his yacht.

* * *

Chester's recovery had progressed nicely, and he had taken to going on long hikes again, at first, he was accompanied by a bodyguard, but lately he was venturing out alone. On one of these hikes, he grabbed his blackberry and texted Ashton – 'Talk?'

A few minutes, later a text came back – 'Wigwam Inn? You name the date.'

Chester replied – 'Tomorrow – lunch in the restaurant?'

'See you then.'

Chester knew this was too public, but quite frankly, while he had begun hiking again, he had not recovered enough to meet at their previous spot. The next morning, he arranged for his cigarette boat to drop him off at the Inn. He arrived at 10:00 and spent a couple of hours drinking coffee on the dock before going to the restaurant for lunch. After a few minutes, Ashton Boyle arrived and walked over to Chester's table.

"You gave us quite a scare, you have lost some weight, but other than that you look pretty good."

"Thanks Ash, Yes, not something that was much fun?"

"I'm glad you contacted me. Since that fateful day, we have been having a shortage of product. With Walter no longer available we would like you to pick up his portion. Are you okay with that?"

"Most definitely"

"I suspect you know it was Walter behind the attempt?"

"I do. But he wasn't working alone! Sean was working with him. I have been able to put together a lot of pieces. It had to be either Sean or Geoff who let The Dyck know we were investigating him. Then it all came together, when I realized the Bean was not the intended victim that day when Geoff and Sanchez were caught up in the crossfire. I was supposed to be driving to the restaurant by myself. We were delayed, as you had just informed us of the large shipment from Montreal. Sean was very upset and now I know it's because he planned on it being me. After our dinner that evening, he went to see The Dyck. There was no reason for this, and more importantly if there was a legitimate reason, why hide it. Finally, he had arranged for the meeting in the Okanagan. Why would The Dyck make contact through him? Sean always wanted to be the head man and it burned him that I was the lead. He must have followed us that day we met at Deep Cove. If I hadn't stopped for coffee, I would not have seen him drive by. Too many coincidences all pointing to him."

Ashton was shocked, "that puts a different spin on things."

"Not really, the purpose for this meeting is to ask for permission. Sean cannot be trusted and must be eliminated. I would never do this without your approval." Then he added, "we will fill the void in product for you."

"Permission Granted." With that, they exchanged goodbyes and Ashton left.

The waiter came around and asked Chester if his visitor would be joining Chester for lunch. Chester replied no, he was just someone he met at a charity ball a while back. He then asked, "what is the special today?" Chester was thrilled it was once again wild halibut. He enjoyed every morsel of the halibut and ordered a very nice bottle of Chablis, and very much enjoyed a glass with his meal. After signing the bill, he told the waiter he could share the remaining wine with the kitchen staff. The waiter was shocked, Chester had only one glass and at $1000 a bottle it meant there was $800 left in the bottle. Chester asked for a double espresso that he would drink on the dock while waiting for his pickup. The waiter put out a large umbrella on one of the outdoor tables and wiped down the chair to dry it. It was, after all, a cold rainy day

* * *

The following day, Chester informed his staff he had decided to finish his recuperation on his yacht. He went to Clarence Hall and asked Anne if she would like to join him. She had been suffering a great deal with the loss of Clarie, and he thought she may like a change of scenery. While he was in the hospital, she apparently made weekly trips to visit him. Once he was out of his coma, she came up to visit him twice. She thanked him, but said she had a few things planned over the next couple of weeks. Chester suggested she join him when she could. It was an open invitation.

The next day, he went to the office and informed them there as well. He once again made arrangements with Nancy to receive updates. He suggested to Geoff and Sean that they come out and spend some time on his yacht while he was recuperating. If they let him know before they arrived, he would make sure his helicopter was waiting for them at the airport. It would be good for the three of them to spend some time together.

He stopped in to visit his friend Ellis on the way back home that evening

****

Two days later, Chester arrived in Athens. After his Canadair Jet touched down and taxied to a private hanger, a car was waiting to take him to his yacht moored at Piraeus, just outside Athens.

Boarding 'The Clarie' brought back memories of the previous summer he had spent with his son. Once again, the memories were good memories interspersed with a few pangs of remorse. He fought back the sadness and chose to focus on the positive. The travel had tired Chester, he was much stronger, but he had not fully regained his vitality. After having a nap, he informed the captain they could leave. Chester liked being on deck when they left a port. For some reason, he found it relaxing watching the shore slowly fade into the distance.

Over the next few days, they worked their way up the Adriatic towards Venice. The first day they stopped in Patras Greece, Chester went onshore and visited the ancient ruins of Patras Castle built by Justinian I. Justinian I was better known for building the Hagia Sophia in Istanbul. He had initially wanted to visit Agios Andreas, but after arriving in Patras, decided it was just another church and instead went to the Achaia Clauss, a winery just outside Patras. He tasted some of the wines, including a red wine it was famous for, called Mavrodaphne. Chester thought it was quite good. He didn't particularly like Greek wines, but this one was unique. It was a sweet dessert wine and Chester decided to pick up a case for his cellar.

For the next few days, they worked their way up past the Ionian Islands and the Albanian coast. They stopped at Dubrovnik briefly, before continuing on to Venice. Chester filled his days catching up on work, doing a lot of reading, watching several movies, and of course the requisite two sessions of physio every day. He had plenty of time to think.

Since Clarie's passing, something inside Chester died too. At first, he thought he wanted to step back and just live out the rest of his life traveling and thinking about what might have been. Despondency had overwhelmed him, his spirit had been assaulted with gloom and he felt, he may never rise above the gloom. Now, he still felt like something was permanently broken, but his zeal for life had returned. Perhaps not as strong or in the same way as it was when Clarie was around, but still it was burning in his essence.

Ironic, he thought, that betrayal and a near death experience somehow healed the despair he felt since Clarie's death. His fight to recover re-instilled his own vim and vigour. Sean had hurt him badly. Ironically, that fact also reignited the fire that was waning. He decided it was time to act and get on with life.

He picked up his Blackberry and sent a text to both Sean and Geoff – 'Senior partners meeting, new developments. Meet on my yacht. Will be in Venice in one day, will wait for you there. We will travel to Malta on The Clarie, should take a week or so. Stay as long as you wish, lots of food, wine and booze.' Geoff would arrive the day they made port in Venice. Sean had some matters to attend to and would be arriving two days later.

* * *

Chester was sitting on the lower covered deck of The Clarie, watching the tourists hustle and bustle taking in the sights. He was struck by how other cities always compared themselves to this city. The Venice of the north, the Venice of the East etc. He couldn't really understand these comparisons as this gorgeous city spread out in front of him was incomparable.

Chester noticed a Maserati Quattroporte pull up to the dock and he knew it had to be Geoff. Chester was not what you would call an aficionado of luxury cars, but he recognised a Maserati as he owned one several years ago. The driver went around the rear of the vehicle and opened the door. Geoff got out and immediately stretched his arms over his head, like he was trying to grab the sun that shone brilliantly over an azure Italian sky.

Chester stood up and walked towards the edge of the deck, past the area shaded by the upper deck and into the sunshine. He waved towards Geoff. Somewhat groggily, Geoff looked around taking in the splendour, then he noticed Chester waving from a yacht moored on the docks and waved back. He spoke with the driver and started down the private dock towards The Clarie. Chester sent one of the stewards out to pick up Geoff's luggage and give permission at the security desk for Geoff to enter.

As Geoff came aboard, he looked around and said, "Okay, now I understand why you like this lifestyle. This boat is spectacular."

Chester laughed, as he shook his head, "Ship, my friend. Welcome." They embraced and joyfully patted each other's back.

"It has been a long day for you already. Are you hungry or thirsty? Would you like to rest for a while?"

"Rest, hell no. That's the great thing about the charter service, I actually had a good night's rest. The plane had a queen-sized bed on it, and fortunately we escaped any turbulence, so I was able to sleep very well. I am fresh as a daisy. I would love a coffee and a tour though."

"Latte, correct?"

Geoff nodded. The steward left and returned with a latte on a tray along with various types of sugar. Geoff added some raw sugar and looking towards Chester said, "lead on, my good man."

Chester proudly guided him throughout the yacht and pointed out where Geoff's stateroom was located. His suitcase was already in his room and an attendant was busily unpacking his suitcase. After touring the ship, they returned to the lower deck. Geoff saw the hot tub and decided this would feel very good, he went to the change room and inside found several pairs of both men's and women's bathing suits. Locating his size, he changed and returned to the deck. A couple of minutes later, Chester arrived wearing his trunks also.

Even though the upper part of Chester`s thigh was covered with his swimming trunks, there was a nasty red scar that started at his knee and traveled up and under his trunks. Additionally, Chester was noticeably thinner and had a few other scars on his torso, but nothing as glaring as his thigh. Chester noticed Geoff looking at his scars and said, "courtesy of The Dyck."

"You have also lost a fair bit of weight."

"I've gained ten pounds since coming home. Recovery is still a work in progress, but I am much better than I was. Let's enjoy the hot tub. Want a beer?"

As they crawled into the tub, another steward came and asked Geoff what sort of beer he wanted, "Guinness, of course."

They sat there for an hour or so while soaking their stresses away. They decided to eat on the ship that evening and after dinner go into town for a few cocktails. After Geoff had enjoyed several beers, he decided he could use a nap before dinner. This was fine as Chester had his physio session and his physiotherapist acted like a drill sergeant.

Later that afternoon, Chester had showered, dressed and was out on the deck when Geoff arrived, stating he'd had a great afternoon nap. He sat at the table beside Chester.

Chester looked at him, "I'll bet you're wondering what the meeting is about?"

"Yes, however I know better than to ask you. You will tell us when you are ready."

"Well, I had a meeting with Clubman just before I left. He wants to double our quota once again."

"Holy Shit, Chester, that's a lot of product – and mountains of cash."

"Can we handle it?"

"Yes, we may have to start using the submarine system, as I am not sure we can increase the toy factory that much."

"Toy factory?" Chester gave a curious look.

"It's what we have started calling it. Better than plastic disassembly rendering system."

Chester laughed, "Yup, you're right there."

"So, does this mean you have made a decision on the future?"

"Yup."

"But you're not ready to talk about it. Am I right?"

"Yup."

They had dinner that evening which the chef prepared for them in honour of Geoff's arrival. Geoff loved lamb. The chef slowly roasted a rack of lamb with fresh herbs foraged locally. Of course, it was served with a special risotto dish called risi e bisi, a local speciality, paired with a very nice Masseto from the Tuscany region. After dinner, they went into town to a club recommended by a fellow mariner Chester met at the pier. This club had an excellent selection of vintage wines, ports and Cognac. Instead of playing head-banging music, this club was known for its classical music. A tenor was the feature act.

Geoff was singing his own version of an aria, as the alcohol had somehow turned him into a tenor. They weaved slightly as they walked down the pier toward The Clarie. Chester had a couple of cognacs and several soda waters, Geoff on the other hand, had imbibed with several additional cognacs, a few ports, and many cocktails. They had a wonderful evening, just like the old days when they were carefree and enjoying each other's company.

Tomorrow, Sean would arrive.

***

The following morning, they had a late breakfast at St. Mark's Square. There was an open-air restaurant that was packed in the summer, like sardines in a can. Tourist season wasn't in full swing yet, so being a warm morning they decided to enjoy the city. Sean had arrived and was on route to the restaurant. Geoff was nursing a bit of a hangover as he gingerly soothed his aching head with a cappuccino smothered with honey. Chester looked up and saw Sean walking down the square towards them. He stood to let him know where they were.

Sean exchanged greetings with Geoff and Chester and said, "This place is gorgeous, I can't believe I haven't been here before."

"One of the wonders of the world," Geoff retorted with a wry smirk.

Sean laughed as he looked towards Geoff, "bit of a tough night buddy?"

"Too many cognacs ... and ports ... and whatever else I drank."

Chester and Sean both laughed.

Chester spoke, "after breakfast we can go back to the yacht and you can rest, or we can do the tourist thing and view some of the sites in Venice. We can rent a gondola, so we do not have to walk too much. You guys decide."

Both agreed going to the yacht and getting a little rest in before doing the tourist thing would be nice. They ordered breakfast and like the old days, they laughed and talked and generally acted like their friendship was still intact. After their meals were served, Chester informed Sean about his meeting with Clubman and the increased volume of their quota. Sean asked if they could handle the volume and Geoff reassured him they could. After eating and heading to the car, Geoff said, "we need to do this more often."

Chester could tell Sean was a little tentative at first. They hadn't spent any time together outside of work since the scuffle. Obviously, Sean believed Chester's invitation was his way of extending an olive branch. However, as their extended breakfast turned into a business discussion, Chester could see Sean was becoming more relaxed.

Back at the yacht, Chester and Geoff toured Sean around. Sean's stateroom was two doors down from Geoff's. Chester said, "we all know how Geoff snores when he's been drinking. So, I decided to put a little separation between him and the rest of us. Since I suspect there will be plenty of drinking." They all laughed again, and Geoff and Sean retired for a rest.

When they woke up, they had a brief lunch, then headed back toward the city. They had arranged a gondola to tour them around the city, they visited the Doge palace, St Mark's Basilica and of course, all the bridges and canals that meandered through Venice. Three long-time friends enjoying spending the day laughing and simply enjoying each other's company.

That evening, The Clarie left Venice and headed south along Italy's eastern shore. They leisurely sailed down the coast and made many stops in different sightseeing locales. Sean had done some scuba diving and they stopped at San Nicola di Tremiti which is a small island off the coast well known for renowned diving. The engineer onboard was an experienced diver, so he dove with Sean.

Sean was thrilled and the excitement of the dive created a glow about him. They anchored just outside of Lecce, which is on the heel of the boot of Italy. The following day, they would head for Malta.

* * *

The next day proved to be a very lazy day spent sunning, talking and a great deal of laughing. Shortly after lunch, they began drinking. Chester had several gin and tonics, though they were mostly tonic with a splash of gin. Enough for flavour but little more. By dinner time, the bottle of Tanqueray remained almost three-quarters full. He had a glass of wine with dinner. He appeared to be tipsier than the volume of alcohol would dictate.

Geoff and Sean were quite intoxicated by dinner. After dinner, they lounged on the lower deck as the sun gently tripped the light as it eclipsed the horizon. After an hour, the enveloping darkness of the night conspired with the rhythmic hum of the engines to coax Geoff into a nap. As he lay deep in slumber on a chaise lounge, Sean was swaying at the rear railing just looking out over the blackness of the sea. One of the attendants witnessed Sean was quite inebriated, and, swaying dangerously close to the railing, asked if he was alright and if he could bring him a chair. Sean indicated he was fine and just enjoying the gentle roll of the ocean. The attendant returned to his duties.

Chester was seated at a chaise lounge close to Geoff. Geoff was making a cadenced whistling type of noise with his mouth slightly agape. With Geoff deep in slumber, Chester looked around and noted all the attendants were occupied somewhere else on the ship. It was just the three of them on the deck. He reached under his chair and located a pouch that was fastened under his chair. He located the flap of the pouch and removed a small device he had picked up from his friend Ellis a couple of weeks earlier. He removed an object that looked like a piece of bamboo about the length of a cigarette. He quietly and slowly walked towards Sean who was swaying with the motion of the sea. As he stealthily approached to within a few feet, he once again looked over his shoulder to ensure their privacy, then holding up the pipe, blew the curare laden dart towards Sean.

Sean was stunned as something stung him on his neck. He slapped at his neck to swat the offending insect and saw Chester standing beside him. "Damn mosquitos," he said.

"I have never forgotten it's because of you that my son died."

Sean was suddenly jolted back to sobriety and tried a calming tactic, "seriously Chester, it's more my Mom's fault than mine."

"That may be … but, it wasn't your Mom that conspired to kill me."

Alarm was written across Sean's face, "What the fuck are you talking about?"

Calmly Chester replied, "I know you tried to have me killed the day the Bean was assassinated outside our office building. Pure fucking luck they got the Bean instead."

"No fucking way," Sean protested.

"And you conspired with that fucker, The Dyck, to have me assassinated at our meeting in the Okanagan."

"Now you're going too far! Why would I have my shoulder shot to pieces."

"Marci and the co-pilot Peter didn't know you were in on it. They were just working for The Dyck."

"This is fucking ridiculous." Sean spat out.

"And this fucking charade has come to an end," Chester venomously replied, just as he took a swing at Sean. His fist landed squarely on Sean's cheek and he staggered but did not fall. Chester had unleashed such force that he spun about and fell himself. In a prone position, he noticed the curare laden dart lying on the deck. He gasped when he noticed the glass ampule inside was still full. That bastard … he'd slapped it away before the venom could be delivered.

"You fucker … you deserved to die!" Sean snapped back, just as he was balling his fist to take a swing. He reached back and let go with a roundhouse blow that caught Chester on his shoulder.

The blow, while significant, was not what Chester had been expecting. He noticed Sean wincing in pain as the blow struck Chester's shoulder. Then he remembered that Sean's shoulder was blown apart in the helicopter. While he looked fully recovered, obviously his shoulder had not completely healed.

Then Chester noticed the curare dart on the deck and dove for it.

Sean recognised the danger of the dart and dove for Chester. Chester arrived an instant before and in one motion, grabbed the dart while flipping on his back to strike Sean. Sean, seeing the dart, slapped it away with his good hand. The result was his bad shoulder took the brunt of his landing. As he recoiled in agony, Chester rolled away and jumped to his feet. Landing on his feet, his injured his right leg, and partially collapsed from the strain.

Dear God, Chester thought, if this wasn't a life and death struggle this may be a scene played out in a Three Stooges skit: Sean dragging his gimpy arm and Chester was unable to stand on his floppy leg.

Sean screamed and jumped at Chester landing on the chaise lounge Chester had previously been resting on. The chair collapsed and once again, they went rolling across the deck.

Chester looked over and saw Geoff had not been woken. How can he sleep through this? With his good leg, he started kicking at Sean's bad shoulder, while looking about for the curare laden dart. He needed to incapacitate Sean or surely, he was doomed. Sean was bigger and stronger.

Unable to locate the dart, he grabbed a wine bottle that had been knocked over. He swung it at Sean and caught him square in the jaw. Rather than immobilize him, this seemed to infuriate him. He spat out blood and a couple of teeth and with hatred in his eyes he spewed, "Okay, you fucker. It's time for you to finally die!"

"Fuck y …" was all Chester could get out, before the remnants of the chaise lounge came crashing down on him and everything went black.

He regained consciousness moments later to realize Sean was dragging him along the deck towards the rear of the boat. Sean's right arm was dangling by his side as he struggled to drag Chester. Chester was spent. He knew his only chance was to catch Sean by surprise. Sean was spitting more blood and speaking to himself, as he limply dragged Chester.

"You fucker, you fucker, I should have been the boss. Who the fuck do you think you are? Better than me! You think you are smarter than me! Well fuck you … you can tell that to the fishes!"

They reached the railing along the back of the ship. Sean was being driven by fury, having exhausted himself in the struggle. Sean leaned down to get the leverage to toss Chester over the side, as his right arm was dangling uselessly. In that instant, Chester saw his chance. With all the force he could muster, he kicked up with both legs and caught Sean square on the jaw. Sean flew up, both legs elevating above the floor, and flying backwards through the air went over the railing like a rag doll. Chester heard a loud thump and realized Sean must have hit the diving platform below. Looking over the side between the railings, he witnessed Sean lifelessly slide into the deep.

Chester, watching Sean's body float away said "that's for Clarie ... you bastard!"

Like a boxer grasping the ropes in a ring to help himself up, Chester used the railing to pull himself onto wobbling legs. He looked across the deck and saw shattered glass, chairs askew and complete dishevelment. He then noticed Geoff had been knocked off his chaise lounge and was laying askew on the deck. He was still out cold! This was strange! Chester slowly made his way over to Geoff and noticed his skin was very pale. He reached down to touch him and saw the dart sticking in his neck. The ampule was empty, having disgorged its contents into a drunken Geoff. Chester grabbed the dart and threw it over the side of the boat ... he could not find a pulse. He collapsed and started to weep just as several crew members rushed out.

The captain arrived and took control of the situation. They helped Chester onto a nearby chair. Somebody brought Chester a large tumbler of whiskey and he downed it. They were asking him questions, but Chester could not hear them. He noticed a couple of attendants placing Geoff back on his chair. He looked like he was sleeping.

Chester stared straight ahead towards the ocean retreating behind him. He thought how this life of his has cost him everything most dear to him ... Clarie, Geoff and the old Sean. With a tone of disgust, he spat out, "avarice, stinking avarice."

Instead of being pleased with finally rectifying the Sean issue, or even feeling sorrow for Geoff ... he just thought about three buddies sitting on a patio at Granville Island drinking coffee and enjoying each other. Unknowingly, he said out loud, "Those were great days."

From the chair across from Chester, a voice groggily asked, "What days, bud?"

Author Profile

Ronald Reiniger retired from a successful 35 year business career. This freedom enabled his pursuit of a lifelong aspiration, to become a published novelist.

His greatest accomplishment is raising three amazing children with his wife, Carol. They love traveling to new places to experience different cultures. Ronald also loves the simple pleasures of spending time with family and friends.

He grew up in a small town in Saskatchewan and currently resides in Port Moody, BC.